THE RETURN TO ZION

Books by Brock and Bodie Thoene

THE ZION COVENANT

Vienna Prelude
Prague Counterpoint
Munich Signature
Jerusalem Interlude
Danzig Passage
Warsaw Requiem

THE ZION CHRONICLES

The Gates of Zion
A Daughter of Zion
The Return to Zion
A Light in Zion
The Key to Zion

THE SHILOH LEGACY

In My Father's House
A Thousand Shall Fall
Say to This Mountain

SAGA OF THE SIERRAS

The Man From Shadow Ridge
Riders of the Silver Rim
Gold Rush Prodigal
Sequoia Scout
Cannons of the Comstock
The Year of the Grizzly
Shooting Star

NON-FICTION

Writer to Writer

THE ZION CHRONICLES/BOOK THREE

BODIE THOENE

THE RETURN TO ZION

BETHANY HOUSE PUBLISHERS
MINNEAPOLIS, MINNESOTA 55438

The Return to Zion
Copyright © 1987
Bodie Thoene

Cover by Dan Thornberg,
Bethany House Publishers staff artist.

Published by Bethany House Publishers
A Ministry of Bethany Fellowship International
11300 Hampshire Avenue South
Minneapolis, Minnesota 55438

Printed in the United States of America by
Bethany Press International, Minneapolis, Minnesota 55438

Library of Congress Cataloging-in-Publication Data

Thoene, Bodie, 1951–
    The return to Zion.

    (The Zion chronicles ; bk. 3)
    Sequel to: A daughter of Zion.
    1. Israel—History—1948–1949—Fiction. I. Title.
II. Series: Thoene, Bodie, 1951–   . Zion chronicles ; bk. 3.
PS3570.H46R4   1987   813'.54   87–24244
ISBN 0–87123–939–6 (pbk.)
ISBN 0–7642–2109–4 (mass market)

For the Poet,
my Only One . . .

"My soul rises from me
to fly to one sight of you.
How can I live without you?
I cannot."

When the Lord brought back those that returned to Zion,
we were like them that dream . . .
Psalm 126:1

BODIE THOENE (Tay-nee) began her writing career as a teen journalist for her local newspaper. Eventually her byline appeared in prestigous periodicals such as *U.S. News and World Report*, *The American West*, and *The Saturday Evening Post*. After leaving an established career as a writer and researcher for John Wayne, she began work on her first historical fiction series, THE ZION CHRONICLES. From the beginning her husband, BROCK, has been deeply involved in the development of each book. His degrees in history and education have added a vital dimension to the accuracy, authenticity, and plot structure of the Zion books. The Thoenes' unusual but very effective writing collaboration has also produced three other major historical fiction series with Bethany House Publishers.

A special word of thanks to
my husband Brock,
whose invaluable help and
research and plot line
make my work possible.

Contents

Prologue

Anaias was certain now that there was no hope of escape. It was only midmorning, and yet the sky was darkened with a veil of smoke that covered the sun and sky and hid the final destruction of Zion's Temple from the sorrowing eyes of heaven.

Only eighteen, Anaias had, with countless other Jewish pilgrims from the four corners of the world, traveled to Jerusalem to celebrate Passover in this very temple. It was the young man's second journey to Jerusalem. He knew it would be his last. Over a million had died in the siege, they said. The valleys surrounding the city were piled high with the bodies of the dead, and the stench had become unbearable in the heat of summer. Now even the courtyard of the Temple itself—the last Jewish refuge against the Roman Legions of Titus—was packed with the dead and those who would soon join them.

Anaias leaned his back against a pillar in the inner court of the priests and remembered his delight at a view of the Temple only six months before. It had shone in the glow of dawn like a snow-capped mountain, white and gold and glistening. He had turned his eyes away from the brightness of its glory when the morning sun had first touched it. And with the throngs he had passed through the great Corinthian Gates to offer his thank-offerings and prepare for Passover, his head shorn and his heart full of his vow. But all of that seemed long ago now. The Romans had come in pursuit of the Jewish rebels; the city gates had been shut. Anaias closed his eyes at the memory. There had not been time for him to even fetch his cloak or run to hide in the hills. Bit by bit the city had died. The soldiers of John and Simon had not been able to hold off the surging tide of Roman rage. Those who fled the city in search of amnesty from the Romans had been crucified or cut open as the soldiers searched for swallowed bits of gold or jewels.

Starvation had taken its toll among those who remained. At last the city walls had been breached and now, this final day, Anaias knew, the Temple itself would die. Six days before, he had joined the last band in their flight into this courtyard. It had taken eighteen strong men to close the gates. Now the fire of the Roman Legions licked the gold that had bedazzled Anaias only six months before. Molten metal coursed down the surface and sparked the wood beneath to a red-hot flame. Wind carried the sparks ever higher until the Great Temple itself was threatened.

Jewish soldiers who still had strength to draw a sword walked among the people now to put an end to their lives before the gates tumbled to ashes and the Romans stormed the courtyard. Here and there, a feeble hand would raise to beg a soldier for a quick end. Those who remained of whole families of happy pilgrims now offered their throats to the blade and lay down to die side by side. A terrible stillness had fallen over the Temple. The Romans would take a few alive, Anaias knew, for their brutal games and celebrations.

Beneath his cloak, Anaias carried a small silver chest; in it lay the tallith, the prayer shawl his father had given him for this journey. He smiled bitterly at the thought of his parents in Antioch. Would they, too, die at the hands of the Roman conquerors? *No matter*, he sighed, touching the concealed chest. *If it is to be, then we shall stand before our Savior together. And there is nothing happening here that He did not speak of. But I never thought that I myself would stand in the Temple as it was conquered.*

"It burns!" a soldier shouted from across the Portico. He pointed up to the top of the Temple. "The Temple is afire!" Anaias' gaze followed the man's outstretched sword to where tiny flames danced atop the great Holy Place. A thin shrill wail rose up from one of the women who still lived; then the rest of the dying joined her and a cry swirled up from the stones and spiraled up with the smoke.

"My Lord!" cried Anaias, certain now that he was watching the end of the world. "We may all die willingly," he sobbed. "But not your Holy Place! Come now and make an end to our miseries, Lord!" His voice was loud, above all others. Some gazed up into the black sky in search of the Messiah. But heaven was silent.

The inferno around them burned hotter, and the smoke flowed downward, choking even the strong. Anaias felt his head swim with the inevitability of his death. "Father," he cried, "I have not yet prayed in my new tallith. And so it shall become my shroud today, as it would have been if I had lived a full life!" He dropped the small chest onto the pavement where it clattered open and spilled the white silk prayer shawl out at his feet. Bracing himself against the pillar, he leaned down to retrieve it. He lifted it high above his head and the wind touched it. Here was the last thing of any purity left in the city. Its whiteness glistened like a banner against the fumes that encircled them. Its bright, royal blue borders reminded him that there was indeed a sky above them and the God of heaven still reigned on His throne.

"But I am cut off!" he cried out in anguish, arguing with his thoughts. "And so the House of Israel dies with me today!" He was sobbing now, and he buried his face into his father's gift. The moans of the dying seemed far away, and his mind grew numb once again. Carefully, he placed the prayer shawl over his left shoulder, "Hear, O Israel, the Lord our God is One Lord." Then he draped it across his back and covered his head. He raised his eyes to the large doors that led into the Holy Place and to the altar itself. Step by step he picked his way across the bodies, like an angel clothed in white. The dying cried out at his apparition. The wind ruffled his tallith and it billowed out behind him. "You!" shouted a soldier as Anaias mounted the fourteen steps that led to the table of showbread and the golden menorah. "Where are you going?" he demanded. The soldier's sword was drawn and bloodied.

Anaias did not answer him. Behind him the flames roared a victory over the Corinthian Gate. Sparks flew in the wind as huge beams collapsed, and metal ran in rivulets down the cobbled streets. Heavily, Anaias forced his feet to the top step; then he turned to look. Amid the heat waves from the burning gate, Roman soldiers stood in armor, swords and lances poised and ready for the final slaughter. "It took only moments to close these gates," Anaias muttered. "And the whole Roman army could not open them again for six months."

He stared at his fate for a moment more; then he turned back toward the doors of the Holy Place. His step was more certain now as he entered the chamber. He looked above his head at the clusters of golden grapes that hung as tall as the height of a man.

Before him was a veil of gold and purple and azure blue that blended together and in its colors spoke of heaven and earth and sky and sea.

Anaias pulled the tallith closer around his chin and walked forward around the first veil as the sounds of final battle echoed in from the courtyard beyond. To his right was the table of gold where the showbread had rested. Near that was the tall menorah, the lampstand that burned before the Holy of Holies. Just beyond was a table where the incense had burned. Anaias inhaled deeply, catching the scent of cinnamon that had burned here for hundreds of years. Before him was the altar and the purple veil that separated him from the Holy of Holies. A feeling of awe swept over Anaias. He smiled, ignoring a scream that echoed outside. Here was peace—in the heart of the Temple. The Shekinah glory of God had left this place, he knew, but God had once dwelt here. The young man turned in a slow circle, drinking in the beauty of this forbidden chamber. Footsteps scrambled up the outer steps, and harsh, foreign voices filled the vestibule just on the other side of the veil. He breathed heavily, his young heart willing him to live even though hope had died a long time ago.

Touching the fringes of his tallith, he wished for the phylacteries that he had worn on his arms and forehead to pray. But they had been sold for food months ago. He stepped forward to the altar and laid his hands on it. "O Lord!" he cried, "I have no sacrifice to offer you but my thanks for the One you gave for me! Accept my life! Accept my soul, I pray!"

"Who is behind there?" an angry voice shouted. "There is a Jew in there! Swords ready, men!"

Anaias bowed his head and sank to his knees as the veil behind him gave way to the Roman swords. He had returned to Zion to pray and offer thanks. His journey had not been in vain after all. He touched the smooth fabric of his prayer shawl and leaned his cheek against the cool altar as the tallith became his shroud.

PART 1

The Secret

"This is the secret which I hide from everyone. I am the head of only boys and beggars . . . with dreams."

Theodor Herzl

1 Checkpoint

February 3, 1948

The skies above Jerusalem were blue and cloudless. Two days before, the wind had swept over the land from the southeast, bringing with it the warmth of the vast Negev Desert to thaw the frozen ground and relieve the shivering sentries of the Haganah. Today, Tuesday, February 3, they manned the checkpoints around the Jewish Agency in their shirt sleeves. They basked in the sunlight of the late afternoon and talked cheerfully among themselves as they checked passports and papers and waved the battered Agency vehicles past the walls of sandbags and barbed wire.

In theory, all of King George Avenue was in the hands of Jewish Jerusalem. In fact, no place in the city was safe from the Arab terrorists and bombers who had devised ingenious ways to penetrate a Jewish-held strong point to leave their homemade explosives as calling cards. Now, it seemed, only diplomats were immune to the careful scrutiny of Jewish sentries, many of whom only recently had been shopkeepers or taxi drivers or students at Hebrew University. All of Jerusalem was a battleground; every Jewish man, woman, and child was a soldier commissioned to hold the sacred city against the strength of the Muslim warriors of Haj Amin Husseini.

The two olive drab cars from the Jewish Agency were battered, showing the results of a decade of hard driving. Originally brought to Palestine for the convenience of a British officer before the war, they had been used during the days of the blackouts when the Nazis threatened Palestine. Their fenders displayed the scars of close encounters along the gorge of Bab el Wad. The brakes squealed like spoiled children, and the gears growled and complained every time the clutch was pushed in. At last they had been abandoned by the English, consigned to a junk heap near the rail station when all the British war surplus rolled in from the port of Haifa. Rescued by three enterprising Jewish mechanics, these dilapidated hulks became two primary vehicles in the fleet of Agency cars.

Now armor plate covered the shells, and they crept like ancient beetles across the rock that was Jerusalem. Today the sun warmed their interiors until their official drivers blotted sweat from foreheads and unbuttoned their shirts. Both men waited impatiently for the cars at the checkpoint ahead to pass through the line of civilian soldiers who chatted amiably with passengers and drivers alike.

Their destination was the Jewish district of Rehavia just off King George Avenue and past Ramban Street—not more than a mile, but the trip would probably take thirty minutes at least.

Johann Peltz, the driver of the lead Jewish Agency car, gazed in sullen boredom at the center of the steering wheel. At some time during the long and varied history of his car, the cover of the horn button had come off. Two wires protruded from the hub of the steering wheel. With a sniff, he touched the ends of the wires to each other in rapid succession, smiling benignly as the horn hooted the barricade guards to attention. They looked up at him with surprised irritation, then went back to chatting with a shapely woman driver three cars ahead at the front of the line. Again Johann touched the wires together and the noise blasted away at the obstinate barricade. He wished he knew a bit of morse code. He might tell them a thing or two.

Now determined to ignore him, the fellows at the barricade waved the first car through and begged a cigarette and a light from the car next in line.

Finally in disgust, Johann slipped the complaining gears into neutral and set the unreliable hand brake. He sprang from his car and shook his fist in the air, shouting, "AGENCY BUSINESS, YOU SCHMUCK! SCHLIMIEL! YOU IDIOT MOMZER! OFFICIAL BUSINESS FROM THE JEWISH AGENCY! LET US THROUGH!"

The guards flushed and became businesslike as they scanned papers and knelt to examine the undercarriages of the cars in line just ahead. Again Johann slapped the wires together, and two skinny, studious-looking young men rushed from the other side of the sandbags to inspect his car.

"Papers!" snapped the taller of the two.

Scowling, Johann flashed his identification papers, holding

18

them open just long enough for the young man to scan them. "Official business," he repeated.

"Passing through any Arab sectors? I have to tell you, the gangs are out in force. Just got a report an hour ago; pleasant weather not only wakes the butterflies, but the hornets as well, eh?"

"We're only going as far as the Rehavia District, then back. And we're in a hurry. So, if you please?"

The second guard peered beneath the car and into the back-seat. Car bombs had become a favorite device of the Mufti's henchmen, and papers could be forged. This fellow seemed to be in a bit too much of a hurry.

"Rehavia!" exclaimed the guard. "On official business, you say? It's no more than half a mile. You could have walked. It is a bright enough day for it."

"Is this your business?" shouted Johann.

"Your keys, please." The guard was firm. Suddenly suspicious, his smile vanished.

"Blast! Blast you!" Johann boiled. Picking up the scuffed leather pouch he carried beside him, he waved it under the nose of the guard. "I said official business! From the Boss! From Ben-Gurion himself!"

"We have orders to search the boots of all suspicious-looking vehicles. For explosives." The sentry steadfastly held out his hand, palm up.

In the rear-view mirror, Johann watched his comrade, Dan, climb from behind the wheel of the second Agency car. The look on his unshaven face reflected his boredom with the officious-ness of these part-time militia men.

"What seems to be the trouble?" He lit a cigarette as he strolled alongside the waylaid vehicle.

"This momzer wants my keys!" shouted Johann.

"So let the momzer have your keys," said Dan laconically as he leaned against the side of the car.

Two more of the barricade guards lifted their heads from the car immediately preceding the Agency vehicle. Frowns creased their brows as they sauntered back toward Johann.

Johann tore his keys from the ignition and tossed them on the ground at the young guard's feet.

"Who's in charge here?" he shouted. "We have an urgent mes-sage for Professor Howard Moniger of the American Schools of

Oriental Research! From Ben-Gurion himself! This delay is—is—" he stammered in his fury. "I want your names! We've been here twenty minutes while you bask and chat in the sun! I want your names!"

"Papers, please," sighed a young sentry who seemed to be in charge. "So. Search the trunk, eh, Philip? That is the order of the day no matter how red this fellow's face is," he instructed the younger man. He turned his gaze onto the livid driver. "What is your business in Rehavia, please?"

"We have passengers to pick up," interrupted Dan, his voice calm and reassuring. "At the order of David Ben-Gurion, eh? It is good you fellows are doing your job, but we're a bit behind schedule. Here"—he passed his keys to the commander of the group—"hurry it up, will you?" He smiled and took a long drag on his cigarette before he tossed it down and ground it out.

"Just doing our jobs. Too many things have slipped by, you know." The sentry apologized and shrugged as he handed the keys to his second in command.

Dan smiled benevolently. "Of course." He patted the still sputtering Johann through the open window. "Patience, Johann. They're just doing their jobs. Like we are doing ours, eh?"

"We'll be late and there will be trouble with the Boss. While they're here basking in the sunshine, we'll be late!"

"There happens to be a bit of a war on, you know." The young commander's voice carried more than a hint of a British accent. "Can't be too careful, you know."

"Can't be too careful?" Johann sputtered as the long, sleek limousine from the American consulate glided up on the opposite side of the barricade. The miniature stars and stripes waved brightly on the fenders above the headlights. "What about *them*?" He gestured broadly as the Arab driver touched the brakes briefly and the American diplomat smiled out from the backseat.

"They are going to the Agency," the sentry explained, as though his words made further comment ridiculous.

"Yes? We are Agency vehicles! Going *away* from the Jewish Agency, you schmuck! And you hold us up here while you let an American car with an Arab chauffeur drive right through!" His eyes widened as, indeed, the American diplomat waved brightly and the car eased away from the sandbags and barbed wire.

"We are following orders!" the young sentry snapped. "If you want to argue, talk to Ben-Gurion, eh? We knew this morning there was going to be a visit from the American consulate. They say his driver is practically an American himself, he's been working for them so long! You, on the other hand! Nobody told us about *you*! And to my way of thinking, you are acting suspiciously, eh?"

Johann slapped his hand against his forehead in frustration. "I have been with the Agency eight years!" he declared. "You, I've never seen before in my life. Oy gevalt! How long have you been a sentry?" His tone was accusatory.

"Since last Shabbat! And we are just following orders."

"Well that explains it. I haven't driven this way in four days."

"Try and keep your temper now, Johann," instructed Dan before he returned to his vehicle.

Johann nodded in grudging silence as a guard slammed the lid of his trunk and tossed the keys into his lap. "Overdoing it just a bit, I think," Johann muttered as he cranked the reluctant engine to life. "Our own fellows, too."

Four of the militia men waved them through, as though one were not enough to do the job. "Shalom, fellows!"

Twice more the complaining vehicles were halted. Heeding the advice of his comrade, Johann shut off the car and dangled the keys out the window, not speaking a word until the car had been inspected by the unarmed men at the barricades. Leaning his head against his hand, Johann stared disconsolately at the leather pouch on the seat beside him. *Urgent!* Ben-Gurion had told him. *See to it that this gets into the hands of the professor personally! Then load up the whole lot of them. The Rabbi Lebowitz, his grandson Yacov, David Meyer, and the journalist. Ellie Warne. She can make something out of this for the American press!* Johann looked at his watch and drummed his fingers impatiently on the steering wheel as the trunk was lifted for the third time. The horn wires tempted him, but he restrained himself. Everyone was leary nowadays, and there was no use in letting his frayed nerves get the best of him and cause further delay. *Keep your temper, Johann,* he told himself.

Wind chimes made of broken potsherds banged noisily against the windowpane outside Ellie's room. Her ancient green alarm clock ticked with a heavy, uneven cadence as if to remind her that it was almost four o'clock in the afternoon and still she had not managed to put one intelligent word on paper.

Chin in hand, Ellie leaned over the decrepit typewriter and stared forlornly at the blank sheet in the carriage before her. A warm, unopened bottle of Coca-Cola stood to the right of the typewriter. After weeks of lentil soup and weak tea, Ellie had remarked how she longed for a hamburger with onions and fries and a six pack of Coke all her own to drink. At 3:00 this morning, David had arrived back in Jerusalem from an emergency flight to Haifa. He had triumphantly pulled the Coke from his duffle bag and said, "Hamburger with onions and fries with a Coke! Hold the fries! Hold the onions! Hold the hamburger! Sorry, honey, you're going to have to settle for the last Coke in Palestine!" Then he had stumbled off to bed to catch up on three days without sleep.

Now Ellie eyed her treasure guiltily. On the Arab black market, it was worth two chickens and a half dozen eggs. But she couldn't bear to think of one of the Mufti's men guzzling her Coke. Even for two chickens in the pot. So there it sat, untouched. Like the typewriter. She would save it for a reward, after she finished the story. Her photographs of the war for Jewish survival, with the accompanying story, would be sent back to the States, to the *LIFE* magazine Editorial Offices. Where, she wondered, could she even begin to describe the events that were going on here in Jerusalem?

At UCLA she had taken just enough journalism to round out her major as a photo-journalist. Writing was not her strong suit. As a photographer, however, her skill had become recognized and much in demand. Her photographs of battles between Jews and Arabs in Palestine had been splashed across the pages of *LIFE* magazine every week for the last two months. The freckle-faced young coed snapping pictures of pots at her uncle's archaeological digs in Palestine was now a staff photographer for *LIFE* magazine. Three days before, word had arrived that the magazine correspondent had been wounded in a battle near Tel Aviv.

PLEASE FILL IN UNTIL REPLACEMENT ARRIVES STOP SEND COPY WITH PHOTOS STOP ABOUT 1,500 WORDS STOP STU MEBANE EDITORIAL DIRECTOR STOP

For three days she had paced and thought and stared out the window at the bare, wind-whipped saplings that lined the street. Twice she had flown with David over the besieged Jewish Quarter of the Old City to drop medical supplies. Once, she had glimpsed Rachel and Moshe waving up to them.

They were not more than half a mile away from where she now sat, and yet they were as distant as another century or another world. "Where do I begin?" Ellie said aloud. She sighed in frustration, certain somehow that the bottle of Coke would probably never be opened.

Then she picked up a sheaf of her own photographs that were slated to be sent stateside in the morning. Aerial shots showed the isolated Jewish Quarter behind the thick craggy walls of the Old City Section of Jerusalem. Around the tiny cluster of synagogues and domed rooftops stood the tall spires of Muslim minarets to the north. Eastward the massive Muslim shrine stood atop Mount Moriah where once the Great Hebrew Temple had stood. There Jesus had preached of the love of God for mankind; there He had predicted that the Temple itself would one day be razed to the ground. Beyond the Dome of the Rock was the Mount of Olives. To the west of the Jewish Quarter was the Armenian Quarter, with Christian churches and shrines just north of that.

Armenians and Christian Arabs by the thousands had fled their homes in fear of the Mufti Haj Amin and his fanatic followers. As they had abandoned their quarter, the Muslim warriors had moved in and taken over. They blockaded the gates into the Old City against Jewish defenders and lately had even denied convoys of food. Here and there a lonely British outpost perched on a rooftop. Although they were not slated to evacuate until May, the British goal, it seemed to Ellie, was to remain aloof from the Arab aggression that pushed against the narrow borders of Jerusalem. "They want to stay alive long enough to get home," David had explained one evening over dinner. "I know the feeling, and I can't say as I blame them."

Outside the walls of the Old City sprawled the New City of Jerusalem. It was a strange mixture of Arab neighborhoods and Jewish neighborhoods. In a few blocks, here and there, the two peoples had even lived as neighbors. Ellie's photographs clearly showed the places that had been targeted by the Mufti's men. The blackened rubble of Ben Yehudah Street marked the place where David's hotel had been blown up. A few blocks from that was the remains of the Jewish Commercial District.

Even now, Ellie marveled at the astonishing determination of the people she had come to love and admire. *It is no wonder,* she thought as she gazed at the pictures, *that they are called God's chosen. The apple of His eye. They have to be something special to stand up to all this.*

Closest to the walls of the Old City, from the north clear around the outside to the south, the Arab neighborhoods stood like fortresses. Those Arabs who had resisted the Mufti's strongarm tactics had been driven out of their homes by the very men who had claimed to be fighting for them. Arab Palestinians filled the roads leading out of the city. They were refugees now, victims of their own political leaders. In their place came the peasants, the warriors who were indebted to and allied with the House of Husseini. And on their way into the city they had not neglected to blow the water mains into Jewish neighborhoods. Even now, they looted the homes of Christian and Muslim Arabs who had fled the fanatic cries of "Jihad! Jihad! Jihad!"

The story seemed clear enough in Ellie's mind; she simply could not find the words to begin. How could she convey to the people of the United States that a piece of Hitler still rules this holy corner of the world? How could she tell them that without their help there would be no Jews left alive in Palestine; that the threat of Holocaust was far from over?

The wind outside stopped abruptly. Ellie looked fretfully at the alarm clock. Almost four-thirty in the afternoon. David had slept the clock around, and Uncle Howard had been gone with Rabbi Lebowitz and Yacov for three hours. She had hoped to have the story finished when they got back, but she had failed to put even one word on paper. "Dear God," she moaned in a frustrated prayer for help. But she couldn't even find the words to finish her prayer.

A heavy-handed knock sounded on the front door.

"David!" Ellie called, unwilling to get up and break her frustrated vigil.

Again the knocking sounded. *Must be Uncle Howard. Probably forgot his keys.* "David!" she called. "Get up! It's four-thirty! Get the door!"

David did not answer from his room, nor did she hear his footsteps padding down the hall toward the front door.

"Drat," she said, pushing her long red hair back from her face. As the banging became more insistent, she tugged her housecoat around her and quickly scanned her face in the mirror. "Bleary-eyed," she muttered. "Four-thirty and still not dressed. The rabbi will not approve."

24

"Okay!" she called. "Keep your shirt on, Uncle Howard! I'm coming!" On the way past David's room she thumped on his door. "Get up, David! Uncle Howard's home!" Quickly she unbolted the door and flung it open. "It's about time—" she began. The faces of two strange and startled men gazed back at her from the front step. For a long moment they appraised one another; Ellie in her stocking feet, blue jeans and a terrycloth housecoat; the two men in green corduroy slacks and white short-sleeved shirts. Ellie looked past them to the bulky, beat-up automobiles parked at the curb. "You're not Uncle Howard," she said simply.

Johann blinked back at her, then smiled. "No. I don't think I am. Are you Uncle Howard, Dan?" he asked his comrade. Dan shrugged. "Not last time I checked." He stuck his hand out to Ellie. "Dan Schellen. Jewish Agency. And this is Johann Peltz. Also Jewish Agency, eh?"

"Ellie Warne. I'm sorry, I was expecting my uncle."

"You should be careful who you open the door to, young lady," Johann chided. "You never know if it might be the Jihad Moquades knocking."

"You're right. Of course." Ellie stepped aside, allowing the two men into the foyer. "How can I help you?"

"Your uncle, Howard Moniger? He is not here?" Johann surveyed the foyer and peered into the sitting room to the right. He tapped the leather pouch nervously.

"No, I'm afraid not. He took two of our houseguests to Hadassah Hospital for checkups. I expect him back any minute. Would you care to wait?"

"We have a message for him. For all of you, actually. The Boss—Ben-Gurion—wants to see all of you. Is David Meyer here?" Dan asked.

"Sleeping."

"Ah yes. Such a night he had last!" Johann volunteered. "He is almost a hero." He lowered his voice as he stepped into the sitting room. "Except that the guns he dropped fell through the roof and into the only bathtub in the kibbutz and smashed it."

"No one was bathing at the time," Dan added, taking a seat and smiling amiably.

"Is this what you've come here to tell us?" Ellie asked, remaining standing in the doorway.

"I am afraid the message is first for your uncle, Miss Warne. Although you and the others will have to come along with us,

25

too." He looked pointedly at her stocking feet poking out under the cuffs of her Levis. "Maybe you will want to . . ." Dan's smile was almost apologetic.

"Change clothes, eh?" Johann finished lamely.

"Well, I don't think any of us will be going anywhere until we know what is going on, Jewish Agency or not!" Irritation crept into her voice. She did not like this kind of surprise on her doorstep. Especially not with a deadline looming and a major case of writer's block to contend with.

"When the professor gets here, Miss Warne, our orders were to give the letter to him personally," Dan apologized. "This much I will say, if it will motivate you to change clothes, eh?"

"Shut up!" shot Johann.

"It is a little something regarding some friends of yours in the Old City," Dan ignored the outraged look on Johann's face.

"Rachel? Moshe? What is it?"

"Well, I don't know myself," sighed Dan. "Just that some word was received about them. Something important. The Boss seemed quite agitated. Said you were to bring your camera and—"

"You have a mouth like Jonah's whale!" said Johann in dismay. He looked at his watch, then at Ellie's stunned and worried face. "So get dressed, already. We won't have time if you don't hurry."

The sickness of fear and foreboding made Ellie's stomach churn. She hurried from the room and down the hall. She banged noisily on David's door again, then cracked it open and whispered loudly, "David! Get up! Wake up! Something is going on with Rachel and Moshe! They want us all down at the Agency. David, hurry! There's a message from Ben-Gurion."

2 The Gift

Like battle-tested soldiers, the twenty-seven young boys of Chaim Torah School stood at attention before Ehud and Dov, yarmulkes perched precariously on their shorn heads. Their earlocks drooped, and the grime of the Old City Jerusalem Jewish Quarter was thick beneath their nails. The oldest was no more than fifteen, and the youngest was barely five. The coat sleeves and trouser legs were too short on the larger boys; the fabric of the hand-me-downs worn by their younger brothers and cousins was patched and worn thin.

Dov adjusted his wire-rimmed spectacles and inspected the line from the tallest to the smallest. "A ragged lot we have here, Captain!" he exclaimed as he clasped his hands behind his back and rocked on his toes.

At his words, the heels on scuffed shoes clicked together, bony shoulders drew back, and chins lifted even higher.

Grizzled and bearlike, Ehud towered over his diminutive and scholarly companion. Huge and good-natured, Ehud was adored by the boys who now stood before him. He could hardly stroll through the narrow alleyways of the quarter without attracting a flock of youngsters who skipped in his shadow, like sea gulls squawking and circling in the wake of an overloaded fishing trawler. "Tell us a story! Please, Captain Ehud!" they would beg, itching for some morsel of adventure. Always Ehud withheld his stories until the moans and sighs of their disappointment reached a proper proportion, then he would shake his head and submit to their requests to repeat a favorite tale—or perhaps make up a new one. After a month of hearing the exploits of their beloved and now landlocked sea captain, there was not one boy in ten in the quarter who didn't dream of a life on the stormy Mediterranean. And every boy longed to be worthy to serve at the side of this burly hero. Those among them who were privileged to carry Ehud a cup of coffee during his midnight watch were admired and called *chaver*, friend, to the captain. A great honor.

Ehud tucked his chin and tugged his beard as he examined the assembly of eager young soldiers. Their eyes gazed straight ahead, focusing on the back wall of the basement of Tipat Chalev, the community kitchen. As the delicious smell of borscht drifted down from steaming kettles, their stomachs growled impatiently.

"Well?" Dov asked, peering up at Ehud. "Well, what do you think?" His own stomach had begun to complain. "Young troops, to be sure, but more orderly now than when they began training, nu?"

Ehud cleared his throat gruffly, suppressing a smile as he straightened the yarmulke on the head of an intent eight-year-old. "Oy! Such a mish-mosh!" agreed Ehud. "But still they might make soldiers yet, nu?"

"And so, these are the future *talmid chachamim* of Jerusalem. To think that before us stand tomorrow's sages and scholars—sensitive, quiet and humble saints who may perhaps enlighten us on the learning of the great sea of the Talmud! Oy gevalt! To think of it! With such as these we will hold the quarter against the Arabs!"

A ripple of pride moved through the ranks, but Ehud frowned at the reality of the fragile defense of the Jewish Quarter and the thousands of Arab militia men who surrounded them. Ehud tugged his beard again. The tiny band of one hundred Haganah soldiers who had been smuggled into the Old City did indeed depend on these boys to help them in a seemingly hopeless cause: to save the holy places of Jewish Jerusalem.

A red-cheeked boy of five suddenly dug into his pockets and held out his hands. "You see, I stole eight rifle cartridges today, Captain!" he cried. "And the rabbi said I am not a *gonif*, but a patriot, nu?"

"Just like the ghetto fighters in Warsaw." A bigger boy stepped forward, his hands full of pilfered British ammunition.

Suddenly the ranks broke and the schoolboy soldiers swarmed around Ehud and Dov. "I have five bullets!" "I got nine!" "Only four for me, but I shall do better!"

"And the rabbi says in the case of *pikuah nefesh*, in the instance of life or death, such as now, God would wish that we take these English bullets to defend our lives and the holy places," remarked a gangly, red-haired adolescent as he took off his jacket to reveal an entire bandolier of ammunition.

An astonished gasp of admiration echoed throughout the group. "Well done, Joseph!" Dov clapped him on the back. "If you make as good a scholar as you do a thief, then you will be at the top of your class!"

Joseph blushed and spoke in a voice that groaned and squeaked in its quest for manhood. "Talmud says it is our *mitzvah*, our duty, to the holy law of God to do what we must to survive and save our people." Joseph gently placed his treasure into the half-filled crate of ammunition. "We must not die for the sake of a law, eh? But we must live for the sake of God and His Word. If sometimes a man did not have to set aside the law to save himself or his wife and children, I think that probably there would be no Jews left by now, nu?"

"Well spoken, Rabbi!" Ehud guffawed and held out the bandolier for the small boys to touch.

"And so," Dov smiled. "Though we may have to play the part of a thief for an hour, we will together preserve our homes and spend the rest of our lives as scholars, eh?" He sighed, "Ah, to simply be allowed to live as Jews! Now *that* would be paradise!"

"Not for Leo!" a swarthy ten-year-old cried as he knocked a yarmulke from the head of his brother. "Leo, my brother the *momzer*! He *wants* to grow up to be a thief!"

With a squawk the two boys dodged and darted around the room, around and through the legs of the captain, then up the stairs and out the door into the community dining hall. The twenty-five who remained cheered and rooted for their favorite brother, except for the few who could not tolerate either of the little Krepske boys.

Ehud held his hands to his ears against the deafening echo in the basement. "A squall! A gale-force wind! Oy, to be on the sea with a hurricane would be more peaceful than this!"

Dov shoved his spectacles up on his nose and clambered quickly to the top of a wooden table in the middle of the room. "ATTEN-SHUN!" he shouted above the din. Immediately the caterwauling was replaced by the scrambling of shoes on the floor as the ranks formed in two lines once again—the tallest on the left, stair-stepping downward to the smallest. "With such as these we may well save Jerusalem," he muttered, observing the vacant space left by the two brothers.

"Or lose our minds." Ehud cleared his throat in disapproval.

Chests out, chins high and eyes straight ahead, the troops stood like statues as the errant brothers screeched and slammed back through the door. The younger of the two had a firm grip on the earlock of the other, but at the sight of their comrades standing rigidly below them, they froze midscream. They loosened their grip, returned their yarmulkes to their proper dignity, and quickly scrambled down the steps to join the ranks.

"Ha!" exclaimed Ehud, clasping his hands behind his back. "So! Are we a rabble? A mob? Or are we soldiers, eh?"

The reply was unanimous and in ear-shattering unison, "SOLDIERS, SIR!"

Ehud shoved his thick finger into his ear and wriggled it. "Hmmm. Yes. Well, then."

Dov coughed once, then, still remaining on the tabletop, he frowned and stuck his lower lip out thoughtfully. "Yes. Soldiers, I think. So! We have a duty to perform tonight." Eyebrows raised expectantly among the boys. "It is a joyous duty to be sure, and God says it is our mitzvah to rejoice, nu? So tonight, even though times are most difficult here in the Old City, we will rejoice and show the Mufti that our hearts are filled with thanksgiving and happiness yet!"

"Life goes on! Life goes on!" Ehud said loudly.

"You older lads will be assigned guard duty, eh? On the rooftops. As the procession begins, it is most important that you look for snipers, for Arab patrols. You will back up the regular Haganah guards. We can carry only a few candles, but you fellows who are ten and eleven, raise your hands please." Seven boys raised their arms.

Ehud quickly counted. "Seven! By the eternal! Seven boys! A good number, seven; it is a good sign. Seven candles in the procession!"

"Good!" exclaimed Dov. "And now the most important duty to you younger soldiers. It is customary at a wedding to throw rice and nuts at the happy couple, nu?" Heads nodded in agreement. "Yes, well, we have no nuts in the quarter and precious little rice to eat, let alone throw." He coughed and waited for the importance of the statement to sink in. "But! What is a Jewish wedding without rice! We might as well forget the canopy or the rabbi!"

"Or shoot the clarinet player!" Ehud shook his head in anguish at the thought.

"God forbid! And God forbid we should have a proper wedding without rice. So, we have managed to wrestle from the cooks here at Tipat Chalev an entire half pound of rice for throwing at the wedding—on the condition that we bring back every last grain when we are done with it. Rice is as precious as bullets if we are to stand against the enemy."

"Bullets would be easier to throw and pick up," said one of the Krepske brothers.

"You momzer!" shouted his older sibling. "You schmuck! Nobody throws bullets at a wedding!" With a hard jab to the ribs, he accented his point; then as the ranks broke once again, the brothers shrieked and pounded one another as they discussed the issue.

———

"Not on your wedding day, Rachel," old Shoshanna chided as she rocked baby Tikvah and glowered at Shaul, who stood expectantly at the door. "A bride should stay indoors, fasting in private and thinking about what blessings God has given her." Her ancient wrinkled face reflected disapproval as Rachel smiled apologetically and buttoned her coat. "It isn't proper for you to go out alone on such a day. And maybe not safe either! You want the tueval should see you so happy? You tempt the evil eye!"

Rachel looked in the mirror and pulled her shawl over her head. For a moment she gazed in delighted wonder at the face that smiled back at her. "I *am* happy!" she said. "And no matter where I walk now, Shoshanna, I am not alone, eh? God walks with me."

"Oy gevalt!" Shoshanna proclaimed, rolling her eyes. "Hear how she tempts evil to find her!" She touched her fingers to her lips in a gesture that tradition had taught her would keep the tueval, Satan, away.

"I'll take the dog, too, if it makes you feel better." She reached down and scratched Shaul's broad head.

"So take him! I always said a dog is a curse to a Jewish home! He frightens away the poor and the beggars." She rocked Tikvah a little harder.

"Well, I am quite poor," Rachel said. "And he doesn't frighten me one bit." The big dog jumped to his feet and wriggled his tailless behind. He had lost a considerable amount of weight and muscle in the weeks since his wound but he had regained his strength under Rachel's care, and his devotion to her had doubled. "I will be fine," Rachel assured Shoshanna. "And if I cannot go back there, I cannot find the package Grandfather wrote me about and Moshe will not have a wedding present. I have to go. I will only be a few minutes. Take care of the baby, eh?"

Shoshanna shook her head in resignation. "So go! But cover your face so the tueval won't see how you smile!"

"Yes, Shoshanna." In deference to the old woman's wishes she pulled the corner of her shawl to cover the lower half of her face. "How is that?" she asked.

"Good! You look like a Muslim. Satan will have no need to

31

bother you. In this war he is on their side, nu?" There was a twinkle in the old woman's eyes as Rachel hurried out the door and down to the warm, bright street. It was too warm to wear her heavy coat, but she felt almost as if she had to disguise herself from everyone in the quarter. Shoshanna was right, of course; it wasn't proper for her to be traipsing about the city on her wedding day, but Grandfather had mentioned in his letter a very special gift for her to give the bridegroom. Hidden away in a plain wooden box in Grandfather's apartment was a blue velvet pouch, and inside was the only proper gift for a Jewish bride to give her bridegroom. Over half a century before, Rachel's own grandmother had given it to Grandfather as they stood beneath the wedding canopy. *Do not tell your young man you have a gift for him*, Grandfather had written. *The young fellow is so in love with you that he has sworn he cares nothing for a dowry or any gift but that of your love. (Well I remember feeling the same feeling for my beautiful Esther fifty years ago, although I had met her but once.) He asks for nothing, wants nothing but you, my dear Rachel. However, the house of Lebowitz may be poor, but we are too proud to give our daughters in marriage without a gift. And so, in the cupboard above the washbasin you will find the box. What you will find inside is a prayer shawl embroidered by the hands of your grandmother's grandmother when she was a bride in Poland. I wear it proudly on Holy Days. Passover, Rosh Hashanna, Yom Kippur. But now I am a very old man. Your grandmother spoke to me in a dream and said this tallith was for Moshe's strong shoulders. May the Eternal bless you both, my child. Your loving grandfather, Rabbi Shlomo Lebowitz.*

Rachel smiled as she thought of the love and care Grandfather had sent in his letter. Moshe had carried it to her with his own hand, never dreaming what its contents were. There was a postscript the old man had hastily scrawled on the back. *Wrapped with the tallith is a small leather pouch. Your mother sent it with thought of ransom when the first hint of trouble rose on the wind. As I think of it now, perhaps you may have a dowry. Take it, child. It is little enough. My heart stands very near you as you come to the canopy. Grandfather.*

Rachel's heart was full almost to bursting as she opened the door to the cold basement apartment. For nearly two weeks she had kept the contents of the letter secret from Moshe. Today, the day of their wedding, was the first moment she had been left alone long enough to steal away. When Moshe was not near here, he stationed two young Haganah soldiers to stand guard over her. But on her wedding day, she had asked him to let her have time alone—time without men watching and reminding her that her new life was about to begin in the middle of a war.

Shaul at her heels, she shut the door of the dank, dark room and quickly lit the stump of a candle on a rickety wooden table. She laughed out loud and tossed her shawl on the bed. "I will not come to him empty-handed!" she said to her shaggy companion as he wriggled and danced around her, then plopped down out of habit in front of the cold kerosene stove. His yellow eyes followed her to the cupboard.

There were only two shelves inside the weathered pine cupboard. A few pieces of china sat beside a pair of silver Shabbat candlesticks. Beside them was an embroidered Shabbat tablecloth that was probably at least as ancient as the gift she had come for. On the shelf above were a few leather-bound books and four long-stemmed crystal wine glasses. The house of Lebowitz had not always been poor.

Rachel reached out to touch the glasses. She was filled suddenly with the sense that her family now stood around her. Faces smiled. Hands reached out. Mama embraced her and Papa stood proud, but a little sad, beside her. *Mazel Tov! Mazel Tov!* they all seemed to say. *Our baby all grown up and today a bride!* She took two glasses from the shelf and held them up to the light of the tiny candle.

"Maybe Mama drank from this cup on the night of her wedding. And maybe Papa drank from this." She studied the gleaming patterns of the crystal for a moment, then closed her eyes. "Thank you, Lord," she whispered softly, as happy memories of Shabbat meals and family gatherings flooded her heart. "This is the most wonderful day of my life, and I am not alone. Thank you," she said again. She touched the rims of the goblets together and they chimed like bells. "Mazel Tov, my dear family," Rachel said joyfully. "Thank you for coming."

With reverence, Rachel placed the goblets back in their niche; then she pulled a small wooden box from the left side of the shelf. The box was plain, polished olivewood. There was no adornment, and the only elegance lay in its stark simplicity. Top and bottom joined together with such precision that it was difficult to tell that they were not simply one piece of wood. Rachel could not see any hinges, but when her thumbs pushed slightly upward, the lid raised easily.

A gasp of astonished delight escaped Rachel's lips as she gazed at the soft royal blue velvet bag that held the tallith. On its cover was a star of David embroidered with golden thread in an intricate pattern, a filigree more beautiful than any Rachel had seen before. *This is how the star of David should appear*, she thought, remembering the crude yellow patch Jews had worn by order of the Führer. But even then she had been proud to be a Jew—as her father and mother had been.

Beneath the golden star, Rachel clearly recognized the letters of the Shema Yisrael: *"Hear, O Israel, the Lord our God, the Lord is one!"* she read. *"And thou shalt love the Lord thy God with all thy heart, and with all thy soul, and with all thy might . . ."* Her finger traced each letter of the prayer and she smiled as again she felt the presence of God's love for her. "I will try to live this prayer, Lord, because you have shown your love for me. . . ." *And these words, which I command thee this day, shall be upon thy heart, and thou shalt teach them diligently unto thy children . . .* It was this prayer, the Shema, that had been on the lips of every observant Jew who had perished at the hands of the Nazis. Rachel smiled when she remembered that the Germans had thought the words proclaimed, *Long live the Jews!* In a way they had been right. "As far as you are concerned, eh, Lord?"

She pressed the blue velvet to her heart, then touched the golden mezuzah she wore on a leather strap around her neck. *"I have loved thee with an everlasting love."* Rachel repeated the words of the verse inscribed on the mezuzah. The charm and the words had been Moshe's gift to her that first day in the quarter when he had told her of God's everlasting love.

Until then, words about God had given her grief, not comfort, but Moshe's actions reflected the love he spoke of. His love for her had been the mirror in which God's everlasting love had been reflected. She had believed with a faith that came easily and simply: Yeshua was God's gentle anointed one. He was the Messiah she had hoped for and yearned to meet.

In Yeshua, Rachel had found the peace of forgiveness and a joy in living that she had forgotten. And now, dreams that had been long dead were reawakened; tonight she would stand beside Moshe beneath the *chupa*, the wedding canopy. They would exchange vows and pledge their love for one another before

man and God. She felt new and alive in her heart as though there
had been no heartache or years of fear and loss. *God will restore
the years the locusts have eaten,* Moshe had told her once when
she fretted about wasted years. From this moment, Rachel knew
there was only a future for her and Moshe and little Tikvah. The
grim past was no more.

Gently, Rachel opened the drawstring and pulled the white
silk tallith from its covering. Light caught the shimmering fabric.
Royal blue stripes trimmed the borders, a reminder of God's
throne, which tradition said was covered with glowing blue sapphires. Rachel remembered her own father in the splendor of his
billowing tallith on the eve of Yom Kippur. They had stood together on the steps of the synagogue in Warsaw and he had bent
very low and said to her, *Someday, little one, your bridegroom will
wear a tallith that you give him on your wedding day. He will know
that the white and blue are a reminder of God's throne. But no
doubt he will also see the color of your eyes within the blue, and
the softness and purity of your skin in the white. When a man and
woman marry, little Rachel, their love touches the throne of God!*

Rachel shook her head at the clarity of her father's words. It
seemed as though he had only just whispered them to her a moment before. "I remember, Papa," she said aloud, only at that moment understanding the importance of his words. "And I will be
a good wife to Moshe. My life will bring him nearer to the throne
of God," she vowed. "And in the blue of my eyes may he see everlasting love."

At the neck of the tallith was an elaborate *atara*, a band sewn
of intricate metallic embroidery. Atop the atara the injunction of
Num. 15:39 was embroidered in blue: *that ye may look upon it
and remember all the commandments of the Lord.* Shining silk,
blue and gold, made this the most bea..iful prayer shawl Rachel
had ever seen. *It is a gift that is worthy of such a kind and handsome husband as Moshe,* she thought happily. In only a few hours
she would present it to him. The flush of excitement touched her
cheeks and caused her heart to beat faster. She stroked the
smooth fabric and imagined it draped over his broad shoulders,
billowing in the wind as he whispered some wise advice to his
own children—their own children—on the steps of the synagogue! "Thank you, God!" She lifted her head and voice to the
throne she knew was very near.

Carefully, she laid the tallith on the bed and reached deep

into the velvet pouch for the small leather purse that Grandfather had mentioned in his letter. Her heart leapt when she felt the weight of the soft suede pouch. *How many years,* she wondered, *had it been since Mama had sent this to Grandfather, hoping that he might somehow use it to purchase their lives?* She dumped its contents out on the bed, shaking her head in wonder at the gold coins that tumbled out. This must have been their entire savings; yet even as it was received in Palestine, it was too late for them. Only baby Yacov had escaped the camps, death, and humiliation. What her parents had so lovingly saved and hopefully sent to Grandfather was now to provide a dowry for her. She stared at the coins for a long moment. Sadness brushed her as she thought of smiling faces who could not be with her at the wedding tonight. Mama and Papa gone. Brothers gone. Only Yacov and Grandfather remained, yet they could not enter the Old City, even though they were so very near. She would give all her dowry to have them stand by her tonight; just to hear their voices. She closed her eyes and let her breath out slowly. This was not a moment for sorrow. Too many blessings had come to her and she would not insult God by seeming to be unthankful even for a moment! Instead, she prayed, "Let them know how happy I am tonight, God. Share my joy with those I love, though they cannot be with me."

With tenderness, she replaced the tallith; then she counted fourteen coins back into the little leather purse. In her heart, she felt peace and joy as she pictured the blue gleam of sapphires on the mighty throne of God, and very near stood Mama and Papa and her brothers. *Hear, O Israel!*

Truly, she thought as she tucked the tallith into the box and blew out the flickering candle, *I do have so much to be thankful for today.* Dozens of women in the quarter had known Rachel's mother as a child growing up in the shadow of the synagogues and Yeshivah schools of Jerusalem. They had danced at her wedding, wept when she had returned to Poland with her young rabbi husband. Her letter telling of the birth of Rachel had been read aloud in their sewing circle. Rachel's first steps in Warsaw had been celebrated in Jerusalem. *Have you heard? Little Rachel, the granddaughter of Rebbe Lebowitz, is walking already! Such a bright child she is! And so pretty! She looks like her mama at that age, nu?* Her photograph had been handed from one excited *Yiddishemama* to another. These same women had mourned when

Rachel's family disappeared into the Nazi abyss. They had competed to mother the infant Yacov when he had arrived in Palestine in the arms of a Jewish refugee with a note identifying him as Yacov Lubetkin, grandson of Rabbi Shlomo Lebowitz of Old City Jerusalem.

And now, so many years later, when Rachel returned from the grave, they had surrounded her with love and concern, careful not to ask too many questions. All but a few accepted her as a daughter of Zion, returned from an ordeal that had no name and was beyond comprehension. All but a few had quietly welcomed her into the safety of their love while they all lived daily on the brink of annihilation.

Rachel was home, indeed. These women of the quarter had worked to provide her with a wedding gown and a trousseau even as the shadow of a new war invaded their lives. When Rabbi Akiva, as mayor of the Old City, had condemned her as a prostitute for the Nazis, they had covered their ears and condemned him and his cohorts instead of Rachel. She had lived through hell itself and survived to come home, they reasoned. She was the granddaughter of kind Rabbi Lebowitz, the daughter of their playmate and friend. At her wedding she would wear white, and there would be nothing more said about it.

And so a beautiful gown had been made from the fabric and lace of the finest Shabbat tablecloths in the Old City. She had been cared for as they had cared for their own children, and today was a day of hope and rejoicing for them all. Rachel Lubetkin had come home to wed in the same square where her mother had taken her vows. Tonight in the Jewish Quarter there would be dancing and singing and celebrating within earshot of the Arab Mufti and the hoodlums who surrounded them and kept them captive. For the Jewish Quarter, Rachel had become a solitary candle of hope in the darkness of reality. *If she could find happiness after everything, then perhaps . . .*

Rachel breathed deeply, inhaling the smell of Grandfather's pipe tobacco one last time before she called Shaul from his resting place and shut the door. She turned the key in the lock, then shoved it down in her pocket and gazed up at the patch of clean blue sky above her. The wind had stopped, the weather was clear; tonight would be a beautiful night for the wedding.

She tucked her head and hurried up the stairs and onto the street. Colorful banners hung from the windows above where she would pass in only a few hours. On the streets below, sandbags and barricades told yet another story. The wedding procession through the streets would be well guarded, she knew. What few weapons the quarter possessed for defense had been secreted beneath the tiles of rooftops in the event of trouble. Extra ammunition was being collected and placed within easy access of the Haganah defenders. She glanced up to a rooftop where a young Yeshiva student stood watch, scanning the Arab Quarter in search of snipers. His eyes widened when he saw her.

"Does Moshe know you are about?" he called cheerfully.

"Shhh." She put a finger to her lips and hurried by. "I had to fetch his wedding gift!" she explained.

He nodded and waved. "Mazel Tov!" he cried. "Mazel Tov, daughter of Zion!"

Rachel smiled broadly and blushed as she turned the corner and climbed up the stone steps of The Street of the Stairs. Shaul followed closely at her heels, panting as Rachel hurried ahead of him.

Plump and rosy-cheeked, Hannah Cohen stepped from the door of her nearly empty grocery store half a block ahead of Rachel. Her shop was midway along the path of the wedding procession, and she swept the cobbled street with a vigor that stripped off the entire top layer. Her lower lip was out and her brow creased in a frown of concentration. She glanced up at Rachel's approaching footsteps and put a hand to her hip in disapproval. "You're supposed to be home!" she called as Rachel waved. "You want the tueval should see you out and so happy on your wedding day?" she chided. "Look at that smile! No one should be so happy! You tempt the evil eye, Rachel Lubetkin! Your mother, may she rest in peace, would not approve of you out on the streets on your wedding day!"

"I had to fetch Moshe's wedding present," Rachel explained, a little out of breath. "Grandfather had it at his apartment." Rachel opened her coat just enough for Hannah to see the smooth olivewood box.

"Your grandfather's tallith?" Hannah exclaimed with approval. "No finer tallith in the quarter!" She propped her broom against the doorpost and encircled Rachel in an energetic hug. "Mazel Tov, my dear! Your mother would be so proud of you today, God rest her soul. So, she is watching from heaven, eh? Closer to God so He can hear her prayers for you."

"My very thoughts," Rachel said, her face beaming with joy.

"So!" Hannah released her and gave her a gentle swat. "Only a few hours! Go home, already! You have much to do!"

"Shoshanna is watching Tikvah for me!" Rachel called as she hurried away.

Hannah raised her hand in acknowledgment. "Such a beautiful baby! Your Moshe is a lucky man to get such a wife *and* a baby in one day! Don't worry about her tonight—" Her voice grew louder. "Shoshanna will care for her well while you and Moshe get acquainted, nu?"

Rachel blushed at Hannah's meaning, and walked a bit quicker toward the apartment. She hoped to avoid any more encounters with the citizens of the quarter. Word would certainly get back to Moshe that she had been walking alone near Grandfather's apartment. Her heart was so filled with the joy of Moshe's love that she felt she could not bear even one moment of disapproval from him. She wrapped the shawl around the lower half of her face and tucked her chin, looking only at the cobblestones.

"Hello, Shaul!" cried the butcher Ish Kisho from his empty stall. "Nothing for you here today, I'm afraid!" He tugged his gray beard and patted the round belly beneath his white apron. Then he gasped. "And is that Rachel Lubetkin? Rachel the *bride* herself? Oy gevalt! Moshe, your intended, would not like you out on your wedding day alone!"

"I know, Mr. Kisho," she said apologetically. "I had to get something for the wedding, you know."

"Don't smile so big! It's bad luck on your wedding day!" he called after her. "Watch over her, Shaul! This is a very important day, you know! We have slaughtered the last lamb in the quarter!" As Rachel turned the corner, she could hear his voice, "Mazel Tov! Mazel Tov, Rachel Lubetkin!"

She wondered if the Mufti could hear the joy that had only begun to echo through the streets. She felt no fear of evil. She was a child of God now, and her smile was for Him. She hoped that somewhere the forces of wickedness grieved over the happiness that was alive in the ancient Jewish Quarter of Jerusalem, because she was confident that in the streets of heaven there was rejoicing. And in that rejoicing there was victory.

3 The Invitation

His spectacles low on the bridge of his nose, Howard Moniger studied the letter from the Jewish Agency. Ellie and David sat on the edge of their chairs while Yacov huddled beneath the arm of his grandfather, Rabbi Shlomo Lebowitz.

Howard smiled broadly and shook his head slowly. "It seems"—he handed the letter to Grandfather—"that we are all invited to a wedding."

"Yeah?" David sat back, relieved. "Rachel and Moshe?"

Ellie glared at the two drivers, whose smiles faded under her stern look. "You could have at least told us this was *good* news! I thought something had happened to them!"

Johann turned to Dan. "You see, you opened your big mouth and worried them. The Boss will not like it!" Dan squirmed and shrugged.

"Well, praise be to God!" Grandfather raised a hand to the heavens. "They are well! Both of them are well and tonight they are to be wed! You will have a brother now, Yacov! Moshe will marry your sister tonight!"

"But how will we go to the wedding?" Yacov asked. "No one is allowed to pass by the Arab guards and into the Old City."

"A miracle, Yacov!" the old rabbi said gravely. "Moshe has carried a radio into the Old City with him, and so we will hear the wedding as it happens. We will be at the Jewish Agency and they will be in the square at home, but we will hear them, nu? God should have such a machine. It would have saved Him a lot of time from coming down to Sinai. True? Of course true!" He peered at Ellie, whose anger had been replaced by relief. "And *you* will get to see the wedding. And take pictures also."

"Me?" Ellie glanced at Uncle Howard, certain that this was some enormous practical joke. He shrugged in agreement and allowed the old rabbi to finish.

"And *you*"—Grandfather directed his gaze at David—"will drive her in the plane, nu?" He sniffed and tugged his earlock. "Yet another invention God might borrow to make the work of angels less tiring."

"Sure, no problem. But what. . . ?" David looked from Grandfather to Howard.

"Quite simple," Howard answered. "Politics. Politics in the form of public relations. Our friend the Mufti has nearly convinced the world that he and his gang have already beaten the Jews of Jerusalem. He has strangled the roads. Terrorism and sniping are rampant. As far as the United Nations is concerned, their hope of Jerusalem being an International City is about gone. And when that hope goes, so will their support of Partition. They may well revoke the entire plan for a Jewish State unless we demonstrate that we are still alive and well and determined to survive whatever the Arabs dish out. We have a minimal number of weapons, so—Ellie, I'm sure you understand."

She nodded and grinned. "So we are fighting this war like a Hollywood press agent after an Oscar. Is that it?"

Howard cleared his throat. "In a way. I would say that David Ben-Gurion is quite a believer in the power of the press. Quite impressed with what your photographs have done for the cause up to now. Unfortunately the Arab cries for bloodshed and the war of Jihad seem to be drowning us out here in Jerusalem. The Boss has apparently decided that a wedding in the besieged Old City might hit some human interest columns and show another side of the situation here."

"He's right," Ellie agreed, relieved that the problem with her story was solved.

"The Mufti is using terrorism to state that the Jews cannot survive and hope for statehood is dead." Howard continued, "So we must show the world hope and perseverance. Terrorism is nothing more than propaganda. Its goal is to destroy the innocent and along with them the courage and hope of those who oppose it. It is an ugly business, this war of Haj Amin Husseini. He cares for nothing but a victory in the end. My Arab friends have told me with tears in their eyes how the house of Husseini murders Arabs as well as Jews while this madman seeks to become the absolute ruler in Palestine."

"He is the devil himself," the old rabbi agreed.

"We can count on one thing." David shifted in his chair. "Tonight isn't going to be just any old ordinary peaceful-type wedding. The guys on the other side of the wall are spreading it around that the Jewish Quarter is about to give up. They aren't going to like it. Not one bit. Kind of upset their propaganda

41

wagon, if you know what I mean."

Grandfather and Yacov dressed hurriedly for their short drive to the Jewish Agency. Grandfather wore a new black coat and a fur streimel atop his head. Howard had purchased both for him the week before in the new shop of a Jewish tailor who had lost his building in the first riot after Partition had been signed. The old rabbi stood proudly before the full-length mirror and straightened his hat.

"So! Another wedding in the house of Lebowitz!" he exclaimed as he plucked lint from Yacov's coat and straightened his yarmulke. "A day to rejoice! Tuesday is the best day for a Jewish wedding, Yacov. The third day of creation. And God said, *It was good!* Tuesday is the best day for a wedding. True? Of course true!"

Alone in the front room with the Agency drivers, David parted the curtains and looked down into the street. There, gleaming in the sunlight was a shiny, black, unmarked car half a block away. Two men sat in the front seat. The unshaven man behind the wheel blew smoke out of his half-open window, while his tough-looking companion studied the pages of the newspaper. David took in the line of cars, including the battered Jewish Agency vehicles, and chuckled. "Starting to look like a used car lot down there. We're going to have a parade to the Agency, you know."

"That's why we brought two vehicles," Dan yawned and looked around the room. "We're going to split up. The Boss wanted to see which of us the men would follow. Intelligence still hasn't figured out who he is or what he wants."

David let the curtains fall back. "I can tell you exactly who they are. Americans, that's who. They've been on my tail for weeks, except when I'm in the air—and I'm starting to get paranoid about that lately. We had a visit from the American consulate, see, and they warned me that I could lose my citizenship if I fly as a mercenary for a foreign power. I tried to tell them the Jewish Agency is foreign, but it doesn't have any power; and how can I be a mercenary when I'm not getting paid peanuts? And why do you keep saying 'he'? There are two guys in the car."

"We know all about that." Johann dismissed David's words with a wave of his hand. "There is more in play here than who David Meyer flies airplanes for. Someone else is quite interested in what goes on at the professor's house."

"Yeah? What's up?"

"Take another look," said Johann, his words thick with weariness. "Just around the corner, past the street lamp."

Curious, David held the curtains open a crack. An empty car sat by the curb at the intersection just across the street at the end of the block. The car had the same dusty, over-used appearance of a thousand other vehicles in the Holy City. Its light tan finish concealed the true extent of its need for a wash, but the windshield was spotted and grimy. "The tan car?" David asked. "So what?"

"It blends nicely with traffic. The fellow who drives it has been watching this house." Dan stretched with unconcern. "We want to see who he'll follow, that's all. You and the girl? Or the professor in there, eh?"

"Who is it?" David frowned.

"We don't know yet. Our fellow spotted him yesterday afternoon. The Arabs and the British have made quite a diplomatic stink about those scrolls the professor and Moshe Sachar dug up, you know. Arabs claim they were stolen from some Bedouins. British claim they ought to have them in The British National Museum because they were discovered while they are still the Mandatory Government. Quite a row going on at the Agency. Wires flying back and forth."

"You think that's what this is about? The professor doesn't have the scrolls."

"So everyone has heard." Dan shrugged. "We just think it might be nice to see who that fellow is tailing. You, or—"

His bald head shining, Howard Moniger stepped into the room. "Ready to go now? I think we are fit for a wedding!"

"The professor," Dan finished laconically.

———

Howard, Yacov, and Rabbi Lebowitz climbed into the backseat of Dan's car, while David and Ellie sat in the front seat of Johann's car. The unmistakably clean chrome of the American consulate vehicle shone brightly in the rear-view mirror as Johann turned a block behind Dan, then turned again immediately at the next corner as Dan's vehicle continued on a separate route. David eyed the side mirror, hoping to catch a glimpse of the dusty tan automobile. But only the shiny consulate car followed them. Street after street, they drove slowly in a circuitous route toward the Agency. Ellie talked happily, not noticing that some-where along the path they had lost the car carrying Howard, Ya-cov, and Grandfather. Suddenly as they passed the majestic stone structure of the YMCA building, she said, "Hey! If you were a taxi driver, I'd say you were trying to push up your fare! Where's Uncle Howard's car, anyway?"

"Just avoiding the barricades," Johann smiled, then changed the subject as his eyes scanned the rear-view mirror as well. "These American agents!" he scoffed loudly to David. "So obvi-ous!"

"David says that's the idea," Ellie responded. "They are trying to intimidate. David is quite famous back home, and they don't want him to give any other Americans any ideas about fighting in a foreign war. The State Department is upset because it looks like the United States is sending men here to fight with the Jews against the Arabs *and* the British. They think it looks bad, espe-cially for a top war ace like David."

David looked over the top of her head and said to Johann, "Either that fella you're expecting to follow us is very good at what he does, or you can scratch me off his list. The only guys behind us are those two goons from the American consulate. If we had time, I'd like to pull in here at the King David and buy them a drink. Good grief, they're persistent!"

Johann nodded. "That's that." He continued up Julian Way, past the YMCA and then left onto Mamillah Street. On the right, the weathered headstones and monuments of Mamillah Ceme-tery rose, marking the border between the Jewish Section of the New City and the Muslim occupied area. Behind them were the blackened remains of the once-thriving Jewish Commercial Dis-trict, where Ellie and Yacov had been trapped in the first riot after Partition. David felt her shudder as she glanced over her shoulder with an unspoken fascination that she had survived the ordeal. Tenderly, David grasped her hand as he remembered his own terrible fears for her safety. For an instant, as the image of her smoke-smudged face flashed in his mind, he wished more strongly than ever that she were back home in California and away from this mess. He studied her profile: freckles across the slightly up-turned nose; full lips that could either pout or smile in an instant; her wide, lovely green eyes that absorbed the world around her with an intensity that belied the childlike innocence they seemed to display. There was a depth in the beauty of this woman-child beside him, which he had only begun to comprehend. He wanted a lifetime with her to explore the light and shadow within those depths.

His face had softened as he studied her, and involuntarily he reached up and touched her wavey red hair. She glanced up at him and grinned brightly; then, seeing the emotion in his eyes, her own expression grew tender and her heart spoke briefly through a lingering look. They could not speak aloud, but the message that passed privately between them was understood.

"What do you know," David said at last. "Moshe and Rachel are tying the knot." He winked and touched her cheek.

"The rabbi says Tuesday is the best day for a wedding," Ellie answered quietly, her eyes locked with his.

"We'll have to remember that." David raised his eyebrows and touched his forehead to hers.

"Oy gevalt!" shouted Johann as they pulled up to the barricade at the intersection of Mamillah and King George Avenue. "Will you *look*!" He pointed toward the shiny black limousine with the two tiny American flags driving toward them. "Now you watch! It will take us twenty minutes to get through this roadblock, and that momzer and his Arab chauffer will breeze right through on the other side!" He rolled down his window quickly and shouted at the approaching sentries, who looked all of eighteen years old. "This is an Agency vehicle! Official business! We're in a hurry."

"Papers, please!" returned the young sentry as he strolled toward the car with his hand extended.

———

David Ben-Gurion does indeed live up to the translation of his name, Son of a Lion, thought Ellie as she watched him from across his desk. Shocks of white hair stood up like a mane, his face seemed etched into a perpetual growl these days, and his temper was short. It was not out of the kindness of his heart that he had called Yacov and his aged grandfather to his office together with Uncle Howard, David and her. Every action had a carefully considered purpose these days in Jerusalem. Every action was weighed to measure its benefit for the Jewish State.

"You brought your camera, young lady?" he fired off the words like a machine-gun burst. Ellie held her camera up slightly

45

and the old man grunted his approval. "Good. You can take pictures from the air?"

"Yes."

"And we can see what they are about?"

"If David can fly low enough. Then I can always blow them up."

Ben-Gurion raised his eyebrows. "This is not a bombing mission. It is a wedding, nu?"

"I mean I can enlarge them," she explained, certain that no wedding in history had ever been photographed like this one, or received the press coverage that this one would.

"Good." He turned to Grandfather and said in a matter-of-fact tone, "When we received the message in code from Moshe, we debated whether it was worth the use of the shortwave radio batteries in order to cover the wedding. We shall see what kind of story Miss Warne writes for the newspapers, nu?"

The contrast between Grandfather and Ben-Gurion was remarkable—Grandfather in his black coat and stiff black hat, and Ben-Gurion dressed casually in a white shirt open at the collar. Grandfather tugged his graying beard and peered curiously at the man who was the vibrant head of the Provisional Jewish Government. "A Jewish wedding is always a story, nu, Mr. Ben-Gurion?"

"And more so when it takes place behind the walls of a besieged city, Rebbe Lebowitz. You take my meaning." He rubbed a hand wearily across his forehead. "Moshe is like a son to me," Ben-Gurion sighed. "Tonight I will raise my glass with you and toast his bride. And also I will hope that the world will raise their glasses and toast Jewish courage and determination to go on living no matter how hard the Arabs make it for us here in Jerusalem."

"Then we are of the same mind," said Grandfather quietly. "And if Moshe is like a son to you, then after tonight we shall be family, nu?"

For the first time since they had entered his office, the Son of a Lion smiled. "The Old City and the New. We are both Jews." A gleam of understanding passed between the two men. The one represented all that was ancient among the scattered nation of Israel; the other carried the burden of today on his shoulders. And between them both, the hope of the future was rich and alive. *This year in Jerusalem!*

As suddenly as it had come, the warmth in Ben-Gurion's eyes

was replaced by an unspoken worry, and the worry was then concealed by brusqueness. "Well then," he patted his hands on the clutter of his desk. "The radio room is just down the hall. There is a room next to it if you would like coffee while you wait, nu? I will join you later." He glanced at his watch while the others stood to leave.

Touching the patch on his eye, Yacov turned and waved at the harried commander. Ben-Gurion scowled, then grinned and winked at the boy who had sat in silent awe before him. Ben-Gurion returned his small wave, then glanced up toward David as he filed out after the rest.

"David!" he called. "A moment more, please. Yes. And close the door."

David shut the door behind Ellie, then leaned on the bookcase and crossed his arms. Ben-Gurion sat with his head poised as he listened to the retreating footsteps of the rest of the group. "What's this all about, Boss?" David asked. "Why all this big deal about a wedding, anyway? What difference is it going to make?"

The weary lion rubbed his forehead, then sighed. "We are going to lose the Old City to the Mufti," he replied in a toneless voice. "We may even lose the New City if something isn't done soon. We make a brave show here, but that is all. Moshe, his bride, those behind the walls with them, are a sacrifice, I'm afraid."

David snorted, "Then why the big show? What's this all about?"

"They buy us time with their bravado. When they fall, they will buy us sympathy with the world. By then the State of Israel will be newborn and have a chance to live, at any rate."

"Better than the chance you're giving Moshe and Rachel."

"They know the risks. Moshe knows most certainly what their fate will be."

"Still he stays. Nuts. The guy is nuts."

"He is courageous and dedicated."

"And suicidal, if you ask me."

"I did not ask you," Ben-Gurion said abruptly. "As I said, they buy us time. Sympathy for their plight makes the Jews of the United States more willing to help with their money. Even now Golda Meir is traveling to raise money for weapons and machines."

"Airplanes?"

"Yes. And this is where you come in. You are quite a famous American flyer. A war ace. You know people in high places in the aviation industry as well as having influence with other American pilots."

"More public relations, huh?" David said sarcastically, still brooding on Ben-Gurion's comments about Moshe and Rachel in the Old City.

"Of a kind, yes. We need you to return to America for us. This time you will have money. We want you to purchase planes. Transport planes."

"And who's going to fly them?"

"You will find crews."

"Hey, I'm just a pilot." David shifted uneasily. "I came here to fly."

"Your friends can deliver mail and drop supplies to the kibbutzim. We need you to perform a much more urgent task. Men. Planes. We will need them stationed at airfields around Europe by the time the British evacuate. They will have to fly to Palestine the instant Statehood is declared. They will carry our salvation and our survival in their cargo bays, and you will lead them."

"Hold it!" David protested. "I have personal reasons for being here, you know."

Ben-Gurion's mouth curved in a half smile and he looked at the door where Ellie had stood just a few minutes before. "I see. She is needed here, David."

"To cover The Alamo," he said flatly. "I get it. Well, what if I don't want to do it?"

"Then God will raise up another who will. But I think you are the man we need." He absently straightened his desk. "What you do might make the difference between our survival or our fall. There is an old Aramaic saying, *Yakum purkan min shemaya.* It means, *Salvation comes from the sky.* This is a saying you believe in, David."

David looked away from his intent gaze. "Yes, I guess I do."

"Indeed! How many times have you stood in this office and argued for a stronger use of air power? You and your American friend, Michael! It was you who practically resurrected the saying, nu?"

"Somebody else ought to go. Anybody can buy a plane."

"Can anybody . . . just anybody inspire American crews to come fly the planes? The American State Department is terrified that you might go public with your stand and compromise their neutrality with the British."

David shrugged. He was beaten and he knew it, but he didn't relish the thought of leaving Ellie in a country where sacrifice was the order of the day.

"Is Michael Cohen coming with me?"

"He has been sent for."

"How much cash have we got to work with?"

"At this moment, forty-five thousand American dollars."

"What? One new Constellation costs a million! Where can we find new planes for that kind of dough?"

"We aren't talking new."

"Well then decent, at least."

"We aren't talking decent. We're talking able to fly, nu?"

David sighed in exasperation. "This whole deal is nuts, you know that, don't you?"

"It isn't necessary to be crazy in order to be a Zionist, but it helps."

"I'll keep that in mind," David muttered.

Ben-Gurion narrowed his eyes. "So. It's all settled, then. The survival of the Jewish nation is in your hands."

"I'll bet you say that to everybody."

The old lion shrugged. "Yes, as a matter of fact I do." He patted the clutter again, signaling an end to the conversation. "Any questions?"

"By the time I finished asking, Boss, the Mufti would be sitting at your desk."

"A possibility, unfortunately. In a few days I am moving headquarters to Tel Aviv. If anything comes up, contact us there at the red house through the usual channels."

"Deserting the sinking ship? Two months ago in this office Shimon Devon told us all we should evacuate Jerusalem!"

"No! Not one inch of ground will be taken by the Arabs without a fight! Not even the most hopeless of outposts!" The old man flared angrily at David's accusation. "If I could I would post the Jewish Agency on top of Nissan Bek Synagogue in the Old City so I could spit over the wall at the Jihad Moquades! But that would be *all* I could do! So I am going where I can do the most good. Where I don't want to go. Like you! Like Moshe and the girl he will marry tonight! And each of us will offer our lives if we must because there is no other way to save lives!"

"You're right." David gathered up his jacket and stretched slowly.

"Sorry." He stood with his hand on the doorknob for a moment, searching for something more he could say.

Ben-Gurion picked up a sheaf of papers and began poring over them. "Call Dan and Johann into my office on your way out, will you?" The interview was at an end.

"Sure." Quietly, David slipped out the door and motioned to Dan and Johann who sat grimly in the only two chairs in the busy hallway.

Johann looked up expectantly. "Well, it seems our friend in the tan car didn't care to follow either of us."

David nodded. "You sure he's been keeping an eye on the professor's house?"

"Who can tell these days, eh?" said Johann in disgust. "Ninety-nine percent of everyone in Jerusalem is up to something. Maybe the man has a girlfriend in your neighborhood. Maybe he's trying to catch his wife at something. Who knows?" he said again.

"Right. I've started jumping at my own shadow lately," David grinned. "The Old Man wants to see you guys. And I've seen him in better moods, so watch your step."

Dan and Johann exchanged glances. "Now, that's something to make a man jumpy!" said Dan.

4 Preparations

The sun lingered in the west, then slowly began to move toward the horizon.

From the window of his tiny room in the Warsaw Compound, Moshe watched anxiously, for the first time in his life wishing for time to pass quickly. He had not seen Rachel since the day before, and the minutes had seemed like days to him.

"Well?" Ehud boomed from the corner as he slipped on his borrowed dress coat. "I am dressed for a wedding or a funeral. I can never remember which it is when I look at the groom! Ha! You are pale as a corpse!"

Moshe turned around and eyed Ehud from head to toe. "So are you. I always wondered what color you were under all those barnacles."

"Every boy in the quarter is washed by now—at least hands and faces. It's too late to change your mind, Moshe. Your wedding is the only reason they would bathe willingly. If you run away they will hunt you down and lynch you! Ah, marriage!" he teased as he gathered up Moshe's kittel, his white silk wedding robe. "Such a blessed occasion." He tossed the kittel to Moshe who put it on with care. "There, yes," Ehud stomped around him approvingly. "The contrast between the kittel and your skin makes you not look so dead." He tapped Moshe's cheeks playfully. "There may be a little color there after all."

Moshe smiled half-heartedly, not up to Ehud's exuberant humor. He stared intently at his own reflection in the cracked mirror above a washbasin. He barely recognized his own face. Indeed, it was not the face that had smiled back at him only a few weeks before. His thick black beard made him look older than his previously clean-shaven cheeks. Large brown eyes gazed back at him worriedly. "Will she recognize me?" he asked, half to himself.

"Recognize you?" Ehud bellowed. "Why, you only parted from her last night! Recognize you!" he guffawed. "The man has taken leave of his senses!"

"No." Moshe was suddenly embarrassed. "It's just that I never realized how much I look like my father. I never saw him without a beard. He was a Sochet, you know, a kosher butcher not five blocks from here. And from the time I left for the University at Oxford, I haven't had a beard. That's all."

"Well, bridegroom, it wouldn't be kosher for you to shave now, eh? You're in the land of the Hassidim. If we stay much longer, we'll be growing earlocks as well!" Ehud patted him on the back. "It won't matter to your bride once the candle is out, at any rate."

Moshe cleared his throat uncomfortably and turned away from Ehud. "Where is my hat?"

"On your head. Where are your wits?"

"Ehud, does every man feel like this before he marries?"

"I suppose it depends on the circumstance, eh?"

Moshe spread his hands in a gesture of helplessness. "You and I have been through a lot together, Ehud. I need to talk to you a moment seriously."

"Ah. I see." The humor was instantly gone from Ehud's broad, grizzled face. "You are having second thoughts maybe?"

"No! That is yes. I mean I . . . I worry that perhaps here, at this

51

time and in this place marriage is unfair to her. This is no life for anyone. Everything is so uncertain, Ehud. How can we know what tomorrow will bring to us?"

"I have known you for ten years, Moshe Sachar. We have run the blockades, fought Nazis and English, nu? Life has always been uncertain for us."

"That is why I never considered marriage to anyone before now."

"You were not truly ever in love before now, my friend." Ehud scratched his beard and pursed his lips. "I loved my own dear wife when life was kind to us and when it was not. When she was taken and I escaped, I grieved near to death. She and the children are in heaven, and still I love them. And I will tell you this, I would not trade the hours of happiness we had for this world and another lifetime if I had to live without having known them. There is often a grief that comes with loving, Moshe. But it is worth it. Yes. It is worth the lonely hours."

"I wish never to hurt her." Moshe's eyes were full of pain. "Not in my life with her, and not by my death if God calls me to serve Him by dying."

"Leave that to God, then, eh? When He wants you to die is none of your business! How He wants you to live is a matter you should pay attention to. So be happy! There is not a man with eyes who would not give an arm to stand beneath the canopy with such a beauty!" Ehud thumped Moshe hard on the back. "So make *her* happy, already, and stop your kvetching. It is not like you, Moshe. Courage, man! A smile on the bridegroom's pale face, if you please. And hurry, or you will be late to the *badeken die kalla*, the veiling of the bride!"

Before Moshe could say another word, Ehud had shoved him out the door and into the dusky courtyard. On the steps of the Warsaw synagogue, dozens of little boys stood waiting for him, and all around them, Yeshiva students and Haganah men mingled expectantly. A lusty cheer rose up from the men and boys as Moshe drew himself up to his full height and raised his hand in salute.

The blue and lavender hues of the sky deepened as the first full notes of the clarinet drifted high above the walls of the compound. Seven flickering candles were lit and held high as a reminder of the lightning that flashed on Mount Sinai when the bride Israel accepted God as her bridegroom. "There were voices and lightning and a thick cloud on the mountain," Moshe whispered the verses of Exodus softly, as bridegrooms of centuries had done before him. *Teach me to love her, Lord,* he prayed silently. *Show me the way to make her happy in my love. And if it is to be that we walk away from this place alive, give us a long life together as man and wife. Omaine.*

He would have felt happier if the wedding were to take place indoors, but Rachel had smiled sadly and spoken of her own parents who were married beneath the stars in the Old City Square. "I intend to marry only once," she had insisted. "Let the Mufti hear our joy! Perhaps it will give him indigestion!" Her laughter had won his consent, and her one moment of grief over the absence of her grandfather and brother had stirred him to yet another action. The shortwave radio that served as the quarter's only link with the outside world was concealed beneath the table which was to hold the two cups of wine for the wedding.

Moshe smiled as he imagined the look on Rachel's face when she heard the voice of the old rabbi. *Tuesday is a good day for a wedding! True? Of course true!* His cracking voice would echo in the square with a hundred other Mazel Tovs, welcoming what had been a ragged remnant of Israel home to a new life; a new beginning. More than anything else in his life, Moshe wanted to offer Rachel happiness. It had become his goal, his prayer above all others.

Lengthening shadows seemed only to make the candles burn more brightly and the music ring more sweetly in the ancient cobbled alleyways. Above them, blue and white banners waved from window ledges and dripped like the icing on a cake above the vaults that covered sections of the streets. They rounded a corner and passed beneath the dark and cheerless shutters of the home of Rabbi Akiva. There was no good will shining from his house, yet Moshe took comfort in the thought that he was among the few who hated Rachel and accused her of a past over which she had no control. Akiva was nearly the last of those who still believed that negotiations with the Mufti might yield some benefit for the Jewish Holy Places. Akiva's alliance with the Arab Quarter as well as his dogmatic opposition of Jewish statehood had reduced him to a bitter shard of a man. He would not wish them well tonight, but still, Moshe and Rachel together had found room for forgiveness and pity for the man. The white kittel Moshe wore and the gown that Rachel was to meet him in stood for purity before God. They had vowed together that they would not enter into a new life with hatred for anyone.

Sweet Rachel, Moshe thought as he glanced at the heavy wooden gate to the courtyard of Akiva. She had even wanted to go to the once-respected rabbi and share with him the things that had happened to change her life. "You cannot," Moshe had told her. "To share what you have found in our Messiah would only give him more cause to fear you and hate you. We must go slowly, my love. As you know yourself, the name of Yeshua has been a name to fear for our people. First we must *live* and love them as He did; then our words will mean something to them."

An invitation to the wedding had been sent to Akiva, along with a special note to his daughter Yehudit. Both had been returned unopened. Rachel had wept. Not for herself but for them. "They are," she had said, "locked in a prison of their own making."

In the dressing room of the synagogue, half a dozen women of the quarter scurried about, helping Rachel dress or taking turns holding Tikvah, who wailed a protest at the disturbance of her daily routine. Hannah Cohen hovered over Rachel, braiding her long black tresses with tiny white flowers and white silk ribbons.

Rachel held a round silver-plated hand mirror and gazed at her reflection with delighted awe. Blue eyes radiated with happiness and her skin seemed almost to glow with the luster of a creamy pearl in the lamplight.

"Where did you ever find the flowers, Hannah?" she cried with joy.

"They are tiny snow drops, sent by the Lord of heaven on the warmth of the wind," she said, her eyes twinkling with merriment, "to show His approval of your marriage. He provides when there is a need, nu? And what greater need for snow drops than the crown of a Jewish bride!"

Rachel turned her head first to one side and then the other. She could not restrain her smile at the lights that shimmered in her hair. "And what will Moshe say when he sees me, do you think?" her voice was animated.

Patting Tikvah on the back, old Shoshanna's mouth spread in a toothless grin. "Moshe will not want to put the veil over you, I am thinking!"

"And he will be most anxious to lift it off again," volunteered

54

another as she slipped out the door.

"Thank you!" Rachel wrapped her arms around Hannah in a brief embrace. Then she glanced around the room, her eyes touching each smiling face. "Thank you all!" she exclaimed. "There was a time I thought I would never be happy, but this is the happiest moment of my life."

"Ah!" Shoshanna said quietly. "Your mama, may she rest in peace, she would be proud of you this day.

"I remember her wedding day! So frightened, she was! Oy! How she shook! In this very room."

Rachel held out her fingers. They were steady. "See," she said brightly, "I am only happy today!"

"Never was there a more lovely bride!" Hannah chirped. "Not even your mama, may she rest in peace."

"Omaine!" said Shoshanna, pleased at last that the baby had finally stopped crying.

A sharp rapping sounded at the door; then the bright round face of one of the school girls poked in. "They are coming!" she whispered as though she were relaying a deep secret. Then her gaze fell on Rachel and her eyes grew wide. "Ooooooooh!" she said in admiration. She gawked a moment longer until Shoshanna whisked her out and shut the door behind her.

"Are you ready, child?" Hannah put her hands on Rachel's shoulders and smoothed the satin of the puffed sleeves.

Suddenly butterflies seemed to fill Rachel's stomach and she held her hand out again. Her fingers trembled slightly and she was filled with wonder that the moment of beginning a new life was finally here. "I—I," she stammered. "I think I am."

"They come!" the young child burst into the room. "Listen!"

The bustle of the room suddenly stilled and every woman cocked an ear toward the half-open door. Louder and louder, the song of the *Badeken*, the veiling ceremony, approached. Its minor chords seemed to fill the room and the heart of not only the bride but also those women who had been brides in happier times. Eyes filled with unspoken memories, and the faces of the young girls spoke of an impatient hope that someday they might be the one in the long white gown with a crown of snow drops and ribbons. In an instant, young and old were joined together in a happy blending of memory and hope. And at the center of their thoughts stood Rachel. She stood straight and tall, her lips parted, and her eyes wide with expectancy as she seemed to see through the walls and float on the music to Moshe's side. In her mind there was no thought of the past, no thought of the future. There was only *now*. This moment of beginning when God would weave her life with Moshe's like snow drops and silken ribbons.

"Where is my gift for Moshe?" she whispered to the spellbound attendants. Her voice quavered a bit.

"Only a few minutes more my dear!" Hannah did not budge. "They are coming!"

"The tallith!" Rachel said more loudly, suddenly panicked as she searched the room, flinging her clothes from a chair to the floor. Hannah quickly picked them up and shoved them into a closet as Rachel snatched up the olivewood box and peeked in quickly, then placed it on a small round table in the center of the room.

Yet another little girl charged into the dressing room, her pigtails flying and her breath short with excitement.

"He's here! The bridegroom has come, Rachel. Rabbi Vultch stands on the steps of the synagogue. Moshe is very handsome in his white kittel, and Ehud comes with him! Miss Rachel! Captain Ehud is *clean*!"

Rachel laughed loudly at the child's astonishment at that last fact, and as laughter filled the room, Hannah positioned Rachel beside the table, then stepped back along the wall with the other ladies. "Shut the door, child," Hannah said softly. "Then come here that you may not be in the way."

Just as the door clicked shut, the music of the Badeken stopped at the steps of the synagogue. Silence fell heavy on the little room and Rachel held her breath as she waited for the approaching footsteps. Three hard knocks sounded on the heavy wooden door. Then a husky voice called, "The bridegroom has arrived. Who will open to him?"

Hannah stepped forward and with a quick glance over her shoulder at Rachel, she pulled the door open.

Moshe's strong and tall form seemed to fill the doorway. His eyes found her like a man who had been blind and was seeing only now for the first time. Warm and full of his very soul, he spoke to her heart and feasted on her beauty as he waited silently for her to speak.

She drew a deep breath and stretched her hand out to him. "You are he who I have been waiting for. Welcome, Moshe Sachar, to my chamber."

Moshe stepped forward, and stood across from her while Ehud and Rabbi Vultch followed behind him. From that moment, for Rachel and Moshe, there were only voices in the room. Their eyes held each other, never looking away. They could not touch, and yet Rachel felt as though his arms encircled her.

"Moshe Sachar, you have agreed to accept this woman, Rachel Lubetkin, without a dowry. For her own self alone. She comes to you without material goods or chattel. You have agreed to love her as your own flesh. To provide for her. And to keep her forever as your wife. May God witness the ketuba as well as men. Now, whom do you name as witness to sign for you?"

"Ehud Schiff," Moshe replied, his eyes speaking to Rachel.

"And Rachel, whom do you name as your witness?"

"Hannah Cohen," she replied, "and those of my family who surely see us from heaven."

Hannah and Ehud stepped forward to sign the parchment that lay open on the table.

"Have you anything to add to the agreement?" the rabbi asked, not expecting an answer.

"One thing." Rachel smiled at the surprise that crossed Moshe's face. After all, the terms had been agreed to several days before, according to the terms Rachel's grandfather had set down in his letter.

"Oh?" The rabbi asked. "But the document is prepared."

"Only one more thing. The house of Lubetkin has vanished from the earth. And yet, my father has not forgotten me. When he lived and I was only a child, he and my mother saved all they could. It was sent here to my grandfather in order that it might be used to save us. Instead, their savings will be a dowry for me, so that the house of Lubetkin might be proud to give their daughter in marriage."

"But, Rachel, I want only you," Moshe protested.

"My father was a proud man; he would not send me into a new life penniless." Rachel's eyes were soft, almost imploring as she explained. "My father would wish to help the man who is to be his son-in-law. And this is only fitting. Somehow God has looked ahead to this day, and the gold that is given for my dowry was meant for this moment."

Moshe did not reply, but studied the expression on Rachel's face. It was plain to see that it was important to her that he accept graciously the terms and the gift that was offered from beyond the grave. He knew how important it was for the father of the bride to provide for the newly married couple for a while.

"Do you accept this new provision?" the rabbi asked.

"The house of your father, Aaron Lubetkin, was great," Moshe smiled at her, "known for wisdom and understanding of the Torah. The father of my bride was renowned for his charity and kind counsel. I would rather have him beside me for advice than have a dowry. But that is not to be. And so, with all my heart I thank the father of my bride for his generosity, and I promise that I too will care for her with all my heart. The terms are accepted."

Rachel touched the mezuzah that she wore around her neck as Moshe took the kerchief from her and presented it to Rabbi Vultch. *I will love thee with an everlasting love . . .* Rachel believed the promise Moshe had given.

"The terms given and accepted, we can proceed with the veiling." Rabbi Vultch clapped his hands together and rocked up on his toes.

"I have a gift for my bridegroom," Rachel said quietly, reaching for the olivewood box on the table.

Moshe raised his eyebrows in puzzled surprise as if to say, "For me?"

Shyly, she held it out to him. "The words of Ruth were spoken to Boaz, *Spread thy cloak over thy handmaid, for thou art a near kinsman . . .*" Moshe opened the box, revealing the royal blue velvet pouch that held the tallith. A murmur of approval rippled through the group of spectators. "As any bride in Israel offers a tallith to her husband, can I do less?"

"Rachel!" Moshe exclaimed. "It is *so* beautiful!" He pulled it from the pouch and held it high and shimmering in the light. "So beautiful," he said more softly; then, he passed it over her head slowly and, as the light of the candles shone through the silk onto her skin, he whispered, "As it is written by the Prophet Ezekiel, *Your time was the time of love and I spread my mantle over you.*"

Their eyes locked in understanding that excluded everyone else who had gathered in the room. For a long moment, Moshe held the tallith above her; then slowly he lowered it and turned to pass it to Ehud. "Please take my mantle and hurry to the square. Tonight, I want this tallith to be the canopy under which Rachel and I stand together and pledge our love."

Ehud took it from him without a word; bowed curtly and hurried from the room. Hannah took the long lace veil from where

58

it lay draped over a chair. She handed it to Rabbi Vultch, who pushed his glasses up on his nose and nodded. "So!" he said triumphantly. "Before we begin the veiling ceremony, has the bridegroom a gift to offer his bride?"

"Only this," Moshe took her hands in his and lowered his chin as he looked her straight in the eye. "My devotion. My life. Everything I am . . ."

Rachel's eyes filled with tears as she smiled into the face of this strong and gentle man.

". . . and one more thing," Moshe winked at her. "Tonight her brother and grandfather will hear the ceremony on the wireless. Tonight their hearts will stand very near to us. We will hear them say *"Mazel Tov!"* What does the bride say to this?" He grinned broadly at the expression of joy that overwhelmed her features.

"Oh, Moshe!" she cried, throwing her arms around his neck.

Rabbi Vultch wiped a smile from his lips and frowned as the baby Tikvah began a steady wail. He stepped forward and parted the embrace gingerly. "Now then," he coughed. "Time enough for that later, eh?"

Rachel, beaming, stepped back. She shook her head in disbelief at Moshe's thoughtfulness. Moshe shrugged happily at her response, as if to say, *It was nothing, really.* But he knew that to Rachel it was everything she needed to make the night perfect.

Rabbi Vultch completed the readings from Genesis, but Moshe stood rock still with the veil, seemingly unwilling to cover Rachel's beauty. "Yes, Moshe. You should veil the bride now, nu? And next time you see her she will be your wife."

"In that case," Moshe smiled and lowered the veil over Rachel's head.

Rabbi Vultch closed his eyes and raised his hands in blessing as he cried loudly over Tikvah's persistent wail, "O sister! May you be the mother of thousands of myriads!" He lowered his hands and patted both Moshe and Rachel on their backs. "And it looks like your bride has a head start on motherhood, eh, Moshe?"

Laughter filled the room as old Shoshanna shushed and hushed and patted the now outraged baby.

The squawk of the shortwave radio permeated the little room at the end of the hall in the Jewish Agency building. A thin young man with curly brown hair and a schoolboy's face turned the

59

tuning knob as David, Grandfather, Yacov and Howard looked on expectantly.

Ellie stood at the door and watched through the view finder of her camera as Ben-Gurion hurried past tiny offices with frosted glass doors. Dan and Johann followed closely at his heels. The Old Man held a clear glass bottle of red wine in his right hand, and his two companions carried stacks of water glasses with which they would all toast the occasion. Ellie smiled when she noticed that the wine bottle had a screw-on lid rather than a cork, and she wondered if this was wine from Ben-Gurion's own homemade reserve. He raised his eyes toward the doorway just as she clicked the shutter. The bulb hissed and sprayed his face with bright light. His smile disappeared and he blinked hard.

"Aren't you supposed to be in the air taking pictures?" he asked sternly. "You almost made me drop the bottle."

"The wedding is taking place here, too," Ellie returned. "We at least need a picture of you raising your glasses to the bride and groom." He turned sideways and inched past her into the crowded cubbyhole.

"Ah, true. Here at the Jewish Agency we celebrate also," he agreed. "This is important for the publicity." His voice held a kind of false cheer and Ellie turned toward David with a question in her eyes. David stood against the far wall, gazing down grimly at the chipped tiles on the floor. Dan and Johann remained outside the room, but their bodies filled the doorway and somehow to Ellie their joyless faces held a knowledge and foreboding that did not fit the occasion.

Grandfather and Yacov were oblivious to the dark current that flowed beneath the surface of these men. Yacov wriggled and squirmed over the shoulder of the radio operator, and Grandfather eyed Ben-Gurion's wine with approval.

"Your own vintage?" he asked with a slight smile.

Ben-Gurion handed him the bottle. "Mazel Tov, Rabbi Lebowitz," he said. "Made from the grapes of a vineyard I helped to plant my first year here on the Yishuv. We had little but marshland then."

"Ah yes. True. I remember." Grandfather unscrewed the cap on the bottle and inhaled deeply. "A nice wine for Shabbat or a wedding."

"Well then"—Ben-Gurion took the glasses from Dan and Johann—"we should at least fill the cups so that Miss Warne may photograph the toast and be off before it is too dark." He passed the glasses to each person in the room.

"I have a little vintage something myself." Ellie dug deep in the pocket of her jacket. "Been saving it for something special and wonderful." She held up her bottle of Coke. "The last one in Palestine, I'll have you know. For the tee-totalers among us. Uncle Howard?"

Howard's face broke into a grin. There was nothing, Ellie knew, that Howard liked to sip as much as a Coca-Cola. "I was hoping you would share this. But I didn't dare ask."

"And Yacov?"

The boy's eyes lit up. "You could have sold that on the black market, you know," he said. "At least two chickens."

"And David?" Ellie asked expectantly. "Will you do the honors?" She passed the bottle to him, and he seemed to brighten a bit. "This will give you a chance to show off," Ellie teased him.

David looked Yacov squarely in the eye. "Watch this, kid," he said, raising the unopened bottle to his mouth. "A little trick I learned in the Air Force." Gripping the rim of the bottle cap in his teeth, he flipped it off.

"Teach me!" Yacov cried in awe.

"Naw. It'll bust your teeth off." He winked and mussed the boy's yarmulke; then he poured Yacov's glass a third full and split the rest between Howard and Ellie.

"Have you nearly got it?" Ben-Gurion asked the radio operator impatiently.

The young man nodded, and simultaneously, the high squeal of the receiver blended into a strong, almost melancholy note from a distant clarinet. A cry of appreciation rose from the little group and all raised their glasses as Ellie focused her camera.

"Well, then, are we all ready?" Ben-Gurion asked. He nodded at Ellie briskly. "Miss Warne?"

"Any time," she said softly as she studied the tender expression of Grandfather as his eyes filled with deep emotion and he raised the ruby red wine over his head. His eyelids fluttered briefly as he searched for words that would properly contain all the blessings he held in his heart for Rachel and Moshe. *"Ye'hey Sh'lomo Rabbo Min Sh'mayo, Vechayim Oleynoo Ve'al Kol Yisroale. Omaine!* Then he repeated the blessing in English as the radio operator held the microphone close to his mouth. "May there be abundant peace from heaven, and life for us and all Israel. Omaine!"

"Omaine," those in the room repeated and the far away voices of many others replied through the static.

The old rabbi turned to the east, toward the Old City, and raised his glass higher. "My dear granddaughter," his voice quavered a bit. "May He who maketh peace in His high places make peace for you and your husband and for all Israel! And we all say, Omaine!"

Glasses were raised to the lips of those in the room, and each person there seemed for an instant to taste of hope—hope for Rachel and Moshe and hope for a new Israel. Ellie clicked the shutter as Grandfather savored the wine and whispered a silent, private prayer for the young woman who had been through so much and lived to see this one moment of joy. Then she turned toward Ben-Gurion and studied his expression briefly. She held the camera in front of her face and hid the fear she felt at the shadow of grief that flitted across his features. She pressed her finger down on the shutter, grateful for the splash of light that brought his thoughts back to this moment.

"Well, then!" Grandfather cried happily. "Is that my Rachel there on the other end of this machine? Are you there, Rachel?"

After a slight pause, her joyful reply filled the room, "Yes, Grandfather! It is I!"

"Are you well, my dear?" he asked.

"Better than I have ever been, Grandfather!" she answered.

"Then perhaps we should begin the wedding, nu?" He clapped his hands together and gazed happily at each face in the room as though they were indeed gathered around the canopy in the glory of Jerusalem Square behind the walls of the Old City.

5 The Celebration

In the eastern sky, iridescent banners of deep blue and violet blended with the purple of approaching night. Finally, the glowing crown of the sun slipped behind the horizon as the blessings of Grandfather crackled over the radio in the square. Voices raised as one in the cry of "omaine!" And Rabbi Vultch stepped forward to the canopy and opened his silver prayer book.

"As God, the bridegroom, came forth to Sinai to meet Israel, the bride," he said quietly, "so Moshe will come forth to stand beneath the canopy first to meet Rachel."

Soft light filtered through the silk tallith that served as the canopy. It billowed slightly in the wind, and the only sound that touched the stillness of the crowd was a gentle flapping sound as the wind touched and fell away, then touched the canopy again.

Candles in hand, the crowd parted as Ehud escorted Moshe forward to take his place on the left side beneath the canopy. He folded his hands before him and looked over his shoulder toward the back of the square where Rachel waited. He smiled slightly at Ehud, who stood at his left. All appearance of nervousness had left Moshe, and an expression of deep peace radiated from his eyes. All around the square, from the low domed rooftops, young Haganah guards and Yeshiva scholars stood watch with one eye beyond the quarter to the Arab streets, and the other eye cast enviously on the canopy and Moshe.

The music began again, low and mellow, echoing high above the square and into the streets far beyond the walls. It was a song that had been played for a million Jewish brides over a thousand years, and in its melody all the hopes and dreams of the future were contained. Violin and clarinet joined together to announce to a doubtful world that life still went on behind these besieged walls. Hope still existed and was acted upon and lived out in this union of one woman and one man. Memories of other weddings filled the minds of those who watched. Near the front of the group, a woman who had seen Rachel's own mother married cried quietly into her handkerchief.

All eyes turned toward Rachel as she walked slowly forward. Hannah stood on her right hand and Shoshanna on her left. Even beneath her veil, Rachel's blue eyes shone luminous and bright. Her hands trembled slightly, but her walk was steady and in time to the minor key of the wedding song.

With each step, her heart grew nearer to Moshe. His eyes held her up and drew her to him like a strong cord. She felt that there was no one else on earth at this moment. No one but Moshe and her and God, who was busy weaving two souls into one. As she approached within a few feet of the canopy, Hannah touched her elbow slightly and she halted, a captive of Moshe's gaze, until the music stopped.

Once again utter silence enfolded the square. A Holy Presence seemed to hover just above them on the wind. *It is the Shekinah*, Rachel thought, looking upward into the purple veil of the sky. Moshe followed her gaze, then nodded, as if to say he felt it, too.

After a moment, Shoshanna and Hannah took her by the arms and escorted her forward, circling Moshe seven times, as the ancient altar of the Temple had been circled during Holy Days of Old. The audience watched in quiet awe, as though this were the first wedding, the only wedding there had ever been on earth. Each step, each word and movement was so old, and yet now so new and ageless.

As Rachel circled Moshe the seventh time, he reached out his hand to her and the two old women stepped back and stood to the side. For Rachel, there was no past, only now and the future. Rabbi Vultch cleared his throat as she took her place to the right of Moshe, "The queen stands on your right hand in fine gold of Ophir." Moshe looked down at her and winked as if to say, *Well, we finally made it, eh?* She inclined her head slightly in acknowledgment and almost laughed out loud with the joy she felt.

Far in the distance the persistent hum of an airplane engine approached. The words that they spoke to each other and to God alone drifted out over the airwaves into the receivers of short-wave radios as far away as Tel Aviv, and as near as the headquarters of the Mufti himself. But still, their vows were only their own. They sipped together from the cup of joy and then the cup of sorrow, knowing in their hearts that they would share both joy and sorrow as one.

When you hurt, I will divide it with you. When I have joy it will be multiplied as we share it together.

As the rabbi read the traditional blessings, Moshe took Rachel's right hand in his own and slipped a plain gold band on her forefinger. Her hand lingered in his strong but gentle grip until the words of the rabbi ceased and Moshe said quietly, "Not even death will separate us, Rachel." His eyes shone with tears of emotion as he lifted the veil and kissed her tenderly.

The rabbi closed his prayer book and nodded slightly, taking from Ehud a glass wrapped in a white linen cloth. He held it high to show the congregation; then he laid it on the ground in front of Moshe.

Grasping Rachel's hand, Moshe raised his foot and brought it down hard, smashing the glass. A loud cry of "Mazel Tov!" echoed from the congregation, across the rooftops and beyond the walls of the Old City. Music began in instant celebration and as hands clasped together and voices raised in song, Moshe and Rachel Sachar were lifted to the shoulders of their friends. Ehud's loud voice rose above all others as he boomed at his troops, "Now! Come forward, boys, and remember! You must retrieve *every* grain for the kitchens!"

Faces bright and scrubbed almost beyond recognition, the small soldiers of Tipat Chalev rushed forward with their fists filled with precious grains of rice. "Mazel Tov!" They shouted, tossing the grains up in a shower of blessings over Moshe and Rachel. "Mazel Tov! Mazel Tov! Mazel Tov!"

Ehud towered happily in the background with his thick arms crossed proudly over his chest. When the last grain of rice had fallen, he shouted loudly, "A shilling to the boy who picks up the most! A shilling, lads!"

Squeals of delight filled the square as the boys fell to their knees and scrambled to retrieve what would most certainly become tomorrow's supper.

Haj Amin Husseini, Mufti of Jerusalem, sat quietly with his palms pressed together beneath his chin. His steel-blue eyes followed the angry pacing of Fredrich Gerhardt with disgust. Gerhardt, his finest explosives expert. Gerhardt, captain among the Jihad Moquades. Gerhardt, madman, psychopathic killer of Jews, was obsessed now with only one thing: the destruction of the Jewish whore who had escaped him.

"They mock me!" shouted Gerhardt, slamming his fist against the cold stone wall of the Mufti's study. "This wedding! This farce tonight in the Jewish Quarter! It is to insult me! To shame me, Fredrich Gerhardt! It is because of her that I bear this number on my arm. I lived among their stink in Ravensbruk because of her!"

Haj Amin's glare became dull with thought. Were he not so valuable, Gerhardt would die where he stood. Madman! He would throw everything away for the body of a woman.

"I wish to be avenged! Allow me, Haj Amin, to take but a few men into the Jewish Quarter tonight. I will kill them as they dance!"

"And let the world accuse me of assassinating a bride at the altar?" Haj Amin spoke quietly and with control. He lowered his hands to his lap and narrowed his eyes. "You are a fool, Gerhardt." His voice was soft, yet thick with venom.

"A fool!" Gerhardt protested.

"Yes. And you forget in whose presence you stand!"

Haj Amin measured each word, silencing Gerhardt who blinked in the glare of the lamplight like a rabbit caught in the headlights of an approaching car. Haj Amin shook his head from side to side. "You see the obvious. You speak the obvious. So the Jews of the Old City celebrate a wedding tonight. In their tattered coats they defy the strength of the Mufti. But *we* are gracious before the world. We wish the world to see that *we* are men of *generosity*; we wish these vagabonds to *live*. That is why we offer to allow them to leave the Old City with safe conduct."

Gerhardt stared blankly at him, unable to comprehend his plan. "But they mock me, I say."

"Not you, Gerhardt." His lips curled in a smile. "They mock themselves with this charade. They dare us to strike them and so we would look like heartless assassins in the eyes of the world." He laughed at the absurdity of it. "They wish to show themselves brave and us as villains. No, Gerhardt. We are not so foolish as all that. If they hope to draw the attention of the world to their comical little play tonight, then we shall simply direct the eyes of their audience elsewhere in Jerusalem. Attack the Old City *tonight?* Never. The revenge you seek is personal, Gerhardt, and your stupidity wears the fabric of my graciousness quite thin."

"But, Haj Amin! Tomorrow every newspaper in the West will carry this brave little show in their front pages!"

Haj Amin sighed a sigh of exasperation. "Not if we fill their columns with other news." He coughed into his handkerchief and then clapped his hands together in a loud summons. The black, ornately carved doors cracked open slightly and the wizened face of the personal servant of Haj Amin appeared, then nodded briefly. Lifting his chin, Haj Amin spoke thoughtfully and politely. "Basil, if you please, send our young cousin to us."

The servant nodded, backed out and silently closed the doors of the study.

"Who is this person you bring into our confidence?" Gerhardt asked irritably.

A spark of fury glinted in the eyes of Haj Amin; then he tilted his head slightly and smiled serenely as though Gerhardt's arrogance had gone unnoticed. "The son of my first cousin. He is a capable young man. A quick learner, by all reports and, most important, he is one who will serve us with unquestioning loyalty."

A brief knock echoed in the chamber, the doors parted again, and the servant stood with his head bowed before the Mufti. "Haj Amin, your cousin, Yassar Tafara."

"Good. Good. Come in, young cousin, and welcome!" He spread his arms as the young man entered. He had the look of a peasant about him. A mere stubble of a beard covered his chin, and his thick lips smiled beneath a bulbous nose and protruding eyes. The young man bowed majestically and touched his fingertips to his forehead. "Salaam, Haj Amin. My mother sends her greetings."

Haj Amin did not rise, but extended his hand. Gerhardt glowered and leaned against the stone beneath a high arched window. "Salaam, young Yassar. We have found a place for you here in Jerusalem as your dear mother requested. She is well?"

"She burns with the fury of all true patriots against the Jews who invade our land. She says that were she a man—"

"But she is not. And for this reason Allah has granted her a strong son to serve us." He swept his hand toward Gerhardt, whose surly eyes were downcast. "You stand in the presence, Yassar, of a great warrior among our warriors. The man is Fredrich Ismael Gerhardt."

The young peasant bowed low and smiled at the man whose name was known to every Jihad Moquade. Gerhardt did not respond; instead, he brooded at the intrusion. His personal anger had been ignored and now, he knew, he was being mocked by Haj Amin as well as the Jews.

Haj Amin did not look at Gerhardt, but watched the young man's smile melt away at the lack of response from the man he bowed to. "We have need of your advice," Haj Amin stated, interrupting the awkward silence.

"My advice?" The young man touched his fingers to his chest and backed up a step. "My advice?" he asked incredulously.

"We are at times so isolated." Haj Amin dismissed the young

man's modesty with a wave of his hand. "There are times our thinking becomes stifled in the sameness of the men who surround us. Fresh blood is what we need."

"The blood of those Old City Jews," Gerhardt snarled.

"Silence!" Haj Amin shouted. The young peasant's eyes grew wide at the rage of his leader. He backed nearer to the door. "You will be *silent*!" Haj Amin hissed. For an instant longer he glared at Gerhardt; then he smiled serenely again and in a breath, his mood changed back to one of tranquillity. "Yes, Yassar," he smiled. "Tonight, you see, the Jews have broadcast a marriage from the Jewish Quarter of the Old City. No doubt to give the world an illusion that all is well within the gates. This is an illusion that must die before it is born. Some say we should attack and destroy them as they sing." He glanced at Gerhardt from the corner of his eye. "Others . . . contemplate other measures. Your mother has commended you to us as an intelligent lad. What is your opinion?"

"To kill Jews at a wedding?" Yassar said after a long, thoughtful pause. "Would the world not call Haj Amin and the house of Husseini barbarians? To kill Jews the prophet says is honorable. But at a wedding? In prayer? I think not."

Haj Amin lifted his chin and smiled. "What then would you do?"

"It is our goal, rather, to show the world how hopeless resistance by the Jews is. Is this not so?" He shrugged as Haj Amin nodded. "Then tonight we should perhaps push their foolishness from the front pages of the newspaper. Yes?"

"A point which has been discussed," Haj Amin said impatiently.

"Well, the reasoning, then, is simple enough," Yassar said brightly. "I would blow up the newspaper. The *Palestine Post*!" He laughed in delight at his own brilliance.

Haj Amin sat forward and remarked "Even so—a target our commander Gerhardt has himself previously proposed."

Gerhardt blinked in the light as the words penetrated his thoughts of revenge. "It is a good plan." He whispered, already constructing the device that would bring it to pass. "There will be no wedding announcement in the *Post* tomorrow morning. There shall be no *Post*."

"You are indeed bright." Haj Amin remained coolly impressed. "I will want you to go with our friend, Fredrich Gerhardt."

"I need no assistance!" Gerhardt protested.

"You shall be the lad's mentor!" Haj Amin raised his hand to silence any further discussion. "He will learn from you, and you will return him unharmed. Is this understood?"

Gerhardt clenched and unclenched his fists, but did not speak.

The young peasant bowed low before Gerhardt. "I would be most honored to remain under the protection of the commander. Since I was much younger, his exploits of daring for the Reich and for the cause of Haj Amin Husseini have been greatly admired. How humble I would be if only I might be a silent shadow to watch your genius."

Gerhardt eyed him with suspicion, but the generous flattery of the peasant at last conquered the rage and resentment simmering near the surface. "All right, then," Gerhardt said. "But you will watch only, and not move until I tell you to do so."

Haj Amin pressed his hands together and smiled benignly. "Good. Then it is all settled. Go now, Gerhardt. Tell my men what you need for our little exploit tonight."

Wires and detonators and sticks of dynamite circled in the mind of Gerhardt as he walked wordlessly from the study. "Thank you, Haj Amin, for giving me opportunity to prove myself." Yassar bowed again. "I will learn all there is to learn from Commander Gerhardt."

Haj Amin raised an eyebrow and spoke in a voice as low and deadly as any he had ever used. "Learn his methods only. Learn the mechanics of what he does. Learn it until you know it better than he does himself. But do not learn the ways of his mind. Beware of his madness. It has no reason to temper the hatred that has consumed his soul."

Puzzled, Yassar looked after the retreating shadow of Gerhardt. "But he is a great man. A brave man."

"He is a man without vision," Haj Amin countered. "He is a fool who lives only because the Angel of Death uses him to harvest Jewish souls." Haj Amin dismissed the young man. "On your way out tell Basil I wish coffee served here in the study."

———

Arm in arm, Yacov and his grandfather led the way happily down the hallway. "Such a wedding it was!" Rebbe Lebowitz said loudly to every harried member of the Agency staff who happened by. "Did you hear my granddaughter was married tonight in the Old City? Such a wedding! Right beneath the nose of the Mufti, nu? Oy and the music! Wonderful! Wonderful! Ah, that I could be there to dance! Maybe if we stand on the front steps of the professor's house, eh, Yacov? Maybe we can hear!"

Each new greeting of "Mazel Tov!" led to yet more joyous explanation by the old rabbi as they left the building bit by bit.

Ben-Gurion walked slowly beside an amused Howard, who shook his head in delight at the happiness of the old rabbi.

"I wouldn't be a bit surprised if there's another wedding tonight," he confided to Ben-Gurion. "David has been trying for months to convince Ellie to marry him. Nothing like a wedding to lower a woman's resistance, you know. Or a man's. Even makes a crusty old bachelor like me a little misty-eyed."

"David will be leaving tomorrow," Ben-Gurion replied tonelessly.

Howard's expression changed from happiness to deep concern instantly.

"Oh? I didn't know." His voice was full of questions. Ahead of them, Grandfather waylaid a secretary who sipped a cup of coffee and listened with interest to the story of the wedding.

"Yes. Back to the States, I'm afraid." Ben-Gurion ran a hand through his tousled hair. "Important business." He lowered his voice and took Howard by the elbow as they neared his office. "A moment, please, Professor." He pulled him to one side and slipped into his office where he sat against the edge of his desk and crossed his arms. Concern was etched deeply into every line of his face.

Howard stood before the door, unsure whether he should sit or remain standing. "How can I help?" He spread his arms slightly.

Ben-Gurion blew his breath out slowly. "The scrolls," he replied simply. "You know what an issue, politically, they have become. The Arabs insist that you cheated the Bedouins out of them. That you stole them." He gave a bitter laugh. "The British want them for their National Museum. And now, we may have political need of them as well."

Howard narrowed his eyes in thought and sat down in the wooden chair next to Ben-Gurion's desk. "I don't quite understand. You know full well that Moshe and I have decided they will most certainly be used to benefit the Hebrew University. Of course, we are fortunate to have come upon them, but they belong to God first, and then to the State of Israel—as long as we are allowed to keep the rights to study and publish our findings. What possible political connections can they have, except that the Arabs and the British want them? Everyone wants them. No wonder."

"You have them secured in a safe place?" Ben-Gurion rubbed his hand across his cheek wearily.

"Of course. As safe a place as there can be in Jerusalem. Neither one of us has seen them since the day we returned from Bethlehem with them. We have not dared to go anywhere near the scrolls."

"We need them, Professor. The future State of Israel needs the use of these scrolls."

"But why? What possible—"

"I cannot tell you that."

"You can't expect me to just give these to the Jewish Agency without some explanation." Howard's face was filled with astonishment at the request. "They are far too valuable."

"How valuable?"

"Priceless. There is no value one can put on such a find."

"Are they worth, do you think, the price of a Jewish homeland? Are they worth the birth of a new Israel?"

"This is preposterous!"

"Not in the least, Professor. And I tell you. They may be the one thin strand that binds us to our salvation in the next few months."

Howard sat in silence for a full minute. The voice of Grandfather echoed jubilantly outside and the dull ticking of a clock marked the long seconds. "Moshe is as much a part of this as I am."

"Then you know what he would say." The Old Man gazed with unrelenting certainty at Howard.

"Yes, I suppose I do." Howard stared at the tops of his shoes. "He would ask you how you plan to get them out of Jerusalem without the British getting hold of them, or the Mufti capturing and burning them at a public rally. Do you have a plan?"

"Not yet. But I tell you this with a certainty. This country of ours will be born by a series of little miracles. These scrolls are our trump card, and we will find a way to get them out of here."

"And take them where?"

"To the States. To America."

6 Wedding Night

The little plane made one final low pass over the Old City Square, then banked to the southeast so near to the Wailing Wall and the Dome of the Rock that Ellie felt she could almost touch them.

"Funny," she yelled over the roar of the engine, "from up here everything looks so small. The Wailing Wall is like a thin silver ribbon in the twilight and that's all that separates the Jews from the Muslims."

David glanced at her and nodded his head in solemn agreement. He did not speak as he piloted the aircraft south, within moments passing over Bethlehem. Ellie sat with her forehead pressed against the glass of the window. Her eyes were dreamy with peace as she watched lights wink on below them. It seemed as though the very soil of Palestine were a pool reflecting the stars that grew thick and bright as the sun relinquished its final hold on daylight.

"You know, the sun is just coming up in New York," David said with more than a hint of sadness in his voice. "And in San Francisco folks are still snuggled down in bed. Maybe listening to the foghorns in the Bay." He still had not found a way to tell her that he was leaving tomorrow night, leaving her alone in a city where the familiar night sounds were the cracks of gunfire and the unrelenting wail of sirens.

She put a hand on his shoulder and patted him gently, "You're lonesome, aren't you?"

He cleared his throat. "Not for New York. Or San Francisco, either." He looked at her longingly. "I'm lonesome for you."

She rolled her eyes in exasperation, "David! What happens to you when you get up in a plane, anyway? You get so sentimental! How can you be lonesome for me when I'm right here?" She studied his face and her playful smile faded. Finally as he turned the plane west, she said quietly, "You're going home, aren't you?"

He nodded.

"*When*?" Her voice was a cry.

"Tomorrow night."

"Oh, David, *why*?"

"It seems they need me to corral a few more pilots and find some transport planes to fly. The Old Man seems to think I'm the only one."

"Then you have to go," she said heavily.

"Go with me."

"I can't."

"I knew you'd say that," he said, almost angrily.

"If I could . . ." Tears filled her eyes as she stroked his arm. "I wish I could."

"Then marry me!" His words were a plea.

"I thought we settled that. You know I love you."

"I mean marry me *tonight*! Before I go. We'll have tonight. To-morrow. When I come back and this thing is over, we'll have the rest of our lives. But for tonight, we'll have each other." His words came in a rush. He grasped her hand in his and in the light of the instrument panel she could see his blue eyes were filled with pain. "I love you, Ellie. There has never been anyone else for me; you know that. Now I'm asking you. Please. Marry me tonight."

She studied him wordlessly while the engine droned on. His eyes never left her face. His question remained written on his expression. Finally she sighed and looked away across starlit Palestine. "You're just saying all this because of Rachel and Moshe. A wedding does the same thing to me. Makes me want every-thing—right now. But, David, it just isn't practical."

"You think their getting married in the Old City tonight is *prac-tical*?" David scoffed. "The Old Man told me tonight we're going to lose the Old City."

Ellie gasped and looked up. "No!"

"Practical is not what working for a Jewish homeland is all about. Practical would be going home and buying a wedding dress at Bullock's Wilshire and walking down the aisle at West-wood Presbyterian Church. We should have done that three years ago before I shipped out again for Europe. Then you'd be nursing babies and I'd be flying the mail route between Bakersfield and L.A.!" He seemed so full of regret that for an instant Ellie thought he might weep. "But we didn't. And now we're here and—rats! I know we *should* be here! God had every little bit of this figured out. And I believe that now, but, Ellie, don't talk practical. It's just not—" He shrugged as his thoughts became tangled in emotion.

"It's not practical," Ellie finished for him. "And you're right.

About everything. Do you know the times I've lain awake at night and thought about you and me together? I used to read the home decorating magazines and figure out what our house would look like if we ever got married. I wanted the long white dress and Mary and Julie as bridesmaids. And Dad walking me down the aisle—"

"Listen, honey, we can do that too! We can get married all over again if it's still important to you when we're both back home. But for tonight . . . don't make me leave you here unless I can leave all of my heart with you! *You* are home to me, Els! God figured that one out too, I guess."

Ellie breathed deeply and rubbed her hand across her eyes. "I don't know what the air up here does to people's brains," she said at last. "Okay," she replied resolutely. "Okay, I'll marry you tonight. But after the ceremony I have to finish this story and develop these pictures before we go on the honeymoon."

David grinned and stuck out his hand. "Agreed. You're worth waiting for."

They shook hands and Ellie sat back, feeling a tremendous sense of relief and peace. "Have you got a preacher in mind?" she asked in a small voice.

In reply, David banked the plane and turned directly north. "Haifa," he answered simply. "It's a Jewish port. We can even get a decent meal before we go back to Jerusalem!" His voice was animated. "Gosh, Els." He leaned over and kissed her cheek. "You know it's only a little past seven. We can be married and fed by eight-thirty. Back in Jerusalem, on the ground, and at the *Palestine Post* by 10 o'clock! How long will it take you to finish up those pictures?"

"An hour maybe," she bubbled, filled with excitement.

"Well, I got us a room at the King David Hotel." David finished triumphantly. "I thought it might be appropriate, with the name and all."

"You mean you *knew* you were going to ask me tonight? And that I'd say yes?" She leaned back and eyed him incredulously.

"A guy can hope." He wriggled his eyebrows. "And I didn't want you to accuse me of being impetuous."

"Never. After all, I've been waiting for this for three years." She tucked her arm through his and laid her head against his broad shoulder. "Thank you," she whispered, but he did not hear her voice over the roar of the engine.

74

The noise of the celebration followed Moshe and Rachel up the narrow steps and to the stoop of the tiny apartment. Suddenly shy, Rachel looked up at the bright round moon as Moshe fumbled with the lock, then triumphantly flung the door wide. Inside, candles flickered as the night air invaded the room ahead of them. From where she stood, she could see the blue floral curtain pulled back from the bed chamber. Pillows were plumped and waiting, and the quilts turned down. Rachel hung back; her smile frozen on her face.

"Well?" Moshe stepped toward her and took her hand from the rail. "Well, Mrs. Sachar?" His voice was filled with pride as he leaned his face close to hers and tilted her chin upward. She stiffened slightly at his touch.

"Moshe . . ." she began, seized with a sudden, inescapable panic.

He moved nearer to her and searched her face. Gently, he touched her cheek. "I won't hurt you," he said simply, answering her unspoken fears. "I will never hurt you, Rachel. Come." He pulled her easily against himself.

"Moshe . . ." she tried again, but as she opened her mouth to speak, his lips found hers, silencing every objection, quelling every fear. She closed her eyes and let the rush of warmth flood over her. And just when she thought she would faint from the press of his strong body next to hers, he gathered her into his arms and carried her over the threshold and into the candle-lit room. He slammed the door with his foot, then stood there, holding her.

"What is it, my love, my wife," he whispered against her cheek.

"Moshe," she said softly, content now to simply say his name. "Moshe."

He smiled at her; gentleness radiating from his deep brown eyes. "No one ever spoke my name until I heard it from you. You touch my soul. You are the other half of my soul. Oh, Rachel!" He kissed her again and carried her to the bedside. "Say my name again and I will die from the joy of it." He buried his face in the nape of her neck and lay down beside her.

"Then I will never say your name again," she laughed and reached up to trace the lines of his craggy, sun-tanned face. *He is so strong*, she thought, *and yet so like a little boy in his love for me*. There was a pain in his eyes now, the pain of feeling so deep that it stretched far beyond the expression of words. "What is it?" she asked, touching his forehead and brushing his hair back.

He raised his eyebrows in a gesture of helplessness, then shook his head. "Ever since I first laid eyes on you I dreamed of this moment. Dreamed that you might one day be mine. That first foggy morning on the beach I watched you while you slept and I thought you must have been a vision. You are like a ship cutting through the waves when you walk through a room. And the wake you leave always points back to you. I have watched you when you didn't know, and my heart has ached with wanting to touch you." He ran his fingertips softly down her cheek and then to her neck and the top button of her high lace collar. Clumsily he worked to unfasten it.

"Let me help." Rachel brushed his hand away lightly as she began to unbutton her gown.

He reached over to snuff out the candle by the bedside, but she stopped him.

"I want to see your face, Moshe," she said in a small quiet voice. "I want to look into your eyes."

He nodded and smiled down at her. "I understand."

Her eyes never left his face as she unbuttoned her gown. She smiled when his tears of emotion clouded his eyes. "You are a gift to me from God." He breathed deeply, inhaling the sweetness of her fragrance; then he took her hand and kissed it. "Love," he whispered. "My only love. Rachel, my wife." He opened her collar and brushed his lips against her throat.

"Touch me," she sighed.

He kissed her fiercely then, and she returned the fire spark for spark. And for her it was a new beginning, the first time. The first time she was kissed. The first time she was held. The first time she felt the joyous burning of true love's passion. Together their love became a prayer of thanksgiving before God.

———

Small and squalid, the Arab village of Shofat perched on a dusty ridge a mere two miles north of Jerusalem. The women of the town glided through the dark, unpaved streets, and gathered like shadows before the Muslim mosque where they might pray for the success of tonight's mission. They huddled together in their long black garb and whispered to one another as they stud-

76

ied the two men who worked on a stolen Jewish taxi parked across the street from them.

"You see there," said one, as she pointed toward Yassar. "He is the one the Mufti has chosen to do the big job in Jerusalem tonight."

Yassar held the large flashlight higher as Gerhardt stretched on the floorboard and worked deftly with the fuse that wound beneath the dash of the aged blue taxi.

"Did you hear that?" he asked Gerhardt nervously.

Gerhardt answered with a grunt of acknowledgment, then twisted the fuse and threaded it through the hole where the radio knob had been. "Hold the light on my hands," he snapped.

Yassar pulled his attention away from the solemn crowd of spectators and adjusted the beam of light to Gerhardt's hands. "If the women of this village know that something will happen tonight in Jerusalem, then will the Jews not find out? Or perhaps the British or the police?"

Gerhardt shot him a brief, menacing look. "That is why you wear the uniform of the Palestine Police, idiot. If anyone stops you, what are you to tell them?"

Yassar ran a sweaty palm over his khaki police uniform. He briefly touched the brim of his cap, feeling intensely ill at ease without his robes and the traditional head gear of his Bedouin ancestors. "I—I am to say that I am on patrol. Searching for suspicious-looking vehicles. We have a tip that perhaps there will be a bombing tonight."

"Very good," Gerhardt sneered mockingly. "And then what will you do when Brown parks the taxi in front of the *Post* and walks away?" he coached as he positioned the fuse correctly.

Yassar patted his chest pocket, feeling for the small tin of Players cigarettes. "I pull in behind him," he rehearsed haltingly. "Then get out of the police van and light a cigarette. Yes? Then I stroll over to the car and pretend to look it over. Open the door and lean in—"

"Yes, yes." Finished now, Gerhardt sat up and blinked into the light. "Here is the fuse." He snatched the flashlight away from Yassar and shined the light on the stub that protruded from the dash. "Then you take your cigarette and hold it to the fuse. An instant. It will spurt and sparkle, alive and deadly. You have two minutes then, idiot. Only two, but it is a lifetime."

Yassar nodded obligingly, his protruding eyes even wider as

he imagined the scenario. "And then I must get back into the police van and drive away."

Gerhardt leaned forward and grasped the frightened young peasant by his shirt front. "Idiot! You pick up Brown at the next corner. Do not leave him, or he may be apprehended and your identity be found out. Or he may die in the explosion and I have lost a valuable courier. Do you understand?" He menaced.

Yassar nodded and gulped, swallowing another question that plagued his mind. "Commander Gerhardt . . ." he began.

Gerhardt spit at his feet, then clicked off the light and climbed from the car. "Were you not the cousin of Haj Amin—" he muttered.

"Commander Gerhardt?"

"What? What is it?"

"I—I," he stammered and touched his pocket self-consciously. "I have never smoked," he finished lamely. "And I do not know how."

Gerhardt's lips curved back, showing his teeth. His eyes were full of contempt as he plucked the tin of Players from the pocket of his trembling young companion. "It is simple." He placed a cigarette between his lips and struck a match, illuminating his face in a glow that enhanced the evil in his eyes. Lighting it, he inhaled deeply, then exhaled into the face of Yassar. The young man gasped, then doubled over in a spasmotic cough. "You see, idiot, as easy as lighting the fuse."

Yassar's eyes watered and he could hear the twitter of the women who stared at them. He fought to find a clean breath again; then through a choking voice he asked, "And what if we are caught?"

"Then you have failed your cousin, the Mufti."

"And what if your bomb fails to explode?"

Gerhardt pulled the young man up by his shirt front and spoke as smoke escaped from his lips with every word. "I have never failed. You will curb your tongue, upstart, or you will find yourself tongueless."

Yassar coughed again, then gasped, startled by the glare of the headlights of a police van as it topped a small hill in the road and crept slowly toward where they stood. "Are we found out so soon?" he wailed.

In contempt, Gerhardt shoved him to the ground and stepped over him, giving a cursory wave to the faceless driver that approached. Headlights winked out and the van stopped a few feet from where Yassar lay in the dust. "It is Brown. He got the van. Get up, peasant," he commanded, tossing the Players tin back to him.

Yassar scrambled to retrieve the tin, then shoved it back into his pocket as he rose.

"Like candy from a babe!" he heard the excited voice behind the van whisper. It was an English voice. Not a voice like the British officials, but rather like that of the common soldiers Yassar had seen many times in his village. "We ain't got much time, though. They'll be reportin' the van missin', an' 'eaven 'elp the bloke caught in this little beauty. Blimey, though! It was like takin' candy from a babe, it was!"

"Yassar!" Gerhardt hissed. "Get over here!"

Yassar hurried around the front of the vehicle, straightening his cap as he went. "Yes, Commander."

Brown was pale, his skin shining in the night. His black eyes sparkled with enthusiasm and his breath smelled heavily of whiskey. It was rumored that these British deserters were paid well in their deadly errands for Haj Amin—certainly better than the Arab volunteers, who received self-satisfaction as their only reward. Yassar instinctively mistrusted this foul-smelling infidel, and yet he had delivered the bombs of Gerhardt to half a dozen locations in the city over the last few months.

"This is the fellow who will assist you, Brown." Gerhardt coughed into his hand and stared at Yassar with disdain.

Brown wrinkled his face, looking much like a noseless pug dog as he examined Yassar head to toe. "Blimey! 'e's an ugly one!" He exclaimed. "Look at them bug eyes, will y'? Well, 'e don't look like any policeman I ever seen in Jerusalem. Blimey! Just ugly enough 'e might get away wif it!"

Yassar narrowed his eyes and gritted his teeth in quiet anger at the words of the English deserter.

Gerhardt threw his head back in laughter. "Yes. He is the cousin of Haj Amin," he informed Brown.

"Go on!"

"Yes," Gerhardt affirmed as he shined the light into Yassar's brooding face. "And I would be careful what you say about him, Brown. He is your ride to safety tonight, after all, and he understands English perfectly well."

Brown laughed self-consciously and patted Yassar on his now clean-shaven cheek. Yassar drew back from his touch and his reeking breath. "Is that so?" Brown said. "Well, I'll tell y' what, mate." He leered down into Yassar's face. "If I was you, I'd grow me a beard as soon as possible. 'ide me face, I would!" He guffawed loudly and slapped Yassar hard on the back.

Yassar's mouth turned down in disgust as he eyed the half-drunk Englishman. "So *this* is in the service of my cousin, the Mufti, and of Allah?" He said with disdain in Arabic. "And what is this son of a camel paid to serve our just cause?"

Gerhardt answered in Arabic as well. "He is paid in English whiskey and pounds. He is useful to us. Even drunk. Or he would be dead. I am not finished with him," he warned. "So take care you pick him up when you have done your part."

"Then I shall look forward to the time that I might wipe him from my shoe like excrement in the marketplace."

"Blimey!" The Englishman wiped tears of amusement from his eyes. He studied Yassar's face a moment, then said seriously, "Come on now, lad! We got us a job to do on the nasty Zionist Yids, right? I'll mind me tongue. Promise on me honor!" He clapped Yassar on the shoulder and led him toward the waiting taxi. "When I get out of the taxi, I'll stroll easy like to the corner. Give me a few minutes, will y'? I want to be out of sight at any rate. Right?"

"You are drunk," Yassar said with controlled fury.

"Yes! That I am. I am drunk," Brown agreed as he slipped into the front seat of the wired car.

"Are we certain this drunken Englishman can drive the taxi? Can he find the *Palestine Post* and walk from this car to the corner?" Yassar asked Gerhardt.

"Good of the lad to be worried about me!" Brown laughed cheerfully.

Gerhardt replied quietly. "Yes. He is always drunk when he does a job. His hands shake too much to light a fuse. You just do your part and bring him back here or you will answer not only to your cousin the Mufti but to me as well, eh?" He shoved Yassar back toward the van. "Now get in, and remember who you serve."

The young peasant climbed behind the wheel of the police van and started the engine with a roar. As he flicked on the headlights, the black-clad women who lined the street rushed toward the vehicles. Their voices were raised in the shrill, undulating cry that had sent Arab warriors to battle for a thousand years. An old woman swooped from the group. Her eyes were mere slits behind folds of leatherlike skin. In her hands she held a large bowl of goat's milk and with a cry she splashed it beneath the wheels of Yassar's van. "For the glory of Allah and of Islam!" she cried.

"For the glory of Islam," Yassar repeated as he let out the clutch and pulled away. "Allah can use even a drunken English deserter."

"Allah akbar!" their cries followed him. "Allah is great! Jihad! Jihad! Jihad!"

———

Captain Luke Thomas stretched his long legs out in front of him and leaned back against his chair. He pinched the bridge of his nose and made a face as he tasted Howard's pitiful attempt at coffee. Howard sat silently across from him with his chin in his hands.

"Three weeks, Howard, and I'm bound for home," Luke said cheerfully. "One thing I won't miss is this tepid mud you call coffee. Oh, for a cup of hot tea with real cream and sugar, eh?" he smiled, attempting to break the gloom that hovered around Howard. He took yet another self-conscious sip, made a face and set the cup and saucer down with a clatter. "All right. Three weeks," he said at last. "We had planned that I get them out at the end of my tour. Here it is, then."

Howard shook his head gloomily. "They need them immediately, Luke. Not three weeks from now."

"Well, I can't ship them home to Mother in a hat box." Luke twisted the ends of his thick moustache. "She'd use them as kindling to start a fire now, wouldn't she?"

Howard's eyes grew wide with horror at the thought, and Luke laughed loudly at the expression on his face. "Never mind!" Howard exclaimed.

"Ah now, Howard," Luke consoled gently. "It's not as bad as all that. They'll find a way. You know they will."

"I just wish I was sure it was necessary, that's all. My entire life has been spent in search of artifacts. In search of those things the Bible tells about. Proof that it is indeed the undeniable Word of God—"

"And do you think the Lord needs a defense attorney, Howard? Or that you are in possession of the only thing that verifies that He is indeed God?" Luke smiled gently. "We have been friends a long time, Howard, and I have yet to see you take on

81

that big a job. The Lord is His own best defense. The scrolls are important proof, yes, that the Scriptures have not been changed since the time of Christ. But these little items may have been sent into your care for a bigger reason than that."

Howard raised his eyes to the lean, weathered captain. "Well?"

"I have thought all along that they were sent to you because you are the only fellow—you and Moshe, that is; you are the only chaps who would recognize them for what they are. Now you have done that and there is another purpose God has for them, you see?"

"The most important historical find of our time—of all times—is about to become some kind of ransom! A down payment!" Howard said angrily. "And I can't refuse them."

"Consider them a down payment on a nation, Howard. Maybe you have done your part with this particular page in the script. You and Moshe risked your lives for these scrolls. But you must remember whom they belong to originally. The Lord works in strange ways to accomplish His purposes."

Howard nodded, still gloomy at the thought of shipping such treasures to an unknown fate. "I told him I would let him know. That I wasn't sure. That unless he had a surefire way of getting them safely out of Palestine, I would not even consider it."

"Then you can stop worrying. If the Lord has a plan He will provide a way. And you will have peace about it."

———

Rachel lay quietly awake in the darkness and listened to Moshe's deep, peaceful breathing. She was afraid to go to sleep, afraid that the happiness she felt was only a dream and if she closed her eyes it would vanish in the morning light. She laid her cheek against his broad back and snuggled against the contours of his body and wrapped her arm around his waist as he slept. *We fit together like spoons,* she thought. Then she smiled and kissed him between his shoulder blades. *We were meant to be together forever and always. Thank you, Lord,* she prayed silently as the steady, certain beat of Moshe's heart comforted her. *Was I ever anyone else? I have belonged to him only this night, and yet, I cannot remember when I was not his.* She reached up to trace the dark line where his hair curled at the back of his neck. He sighed with contentment at her touch, then whispered her name.

"Rachel?" he asked. "Are you sleeping, love?" His voice was sleepy but rich with happiness.

"No," she answered simply, thinking that even her voice sounded somehow different, like the voice of a woman who *belonged*.

He turned over on his back and enfolded her in his arms, pulling her against his chest. "Can't sleep?"

"I was just lying here thinking," she answered quietly.

"Worried about the baby? She'll be fine with Shoshanna," he assured her.

"That's not it at all," she smiled at his thoughtfulness.

"Are you all right?" he held her tighter, his voice edged with concern.

"I was just thinking about you," she murmured, kissing his chin. "And me. About us, you know. I didn't want to give that up, not even a moment, to sleep. I am so happy, Moshe, that I never want to sleep again." She touched his lips with her finger tips. He took her hand in his and kissed her palm.

"Just now I was afraid to wake up," he said. "I was afraid I had been dreaming and that when I opened my eyes, you would be gone."

Rachel burrowed closer to him, resting her head just beneath his chin. "Now you know why I don't want to sleep."

They lay with their thoughts in silence for a long time. The primus stove hissed and popped in the corner and at the same instant they both sighed happily, then dissolved into laughter. "You see," chuckled Moshe. "Already we even breathe alike!"

"And our hearts beat in time."

"But yours is like a little bird." Moshe laid his hand over her heart.

She put her hand on his chest. "And yours is steady and strong."

He kissed her gently.

"Oh, darling," she sighed. "Can we make the world stop? If only this night would last forever."

"But then," he said, stroking her cheek, "we would miss the joy of waking up next to one another . . . the happiness of knowing that we are not a dream, eh? I want"—he searched for words—"I want to wake up every night a hundred times, just so that I can reach out and find you here beside me, Mrs. Sachar." His voice was full of love. "For the rest of my life I want to come home and see your face and say *'This is not a dream!'* I want to turn around and find your eyes and say, *'She is really mine!'* Your love is such a gift!" He pulled her closer. "Rachel, my wife, my only love!"

She laid her face against his and felt his cheeks wet with tears. *Thank you, Lord*, she prayed again, certain that this was a prayer she would never cease to pray.

7   At the *Palestine Post*

The wind had shifted, bearing down from the northwest as a cold reminder that it was still winter. It pushed at the tail of the Piper, hurrying it back toward Jerusalem, ahead of an approaching storm.

In the cockpit, Ellie snuggled as close to David as she could, linking her arm through his and laying her head against his shoulder. She breathed deeply, inhaling the old, familiar aroma of his scuffed leather flight jacket. On the ring finger of her left hand was a delicate gold band engraved with roses and set with tiny rubies. David had hardly spoken on the flight back from Haifa, but at times would sigh with contentment and reach down to touch her hand and play with the ring on her finger. The steady drone of the engine and a million stars above them made the moments seem endless and dreamlike.

Ellie closed her eyes and nestled against his shoulder. "Oh, David, you were right," she sighed.

"Well, I'm not surprised, I usually am." He grinned and kissed the top of her head. "And what is it I was right about?"

"You really are the most conceited, egotistical . . ." she began, raising her head to chide him playfully.

"You're right."

"But that wasn't what I wanted to say." She settled back in. "This *is* really the most peaceful place on earth, isn't it?"

"Here and now, with you, yes." He touched her gently on the cheek. "I think so."

"Can't we just stay up here? Can't we spend our honeymoon up here?"

"I've been trying to figure out how to make that work all the way back from Haifa!" he laughed. "But you made me promise—first you've got to get your story in, right? First we work. I don't want to start our lives together with broken promises. Besides, take a look."

Ellie sat forward and gazed downward. Fragments of light winked up at them from the earth. "Jerusalem?"

"Uh-huh. Dead ahead. And I want to spend my first night with the woman I love in the City of David." His face glowed in the light of the instrument panel and he winked at her when she smiled coyly at him.

"Darling, anyplace you are is the City of David."

She leaned against him again and closed her eyes, savoring the moment. So many things were unspoken, yet already she felt her heart intertwined with his. There were no more questions in her mind. David was the man God had intended her to spend the rest of her life with. It seemed as though every thought and action in her life had pointed to this hour, this beginning, when they would make two lives into one. She marveled at the clear working of the hand of God. Even before she had known, the blueprint of her life had been drawn, clearly and unmistakably. *When hard times come again,* she prayed silently, *I want to remember this moment. This certainty that my life is in your hands, God. Thank you for knowing me. Thank you for loving me and giving me David. I want to be the best for him.*

Finally David spoke again, interrupting her reverie. "You didn't tell me how you like it."

"Right now I love everything," she answered dreamily.

"I mean the ring," he finished with self-conscious pride.

She held her hand up in the light and twisted the band, studying the soft golden glow with deep satisfaction. Then, as though suddenly struck, she exclaimed, "But where did you get it? I mean, how did you happen to have a wedding band in your pocket on the night we fly off on the spur-of-the-moment to Haifa and get married on impulse? Not to mention the fact that the minister *knew* you and wasn't in the least bit surprised when I showed up hanging on to your coattails and—"

David threw his head back and laughed loudly. He looked at her shocked face and laughed again. "Yep. I'm a real impetuous guy."

"You *knew*!" She pounded him playfully on the shoulder and

leaned back against the door of the plane in mock disgust.

David shrugged and laughed again. "I've only been carrying that ring around in my pocket for about six months. I had it made up at the little jewelers in Chinatown in San Francisco. You know, the little bald guy across from the Far East Cafe?"

"The one who doesn't speak English?" Delighted, she held the ring up and studied it with new appreciation. "And you've had it all this time?"

"Yep. And then I came looking for you. I was hoping, you know, that night before Christmas when I brought you up here that you would say yes. You're the impetuous one in this team, Els. I've had that preacher in Haifa on hold ever since I landed in Palestine."

"You!"

"You held out long enough to get your own way. And just long enough for me to realize even more how incredible you are. Have I told you how much I admire what you're doing?"

Ellie felt a blush climb to her cheeks. David had not often told her what he had felt about her work. "You know," she said brightly, "I was thinking that maybe when this is all over and we get back home, maybe we can open an aerial photography business together. People are always wanting stuff photographed from the air, aren't they? Businesses and cities and mountains. And we can have babies and that little house we talked about and . . ." She threw her arms around his neck and the plane wobbled a bit as she kissed him. "And I love you, David Meyer," she finished quietly.

"And I love you, Ellie Meyer," he returned.

"Does this mean our kids will be Jewish?" she grinned.

"Nope. The rabbis say it has to come from the mother. I don't even count since my grandfather is Jewish. Has to come from the mother's line, see? However, I had something engraved inside your ring. It was spoken by a Gentile woman who became an ancestor to Jesus."

"I don't want to take it off," she said tenderly. "Tell me."

David cleared his throat. "The reference is from the Book of Ruth, chapter one, verses sixteen and seventeen." He paused a moment then began: *"Don't urge me to leave you or turn back from you. Where you go, I will go and where you stay I will stay. Your people will be my people and your God my God. Where you die I will die, and there will I be buried. May the Lord deal with me, be it ever so severely, if anything but death separates you and me."* He finished and raised his eyebrows expectantly. "Well? You

86

like it? When I had it made, see, I thought maybe I'd get over here and you'd tell me to get lost. Go home. I don't ever want to leave you, Els. Not ever." His voice caught and his eyes were full as he studied her expression.

Ellie touched the ring and then laid her hand on his arm. "We will have tonight, David," she said softly. "And then we will have forever. Thank you. I'm glad you found me again. I'm so glad."

David coughed into his fist, as if to clear away the emotion that pushed at his throat. "Of course, Mr. Wong couldn't fit the whole passage on the inside. Just the reference to the scripture. And he spelled Ruth, R-U-F-E. I should have written it down for him."

"And what if I had turned you down?" Ellie teased. "Would you have given it to some other girl?"

He did not smile, but shook his head from side to side. "Nope. I had him put our names after the verse. *For Ellie. Love, David.* I was kind of hoping."

Ellie twisted the band around and around, almost awed by the depth of David's love for her. She had not realized how very much he had cared. She had always known, however, how difficult it was for him to talk about his deepest feelings. As he tapped out a brief message to Jerusalem, she said quietly, "You're pretty terrific. You know that, don't you."

He nodded. "Yep. And always right, too." He banked the plane, circling over the sleepy city. "Watch down there," he said. "You'll see the lights of our landing strip come on in about a minute."

Ellie gazed down at the darkened streets of the Old City as they passed overhead. She breathed a prayer for Moshe and Rachel and smiled inwardly at the irony that she had pictures of their wedding but none of her own. Lights switched on below at either end of a narrow dirt strip. They were the headlights of two Agency cars kept near the hangar for this very purpose. "There they are!" she cried.

"Don't know what we'll do if the batteries ever go dead on those cars." David guided the little bird downward, easing her between rooftops and towers that he had come to know by heart. "Hold on."

Shadows of buildings sped by and Ellie held tightly to her seat as the landing gear nearly brushed the top of the car at the near end of the landing strip. She held her breath until a gentle bump and David's quick actions told her that they had touched the ground of the Holy City once again. He taxied to a stop and cut the rattling engine as a dark figure ran up to the side of the plane. In the glare of the headlights, Ellie recognized a blue denim jacket and the balding head of David's friend, Michael Cohen.

David sat back and looked at Ellie for a long moment. "Sorry we had to come down."

"As long as we come down together. Open the door. Michael is out there."

Through the thin walls of the plane, they could hear Michael shouting happily in his nasal New York accent. "Hey, Tinman! Hey! Open 'er up! Went and got yourself hitched without me."

David pecked Ellie quickly on the cheek and opened the cockpit door. "So much for peace and quiet," he muttered. Then, as Michael extended a meaty hand, he said loudly, "Well, long time no see!"

"Mazel Tov! Mazel Tov! Went and got hitched without me to stand up for you! So the Tinman finally married Dorothy and I wasn't around t' see it!"

David clambered from the cockpit and helped Ellie to the ground. "Well, I had her up there, Scarecrow, and didn't want to give her time to change her mind!"

Michael clapped him on the back and embraced Ellie. "Can I kiss the bride?" Without waiting for a reply he smacked her on the lips. "Mazel Tov!" he said again. "How'd he get you to marry him? What'd he tell you? All lies!" he teased. "Are you going to the States with us tomorrow?"

"No," Ellie said quietly, "I'm staying here."

"Yeah?" Michael asked as a puzzled look crossed his face.

"She's got the war to cover." David slid an arm protectively around her waist.

Michael stood dumbfounded for a moment. "Well. Hmmm. Yeah. Well, I'll watch out for him for y'. So, when's the honeymoon?"

"Tonight," David muttered. "After we finish some work at the *Palestine Post*."

"Well." Michael scratched his bald spot. "This is some kind of wedding night, huh?"

Ellie linked her arm in Michael's. "Listen. I have some work to do. Why don't you guys drop me off and go get coffee or something. I won't be more than an hour. You can keep David company. He'll tell you all about the wedding!"

Michael brightened. "Ah! He give y' the ring! Ain't it a beauty? He's been carryin' it around for months, y' know. Great, ain't it? You two gettin' hitched. Except the Chinese guy that made the ring spelled Ruth, R-U-F-E! Tinman shoulda wrote it down for 'im!"

David tapped Michael playfully. "I told her already."

"And she still wanted the ring?"

"I told her *after* it was on her finger!"

Michael laughed and led the way to the car as Ellie and David, holding hands, followed after him.

Bored with their vigil and cold now with the fresh wind that had sprung up, Johann and Dan sat in the darkened car and watched the Piper land. For hours they had waited for the return of David and Ellie; their only instructions from the Old Man had been to "keep an eye out for them." Talking about wives and children had grown tiresome after the first two hours. Now they simply smoked silently and watched as David and Ellie piled into the car with Michael Cohen and started off across the field to the south and Gaza Road. Johann grasped the keys and started the car, then flicked his last cigarette out the window and reached to turn on the headlights.

"Wait a minute." Dan put a hand out and stopped him. "Let's watch a minute longer."

The headlights of Michael Cohen's car bounced and jostled over the plowed dirt strip, and as soon as it turned onto Gaza Road, yet another set of headlights flicked on a block away and followed slowly after them.

"It's those American fellows," Johann said. "Who cares?"

Still Dan held his hand out and watched. "Wait," he said quietly.

"What for?" Johann asked with irritation. "David Meyer and Miss Warne are in the lead car. The Americans are follow . . ." His voice trailed off as yet another set of headlights came on just beyond the airfield at the Monastery of the Cross.

"Wait," Dan said again.

Johann frowned and wiped his lips with the back of his hand. "Who?" he asked.

"Maybe our friend in the tan car? Hard to tell in this light, but look." He squinted and leaned forward. "He is following them most certainly, nu?"

The headlights pulled out from the narrow drive to the Monastery and trailed at a safe distance from the sleek black sedan of the Americans on David's tail. "It's a parade." Johann shook his head in amusement.

"Our turn to join it, then." Dan pulled the headlights on and Johann rounded the corner of Ramban and headed toward the Gaza Road. The street was unlit, and passed through the Rehavia District where it curved gently toward King George Avenue. As Johann drove, Dan leaned his elbow against the dashboard and stared intently at the dim taillights ahead of them. The car from the Monastery was indeed light in color, and its driver touched the brakes whenever the American car's brake lights flashed.

"There's a barricade ahead," said Johann softly. "We'll see what he does."

A full block ahead of the thick ring of sandbags and barbed wire that protected the Jewish Agency building, the monastery car slowed and turned, taking a different route than David and the Americans.

"False alarm," Johann stated, breathing a deep sight of relief. "Look, he's turned off on Ramban."

Dan stared suspiciously after the retreating vehicle. "Ramban Street?" he exclaimed. "If the fellow wanted to come to Ramban Street, why didn't he drive toward us when we were parked down at the other end? Why drive all this long way around?"

"Well, that meshuggener Michael Cohen did!" Johann exclaimed.

"He is from New York. How can you expect him to know where he's going?" Dan scratched his head and peered after the car, which slowed again and turned onto a side street.

Johann shrugged. "It was nothing."

Dan did not reply, but settled back in the seat as they approached the barricade where the black sedan was just passing through.

Johann smiled at the sentries and held out a slip of paper signed by the Old Man himself. Without a word, they saluted and let them through. "It is ridiculous," Johann said at last as they sped past Ben Yehudah Street and Zion Square. "David knows the Americans follow him. They know he knows. Both of them know we are following them, and we know they know. So what's the big secret? We should all park and have a cup of coffee! Does this make sense?"

Dan did not reply; instead, he lit another cigarette as Johann pulled to the side of the street and parked within full view of the Americans and the vehicle of Michael Cohen, which stopped directly in front of the red stone building of the *Palestine Post*. David climbed out of the front seat and helped Ellie out, escorting her up the front steps. There, he gave her a long, lingering kiss and opened the front door for her. She disappeared inside; then David turned around, made a tremendous sweeping bow and waved first to the Americans, then to Johann and Dan. Leaping down the steps, he thumped the hood of the car and climbed happily back in. As Michael pulled away from the curb, the black sedan eased after them.

Johann rolled his eyes in exasperation. "How long, O Lord?" He reached to start the car.

"Hold it," Dan said quietly. "Maybe we should let the Americans chase after David for a while. The Old Man told us to keep an eye on both of them, nu? He meant the girl, too. Let's stay here. David will come back. If she's in there, he will not be far away. True?"

A full twenty minutes passed before a blue taxi came into view. Slowly it crept along the street as though searching for an address. It rolled past the *Palestine Post* building, then braked to a stop. After a moment's hesitation, it slid into reverse and parked directly in front of the stone steps with two wheels over the curb.

"She's called a taxi," Dan speculated.

"A drunk one at that," Johann said sarcastically. "Must be from New York. Doesn't seem to know where he's going."

Dan shook his head as the taxi driver lunged from the front seat of the vehicle. He seemed to sway for a moment, steadying himself against the bumper of the car.

"Drunk," Johann said with irritation. "Shameful. Get the momzer's license number, Dan."

Dan shook his head again at the thought of a drunken Jewish taxi driver. "Well, we can't let her ride home with him," he remarked. "She'll be killed quicker than going for a stroll in the Arab Quarter, eh?"

The drunken driver squinted his eyes and peered back toward King George Avenue. For an instant, he seemed to smile, then he turned on his heel and staggered away, leaving the door of the taxi wide open.

"Now what?" Johann asked as the man quickly disappeared in the shadows beyond the *Post* facade.

"Well, we'll just have to take her home. When she comes out we'll tell her we were to keep an eye out for her safety and—"

Only a moment passed until a van clearly marked *Palestine Police* rolled to a stop behind the taxi.

"Someone already reported him," Johann said, and Dan nodded in agreement. "He'll have his taxi towed away. He'll come back here in the morning and the thing will be gone."

"I hope we're not here to see it," Dan yawned.

Both men watched with an interest born of intense boredom, as a small, nervous-looking policeman stepped from the van. He seemed to search the streets almost furtively and as his eyes fell briefly on their car, he looked away quickly and searched his pocket for a cigarette. Even from across the street, Johann could see the officer's hands tremble slightly as he placed the cigarette between his thick lips, then patted his pockets looking for a match. "Well, this fellow is in bad need of a smoke," Johann observed drily.

"He needs a light," Dan chuckled at the frantic way the policeman plunged his hands into his pockets and looked wildly up the street in the direction the drunken taxi driver had gone.

"Good grief, Dan, get out and give the man a light," Johann nudged his partner. "I've seen you that frantic for a taste of nicotine before. Have some pity, man!"

"Have pity yourself," Dan said in a surly tone. "It has gotten cold out there. He'll come over in a minute and ask."

"No need," Johann pointed nonchalantly up the walk. A slender man in a brown pin-striped suit strolled toward the distraught policeman. His face was concealed beneath the wide brim of a brown fedora, his hands in his pockets. He nodded briefly to the policeman, then pulled a silver lighter from his suit pocket. A small flame sputtered to life and held steady as the grateful policeman leaned toward it and took a long drag on his cigarette. He immediately doubled over in a fit of coughing, and after only a moment of hesitation, the man in the brown suit walked past him and melted into the shadows.

"That fellow is in terrible shape," remarked Johann as he

squinted at the policeman. "Someone with such a cough should give up smoking, nu?"

"So tell his mother." Dan looked away, bored with the whole episode.

"Look at the way he puffs. Like a smokestack!" Johann watched with disdain as the policeman walked toward the taxi. "So give the momzer a ticket, already. Illegal parking. Drunk driving."

"Who cares," Dan said. "Go get the girl and tell her we'll give her a ride home."

"Wait a minute." Something in the tone of Johann's voice caused Dan to turn his eyes back to where the policeman leaned in through the open door on the driver's side. "What's he doing?"

The policeman stood up and slammed the door of the taxi; then he threw the cigarette to the sidewalk as he hurried to the van. The engine was still running, and he jumped in and roared away. Suddenly, at the same instant, a light dawned in the eyes of Dan and Johann.

"Dear God!" shouted Johann as he jumped from the car. "I'll try and get the fuse! You warn the girl! Run, Dan! Run!"

With a cry, Dan sprang up the steps and crashed through the doors of the *Post* building. "Get down! Everyone get to the floor!"

And as Johann flung the door of the taxi wide and lunged onto the front seat, a sickening flash tore at the night and shattered the windows of houses as far as twelve blocks away.

———

David had just reached his empty cup out to the passing waitress when a distant explosion rammed through the streets and rattled the windows and the stacks of plates at the Atara Cafe.

Michael cursed loudly and slammed his cup down on the table. "Not again!" he said bitterly. "Holy mackerel! Tinman, won't it be nice to have a couple weeks vacation from this stuff?"

Several of the customers leaped up and darted out the door into the dark street to search the skyline for flames and a clue as the latest target.

David listened to their frantic shouts and harried questions and rolled his eyes. "You know this will probably ruin our plans," he whispered hoarsely. "I've married an ambulance chaser with a camera!" He ran his fingers through his close-cropped hair in frustration. "She's at the *Post*, too. Don't think they'll let her get out of there without wanting her to go take pictures of this."

"Maybe it's a gas line," Michael offered hopefully.

David raised his hands in solemn surrender. "We'll see." He stood up and dug down into his pocket for a coin. "I'll call her. We should start this marriage off right. I'll be firm. Tell her this new explosion was not part of the deal." David made his way through the now deserted cafe to the telephone at the rear of the room.

"Looks like someplace near the heart of the city," a frantic man in a rumpled suit called through the door as David dialed the number of the *Post*. A busy signal buzzed insistently on the other end of the line. He waited a moment, then dialed again. Once more the line buzzed a busy signal. David slammed down the receiver and waited another thirty seconds, certain that everyone within earshot of the explosion was calling to notify the *Post*. Outside in the streets, ambulances screamed by and David could see a few alarmed and curious citizens clustered outside. He double-checked the number and dialed carefully. Again a busy signal greeted his ear. He held the phone at a distance for a moment, and watched as the frantic man in the rumpled shirt stuck his head in through the front door and shouted. "The *Post!*" he cried, his eyes wide with horror. "They've blown up the *Palestine Post!*"

———

Sirens and screams mingled and reverberated through the streets like hollow echoes of a nightmare. David ran, pushing his way through the crowds of the injured and onlookers who clogged Halosel Street and Zion Square. Wounded staff members staggered out the gaping hole where the doors of the *Palestine Post* had been. The scorched logo of the newspaper was blasted in half and hung among the wreckage like a torn flag.

The acrid smell of sulfur stung David's eyes and tears streamed freely down his cheeks. But they would have flowed even without the smoke. Vaguely, he heard the voice of Michael calling his name from far behind him in the din of human misery and the roar of the bullhorns. And always, always he heard someone's voice shouting the name of Ellie. It was his own voice, but he did not recognize it anymore.

Glass crunched beneath his feet. Twisted balconies hung crazily above the heads of the throng. Policemen and volunteers pushed the people back, warning of the danger from the certain collapse of the front wall of the now burning *Post* building. And everywhere there was blood. Blood on the faces of the weeping wounded. Blood on the hands of those who reached to help them. Blood trailed across the pavement in little drips and sticky puddles. Smoke. Lights. Policemen. Sobs and cries.

"Ellie! Ellie!" David called and his words were crushed and smothered even as they left his lips. "Ellie!" he sobbed as the sound of his voice mingled with the others in one collective groan.

"Have you seen her?" he asked bleeding staff members that he recognized. Heads shook an unspoken reply. "Have you seen Ellie since the explosion? Have you—?" Then he pressed on to another group—crouching, holding broken limbs and bleeding heads as they waited for an empty ambulance.

"Get back! Get back!" A uniformed policeman shrilled as he herded the people away and the flames danced atop the shattered building. "She's gonna collapse! Get back, I say!"

"Ellie!" David called. Then he recognized the stooped figure of the matronly secretary who had always been so kind to Ellie. The woman's clothes were torn, and she wiped her eyes on a sooty handkerchief. She seemed to have only minor scrapes, but she cried quietly as she stared at the inferno that now leaped from the broken upper-story windows. David pushed through a little crowd of people gathered near her.

"Have you seen Ellie?" he begged. "Ellie Warne? Have you seen her?"

The woman sobbed louder now and shook her head from side to side. "So useless," she said. "So senseless." Then she raised her hand shakily and pointed toward the *Post*. "In there," she wailed. "She was in there."

A wave of nausea swept over David and he whirled around toward the building. "NO!" he screamed like a wounded animal. "Ellie! Ellie!" He started toward the teetering facade of the building and was met with the strong resistance of two guards of the Palestine Police.

"You can't go in there," one warned. "There is no one left alive in there."

"Ellie! My wife is in that building!" David felt he must surely be having a nightmare, or that he had died and the heat of the flames he now faced were those of hell itself. But the flames were still not as hot as the anguish that burned him, scorching his soul and consuming his hope. "Don't you understand?" His words were imploring. "My wife!"

"No, son," the older of the two men put an arm around his shoulder. "You can't go into the building." He talked quietly and led David like a small child away from the danger.

"David!" Michael cried as he bobbed among the crowd. Spotting him with the policeman, he waved broadly and inched his way toward him. "David!" he said breathlessly. "I've been looking all over for you!" David did not take his eyes from the flames.

"He says his wife is in there," said the policeman, frowning as his eyes rested on the building.

Michael nodded his head in agreement and took David by the arm. "Come on, pal," he said gently. "There's nothing for you here."

David nodded and put his hand over his face for a moment as the reality of what had happened sliced him open and left him to bleed without hope of comfort. He did not call her name again, but her face smiled up at him in his mind. The sun caught the radiance of her copper-colored hair, and her soft arms encircled his neck. Michael took his arm and led him through the wounded and the spectators away from the heat of the inferno. Behind them the flames reached high and roared a victory as the building collapsed upon itself. The thoughts that he would not see her again or hear her voice filled him with an emptiness that was itself a kind of death. Numbness crept over him. *Maybe I will wake up*, he thought. *Maybe this has not happened.*

Michael led him to a dark street corner away from the calamity. "Stay here, buddy. I'm going to go get the car, huh?"

David nodded and leaned against the cold metal of an unlit street lamp. Michael jogged quickly down the street and disappeared around the corner. Moments later, the headlights of a car appeared, blinding David. The car sped toward him and screeched to a halt at the curb.

A portly man with a round, moon-shaped face got out and stood by the open door of the automobile. "David Meyer?" he demanded.

David nodded, silently. "I don't want to play," he said simply. "No more cops and robbers. So whoever you are and whatever you want—"

The man pulled out his wallet and opened it, then walked to where David stood. "Feldstein. Jewish Agency," he said crisply. "You will come with us now, please."

"No thanks. I've got a ride. All the way to the States."

"You will come with us now, please." The man was insistent. "Your life may be in danger."

David stared at him through dull, uncaring eyes. "My life is over, Feld-whatever. So leave me alone." His words were slurred, as though he had been drinking.

"You're drunk," said the man sharply. "Get in, I say!"

"Get lost."

The man lowered his voice to an intense whisper. "Get in, you fool."

"Leave me alone!" he shouted, lunging for the man and grabbing him beneath the throat. "Haven't I done enough—given enough? And for what?"

"Shut up!" the man said in a garbled voice. "Let go of me and get in the car, will you?"

David shoved him hard, throwing him back into the front seat. Then he slid into the back seat of the vehicle. "Sure," he muttered wearily. "What difference does it make, anyway?"

As the car sped away, Michael Cohen drove carefully around the corner. His eyes scanned the place where he had left David, then he cursed and slammed on the brakes. Jumping from the car, he searched the streets for his companion. "I never shoulda left him," he mumbled to himself. "Never."

8 News

In the dim light of a lantern, Moshe and Ehud huddled over Dov as he fiddled with the shortwave radio. Faintly audible voices drifted in and out as the receiver whined and growled and popped.

"Are you *sure*?" Moshe demanded, his jaw set and grief etched deeply on every line of his face. "Are you certain that's what you heard, Dov?"

"Read it yourself." Dov handed back a torn slip of yellow note paper. "I wrote down as much as I could pick up."

Moshe studied the scrawl, barely able to focus on the words, let alone make his mind accept them. . . . *woman photographer*

. . . assignment . . . LIFE magazine . . . killed . . . bombing of Palestine Post . . . body to America . . . notification of next of kin . . . U.S. State Department . . . "God," Moshe said quietly. "Merciful God." He squeezed his eyes tight and pressed a hand to his forehead. Ehud took the slip of paper from his hand and read the words silently over and over. Only the radio moaned as the men stood silently absorbed in their own thoughts. At last Dov turned back to the protesting dial and worked it with the care of a safecracker hoping to open the vault of a Swiss bank.

Ehud, shadows deep on his craggy face, put a hand on Moshe's shoulder. "I am sorry, Moshe," he said in a hoarse whisper. "It can only be the little shiksa, eh? Your Ellie Warne. I am sorry." He patted Moshe awkwardly.

Moshe still did not open his eyes, as though he hoped he was only dreaming, that soon he would wake up and this would be a nightmare which vanished in the light. "What . . ." he groped for words. "How will I tell Rachel?" The radio whined again, then screeched, concealing Rachel's footsteps as she descended the ladder behind him.

"Tell Rachel what?" she asked brightly. Moshe could see her smiling face in the lamplight. Over her arm she carried a wicker basket covered by a red napkin. "I brought breakfast. They told me you were here—something about the radio—"

Moshe's expression was concealed in the shadow. He did not answer, but as she stepped from the ladder, he took her in his arms and buried his face in her neck. He fought to control his emotions, filled with visions of the bright, brave little redhead who had come to mean so much to him. *So alive. So vibrant. So full of joy and love. Could one such as this be gone?*

Moshe's grief was so profound that Rachel could only think of his comfort. She dropped the basket and cradled him like a small child in her arms. A full minute of silence passed, with Ehud leaning against the damp stone cellar wall in despair. His eyes were blank and riveted to the floor. Dov continued to argue with the obstinate radio. Rachel ran her fingers through Moshe's hair, afraid to ask what grief had touched him in this tomb-like setting.

At last she whispered, "What?" Moshe did not reply; instead, he turned his head deeper into her shoulder. She could feel that the fabric of her dress was damp from his silent tears. She turned her gaze to Ehud's disconsolate face. "Ehud?" she asked.

Ehud looked up and his face, she thought, seemed suddenly

old. Sorrow deepened every line and pulled the corners of his mouth downward. Reluctantly he held out the yellow notepaper.

Rachel took it from him, yet held it at a distance for a long moment until she breathed deeply and found the courage to read its grim message. She moaned softly at the words: *photographer . . . LIFE . . . killed . . . bombing.* She shook her head slowly from side to side, trying to comprehend what the death of Ellie Warne would mean. An empty hole opened up in her heart when she realized that never again would she see her friend or hear the sunny voice chiding her to be careful. "Moshe!" Rachel cried, letting the note slip from her fingers and fall to the ground like a dead leaf. "Oh, Moshe!" He held her tighter, awake now to her profound sense of loss. "I told her she couldn't come here to the Old City with me! I was afraid she would be hurt. I was afraid for her, and I didn't want to say good-bye again. I never wanted to say . . . Moshe! Moshe!" She said his name again and again as sobs shook her slender shoulders. And now he held her and stroked her head gently.

"Hush now, my love. Hush, my sweet Rachel. She is safe now. Our little Ellie is home with God."

Ehud looked away and brushed a tear from his face with a calloused thumb. Dov did not look up, but sat remembering the final embrace of Rachel and her redheaded friend that rainy night when they had entered the Old City. At last a voice came over the radio, clear and clean in a crisp British accent.

"Tragedy again struck the Holy City of Jerusalem last night when a car bomb disintegrated the building of the *Palestine Post* newspaper. At a quarter past eleven, the bomb exploded, shattering windows for eight blocks in the Jewish sector of the city. Even with the lateness of the hour, there were many casualties. Two staff members were killed, and one American woman photographer on assignment for *LIFE* magazine was killed when the darkroom in which she worked collapsed on her. The bombing of the *Palestine Post* is but another in a series of tragedies that has rocked the city of Jerusalem. The body of the American killed will be taken back to the States for interment. Her name has not yet been released, pending notification of her next of kin in the U.S. However, a spokesman for the U.S. State Department commented that he expects the body to be accompanied home by the woman's husband, who has been employed here in Palestine by the Jewish Agency."

"Is that enough?" Dov turned and snapped off the radio. His chin was quivering with compassion he felt for his friends as the reality cut deeper and deeper into what had been their joy only the night before.

"Yes." Moshe's voice was toneless. "It is enough." Gently he lifted Rachel's chin and gazed into her eyes. With his fingertips he traced her tears, certain that the grief she felt outstripped his a thousand-fold.

"I should have let her come with me," Rachel cried softly. "Moshe, I should have let her come."

He shook his head and forced himself to reply. "No. Her life was in God's hands. As are yours and mine. It is for Him alone to say when we are to join Him, eh?"

"Oh, Moshe!" Rachel clutched him fiercely. "Please promise me! Promise you won't leave without me! Please don't leave me here alone, not again! Not again!"

Moshe took a deep breath and looked up at Ehud. "Can you take care of things awhile? I'm going to take her home."

"Stay with her." Ehud's voice was soft and thick with emotion. "We will be fine."

"Yes. Have the fellows finish cutting the basement passages, if you will." He held Rachel very close for an instant more, then kissed her on the cheek. "Come now, love. I will take you home."

Ehud stepped forward and extended strong hands to help her up the ladder. "God bless you, Rachel!" he called after her. Then he sighed. "I have lived too long."

Moshe patted him on the back. "A little longer, if you please." Then he ascended the ladder after Rachel.

Dov called after him, "Hey, Moshe, do you want me to confirm this with the Agency?"

Hesitating for a moment on the ladder, Moshe frowned down into the shadows. "No," he said. "They will only tell us again what we don't want to hear."

Sergeant Hamilton crossed his arms and leaned heavily against the windowsill in Luke's quonset hut office. His eyes were narrowed to angry slits as he fixed his eyes on the glowing dial of his captain's ancient Philco radio.

". . . woman photographer on assignment for *LIFE* magazine

was killed when the darkroom in which she worked collapsed on her..."

"Well, them hooligans of the Mufti 'er paintin' their slogans with the blood of innocents, that's for sure, Cap'n! And such a lovely girl that Miss Warne was, too! Did y' know the night of the bus wreck she give 'er own coat and field boots to that Jewish girl what went on into the Old City! And in such weather! Me an' the lads noticed what a kind-'earted girl she was. There's no denyin' it! Cold-blooded murder is what that is!" He looked for a place to spit, then pulled up the window and spat angrily outside.

His eyes dull, Luke watched as the portly sergeant slammed down the window again and turned to glare threateningly at the radio.

Luke leaned back in his chair and shifted his gaze to the untouched cup of tepid tea that sat on his desk blotter. The newscaster droned on for what seemed like the hundreth time that morning. Still, Luke could not find it in his heart to accept the dreadful certainty of his words . . .

"Her husband was among the first to arrive on the scene. The American flyer could not be found for comment for the press . . ."

"Small wonder," Ham muttered. "They say the poor bloke wouldn't even be able to recognize 'er! Aye! It'd be enough t' put a sane man in an asylum. Blimey!" Ham shuddered and Luke shot him a glance, imploring him to hold his peace. "Sorry, Cap'n." Ham sniffed.

". . . U.S. State Department reports that the airman has resigned his position with the Jewish Agency and will be accompanying the body back to America . . ."

"Poor David," Luke whispered quietly. Then he prayed silently as Ham brooded and the news continued. *God, comfort David. He is a soldier, like I am, but Ellie's death, so senseless, must be nearly beyond bearing. Make the lad strong, Lord. Remind him of the only true hope.*

In Luke's years as a soldier, he had fought shoulder to shoulder with men who had followed him into battle and had fired their guns while they cursed and prayed. Many had fallen still and lifeless an instant later. How often had he closed the eyes of the dead or called for a medic to tend the wounded, then scrambled from the dust to fight again? But this was beyond understanding. "It does make a man weary, Ham," he sighed heavily. "It makes a chap wonder what purpose there can be in the death of one so young and beautiful and full of life."

"Aye, Cap'n Thomas. It makes a man wonder." The usually ruddy complexion of Ham was pale and waxy. "But will y' look at this!" He held up a mimeographed sheet bearing the logo of the *Palestine Post*. The headlines read: *Jihad Terrorists Bomb Post!* "Why, it's somethin' a man can admire, Cap'n Thomas, the way them Jews manage to keep on! Terry told me they pulled this little mimeograph out of the rubble an' set it up in a 'ouse down the lane. An' will y' look at this! The Arabs blow up the *Post*, but 'ere's the *Post* on the newsstands all the same! They got nothin' but courage, but they've enough of that to build a nation, I'd say."

Luke took the pitiful rag of a newspaper from Ham's outstretched hand. "You're right," he said, smiling slightly. "They are men and women to be admired."

"Ah well, they 'ave their share of gangsters among the ranks, to be sure. I ain't forgettin' the bombing at Jaffa Gate, but I'm thinkin' it won't be the gangsters runnin' the Jewish State in the end. Now, if the *Mufti* wins!" he exclaimed, "there's an assassin for you! And 'e would make himself king."

"Yes. I thought we fought the last war to be rid of all the little Hitlers. I cannot understand why the government doesn't face up to what we're dealing with."

"Parliament!" Ham sniffed in disgust. "They ought to spend a day in the Old City! 'ear that Cap'n Stewart who replaced you is lettin' the Arabs do as they jolly well please in there an' those old rabbis are hangin' on by their teeth! Makes a man wonder if there's any justice short of *this*!" Ham reached over and lifted the largest artillery shell from the display on Luke's bookshelf. "At least with these we knew what was comin', didn't we, Cap'n? Not like a bundle of TNT in the boot of an automobile!"

"Somehow a shell from a field gun does seem a bit easier to deal with. Soldiers firing at soldiers."

Ham cradled the large shell in his arms. "I remember the day this one came screamin' in, eh, Cap'n?"

"Battle of El Alamein."

"Aye, and we knew we was done for. Right on target she came for us! Screamin' in! Landed a few meters away, she did. Thump!

102

That's all. Thump! An' you picked yourself out of the sand and said to the rest of us—"

"Dust yourselves off, lads. God has decided to let us stay here a bit longer," Luke finished, the incident fresh in his mind.

"Aye. An' when the battle was done you shoved the disarmed dud into an empty shell casing and gathered those of us as was left an' we bowed our 'eads in thanks. He shook the heavy shell. "What y' keep in 'ere now, Cap'n?"

"Personal papers."

"Well, it's a fine reminder of who's in charge." Ham set the shell back along the long row of display shells. "155 millimeter," he said in wonder. "She would 'ave blown a whole block full of *Palestine Posts* if the Lord 'adn't been watchin, eh, Cap'n? Made a believer out of me!"

Luke cleared his throat and said quietly, "Then we have to believe that He holds the lives of all His children in His hands, Ham. Pray for David Meyer when you think of it, will you? And for my dear friend Howard Moniger, her uncle. They must be in pieces over this."

"Aye. I'll pray God gives 'em some comfort. Terrible. An' if ever there was a moment when a man would wonder if God has a plan, this kind of grief is the moment." He shook his head and stood with chin in hand. "Aye. I'll pray God uses this somehow."

A sharp knock on the door interrupted their conversation. A young soldier opened the door and poked his head into the small, cluttered room. "Captain Thomas?" He extended a white envelope in his hand. "A message for you, sir."

"Yes. Turn off the radio, Ham," he instructed, motioning for the soldier to enter.

"A young Jewish boy brought it in." The soldier approached and laid the envelope on Luke's desk. "A young Jewish boy with a patch over one eye. He said it was most urgent you read this yourself. I didn't want to bother you but . . ."

Luke was careful not to let any emotion betray him. He folded his hands and dismissed Ham and the messenger with a nod, returning their salutes. "Thank you, Sergeant. I appreciate your comments on the matter," he said quietly as Ham slipped out the door and closed the door after him.

Alone in the room, Luke stared at the black scrawl on the outside of the envelope. It was Howard's handwriting. His stomach churned for an instant, and he took a deep breath as he picked up the letter and held it between his fingers. He opened it carefully, cutting the seam of the envelope with a broken bayonet that served as a letter opener. Inside, a small scrap of notepaper was folded in half. With a sense of Howard's grief, he opened the note and read quietly: "My Friend: The time has come to *praise the Lord and pass the ammunition.* Goldman's Mortuary before nightfall. Howard."

Luke read the words again and again, certain of their meaning, yet unable to comprehend that the password he had waited two months to hear had finally come on the heels of such a tragedy. *Praise the Lord and pass the ammunition! Goldman's Mortuary!* The message could mean only one thing.

Luke rose slowly and pulled the shade on his window. Then he locked the door to his office and stood for a full five minutes silently contemplating the row of artillery shells on his display shelf. "They have found a way," he said at last. The steady beat of his heart sounded in his ears as he picked up the large projectile that Ham had held so casually only a few minutes before. He pulled off the pointed head and laid it on the desk. Then he reached into the depths of the shell and pulled a carefully wrapped and sealed package from the inside. With reverence he placed the package on his desk blotter and unwrapped it layer by layer until at last the weathered brown edges of an ancient scroll were revealed. He touched the leather with a sense of awe, conscious of the age and value of the scroll, but even more aware of its meaning. "So, God," he whispered. "You found a way to save them. A way to get them out of Jerusalem safely. Thank you, Lord," he said with tears in his eyes. "Thank you."

———

Bowing low on the prayer rug that had been a gift from his father, Haj Amin finished his morning prayers. Sun glistened through the high windows of his private mosque, and outside the call of the muezzin filled the courtyard of the Dome of the Rock. Haj Amin bowed reverently one last time to the east, then he stood slowly and watched as one of his bodyguards rolled up the treasured rug. He smiled serenely, confident in the fact that Allah had heard his prayers and was indeed with the Jihad Moquades who swarmed to Jerusalem from every village in the surrounding Arab nations as far away as Iraq. Last night's destruction of the *Palestine Post* had been a triumph, a stunning victory that proved the Jews of Jerusalem had no hope once the British evacuated. By tomorrow at this time, the Mufti knew, every newspaper in the world would have editorial pages filled with indictments against Partition and against Jerusalem becoming a city governed by the United Nations. With each new act of terrorism committed by Palestinian Nationals, the world resolve for a Jewish homeland slipped further from its foundation. Fear was a weapon that would in the end take a greater toll against the Jews than bullets.

He sighed with contentment, then turned slowly around, studying the mosaics of the mosque as though he were seeing them for the first time. Soon enough, the Jews would sue for peace. Soon enough, the world would ask for his help to calm the violence that seemed to be so unplanned, so spontaneous. He alone could bring the angry peasants of Palestine back to order. He turned to where the light beams filtered from the windows to the tile floor. They seemed to be like ladders leading into heaven. *It must have been such a day,* he thought, *when the Prophet Mohammed and his steed flew from this place into Paradise. It was he who declared our war against the Jews and now I, Haj Amin Husseini, will finish it.*

It was a quick walk back to his residence, down a cold flight of ancient stairs to a passageway from the Temple Mount to the Mufti's Jerusalem home. The foundations of the house were the very stones upon which the meeting place of the Jewish Sanhedrin had stood nearly two thousand years before. *Had not the one they called the Christ stood here in secret judgment by those Jews? And the one called Paul? And now it is I, the Mufti of Jerusalem who rules from this place. Further proof that there is no God but Allah, and Mohammed is his Prophet.* Haj Amin gazed with satisfaction at the ancient stone pillars and the steps that led upward into his office. Seven men followed silently behind him in a ritual that had been performed by every Mufti since the days of Saladin. The stone steps had no rail, but Haj Amin touched the damp wall worn smooth by a thousand years of Muslim rulers who touched these stones morning and afternoon on their way to prayer. *What right have the Jews to claim this land?* thought Haj Amin, remembering how ancient the Arab claims were to Jerusalem and the land of Palestine. *Only by the grace and kindness of followers of the Prophet were the beggars allowed access to their Western Wall. Only we allowed them to build their pitiful huts in the shadow of their former glory. But the kindness of the*

Arab world has evaporated in this injustice. And now they will leave or perish where they stand. Palestine, so long ruled by men from faraway nations would once again be united, Haj Amin had vowed in the morning prayers. It would be united under his leadership as the Kingdom of Haj Amin Husseini.

He turned the brass knob on the weathered door at the top of the steps. Inside the Mufti's residence, his servant stood beside his desk with a steaming pot of coffee in hand and a small cup on a silver tray heaped with pastry. On his desk lay a copy of the newspaper from Cairo, and the local Arab daily from Jerusalem.

As his small entourage left the room, Haj Amin sat down in the large leather chair and opened the paper. *Jewish Newspaper Destroyed! American Photographer Killed in Blast!* The name of Ellie Warne was not mentioned, but Haj Amin was well aware of which American woman now lay in pieces in the Goldman Mortuary. He laughed softly as the servant poured his coffee.

"The news is pleasing to your excellency?" the servant asked.

"Most pleasing!" Haj Amin said as he scanned the columns. "The son of my cousin has done well! Not only is the Jewish propaganda sheet in ruins, he has managed to destroy that pest of an American journalist as well. We had hoped that she might lead us to the scrolls, but it is a small matter. There are others who are likely to show us the way to them." He sipped the coffee and grimaced at the heat of the black liquid. "Are Gerhardt and Yassar nearby?" He reached for a honey-filled pastry.

"In the outer waiting room, Excellency." He nodded his turbaned head and stepped backwards to the door. Haj Amin did not look up as the servant slipped quietly out and shut the door behind him.

Moments later, as the Mufti read the reports and studied the photographs that were splashed across the pages, a soft knock sounded and Yassar and Gerhardt entered quietly to take their places on opposite sides of the small office. A full minute passed before Haj Amin looked up into their brooding faces. A smile flitted across his lips. "I see you still do not like one another?" he said. Then he waved his hand as if to dismiss such a small insignificant detail. "It is of no consequence how you feel. You have done well. Both of you. You are to be congratulated. The American woman is dead. The *Post* out of business."

"Not quite, Haj Amin," Gerhardt said sullenly. Then he pulled a folded sheet of paper from his shirt pocket. Carefully, he smoothed it out and laid it on the blotter before the Mufti. Haj Amin picked it up gingerly by its corner; then he cursed softly as he read the logo at the top of the mimeographed sheet. *The Palestine Post. February 3, 1948.* The headlines screamed, *Jihad Terrorists Bomb Post!* Angrily, he studied the dimly printed words on the facsimile of a newspaper before him. At last he spoke. "Apparently we did not kill enough of them." He breathed deeply. "However, we have made our point."

"And they have made theirs." Gerhardt's face was hard and grim. "They have said it does not matter what action we take, they will continue on."

"Then we must say again that nowhere they are is safe." The Mufti's voice was low and malignant. "Don't you agree, Yassar?"

"Ha! That imbecile! He was barely able to—" Gerhardt began to ridicule him.

"Enough!" Haj Amin shouted. "I have heard the report—last night from one of our agents. Yassar did not panic. He was unafraid, and most importantly, he carried out the deed! You will say no more!"

At the words of Haj Amin, Yassar squared his shoulders and looked Gerhardt straight in the eye. "I think we should be more bold, next time," he said, "I—I think perhaps to kill Ben-Gurion. To destroy the Jewish Agency building itself would be a worthy goal."

Gerhardt rolled his eyes and leaned back against the wall. Everything in his manner was full of derision for this thicklipped peasant of Haj Amin's. "And who will light your cigarette this time?" he scoffed. "If it hadn't been for Mont—"

"Silence!" Haj Amin shouted, jumping to his feet and spilling the thick black coffee over the newspapers. "You were told never to mention the name! Never!" he hissed. His eyes were red with rage and his lips were tight as he fought for control. "You fool!" he whispered angrily. "In a word I could wipe you from the face of the earth. Your indiscretion has cost me time and time again. I do not know how long my patience will tolerate your insolent stupidity!" He pounded his hand on the desktop and sank slowly to his chair.

Gerhardt was white with outrage and with fear of the power held by the man he served. Yassar crossed his arms and smiled with satisfaction at the reprimand Haj Amin had given Gerhardt.

Somehow all the insults of the night before in Shofat seemed small by comparison.

Haj Amin regained his composure, noticing for the first time the overturned coffeecup. "Yassar," he said quietly, "you are dismissed. Fetch Basil for me. Tell him there has been a bit of an upset in my office."

Yassar nodded and started out the door. His thick lips parted in a triumphant smile at Gerhardt.

"And, Yassar," Haj Amin said pleasantly, "it would please us if you would master the use of tobacco."

"Yes, Haj Amin," agreed Yassar, suddenly humbled and curious as to how the Mufti knew the events of the night before. He hurried out the door as Haj Amin directed his venom once again at Gerhardt.

"I keep you under my protection only as long as you are of use to me. If you wag your tongue once too often, Gerhardt, you may find you have no tongue to wag."

Gerhardt's eyes met his. The shadow of fear crept across his features and he nodded in reluctant agreement. "Yes, Haj," he said, suddenly humble before his master once again.

"I suffered the loss of two good men on account of that Jewish whore you pursued. Useless. You knew as well as I that we will have her body when we have the Old City. Soon enough! Now, I say, I will not have you misuse this member of my own family for your glory and benefit. Yassar will not be harmed. The ridicule will cease. And you will teach him well all those things you learned in the service of the Führer." His words were controlled, almost gentle, as though he were explaining a simple problem to a young child. "Do you understand, Gerhardt?"

"Of course," Gerhardt said fearfully.

"As for the other matter. Montgomery is of more value to us than you are at this point. That name will not be uttered or even thought by you again. There is too much at stake for you to dash it all by a careless word. Is that clear?"

Gerhardt shifted his weight uncomfortably and nodded in absolute submission. "Forgive me, Haj," he whimpered. "It is the woman, you see. The humiliation. They left me in the sewer to die. For days I wandered and my mind . . . I forgot what we fight for. I forgot my purpose!"

"Perhaps you would like to spend some time away from Jerusalem?" Haj Amin responded. "Yes? Perhaps your thoughts would

flow easier as you consider the problem of the Jewish Agency...
Perhaps you would be happier for a time working with Kadar?"

Gerhardt raised his eyes quickly. Hostility and anger once again replaced his remorse. "He is only half a patriot!" he shouted.

"Because he does not hate the Jews with your fervor?" Haj Amin was amused at the reaction. "Well then, perhaps you may help him find his true passion. He holds the pass of Bab el Wad, now, guarding the road against Jewish convoys. It is our wish that you join him in the village of Kastel and direct your great talents to stopping completely all Jewish traffic into Jerusalem. And when you have devised a plan for the Jewish Agency, you will be welcomed back with us in Jerusalem." His words had a finality to them that caused Gerhardt to shrug in helpless acquiescence to the will of Haj Amin.

As the servant hurried in to mop up the remnants of the Mufti's rage, Gerhardt bowed low and, with a flourish, left the room committed to obedience or death at the hands of his benefactor.

9 Where Is God?

"I have come for Tikvah," Rachel said in a whisper laden with emotion.

Old Shoshanna stood in the doorway like a statue and studied the beautiful young face that had been filled with joy only the night before. Now, grief lingered on Rachel's features and tears clung to her long eyelashes. "What is it, child?" The old woman's voice brimmed with compassion. "My dear? Has he hurt you?"

Rachel shook her head and pursed her lips in a silent attempt to contain her emotions. Shaul rose from the floor behind Shoshanna and stretched; then he sidled up to Rachel and bumped against her legs. "It's not—" Rachel almost choked on the words.

Shoshanna patted her gently. "You are not the first bride who has wept on the morning after her wedding," she said quietly. "And you will not be the last. But things will be better, you will see," she sighed. Then she looked past Rachel to where Moshe hurried toward them up the street. She scowled back at the worried expression on his face.

"Please," Rachel whispered through deep, difficult breaths, "may I have my baby?"

The old woman raised her chin and peered down her nose at Moshe. She stuck out her lower lip in distinct disapproval, certain that it was he who had caused sweet Rachel this grief. "Well, and here comes your bridegroom," she spat.

Moshe was out of breath. "Rachel—" He stretched his arms out to enfold her. "I am so very sorry." She leaned heavily against him.

"Do not speak gently to me now," she whispered, "or I shall weep here in the street."

He looked into Shoshanna's angry face. "Good morning," he said quietly.

"Is it?" she asked, glancing at Rachel protectively. "Well! I think not."

"No, Shoshanna." Rachel wiped away a tear that had escaped. "I know what you are thinking. It is not Moshe. No. It is—" She could not finish as the grief she felt swelled in her throat and stopped her words.

"We have had bad news." Moshe stroked Rachel's hair, as he explained to Shoshanna.

"Not the rabbi, God forbid!" The old woman's face changed from anger to sympathy in an instant. "Not Rebbe Lebowitz or little Yacov!"

"A friend. A very dear friend in the New City. The little shiksa who came here with Rachel and Yacov the first night; do you remember?"

"The red-haired girl?" Shoshanna clucked her tongue and reached out to touch Rachel's shoulder. "Oy! What next?" she cried. "Such a time this is to be alive. My dear, my dear!"

Rachel wept openly then, unable to hold in her feelings any longer. "Ellie!" she cried. "Oh, Moshe. Make it not be so." She clung to him as silent sobs shook her shoulders.

"I'll take her upstairs," Moshe said quietly. "Will you bring baby Tikvah?"

"Of course," she said, reaching out to pat Rachel once again. "The baby will help." She turned away as Moshe led Rachel up the steps to the apartment and Shaul followed mournfully behind.

Little Tikvah squirmed as Shoshanna changed her diaper; then the baby wrinkled her face and squawked angrily at the inconvenience of being waked up in the middle of a peaceful morning

110

nap. "Shush now, little one, your mama has need to hold you now. You are her joy in a world of sorrow, little Jewel, so come. Shush now." Shoshanna wrapped her in a warm soft blanket and held her close against her shoulder as she hurried out the door and up the steps. She tapped once on the door, then entered without waiting for an answer. Tikvah still wailed unhappily, as though she sensed something was very wrong. Moshe pulled up the shades and started to take the baby from the old woman, when Rachel stood and stretched out her arms to take the child.

Wiping her own tears on her sleeve, Rachel cradled Tikvah, who gazed up into her face. "There now, my love, don't cry. Don't cry anymore, little Tikvah. Mama is here now." She turned to walk the length of the room, then back again, as Moshe and Shoshanna watched helplessly. Tears streamed freely down Rachel's cheeks, and yet as her eyes drank in the beautiful face of the child, her grief lessened.

"I will come down for the baby's things in a bit." Moshe ushered the old woman to the door. "Thank you for your kindness."

"It was nothing," Shoshanna whispered. "She will be all right." She touched the sleeve of Moshe's shirt. "She is a strong young woman." Her eyes followed Rachel as she paced the floor. "But such a time we live in, nu?" She laughed bitterly at the ridiculousness of her own words. "For Jews it has always been such a time."

Moshe nodded in agreement, and shut the door behind her, thankful for her concern. He turned and leaned his back against the doorjamb, uncertain what he could do to comfort Rachel. His own sense of loss seemed minute by comparison with the overwhelming grief that had encompassed the life of his lovely young wife. *God, give me words of comfort,* he prayed.

Rachel sat down in the rocking chair and held the baby close against her cheek. Tikvah sighed with contentment at being nestled safely in Rachel's arms once again. Shaul lay in a patch of sunlight beneath the window and watched with soulful, uncomprehending eyes.

The clock ticked off long minutes, and the squeak of the rocker kept time. Moshe did not move or speak until at last, Rachel raised her eyes to him. "This is not what I wanted for the first morning of our marriage," he sighed.

"What is to become of us?" Rachel's face was full of anguish. "What kind of world will my baby grow up to?"

111

"A better one, I hope than our parents bequeathed to us. Perhaps a smarter world? A world that will one day say *never again*, eh?"

"When?"

"Perhaps in her lifetime." Moshe stepped forward and leaned down to kiss the velvet head of the sleeping Tikvah. "That is why we are here, in this place at this time. That is why so many have suffered and died for so long. Because we all hope that someday—"

"Why not now?" Rachel's voice sounded small and lost.

"I have asked myself such a question every time I have seen the face of a child who has suffered, or a woman who has lost husband and children and still has to go on putting one foot in front of the other. I have asked God *why* when I remember how you yourself have suffered. I have no answer but this, Rachel—" he began.

"Can there be an answer?" Her voice was weary and full of all the old doubts and fears. "How long have our people waited and suffered and looked for the Messiah to come and redeem us? When will He come, Moshe? When will this end?" Then she said angrily. "Why does He wait?"

Moshe sat down on the edge of the bed across from Rachel. He clasped his hands together and leaned forward to study her face as he searched for words. "You believe as I do, Rachel, what the Prophets spoke about our Messiah. What Isaiah said in chapter fifty-three, that He would take the sins of all of us upon himself. He has done that. He offered His life willingly to redeem us from our sins."

"I believe that, Moshe." Rachel gazed tearfully at Moshe's strong hands.

"That much of God's work has been done. How sad it is that through two thousand years, men have added to it and changed it until the beautiful simplicity of God's plan has been distorted. And yet, it is not surprising, is it?"

Rachel smiled sadly at the memories of men who behaved so inhumanly and excused their behavior against Jews by calling them Christ killers. "I was always surprised," she said simply, still unable to comprehend such acts of barbaric brutality.

"Do you remember the old proverb, *If God lived on earth, people would break his windows*?"

Rachel smiled and nodded slightly. "My father said that many times."

"Is it so surprising that when Messiah came, first He was cru-

112

cified, and then when being a Christian became acceptable, the very One they crucified became a cause to murder others? This is a terrible time. Yes. And yet it is no different than it has always been. Yeshua said that His kingdom was not of this world. He took our sins upon himself so that we might be a part of a greater kingdom, Rachel. Unfortunately, we still have to live in this world. We have to suffer, as He did, because we live in a world that belongs to God's eternal enemy, Satan. He has killed and murdered in the name of the Holy One of Israel. Why? So that God's own people will fear the very name of our Messiah and run from Him. We are in a war here in this world, Rachel. But it is a battle that is bigger than that which is fought for land. This is a battle that is fought with fear and despair and hatred and lies; in the end it is fought for eternity, and the prize is the souls of mankind."

Rachel laid her cheek against Tikvah's and breathed the baby's sweet breath. "But so many innocent ones have been slaughtered, Moshe. Where is God in all of this?"

"He is still here. Still holding ground in this kingdom of darkness." He frowned and hesitated a moment, searching the depths of his heart for what he truly believed. "Some time ago, I walked through a cemetery," he said slowly. "I saw a tiny headstone. On it was the name of a child, a little girl who had died when she was only three. A lamb was on the headstone and the words beneath her name read: *First word*, and the date when she had spoken. Then, *First step*, and the day she had walked. Beneath that it said, *Gone to heaven*, and the date she had died." He studied Rachel's face as she clouded up and clung closer to Tikvah.

"How her mother must have grieved!" Rachel's words were full of pain and compassion for the unknown woman who had buried her precious child.

Moshe nodded. "Those were my very thoughts," he agreed. "I stood beside the grave of that little one and I read the date of her death. It was, I believe, 1907."

"So long ago."

"And I thought of the tears and grief that had been shed at that very graveside. Then I looked down at the tombstone beside her tiny lamb." He smiled gently and reached out to touch Rachel's hand. "Beside her was the grave of her mother and her father. The words on their headstone said simply: *United.*"

Rachel sat silently for a long time, drinking in Moshe's words. A feeling of peace filled her as she thought of her own family. "I

113

think I understand," she said thoughtfully.

"Time has a way of leveling all grief, Rachel. And our Lord has promised that someday He will with His own hand wipe away all our tears. All. No more sorrow and no more tears, eh?"

"In the meantime we still live here," she said softly. "And we wait."

"Yes. And when Yeshua walked this earth, He wept for us as well. Because He knew our battle is not against flesh and blood but against those powers of darkness who would destroy our lives for eternity. Someday, we will all stand before God, Rachel, and He will ask us whether we had a victory over despair and hopelessness. Satan will say to Him, *There, you see! I did these things to them in your name and so they cursed you to your face!* And the Lord will turn and say, *You did evil to my servant Rachel and still she believed me. Still she called upon my name. Be gone, Satan! My warriors have won this battle for me.*"

Rachel pondered his words, then closed her eyes in gratitude at the healing he brought her. She remembered the words of Job when his friends accused him of sin as he suffered for no purpose that he could understand. "For I know that my Redeemer lives," she quoted softly, "and that in the latter days He will stand upon the earth."

"Perhaps sooner than we think," Moshe agreed. "But first the Prophets said that the remnant of Israel will return from the four corners of the earth. That they will make the desert bloom, eh? We will see our Messiah return to Zion this time as a King. It is promised in God's Word. Maybe in Tikvah's lifetime. Maybe we will see it, too."

"I hope so, Moshe." Rachel gazed into the baby's sleeping face. "I will pray so."

"We must continue to trust, my love. That there is a purpose and a plan for everything. God is paying attention and, though we may grieve now, the whole story is not known to us yet." Moshe took Tikvah from Rachel and laid the sleeping child gently in her cradle. Then he took Rachel by her hand and lifted her, enfolding her in his warm embrace. "And for now, we have this brief moment when we are alive on this earth and together. And we have the hope that this love we share here is only a shadow of the joy we will have for eternity. I love you, Rachel Sachar," he whispered in her ear. "I love you with an everlasting love."

PART 2

The Dream

"Dream and deed are not as different as many think. All the deeds of men are dreams at first, and become dreams in the end. . . ."

Theodor Herzl

10 Plans

His face expressionless, Ram Kadar stared across the table at Haj Amin Husseini and Gerhardt. He wore a soiled green khaki uniform beneath his long, flowing robes. Concealed under his shirt was the silver crescent medallion that marked him as honored among the Mufti's servants, and a Walther pistol was tucked into his belt. Only two hours earlier, word had arrived at the fortress of Kastel that overlooked the pass of Bab el Wad. Kadar had left his command in the hands of a junior officer and left immediately for Jerusalem. He had welcomed relief from the monotonous duty that had been his for four long, cold weeks. Now, as he sipped tasteless coffee and listened to the benevolent words of Haj Amin, he wished he had not come.

". . . and so, we feel the services of Commander Gerhardt will be put to good use in Kastel. The convoys will be more completely annihilated under his skills."

Kadar fixed his eyes on his cup and tapped his finger on the dainty handle with an impatient flick, like the tail of an annoyed cat. "No Jewish convoys have gotten through from Tel Aviv. Not in four weeks. None at all."

Gerhardt corrected him. "Two have. With the help of the British."

"Those were British convoys. We would not dare to attack them openly when they are by their very indifference already helping our cause." An edge of anger crept into Kadar's voice. He swallowed hard, then raised his cup to his lips with a shaking hand.

Haj Amin leaned forward and tapped his fingertips together. "Be they Jewish trucks or British, the Jews of Jerusalem still eat. History teaches us that when the larder is bare, the battle is lost. If the Jews are hungry enough, they will capitulate to us. Remember, Gerhardt, how the Gestapo promised them bread and jam in Warsaw?"

Gerhardt threw his head back in a rare laugh. "Thousands of them lined up willingly for a trip to Auschwitz! This was the Führer's own idea. And once the Jews got to Auschwitz, there was only one way out—up the chimney!"

Kadar smiled tolerantly, then said to Haj Amin, "I think the more pertinent issue is simply that the United Nations know that we control the pass and thus control the flow of food into Jerusalem, not that we are barbarians bent on the destruction of every Jew."

"While they live they are a threat to us!" Gerhardt flared. "The Koran commands that we destroy them and all unbelievers!"

"We know well what the Koran teaches, Fredrich," Haj Amin said soothingly. "You are both chosen to fight one enemy, not each other." He sat back and eyed them both benignly. "So. It is settled then. We have made our point here in Jerusalem. I think the world will tremble when we completely control Bab el Wad. The 100,000 Jews of Jerusalem may even find themselves lined up for jam and bread."

"And then they will find themselves in the sea," Gerhardt said. "Or up the chimney."

"Time enough for that," Haj Amin replied, studying the distaste that flickered over Kadar's face. "When we are given what we want, we may even feed them. For a while. But for now we must demonstrate our power. Do you agree, Kadar?"

"Inch Allah," he muttered. "If it is his will."

"And my will as well," Haj Amin said coldly.

Kadar bowed slightly in acquiescence. "Of course."

"Well, then. It seems to be settled. Gerhardt, you will go home now and gather what you need. Tomorrow morning you will leave the city quietly with Kadar."

Gerhardt stood and touched his forehead, bowing with an elaborate gesture. "I will serve you even with my life," he said with new fervor.

"*Al-hamdu lillah*! Allah be praised that I have been given a servant so willing and skilled," Haj Amin responded, nodding his head in humble acknowledgment.

Gerhardt turned on his heel and left the room with his head high, certain that he was once again in the favor of the Mufti.

Haj Amin watched him, his smile melting away to a gradual displeasure. Moments passed, and when the Mufti was certain that Gerhardt was out of earshot, he said with venom in his voice, "A soft tongue can take milk from a lioness. Flattery is a balm to Gerhardt. He is my creature. Flattery and a whip have chained him to our portico." He leaned forward and smiled into Kadar's now-softened features. "You hate him."

"A small word for emotion so strong," Kadar replied without emotion. He had accepted the decree of Haj Amin that Gerhardt must go with him to the pass, even though the very presence of this demented creature revolted him to his core. He had always considered the half-breed Gerhardt to be only half-human. Now, through the months since Gerhardt's arrival in Palestine—smuggled on board a ship of illegal Jewish immigrants because he, too, bore a number on his forearm—Kadar had come to believe that there was no remaining vestige of humanity left in the shell of Fredrich Gerhardt.

To call him an animal seemed kind. He was more like a twisted shadow leering from the mouth of Hades. His breath smelled of death and his eyes found delight in only the most vile of deeds. He was no patriot of Islam. The words *Jihad! Holy War!* were but another excuse to murder. He was no soldier. He was an automaton whose fingers tinkered with detonators and instruments of death the way a schoolboy doodled on his notepad when he daydreamed. Destruction was not simply second nature to Gerhardt; it was his whole being and cause for existence. And yet, for all of this, the men who swarmed to fight against the Jews respected and feared this demon.

"Gerhardt is a great benefit to us," Haj Amin interrupted his reverie. "A great example of daring and courage." When Kadar did not answer, Haj Amin sipped his coffee and added, "Of course, the lioness can at times turn hostile, even when the tongue is soft. Gerhardt is a madman, of course. If this were not a time of great struggle, we should find a quiet cell for him and throw away the key."

"I do not trust him," Kadar said sullenly.

"Nor do we," the Mufti replied.

If the news that Gerhardt would join him in Bab el Wad had taken Kadar's appetite away, then the whispered words that followed were enough to revive it again.

Haj Amin sat back for a moment, gazing thoughtfully into the shadowed vaults of the ceiling above them. Then he leaned forward and put his elbows on the table. "Our comrade Gerhardt has come near to outliving his usefulness. We have an apprentice working at his side, a member of my household. No doubt it will not be long before he is ready to take over this function. I will send the young man to Kastel with Gerhardt. Watch over him. I fear Gerhardt will take his life in some devious way. The boy lit the fuse last night. It was supposed to burn for two minutes but exploded a mere fifteen seconds later. No accident, I am sure."

"Gerhardt is jealous of everyone."

"He is popular. A hero."

"A butcher."

"He would make a good martyr for our cause, do you agree?" Kadar nodded and smiled a thin smile. "A suitable goal."

"His death would stir the passions of the mob." Haj Amin leaned back in satisfaction as though the deed were an accomplished fact. "He craves that woman, that Jewess. His foolishness cost me two of my best men, and he would have machine-gunned a Jewish wedding last night had I not stopped him. He can no longer see the difference between political aims and personal revenge. Before he becomes an embarrassment to us . . ." He pondered a moment. "You must send word when you think his assistant is competent."

"Soon, I hope."

"It must appear that Gerhardt dies bravely, even *unjustly*, at the hands of the Jews. You take our meaning."

"We will give him a death befitting a martyr."

"Good. And the people will grieve. Then they will rage, and Gerhardt may accomplish his goals more in death than by his bombs." Haj Amin sighed in contentment. A difficult matter had been solved with a minimum of stress. He smoothed the brocade of his jacket and dismissed the subject with a wave of his hand. "So," he said, introducing yet another topic. "Still another matter has arisen that needs your attention." He left the remark to dangle like bait to Kadar's curiosity.

"Yes?"

"Your friend Montgomery is in Jerusalem." He smiled openly at the surprise on Kadar's face. "A servant such as this is of more use to us here than in Cairo prowling around the court of that British puppet King Farouk. That domain is little help to us now. It is filled with English marionettes, and soon enough their strings will be severed." He drew a finger across his throat. "Farouk will die. As Ghandi died last week. When independence finally comes from the British Empire, Farouk's own people will assassinate him. Just as the people of Ghandi did."

"The fellow who killed Ghandi was a madman, they say."

"All it takes is one. Like our friend Gerhardt." He sighed again at the thought. "Oh, well." He clapped his hands and a servant entered, carrying a steaming samovar of coffee. "So. As I was saying, your friend is among us." He waited until the servant slipped quietly out before he continued, opening a drawer on his ornately carved desk. "Tonight you will see Montgomery and will take this." He tossed a heavy bag of coins to Kadar.

"A pretty payment." Kadar opened the mouth of the pouch and gazed in at the golden coins.

"A small token for very pretty service, yes?"

Kadar nodded and smiled. "Indeed."

"Already Montgomery's presence has made an impact here. I have one more gift to offer." He pulled a small golden box from the drawer and passed it to Kadar. "Open it; go on," he urged, very pleased with himself.

Filigreed roses and thorns twined around an arabesque trellis on the sides and top of the box. By its weight, Kadar knew that the box itself was made of gold. He opened the lid to reveal a crescent-shaped medallion like his own, only gold and encrusted in tiny diamonds. He looked up questioningly. "Beautiful," he whispered.

"A fitting gift for one who has done our future kingdom such great service. Please convey our pleasure when you speak to Montgomery. We have had almost hourly reports from the little spiders who creep to our doorstep, but we will most likely not see the one who sends them until this war is over."

"That was part of the agreement for Montgomery accepting work in your service, was it not?"

"I cannot trust the spiders to take this"—he motioned toward the box—"I dare not trust them. However, since you have had such long and familiar acquaintance—" He did not finish. "I had thought I might wait and present this medallion at a special ceremony. But who knows how long that might be, and after last night's service and this morning . . ."

Kadar snapped the lid of the box shut and looked at his wristwatch. "The time . . ."

"Of course," Haj Amin nodded as Kadar stood up. "It is short. Always too short."

––––––––

David Ben-Gurion balanced the telephone between his ear and his shoulder as his hands sifted through the stacks of reports and requisitions on his desktop. On the other end of the line, the United States Ambassador confirmed the final arrangements for shipping the coffin of Ellie Warne back home. David would fly the coffin to Tel Aviv, and from there to Rome; then it would be shipped to New York on a commercial airline.

The Old Man nodded and scribbled down the flights and times of departure and arrival. "Yes," he nodded. "Michael Cohen will accompany Captain Meyer and the body. Other representatives of the Jewish Agency will be there to meet them in New York." He hesitated for a moment, scanning a letter before him as the ambassador talked on. "Yes, of course. We felt very much like the young woman was one of our own. It is a great tragedy, indeed. We have sent out condolences to the girl's parents. Yes." He looked up then to where Howard paced nervously back and forth in front of the desk. "No. I believe her uncle wishes to remain here in Jerusalem. This has been his home for nearly thirty years, after all."

Howard did not acknowledge the mention of his name; instead, he continued to pace grimly, without looking up. "I will tell him when I see him," Ben-Gurion finished, hanging up the telephone.

At last Howard stopped, plopping down in a chair in front of the Old Man. Lines of exhaustion and strain coursed across his normally pleasant face like a road map. "Well?" he asked quietly.

"The American Ambassador sends you his sympathy."

"And?"

"And the coffin will pass through American customs sealed. I cannot speak for Rome. I explained that there was not enough left of the body to examine."

Howard frowned and rubbed his hand across his dome at the thought.

Ben-Gurion brushed his discomfort aside and continued. "If you feel you would like to go along . . ." he offered.

Howard shook his head. "David can handle it," he answered, his voice tense. "I am worried about Ellie's parents. When they hear—"

"We have sent a wire in code from Tel Aviv to Rome, then New York. It should arrive in Los Angeles within the hour. Our man will personally go to speak with Miss Warne's parents—"

"Mrs. Meyer. As of last night she became Mrs. Meyer," Howard corrected.

122

"At any rate, the instant the message is received our man will go to them. Believe it or not, Professor, our cable system works much faster than the conventional one. They will be reached before the American Embassy sends its first word on Ellie's death."

"Good. They must be warned. I don't want any more grief than is necessary in this."

"I am sorry it has to be done this way," Ben-Gurion shrugged apologetically. "If you can think of another way to smuggle the scrolls out."

Howard shook his head. "You can understand my apprehension. I simply wish this grim business did not have to be done at all."

"No one will question. No one will be eager to search the coffin of a bombing victim. And I think young David can carry it off."

"He was like a ghost." Howard closed his eyes briefly at the memory. "It will take him a few days to get over the shock. He won't have any color in his cheeks until this is over, I'll wager. After all, if it hadn't been for that fellow Dan, it really could have been her in that box."

"Quite." Ben-Gurion stared at his hands. "We have been unable to find even a trace of Johann Peltz."

"Will Dan be all right?"

"He lost a considerable amount of blood. They called from the clinic about half an hour ago. He has over one hundred stitches from the glass, but he's talking and lucid. Feeling well, considering. He only vaguely remembers bringing Ellie here through all the smoke and confusion. Somewhere in all of it he says he figured out that the third man, the fellow who lit the cigarette, may have been trailing Ellie. Indeed, she may have been the target. There is no way at this point to be sure. At any rate it is better for her now if they truly believe she is dead, eh? We can get her out of the country later."

Howard nodded wearily. "If we can pry her loose from Jerusalem."

"After last night, David may have a thing or two to say about it, eh?"

"Probably less than you think. Do you realize that the only way she agreed to play dead is if you also sent a wire to *Life* Editorial staff telling them that she is indeed alive and well and participating in undercover work for the biggest story of all time?"

"In a way, she is right."

"She is worried they'll send another photographer out here to take her place."

Ben-Gurion tapped the folder of photographs on his blotter. "When they see these"—he shook his head in wonder—"they would not dare. And David can deliver her last work in person. Along with the story she is posthumously writing right now." He chuckled and leaned back in his chair.

"Yes," Howard replied, proud of her spunk, but unhappy because of the danger it led her into. "She was always a bit of a daredevil, I'm afraid. I wish she were less so. So does David, poor lad. I doubt that any man in the history of the world ever had a worse wedding night."

"The important thing is that she is safe. We will have a team looking into the identity of that third fellow. He may well have been a passerby, not following her at all. Still, better to be safe, eh? We will keep her here until the coffin is through customs and the treasure is in safe hands. By then we should know whether your niece was a target or merely at the wrong place at the wrong time."

"She has a remarkable ability to stumble into things." Howard's voice was full of frustration. "I suppose that is why she always insists on carrying a camera."

"Before this is over"—the Old Man leaned forward and picked up the stub of a pencil—"she may well have opportunity to cover the greatest story of all time." He tapped the lead point impatiently on his desktop map of Palestine. Again and again the pencil touched the red line that marked the narrow Arab-held gorge of Bab el Wad and the only road to Jerusalem from Tel Aviv. "Jerusalem may well become another bloody little Leningrad, another . . ." His voice trailed off.

"Another Alamo?" Howard finished.

Ben-Gurion nodded. "If we can only hold the Arab armies here long enough to supply the rest of the Yishuv with weapons after the British leave." He turned his intense gaze full on Howard. "Yes. Like your American Alamo. What journalist would not have wanted to be in the middle of that, eh?"

"No doubt, if my niece had been in Texas, the armies of Mexico and the faces of the few men who held them off would have been recorded on film. One of these centuries," he laughed bitterly, "all these photographs are going to make archaeologists obsolete."

"And why," Ben-Gurion questioned, squinting curiously, "when you know what may happen when five armies surround this city . . . why does this archaeologist stay here?"

Howard answered without hesitation. "Didn't you explain it to the American Ambassador for me?" He smiled and leaned his arm against the Old Man's desk. "This is my home. My life. Thirty years I have lived and worked here. If I leave, I may never see Jerusalem again. If I stay, all the more reason to pray for peace here."

"You may not be a Jew, Professor, but I see you are a Zionist nonetheless, eh?"

Howard nodded and silently gazed out the window to where the morning sun bathed the pink stone of the Old City in light. "My heart has found a home here," he replied. "Among the shadows of the glory that once was, and the glory that will be again. And in this terrible hour I simply tell myself that we are all—all of us—waiting for the fulfillment of a promise God made a long time ago. That is why you are here, isn't it?" Howard's eyes met the Old Man's steady gaze and held it fast.

"Of course," he answered. "Such a dream makes everything else seem quite small by comparison. Even the sacrifice of my life would seem a small price to pay. And yet, it is to *save* lives that we fight. We can be the hands that help God make little miracles happen. And when we can do nothing more, then He will bring the bigger miracles to pass. There will be a safe homeland for us." He pressed his fingertips together. "That much is promised. But it cannot happen unless men and women are willing to sacrifice even what they hold most dear. I consider your willingness to loan us the scrolls yet another sacrifice, yet one more small miracle."

"I wish I could take credit for this miracle," Howard grinned. "But the explosion is simply one more example of God turning an evil act around and using it for good. When you called me last night and explained what had happened, your plan, there was little I could do but give the okay. After all, if Ellie and David agree, who am I to say no?"

A light tap sounded on the door and the soft-looking man who had picked David up from the street the night before poked his head into the office. "She's finished," he announced without ceremony. "Captain Meyer is with her. Would you like to have a word with her, Boss? And with the captain, too? He's still edgy."

The Old Man sighed heavily and without a word led Howard

down three flights of stairs to the cold, dank basement storage room where Ellie had been hidden away since minutes after the dreadful explosion.

A single light bulb hung from the water-stained ceiling, illuminating the tiny cubicle. Stacks of boxes were piled high in one corner, and against a wall was a typing table and a heavy antique typewriter. Beside it was a neatly typed story and on the other side were prints of the wedding and the immediate aftermath of the *Palestine Post* bombing.

Exhausted by her ordeal and a full night's work that had followed, Ellie huddled beneath David's outstretched arm. She was still wrapped in a coarse army-surplus blanket that covered her ragged and dirty clothes. David was filthy; smudged with his own sweat as well as soot and blood from the wounded. His face was set in grim anger—anger directed first at the Arabs, then at the Zionists, then at Howard and himself for submitting to such a plan, and last of all at Ellie for not being safe back home in the States. Coupled with all that was an immense sense of relief that he had found her unharmed in the Jewish Agency darkroom, working on film that she had rescued before fire had taken its toll on the *Post* building. He felt completely drained of strength, and more than anything, he wanted to find a warm dark corner to curl up in—with Ellie, of course. He gave the Old Man and Howard a dark, threatening look as they opened the door. Putting a finger to his lips, he then motioned to them to come in quietly. His bride was sleeping soundly against his chest.

The Old Man nodded and tiptoed to the papers by the typewriter. He picked them up and skimmed through them as Howard glanced through the photographs, in awe of what Ellie had managed to capture on film. He studied the photographs intently; the first of which must have been taken only seconds after the blast. The interior of the building showed little structural damage. Paper and equipment and people were on the floor. In the next of the series, staff members pulled themselves up to help their wounded comrades. Then a small flame shot up from the stairwell to the basement. Next the bleeding, stunned face of Dan was clearly visible as he staggered toward her. She had turned to take one final shot as they had exited out the back door and flames soared higher, finally engulfing the building. Ellie had explained later that the darkroom where she had been working had been nearly impervious to the blast. She had escaped

126

with little more than a headache as the bleeding Jewish Agency guard had hurried her quickly away from the scene.

Ben-Gurion rubbed a hand across his lips as he finished her story. "Another small miracle," he said softly. "And this girl claims she cannot write well?" He handed the story to Howard, who in turn gave him the photographs. He glanced through them and gave a low whistle. "She is quite remarkable."

"A candidate for a Pulitzer, I would say," agreed Howard.

Without opening her eyes, Ellie sighed and said, "Is that praise I'm hearing?" she asked sleepily. "I guess I can wake up for that." She sat up and blinked.

The Old Man waved the photographs at her. "Quite remarkable, young lady. Quite."

She looked up at David, "Another case of right place, wrong time, huh, David?"

"Definitely," he answered. "I had planned a few fireworks of my own for last night. Somebody got carried away."

"Oh!" Ellie sat bolt upright. "Is Dan okay? The poor guy was bleeding all over, but all he could think about was getting me out of there. He ought to get a medal or something."

"He will recover. Johann was, of course, not so lucky."

"I'm sorry," Ellie said softly, leaning back against David. She stretched out her left hand and stared painfully at her empty ring finger. "And me! Here I was crying because I lost my wedding ring."

"You are among the lucky ones," the Old Man said. "And you will certainly be safe here." He glanced around the tiny cubicle.

"Well, it's not much better than a cell at Acre Prison," David frowned at the accommodations.

"So it's not the King David Hotel, but I'll be all right here until you get back." She looked pointedly at Ben-Gurion. "As long as I don't lose my job over it. Remember! You promised me an exclusive interview. Me first. Got it?"

"Payment of a great debt, young woman," he promised, bowing sharply.

"In that case"—she stretched and yawned—"David, I'll need all my Zane Grey novels and Uncle Howard's copy of *War and Peace*, and a couple of nightgowns and some clothes. And my Bible." She smiled up at his unshaven face and batted her eyelashes at him.

"Anything else? Look at her, would you? Married twelve hours and already a slave."

"You were that already," she stated, kissing his cheek. "And since you asked, darling," she added, emphasizing the word *darling* in her finest Greta Garbo voice, "why don't you take a bath while you're at it?"

David shrugged and stood up. "Right. And I suppose you want me to go find your wedding ring?" he joked sarcastically.

Howard patted him on the back in mock sympathy. "Just like her mother," he said.

"My own fault," David replied. "I signed up for the duration, you know. I just didn't expect to spend my first hours of wedded bliss in a bomb shelter." He shook his head in frustration. "This is like Humphrey Bogart in *Casablanca*, you know? 'Out of all the joints in all the woild, she had ta walk inta mine.' " He winked at her, and relief seemed to radiate from his eyes. "Nightgowns. Zane Grey. Bible. Right?"

"And toothbrush," she added.

"And David," the Old Man warned, "watch yourself. The streets are filled with journalists—"

"No doubt wanting a crack at the bereaved husband," Ellie interrupted.

"Remember you are a man in mourning, eh? The less said the better." Ben-Gurion stretched out his hand.

David nodded. "If I get into trouble I'll think about how I felt last night when that building came down." He turned to Ellie and drank in her smiling face. "I thought she was a goner. I won't have to fake it, gents. That scared the wits out of me, you know?"

"She's safe now, David," the Old Man assured him. "The Agency is a fortress. I have two guards assigned to her. And we are doing our best to learn the identity of the fellow who helped the terrorists."

"That all ought to be comforting. But somehow. . ."

Ellie stood then, her blanket dragging the floor. She looked straight up into his worried face. "Listen, pal," she said with tears shining in her eyes, "I'm going to be okay in here. Me and Zane Grey. Who knows, maybe they'll give me time off for good behavior. You're the one who's going to be out there on the streets, right? If they were after me, they might want you, too."

"Who me? I resigned." He winked, then took her in his arms, amused somehow that she was as worried about his safety as he was for hers. "How many German fighters did I shoot down? You think I'm going to let some Arab get me now after everything I've been through to stay alive?"

She nuzzled against him. "So who's worried about Arabs?" she asked when she found her voice again. "Watch out for the press, okay?"

11   Angela

David moved cautiously through the smoldering ruins of the *Palestine Post* building. A dozen others, cleanup crew and scavengers, worked among the rubble, and a British Army bulldozer roared loudly as it rearranged the heaps of wreckage in the street. David had promised one hundred American dollars to the first man who happened upon Ellie's wedding ring. So far their seemingly hopeless search had proved fruitless.

David stepped carefully over a charred typewriter, then shoved it over with the toe of his boot. Layers of black ash moved beneath it. For the first time in half an hour, he raised his eyes from the floor and looked up at the endless mess surrounding him. He sighed and shook his head. "Useless," he muttered. "This is one bill I won't be paying."

Behind him, a woman's soft voice spoke in a clear British accent. "What are you looking for, Captain Meyer?"

David whirled quickly around to face a tall slender woman of about twenty-five. She was dressed in a tweed skirt and long jacket and wore brown pumps that seemed dangerously out of place in the wreckage. Her chestnut brown hair was pulled back in a bun, and wide full lips were parted in a sympathetic smile. David saw his own filthy reflection in the lenses of her sunglasses. She was pretty in an intelligent-looking way, and on any other day, David might have looked twice. But not this morning. He stared wearily at her for a moment, then, without answering, he turned his back on her and moved slowly toward the back of the building.

"Captain Meyer," she called after him, "I was a friend of Miss Warne's."

He stopped and stood up, his arms hanging limply at his sides. *Press*, he thought. "I'm looking for her wedding ring," he replied.

"May I help you?" Her words were almost imploring.

"Sure," he said bitterly. "One hundred bucks to the first person who finds it." He gave a short laugh.

"Have you looked in the darkroom?" she asked quietly, picking her way toward him like a cat stepping through a puddle.

He turned and appraised her again. "You came down here to help me find Ellie's wedding ring, huh?" he asked.

"No. I told you. I was a friend of hers."

He raised his eyebrows briefly and nodded. "Is that so?" He did not try to conceal the sarcasm in his voice. "What's your name?" There was an anger in his tone that caused her to stop short and tilt her head slightly in curiosity at his hostility.

"Angela St. Martain."

"Never heard of you," he said curtly. "You're press. Good grief. I can spot you vultures a mile away." His eyes fell accusingly on the yellow lined notepad that protruded from the top of her purse.

"Well, yes. I am with the *Thames Courier*, but—"

"No buts, lady. Get lost. Beat it. I told you guys no comment." His voice was loud. Several of the men cleaning up the debris looked up anxiously.

"I knew your wife from school," she protested, looking as though she might cry.

"Spent some time at Stanford, did you?" David lowered his voice as he remembered Ellie's warning to beware of the press.

The woman frowned and raised her chin questioningly. "Stanford? No. UCLA. I was a couple of years ahead of her, but I remember what an excellent photographer she was even as an underclassman."

David appraised the woman, still not willing to let his guard down. She did indeed seem to know Ellie—or at least know something about her. "You can see how much good that did her." He kicked a fallen timber, sending a spray of ash into the air. "This is no place for a woman. And you won't find Ellie here, so maybe you ought to go back to UCLA or England or wherever you're from . . ."

She nodded quickly and looked down at the blackened rubble. "I didn't mean to intrude. I am sorry, Captain Meyer. This is a great tragedy for you." She glanced quickly around at the destroyed newspaper office. "For all of us. She truly was a great photographer, and a lovely. . ." Her voice trailed off as David silently continued his search for the ring. His face was grim as the realization of how near Ellie had come to death once again filled him.

The woman watched him for a long, silent moment, then she said quietly in a voice edged with compassion. "The darkroom is back there, you know," she pointed.

David raised his eyes to the small cinder-block cubicle that hugged the remaining back wall near what had been the rear exit of the building. It was scorched, and a heavy metal door hung crazily from its bottom two hinges. David pressed his hand to his forehead as the memories of the night before washed over him with a wave of nausea. He swayed for a moment, oblivious to the sound of the woman's footsteps moving toward him. She placed a hand gently on his shoulder.

"I'll go look for you, Captain Meyer," she said softly. Then she moved quickly toward the darkroom.

David raised his eyes to watch as she reached out and touched the cinder block walls of the room. She scanned the uppermost stones as though examining their structure for safety; then she gingerly pushed past the door. Inside, developing trays and broken bottles of chemicals littered the floor, but this one tiny corner of the *Palestine Post* was unscarred by the inferno that had raged.

David frowned and regained his composure, then walked to where the woman picked through the fallen contents of the darkroom. He stood at the door and imagined his beloved Ellie inside this room last night. Again, he felt dizzy, and he leaned heavily against the doorjamb.

"What exactly are we looking for, Captain Meyer?" she asked gently.

"Wedding band. Small. Gold with rubies. We were married last night, you know," he offered involuntarily as though her kindness had taken him off guard. "You going to print that?" He regained his sharpness, and narrowed his eyes. She did not look up or acknowledge the bitterness of his words.

After several minutes of silence, she lifted a toppled drying rack and gave a small cry of delight. There, amid slivers of shattered glass, lay the wedding ring that Ellie had worn for only a few hours. "Here we have it, Captain!" she exclaimed, picking it up reverently and carrying it to where he stood. She held it between her thumb and forefinger and dropped it into his upturned palm.

"Thanks," he whispered, remembering the joy with which he had given it to Ellie. "Guess I owe you a hundred bucks," he smiled slightly.

"A cup of coffee sometime perhaps?" she smiled. "That is enough."

"Are you going to print this?" he asked, all anger gone from his voice.

"I think not."

"Then I owe you double." His hand closed around the ring and he slipped it into his pocket.

"Perhaps you really will have a story for me sometime." She brushed the dust from her hands and stepped past him. Her tone was injured and David felt ashamed. Ellie would not like him talking to her friend like this.

"Sure. Maybe sometime. If you want to come to the States and write about an ex-fighter pilot turned commercial pilot or something." He shrugged, then wiped his hand across his cheek. "Look . . ." he began. "I didn't mean to get short with you back there. I just . . . It's just been one rotten night. Okay?"

"I understand," she smiled tenderly. "I truly am sorry for you, Captain. She was quite good at what she did."

David nodded and sighed deeply, then looked away. "Right. The best."

The woman lifted her hand in farewell. "I'm going to hold you to that cup of coffee someday."

David responded with a half smile and raised his fingers slightly. "Good luck." For a long moment he watched her as she moved through the rubble toward where the bulldozer rumbled on Halosel Street. Once she turned around and he waved again, careful not to smile too broadly. Finally she walked from his view and down toward the central district of town. He sighed a deep sigh of relief and wiped sweat from his brow; then he patted his pocket and announced in a loud voice: "The contest is over, boys! We found it."

The final decision as to who would know Ellie's whereabouts

132

and who would not had been made in the dimly lit office of the Old Man the night before. The fewer who were part of the charade, the better. The more genuine grief displayed in public and seen by the press, the better. David himself had been frightened badly enough by the events at the *Post* that he had no doubts he could play the part of a grieving husband well. Ellie's safety and that of the true cargo in the coffin depended on it. Michael Cohen, on the other hand, was to be excluded from the true facts of Ellie's whereabouts and physical condition. That decision was bordering on cruelty, David knew, but in the final analysis, it was the only safe choice to be made. Michael would not be told that Ellie was alive and well at the Jewish Agency.

After five years of friendship, David had learned that the honest frankness of Michael's manner made it nearly impossible for anyone who met him not to know that he knew something he should not tell. David was certain that Michael must have been the kind of child who, watching his older brother rob the cookie jar, had been blamed for the misdeed by virtue of the fact that he wore the guilt of knowledge all over his face. Others might lie boldly and then forget about it. Michael Cohen might lie boldly, but the truth would then climb to his shoulder and shout suspicion into the ear of the hearer. Michael was indeed *a man in whom there was no guile.*

But this was a time when guile was the better part of valor, and so, as far as Michael was concerned, Ellie lay still and lifeless in a cold metal coffin in a back room of Goldman's Mortuary. The terrible grief reflected on his face was real. Tears of sympathy lingered just beneath the surface of his open features. Anger seethed behind his normally pleasant face, and as far as he was concerned, David was a broken man; a man in shock; a friend who needed his protection against the vultures who circled in search of a story. In this desperately dangerous undertaking, the decision had been made. The honest grief of Michael Cohen would speak more than a thousand falsehoods. David simply would not speak at all, and his silence would hopefully convey a message to those who watched him. When the time was right, when Ellie was safe and the scrolls were safe, David would whisper the truth into Michael's ear. Again, David was playing the heartless Tinman to Michael's brainless Scarecrow. He could only hope that Michael would understand and forgive when the facts finally came to light.

This morning, Michael sat uncomfortably in a powder blue velvet Victorian chair in the foyer of Goldman's Mortuary. He leaned his cheek against his hand and studied the oil painting on the wall opposite. Two happy angels flanked an empty tomb and raised their arms in righteous salute as two women bowed fearfully before them. He squinted and squirmed uneasily, aware that he sat in the Gentile foyer of a facility that served Gentiles and Jews alike from opposite sides of the street. He had once had occasion to wait in the Jewish building, where a painting of Moses on Sinai had comforted the mourners. He had never thought of Ellie as a Gentile. But then, he had to admit, he himself did not make such a great Jew. By the standards of the religious Jews, he was *Apikorsim*, an apostate. He always managed to remember that at times like this—but even so, he would have felt more comfortable looking at Moses on Sinai.

He was dressed in a suit and tie—borrowed. And he sat here as a representative for the family. For David. So far he had told three distinguished members of the press that there was no comment, that the family wanted to be left alone in their grief. David was resting at an undisclosed location. They would both accompany the coffin back to the United States. Yes, David was finished helping the Jewish Agency. All he wanted was a little peace and quiet and time to recover, so thank you very much and goodbye. The men had nodded respectfully and left, waiting until they reached the sidewalk before they scribbled their notes.

Howard Moniger had come in just a few moments earlier, and a tall, lanky British captain had followed, carrying a satchel under his arm. They had been ushered through the dark walnut door and down a long hallway through yet another door. Michael was quite certain that David would not come here at all.

He glanced up from his morbid vigil as the front door swung open and a tall young woman in a brown tweed suit walked into the foyer. Her mouth was turned down slightly at the corners, and her eyes were hidden behind large sunglasses. She clutched a handbag in front of her and stood uncertainly as the door closed behind her. Smiling nervously in the heavy silence, she swallowed hard and turned her face to where Michael sat.

"Excuse me." Her voice was apologetic. "I was a close friend of Ellie Warne."

Michael stood and straightened his tie; then he extended his hand. "I . . . I'm a . . . a friend also. Of the family," he faltered. "They asked me to—"

"I just would like to say goodbye." The young woman's voice broke and she quickly pulled a handkerchief from her purse and dabbed her eyes.

Michael rubbed his head and looked up toward the ceiling, as though imploring a higher power to help him deal with this obviously distraught female. Newspaper men were one thing. The tears of a woman were quite another matter. He sighed and stepped a little closer. "Do you . . . why don't you sit down?" he offered kindly.

Without a reply, she accepted his offer and sat down gracefully in his chair. She crossed her shapely legs and Michael looked away, filled with remorse that he would notice legs at a time like this. "My name is Michael Cohen," he said quickly.

"Michael," she said with feeling. "Of course. She spoke of you often."

"She did?" He felt a lump in his throat.

"Of course," she sniffed. "You are . . . you were . . ."

"Her husband and I went through the service together," he volunteered. "She was somethin', that girl." He pursed his lips. "She really was somethin'."

The young woman nodded. "We went to school together." She tucked the handkerchief back into her purse. "UCLA."

"No kidding?" Michael smiled. "I never would have guessed. You with your accent and all."

"Oh yes," she sighed and leaned back. "When the war broke out my parents sent me to America to school. The blitz, you know."

"Yes. My Uncle Sam sent me to Europe," he smiled.

"And you met David there?"

"Yeah. He is quite a guy." He lowered his eyes. "This is terrible. Terrible. He isn't himself, you know. Like he's mad at the world."

"One can't blame him." She reached for her kerchief again. "Where is he now?"

"I don't know. Home maybe. Sleeping it off. I don't know. We've got quite a trip ahead of us the next few days."

"When are you leaving?"

"Tonight. I think. If everything is ready, you know."

The young woman let her eyes fall on the heavy walnut door that led to the viewing rooms. "I see," she whispered. "Do you

135

think I could . . . see her?" Her voice was almost inaudible.

Michael shook his head slowly. Then he wiped his eyes on the back of his hand. "No. Closed casket, you know."

The woman leaned forward in the chair and covered her face with her hands. "My God!" she said. "Oh, dear Ellie! The radio said the darkroom collapsed on her! Poor Ellie! Dear Ellie!"

Stepping close to her, Michael patted her on the back awkwardly. "It's awful," he clucked his tongue. "I know how you feel. Her uncle is back there with her body now. Getting the details ironed out." The woman did not reply. "We'll leave tonight for Tel Aviv. Then we'll catch a trans-Atlantic to New York from Rome tomorrow night, 9 o'clock." The woman still did not reply, but kept her hands over her face as Michael continued to speak. "They said they'll try and get the coffin through Customs sealed. They don't even want *those* guys to open it, you know?" He shook his head solemnly. "They aren't embalming the body, I guess and . . . well, you know. None of this is very pretty. David is just about crazy. Last night some guys from the Jewish Agency picked him up right off the street when all I did is leave him to get the car. You know, they could have been anybody and he went with them, you know? I didn't find him for two hours until I stumbled into the Agency and there he sat. Just staring. He hasn't said a word to me. Not a word. The Old Man told me to go take a bath and took this suit right off the back of some clerk. And here I am. Fending off the reporters. Every one of them after a story, you know?" He frowned and stopped patting her shoulder as she wiped her eyes beneath the sun glasses and stood slowly.

"The world will miss her," she sighed.

"You went to school together, huh?" Michael suddenly realized that he had not stopped talking since she walked through the door.

"UCLA School of Journalism."

Michael scratched his head. "Are you a—"

"*Thames Courier.*" She flipped out a compact and studied her reflection for a moment. "I have been in Cairo for several months. Just passing through, and wanted to stop and see my old friend."

"Well, do me a favor, will you?" Michael looked pained. "Don't write about this, will you not? I mean I wasn't supposed to—"

"Mr. Cohen, I hope you think better of me than that. I didn't come here for a story." Her face clouded up again and she looked away. "Thank you." She bit her lower lip. "You have been a comfort to me." She put her fingers against her lips and turned slowly from Michael.

"Any time," he said sadly as she walked out the door. He sat down heavily on the blue velvet chair and only then realized that he had not gotten her name.

12   As Time Goes By

A bundle tucked under his arm, David made his way down the metal steps into the broad, dark corridor of the basement at the Jewish Agency building. His boot heels clanked loudly and echoed the length of the corridor. Thick steel pipes hung like rusty garland from the low ceiling and he had to duck several times as he made his way toward the far end of the basement. Steam from the furnace hissed and boiled upward as water from plumbing swished by in the other direction. Naked light bulbs dripped through the maze of pipes at ten-foot intervals, creating an atmosphere like an interrogation scene David had watched in a Grade-B detective movie.

Small rooms with gray steel doors lined each side of the hallway. Crates of typing paper were stacked beside one, and a broken desk chair leaned against another. Dust coated the chair and David could not help but wonder how long it had been consigned to the gloomy storage area. Thirty feet beyond that, two muscled, tough-looking Agency guards played cards beneath a light bulb. They both looked up at the sound of his approaching footsteps, then in unison looked back at their cards. They had the look of men who had accidentally fallen down a deep hole and were unable to find a way out. Their eyes were red-rimmed and bleary; three days growth of beard bristled on their chins, and they slapped their cards down on the discard pile and drew with such vengeance that David was sure they must have had nothing else to do but play gin for weeks. An unlit cigar hung from the mouth of the largest of the two men; the man, David noted, had arms like an oak tree and fingers as thick as a Coney Island hot dog.

"Hi, fellas!" David called brightly as he neared them.

Neither man answered as they gazed with stony intensity at their hands.

"Playing gin, huh?" David tried again, bumping his head on a light bulb that sent it spinning in circles. "Watch it," the big man mumbled.

"New York," David said. "You're from New York, huh? Recognize the accent anywhere."

"What of it?" snapped the tree, slamming his card onto the pile.

"Recruited from the mafia, right?" David stopped and grinned as the guard stared menacingly up at him.

His partner eyed the card on top of the pile, then scrutinized his own hand for a long moment. The big man snorted and turned his head sideways, then narrowed his bloodshot eyes to appraise David suspiciously. "Yeah. And who're youse?"

"The husband," David replied brightly.

"Ah-ha!" cried the partner, snatching up the discard. "I got it! Three of spades! GIN!" He slammed his hand face up on the crate.

Outraged, the big man opposite him sprang to his feet. "Yeah? The husband, huh? Well, we got orders nobody in and nobody out. Unless youse got proof, we ain't supposed t' let nobody in, see?" He clenched and unclenched his fists and stood like a grizzly bear guarding his lunch.

David rubbed a hand across his freshly shaved cheek and looked from the grim face of first one guard to the other. "Glad to see you guys are on the job. She'll be safe with you all right."

Neither man replied, and the smaller of the two stepped closer as the big man stepped between David and the door and crossed his arms. His lower lip worked the cigar stub, which wagged at David like a finger.

"Hey, guys, honest. I'm the husband!" David said innocently.

"Yeah, well, ain't nobody s'posed t' go in there. She's s'posed t' be dead, y' know," said the small man.

David looked at the heavy steel door and frowned. "Well, look guys, if you need me to go get Ben-Gurion or something." The knob to the door turned slightly and opened just a crack.

Ellie peeked out and smiled broadly, her red hair and vivacious green eyes a colorful relief to the grim environment. "Ellie! Honey! I got your stuff. Your toothbrush and the nightgown and . . . gosh it's good to see you! Tell these goons who I—"

"Is it okay now, Ellie?" asked the big man gently, his face melting into hound-dog adoration.

"Thanks, fellas," she said brightly. "I've got it all ready now; you can let him in in a minute, Eddy."

Both guards were smiling now, their bulldog faces transformed with delight over the arrival of David. "Mazel Tov!" The oak tree stepped forward and pumped David's arm vigorously. "Mazel Tov, Captain Meyer! Youse got quite a goil in there, y' know?"

"Yeah." David was puzzled and relieved.

"Close your eyes, David!" Ellie bubbled. "Hold him just another minute, Herman, until I say let him in!" She pulled the door shut and David closed his eyes, feeling like a kid at a birthday party. The guards chuckled at their conspiracy and grasped David, one on each arm.

"Hey, Els!" David called loudly, "when do I get to unwrap the presents?"

"Just a minute, Captain Meyer. Youse ain't gonna ruin this. She's been workin' on it since this morning, y' know?"

"Hey, Els?" David called again, rocking on his toes and feeling a giddy rush in the pit of his stomach.

Suddenly, from behind the door, he heard the crackle of a phonograph and a mellow voice rising on the swells of an orchestra.

You must remember this,
A kiss is still a kiss,
A sigh is still a sigh . . .

With his eyes closed, the guards led David forward and he heard the door open and the music grew louder.

"Okay, boys," Ellie said authoritatively, "I got him." She took his hand as they released him. "Thanks!" she called, tugging David into the room and shutting the door after him. "Keep your eyes closed," she warned.

The smell of perfume filled his senses and as the song played on, he reached out for her. She pushed his hand away and stood back from him.

"Els, honey," he said feeling his head spin.

139

"Don't open your eyes yet. You'll ruin it!" He heard the squeak of a bed spring as she sat down.

A kiss is still a kiss . . .

A sigh is still a sigh . . .

The record crooned on. Dim light shone through David's eyelids and he instinctively directed his head toward that.

As time goes by . . .

"Okay, King David." Her voice was low and quieting. "Open your eyes."

David opened his eyes and stood speechless at the transformation in the tiny cinderblock room. A tall tapered candle burned brightly on a wooden crate covered by a lace cloth. Ellie sat on the edge of a sagging bed, her face awash in happiness at seeing his expression. She wore a pastel blue silk nightgown, outlining her lovely form. David gave a low whistle, his eyes unable to absorb anything but her. He tossed the bundle of personal belongings and clothes onto the bed next to her and stepped around the makeshift table until he stood before her, and she smiled up at him.

"You are wonderful, you know that?" he said softly.

"You haven't commented on the sign." She motioned to the wall behind her.

David looked up, for the first time noticing the large butcher-paper banner that proclaimed, *HONEYMOON SUITE, KING DAVID'S HOTEL!!!* Travel posters of the pyramids of Egypt and the Eiffel Tower flanked it, and the room was decorated with bouquets of flowers made from toilet paper. In the corner, a dilapidated crank phonograph clicked and popped as it sang to them, and a bottle of red wine and a loaf of fresh white bread and thin slices of cheese waited on a round silver tray.

David took her hand as he shook his head in amazement. "But how—"

"The boss's secretary. I told her how we had planned to spend the night at the King David last night." Her voice sounded wistful. "Well, she was just wonderful. The Old Man even rounded up another bottle of the stuff he calls wine. I sneaked a sniff, and I think we might be safer to pour it down the sink. Maybe we ought to see if someone around here can change wine back to water . . ."

David was hearing her voice, but no longer listening to her

140

words, He touched her cheek, then bent down and kissed the top of her head.

. . . and when two lovers woo,
they still say . . .

David sang the words off-key, "I love you-u-u.
On that you can rely-y-y.
The fundamental things apply,
As time goes by-y-y."

"You know, Humphrey Bogart didn't try to sing it to Bergman," Ellie teased. "He hired a piano player."

"I didn't expect this, you know?" He pulled her up to him and held her close. "Like the Old Man said, I'm supposed to be in mourning."

"Just wait until you have to say goodbye," she said. "You won't have to fake a thing." She laid her head against his chest and began to hum the melody of the song as they danced in a small circle.

"I kind of figured we'd have a honeymoon when I get back in a couple of weeks," he said in quiet awe.

"I didn't want to wait two weeks for you," she whispered in a barely audible voice. She lifted her face to him and he searched her eyes, then kissed her tenderly. "I promise, David. We can do this again when you get back if you like."

David sighed with deep contentment. "Then I'll hire a piano player."

———

Four hours later David stood barefooted in the center of the little room. "You were right, you know. Having to leave you like this—I won't have to pretend to grieve." He sighed and shook his head. "When I get back we really are going to the King David Hotel."

"I'll be looking forward to it," she said as she moved into his outstretched arms.

"What I'd really like to do is take your body to New York—in its current state of good health, of course, and replay this afternoon at the Biltmore Hotel."

"I'd love to take you up on that." She lifted her face to his, then she gasped. "Who *are* you taking to New York?" She stepped back and paled a bit at the thought of the true occupant of the coffin.

141

"An old goat," David grinned.

"How irreverent, David! I mean, to talk about a human life like that! An old goat!" She was indignant now.

"Hold it, Els." He plopped down on the sagging bed and pulled his socks and boots on. "I mean in the literal sense, we've got an old goat in the coffin. Word is out that there wasn't enough of . . . the body to embalm, right?"

"What are you getting at?" She frowned and pursed her lips.

"If some wise guy in customs wants to rummage through the casket, he'll wish he hadn't opened the lid. At least that's what we're hoping for."

She wrinkled her face in disgust at the thought. "Oh. Oh yuk. They are going to think that's *me*!"

"Not real flattering, I'll grant you. But it ought to be effective. This is a *ripe* old goat." He laughed as Ellie blanched and sat down beside him.

"Don't tell me any more. Please." She gulped. Then she put her hand to her lips and frowned. "The poor old thing. Was it already dead or did they kill it just for this. . . ? How awful."

"Think of it as a sort of hero. The unknown scapegoat. We'll erect a monument."

"I guess it's better than the alternative," Ellie said softly. "It really could have been me."

David's smile melted away instantly as he looked at her. "You could have gone the rest of your life and not said that," he replied after a long moment. "I haven't been able to think of anything else. Today I went back to look for your ring . . ."

Her expression grew tender. "You did?"

". . . and I was standing there talking with that reporter friend of yours and I got sick. Dizzy. You know? Just remembering last night."

"What reporter friend of mine?" Ellie looked alarmed.

"Some dame. Said she went to UCLA with you. Quite a looker."

"Who?"

"Her name is Angela Saint something . . . British accent. She seemed to think the world of you—"

Ellie's eyes grew wide. "Angela St. Martain? Here in Jerusalem?"

"You really know her, huh?" David grinned and shrugged. "I wasn't exactly cordial to her."

142

"Well, she was only the best reporter at UCLA. Graduated two years ahead of me and flew off to cover the war. Italy. Crete. Cairo. My gosh, we all envied her." Ellie smiled wistfully. "And you mean she remembered me?"

"You should have heard her rave about your work . . . what an obituary she's going to write for you!" he teased.

Ellie tossed a pillow at him. "It's kinda nice knowing I'm appreciated while I'm still alive."

David looked at her, and emotion flooded his face. "I can vouch for that." He reached out to touch her cheek and the two stood in silence as they searched one another's eyes.

At last Ellie spoke. "You went back to look for my ring?"

He reached into his pocket and pulled it out, holding it up triumphantly. "I wanted to make an honest woman out of you."

His smile returned, and he decided not to tell her Angela found it.

In awe, Ellie took it from his hand and touched it to her lips. "David," she whispered.

"You're supposed to wear it, not eat it."

"Will you put it on for me again?"

"As many times as you want." He pulled her to her feet, then took her left hand in his and looked into her eyes. "With this ring I pledge my love and my life to you for as long as I live." He slipped it onto her finger and held her hand gently in his. "Thank you, Lord, for giving all this to me," he breathed quietly. "And thank you for being my wife, Els. If it weren't after four o'clock I think I would probably be the happiest man on earth, you know?"

Ellie nodded and bit her lip. "Hurry back to me, David." She smiled bravely, but tears welled up in her eyes again as she studied the pain on his face. "God keep you safe for me. Please, God . . ." She leaned her head against his shoulder and sighed.

A firm knock sounded on the door, and a voice said loudly, "Time, Captain Meyer."

"Yeah!" David barked his reply. "I'm coming." Then he said quietly. "These guys must have been guards on death row in Sing-Sing. That's how I feel anyway. Like my whole life is right here in this little room with you."

"And mine is going out the door with you." She threw her arms around his neck. "Be careful," she begged. "Please."

He nodded but did not reply; instead, he kissed her one last

143

time. He held her a moment longer until the knock on the door sounded more insistently. She stepped back from him, and he reached for his leather flight jacket. He started to put it on, then handed it to her and shrugged.

"Keep yourself warm while I'm gone." His clear blue eyes were full of unspoken words.

Ellie nodded and pulled the jacket on, tugging the long sleeves up over her small hands. "I will."

"Time, Captain Meyer!" the voice insisted.

"Okay!" he called angrily. Silence filled the room and David stepped forward to hold her one last time. She felt weak and small in his embrace. He kissed the top of her head, then without a word, he turned and left the room.

Ellie stood alone in the center of the room, her arms loose at her sides, with the steady thump of the needle on the record her only company.

13 Leaving Jerusalem

A heavy, lead-gray line thickened on the afternoon horizon and swept toward Jerusalem from the sea. Harsh wind swept away the pleasant warmth of the sunlight, and soon the mountains around Zion were capped by towering black pillars of thunderheads.

David stood near the ramp of the mortuary and studied the threatening sky as the coffin was wheeled down to the van. Howard stood beside him, his arms crossed and his gaze fixed worriedly on the sealed metal casket. Across the alley, an intrepid band of journalists scribbled notes and snapped pictures under the disapproving stare of four strong American Embassy guards and a group of eight Jewish Agency men who had come down to help.

The coffin slid easily into the back of the long van. David adjusted the sunglasses he wore and stepped to one side as the doors were shut. Michael wiped a tear from his eye and patted David solidly on the back, as David took care to gaze solemnly at the pavement. The two men from the American Embassy who had trailed David and Ellie for weeks approached him in unison and offered their hands in condolence. David simply nodded and looked all the more distracted as the shutters of a dozen cameras clicked. He looked up briefly, noting that the face of Miss St. Martain was not among the reporters. A short, plump man, with a shirt that bulged at the middle and a tie that hung crazily to the side of his bulk, pushed thick glasses up on his nose and broke from the group to hurry toward where Howard stood.

"Professor Moniger!" he called, a serious frown marring his round, red-cheeked face. "Mr. Meyer! *Captain* Meyer, excuse me please!" He launched into a series of questions as the others followed and clustered around.

David held up his arms as though he were surrendering, but he said nothing. Howard was kinder in his response. "Sorry, fellows. This has been an ordeal. Maybe later." Questions continued to fly from every quarter.

Michael tugged at his starched shirt collar with his forefinger, and stretched his neck uncomfortably like a turtle about to snap. "Why don't you guys can it?" he said angrily as he stepped between them and his friend. "Beat it! Can't you see this is a bad time? Holy mackerel! Haven't you got no manners?" He quickly ushered David to the waiting American Embassy limousine and nudged him into the backseat after Howard. As the door slammed shut behind the two men, Michael turned on the reporters like a mother hen warding off predators. His arms were spread wide and David rubbed his hand across his lips to conceal a smile as Michael let loose with a few epithets learned, no doubt, from his tough West Side New York upbringing. ". . . so print that in your lousy newspapers, y' bums!" he yelled.

"You were right about Michael," Howard blinked innocently.

"Great, isn't he?" David remarked under his breath. "I just hate to think what he'll call me when we let him in on the secret."

Wordlessly, the Embassy driver opened his door and slid behind the wheel. He was Arab, David noted, dressed like an American. He looked in the rear-view mirror at David and Howard, and for an instant, David thought he saw some collective sense of guilt in the man's sympathetic brown eyes. For a moment, David wanted to pat him reassuringly on the shoulder and tell him everything was all right. It was an urge he knew he would have to curb over the next few days while the world turned its eyes on their long journey home. He would not open his mouth. Undoubtedly Michael would say enough for both of them.

As the small caravan of official vehicles followed the van carrying the coffin through the streets of the city, David was astonished and touched at the people who paused and waved or nodded their heads in salute to Ellie Warne. Her work had been well-known and admired in the Holy City. He made a mental note to relate her own funeral procession to her when he returned. English soldiers stood to attention and saluted, mothers pointed the procession out to their children. Bearded old men stared solemnly and young women wiped their eyes.

Barricade guards stood to one side and reached out to touch the van that carried the remains of the little American shiksa who had captured so many of their faces on film.

"She would be pleased," Howard said softly and the driver glanced into the mirror, then quickly away.

"The Ambassador thought it would be nice," David replied with a sigh. "Sort of a last tour of the city." He was certain his words would be repeated by the driver. "Thoughtful of him." Foremost in his mind was that it was also the very best possible kind of public display. The events of the day would be repeated in every Muslim meeting place in the city, including the drawing room of the Mufti. No doubt he would call off his dogs—for a while, at any rate. Give them time to get the cargo safely to its destination.

The tall tower of the YMCA building loomed ahead of them as they turned onto King George Avenue. It was a reminder to David that soon enough he would be seeing another tower built by the same architect that had built this one. A smattering of rain sprinkled the windshield as David thought about the day he and Ellie had stood atop the Empire State Building in New York, never dreaming that they would one day climb the one hundred and twenty-foot observation tower of this building in Jerusalem to discover it was designed by the same man. "Small world," he muttered, repeating Ellie's words. "All hooked up together, aren't we?"

Howard nodded, not quite certain where David's comment had come from and not willing to probe. The wipers lobbed slowly back and forth as the vehicles moved down Ramban Street toward the airfield. David and Howard remained in the car as the Jewish Agency men unloaded the coffin and carried it to

146

the waiting Stinson aircraft. One seat had been removed to facilitate its loading, but still they had to maneuver carefully to cram the coffin into the cargo area.

The driver stepped out of the vehicle and stood discreetly near the front bumper as Howard and David watched Michael issuing orders beneath the wing of the plane. His borrowed suit was drenched, and damp hair clung in wisps around his bald spot. Across the field, yet another knot of journalists huddled beneath black umbrellas.

Michael pulled out a handkerchief and blew his nose hard, then gazed forelornly back toward David and Howard.

"I think that means we can get out," David said as he reached forward to the door latch.

Howard clasped his arm and grinned, "Do me a favor," Howard said. "Don't let your friend suffer any longer than you have to, will you?"

David raised his fingers in a Boy Scout salute. "Scouts honor, Howard. But honestly, isn't the guy great?" He shook his head in wonder at the honest emotion that radiated from every pore of Michael Cohen. "Who could doubt, right?"

"Ellie will have to bake him a cake or something when you two get back."

"C'mon, Howard! Not that! Isn't this bad enough?" he chuckled.

Howard put a finger quickly to his lips as the door opened behind David, and Michael poked his head into the car. "Right, buddy." He extended his hands to help David from the car. "Loaded. We'd better get out of here before the weather gets any worse."

"Stay in the car, Howard," David lowered his voice. "No use you getting wet."

Howard drew his breath in and let it out slowly as he looked past David to the dull gleam of the coffin. *Two thousand years, Lord,* he prayed silently. *You kept them safe for two thousand years . . ."* The prayer remained unfinished, but was a request nonetheless for God to oversee this small mission. "Take care," Howard shook David's hand. "God go with you."

"And stay with you," David returned. The men locked eyes for a long moment of understanding. David was leaving his heart in Jerusalem, while he took Howard's away to America. Ellie had been right; it would not be difficult for David to play the bereaved husband.

"Hurry back," Howard called as David slammed the car door and sprinted through the downpour to the plane.

———

A pale blue haze of smoke hovered above the heads of those men who had found shelter from the rain in the Son of the Prophet coffeehouse on Doud Street in the Old City. Thick Turkish coffee was served in tiny cups, and a tall water pipe was brought to the table of Ram Kadar. The mouthpiece was dipped in scalding water by a smiling, gap-toothed waiter, who then handed it to Kadar with a flourish.

The red keffiya Kadar wore on his head was damp, and his robes were wet at the hem and across the shoulders. His appearance was like that of a thousand peasants who flocked to Jerusalem, but there was an air of authority about him that caused the waiter's smile to dim slightly and the bow to deepen. Kadar had come to this place, cloaked in the guise of obscurity, to meet with Montgomery. This same Montgomery he had known well since the pre-war days in Cairo, but in a public place, Kadar knew, Montgomery would seek him out. Montgomery, master of disguise and deception, would surprise him once again with the thoroughness of yet another identity. *It has become a game,* Kadar mused as he puffed the cool smoke of the pipe. Throughout the years of Nazi occupation, Kadar had been the one link between Montgomery and the German Command. Vital information on British military operations in the vast sands of Northern Africa had been carefully garnered by this one called Montgomery, then passed quietly along in meetings like the one tonight. Always, Kadar had studied faces and gaits and the slope of shoulders of everyone who came in. Even knowing the true identity of Montgomery had not enlightened him as to the final shape of the one who would sit quietly beside him, pull out the ornate silver lighter that had been a gift of the Führer, and light a Players cigarette. *Perhaps,* Kadar thought, *even the spiders who brought messages to the door of the Mufti had not been messengers at all, but different faces of the same person, whose true features were hidden beneath putty and powder and tattered robes.* Kadar glanced around the room, ruling out the obviously obese or desperately thin among the crowd. The fleshly hands of the portly and the boney fingers of the aged were difficult to imitate. Shoulders could be padded, a confident stride could be altered to a limp, but the *hands* were nearly impossible to change. Montgomery would shove them deep into pockets, Kadar knew, then, when ready, would take them out, cradling the lighter in slender strong fingers. Only then would Kadar be certain.

The room was warmed by the press of men who had gathered to hear Abu Nafur, the *rawi*, or storyteller, who mesmerized his audiences each night with a different tale. Kadar sat on a long carpeted bench between two old men in long robes with red tarbooshes on their heads. Kadar studied each of them for a moment, satisfied that neither was the one he looked for.

"The weather is grim once again," one of the old men smiled with yellowed teeth in response to Kadar's gaze. "Seventy winters have I seen, and none so unpredictable as this."

"And so the Zionist trucks cannot move upon the roads for the mud, yes?" He puffed his pipe. "Allah is wise and just. And he gives us camels with which to move our supplies."

A hush fell over the room as the *rawi* entered and slowly climbed the steps to a small wooden platform where an elaborate Persian rug hung as a backdrop. Abu adjusted his fez and donned his wire-rimmed glasses; then he opened the book of Antar in front of him and in a booming voice, he began the story. Kadar searched the faces of the audience as Abu recited the story of Antar, the ancient hero who conquered all for the sake of love. Eyes grew wide and faces intent on the words of the rawi. Surely, if Montgomery were among the crowd, cool boredom would radiate from those confident eyes. *Perhaps*, Kadar thought, *I can guess from the expression*.

"To prove his love for the fair damsel Abla, Antar would fight the lion . . ."

"Ahhhhhh!"

"But to prevent him from escaping, his feet were bound by the terrible Munzar, the villain . . ."

"Ya Allah!" The crowd chorused. "Oh, God!"

"The lion sprang, looming large as a camel, but Antar met him in midair with his sword and cleaved him in twain!"

"Ya Allah! Ya Allah! Ya Allah!"

Kadar sighed and sat back, confident that Montgomery would find him. As the audience shouted and cheered, Kadar was silent.

An old Bedouin squeezed in between Kadar and the other old Arab to his right. Kadar inched over at the strong smell of sheep dung that radiated from the man. Out of habit, he glanced at the man's hands. They matched his old, sun-splotched face. His skin seemed like leather, and his wet keffiya was faded from the days in the sun. Kadar glanced away from him and continued to scan the others in the room. In the far corner, a slender man stood in the shadows, his clean white keffiya and unspotted robes seemed out of place among the common men of the coffeehouse. He wore thick glasses that reflected the light of the lamps, and he stood with his arms crossed, watching the rawi with little interest.

"Ya Allah!" shouted the little man beside Kadar. "May Allah sever their heads!"

Kadar studied the man in the corner intently. He was unable to see the hands. They were hidden beneath his robes. *This must be . . .* The man looked curiously toward Kadar's frank stare. *Certainly this is Montgomery.* Kadar started to rise, when the aged hand of the old bedouin touched him lightly on the arm. He gestured toward the bowl of Kadar's now cold water pipe.

"I see," he hissed. "The ember has died in your bowl. No need to fetch another." He held up his wrinkled, spotted hand. Then he reached deep into his pocket and pulled out a silver lighter.

Montgomery! Shock was written on Kadar's expression. He glanced to the man in the corner, then back again into the amused brown eyes that laughed from behind deep folds of skin.

The lighter flickered to life and the old man leaned forward and touched the flame to Kadar's tobacco. "It is nothing," the voice whispered. "All in the hand."

The crowd continued to shout and cheer their hero in his exploits. "Amazing," Kadar shook his head as he whispered.

"The hands, eh?" The reply came in perfect Arabic. "You have been complaining about the hands."

"So *old*," Kadar wondered.

"Not so very difficult." The voice was a husky reply. "And unchanged beneath it."

"You frighten me." Kadar frowned slightly as he studied the strange face beside him.

A slight smile wrinkled the dark face like a road map. "And so I should. Did you bring it?"

Kadar nodded and fumbled in his pocket for the payment Haj

Amin had sent along. "All you asked for and more," he whispered furtively as he passed the pouch and a small heavy bag filled with cinnamon. "A gift. Beneath the spices."

Montgomery slipped the two items into the generous pockets of the flowing robes that concealed even the shape of the body beneath it.

The rawi boomed on over their words, ". . . Antar rode among them, his sword glinting in the sun . . ."

"My thanks to him," Montgomery replied. "All is not as it seems. The death of the American girl . . . I am leaving the city. Tell him perhaps I will return with a gift for him." The shell of the old man rose. The meeting was at an end; Montgomery shuffled away through the audience. Kadar did not look after the form of the old Bedouin, but stared at the rawi who sweated as he recounted the battle of Antar. A moment later, when Kadar turned his eyes back to the place he had last seen Montgomery, he could find no trace of the aged Bedouin who had taken the precious offerings of Haj Amin. For an instant he was seized with a doubt that perhaps that had not been Montgomery at all. He frowned, then lifted the mouthpiece of the water pipe to his lips. The tobacco glowed as he inhaled. And he breathed relief as he remembered the lighter.

". . . and so Antar had vowed that he would die for his lady, but Allah had willed that he would fight but not die . . ."

"Allah akbar! Allah akbar!"

———

The flight to Rome passed in silence. Occasionally, Michael sighed and cast sidelong looks at David. Once he asked David in a soulful voice, "You want to talk about it, Tinman?"

David looked up from the controls, raised his eyebrow and said sternly to Michael, "Nope. And neither do you. Not to anybody. Especially not the press. Got it?"

Offended and hurt, and not a little guilty at the thought of the woman he had spoken to at the mortuary, Michael shrugged and leaned against the door of the cockpit. "Sure. What do you think I'm going to say?" Then he stared out the window into the murky darkness for the remaining three hours of the flight.

There was plenty David would want to tell Michael later, but for now, the less said the better. Ellie had been right, at any rate; David did not have to pretend to grieve for her. He was only a few hours from her and he felt his bones ache from missing her. He was irritable and angry all over again at the charade that kept him from her.

Once, as he remembered their afternoon together, David began to hum the tune, "As Time Goes By." Michael had turned and looked at him so sadly that David thought Michael would burst into tears. David fell silent again, only daring to open his mouth about the weather conditions and the headwind that slowed their flight and consumed their fuel.

When at last the lights of Lido Airfield loomed into view, Michael looked at his watch and croaked, "Nearly midnight. When is the plane leaving for New York?"

"Three," David answered through a yawn.

"You'll have a little time to get some shut-eye then," Michael said in a voice laden with empathy and tenderness. "I'll uh . . . I can take care of uh . . ." He hesitated and fumbled for words. "I'll see to it that they get the uh . . . the . . ."

"Coffin?" David asked. "Are you trying to say *coffin*, Michael?"

"Yes." Michael squirmed. "I can get it loaded onto the New York flight."

"Nothing doing," said David as he lined up with the runway. "I'm staying with her."

"Sure, Tinman," Michael gulped and scratched his nose uncomfortably, determined not to mention another word unless David spoke first.

"I could sure use a sandwich and a cup of coffee," David said as the bright lights of the runwa rose up to meet them.

Michael was encouraged by this sign of life in his grief-stricken friend. "Sure, Tinman! We'll get you a sandwich. Coke or Coffee? Whatever you want, buddy."

"*She* liked Coke," David said soulfully, unable to resist watching Michael gulp and wrinkle his brow. David was certain now that Michael would not mention Coke again until he knew that *she* was not really inside *it*.

The wheels touched down with a gentle thud, and David taxied to a small hangar on the outskirts of the airfield. A bright light burned in the window of the tiny office, and before the propellers stopped churning, David and Michael were greeted by two smiling men named Claudio and Irving. The two young men manned the lonely outpost that all hoped would become the European base of operation for a Zionist air force. Tonight, however, the Stinson would be the only plane in the hangar.

Claudio was a native of Rome, and spoke only minimal English. Irving was a New York-born Jew from Brooklyn. He spoke Italian fluently and interpreted Claudio's comments with a heavily laced Brooklyn accent.

David suspected that the two men had been informed that the remains of Ellie Warne were not really inside the coffin, but neither man mentioned it or asked questions. They chatted, instead, about the weather and the political climate of Italy while David munched on the sandwiches so graciously provided by Claudio's wife. Michael, on the other hand, brooded in silent disapproval at the disrespect these two fellows showed in the presence of his grieving friend.

"The Italian police might show up," explained Irving, stuffing salami into his mouth. "To take a look inside the coffin."

Michael shot him a grim look; Irving said *the word.* "Why would they want to do that?" Michael snapped.

"I dunno. Maybe they're morbid. Ha!" He sipped his coffee. "Naw, just jokin'. The whole country's gone nuts, y'know. They're havin' elections. Christians against Communists and the whole place is paranoid about the Reds. Who knows? They might think youse guys are smugglin' guns or something. That's why we've got ol' Claudio here."

Claudio perked up at the mention of his name. "Si."

David did not reply, but studied his sandwich. Michael glowered as Irving nudged him in the ribs. "They're in for a real surprise if they crack that box, ain't they?"

Michael narrowed his eyes in disgust as Irving rattled on. He was obviously a man in need of exercising his mastery of the English language. "Yessir. Claudio can handle the coppers. Can't you, Claudio?"

"Si!" Claudio poured himself another cup of coffee and looked out the window to where a small baggage cart trundled toward the hanger. He spoke rapidly in Italian, and Irving stood quickly and went to the door.

"Well, we shall soon see, anyway," he muttered.

A small, uniformed officer in jack boots sat next to the driver of the cart. He hopped from beside him and strode into the office. Claudio greeted him in rapid Italian exclamations, which Irving interpreted.

"He wants to see your passports." The officer held out his

153

hand and snapped his fingers as David and Michael rummaged for their passports. As Claudio continued to talk, the officer scanned the documents and fired questions as quickly as Claudio could answer.

"He wants to know why you brought the body to Rome. Claudio told him you're taking it back home to the States for burial. He says your passports are in order. He wants to know if the dead woman was a Jew."

David shook his head, "No."

The officer looked at him and rattled off yet another string of questions.

"He wants to know what she was doing in Palestine, then."

"She was with me," David answered and his words were relayed back to the little man.

"He asked if you are the husband. And if you are a Jew," said Irving quietly, growing irritated at the nature of the questions.

"Tell him *si*, and *si*," David nodded.

The officer clucked his tongue and handed the passports back. Again he spoke, this time looking directly at David.

"He wants to know why any man in his right mind would take his wife to Palestine," Irving said. This was not a question Claudio could answer. "Be careful how you answer him. It is best to keep smiling, pal, even if you want to punch the guy in the nose."

David frowned thoughtfully. "Tell him she was a devout Catholic dying of a rare disease and she wanted to make a pilgrimage before she died."

As the words were repeated, the officer crossed himself and his demeanor suddenly changed to one of considerate attention.

Twice, as the men wrestled the coffin from the stubborn cargo area of the Stinson, the officer patted David on the back. He removed his cap and stood back respectfully as the metal coffin was placed carefully on the baggage cart and trundled off toward the waiting DC-4 passenger plane on the tarmack.

David followed closely behind and watched while the coffin was lifted into the cargo hold. The officer shouted directions to the baggage men and Irving nudged David and whispered quietly as the men crossed themselves, "He just told 'em she died on a pilgrimage to Jerusalem. Good luck, pal. Bring us back a few big ones to put in the hangar, will ya?"

Michael wiped a tear from his eye as the coffin slid out of sight into the bay. The pockets of his jacket were stuffed with sandwiches for the flight and he carried two bottles of Coke. "I got us a couple of . . . *these*," he said respectfully to David.

"You mean Cokes?" David could not resist smiling. "You're a good man, Michael. If Ellie were here, I'm sure she'd fight you for them."

"I only wish she could be, Tinman," sniffed Michael as the bay door closed.

"You and me both," David said, suddenly missing her more than ever. He pulled his flimsy jacket collar up against the chill that made him shudder.

"Where's your flight jacket?" Michael asked, noticing for the first time that David was not wearing the jacket that had almost become his trademark.

"I left it with Ellie," he answered softly, then alarm gripped him as he realized the slip.

But Michael didn't question David in the least. "Yeah, pal," he commented quietly. "I guess you want somethin' special to be—uh—buried with her, right?"

Michael gulped hard and yet another tear escaped from his eye. Now the word *jacket* would be a word to avoid, along with *coffin* and *Coke*. David had the sinking feeling that the fourteen hours to New York would be long and awkward.

14 Forgiveness

In the soft light of pre-dawn, Moshe opened his eyes and lay quietly in the stillness. Rachel was still sleeping soundly, snuggled against his back, her arm around his waist. He was afraid to move, afraid he would disturb her; but he reached down and held her hand in his. At his stirring, she nuzzled closer against him and made a contented sound, like Tikvah after she had a good meal and was drifting off to dream. *My two little girls*, Moshe smiled.

The hiss and pop of the primus stove had long since ceased, and the room was cold. Reluctantly, Moshe slipped out from under the blankets and shivered as his bare feet touched the cold floor. He tucked the blankets around Rachel who murmured his name in a groggy question, "Moshe?"

"Go back to sleep, love," he whispered. "I am just checking the baby."

She sighed and rolled over, instantly returning to slumber. Moshe reached between the blankets at the foot of the bed and pulled out his warm trousers, quickly slipping them on. Then he groped for his socks and shirt which were also warmed beneath the blankets. He dressed hurriedly, then leaned over Tikvah's cradle. Only the crown of her head poked out from beneath the quilts, and Rachel had made certain that she wore a knitted night cap against the cold. With his thumb, Moshe lifted the down quilt slightly to gaze at her face. Her long black lashes reminded him so much of Rachel's, and her creamy complexion and rosy cheeks radiated health and contentment. Wisps of jet black hair poked out from the pink cap, framing the tiny face that seemed remarkably like his beloved Rachel.

The baby sighed deeply, drawing her breath in little jerks and moving her rosebud mouth as though she were dreaming of a warm bottle of milk. Tenderly, Moshe let the cover fall back. He stood for a moment, gazing at the top of Tikvah's head, and then he looked over to Rachel's hair fanned out across the pillow. "God," he whispered, unable to find words to express his thankfulness. "Of all your creation, you have given these to me."

He shuddered in the morning cold, and took his jacket from the back of the rocking chair. He would not light the stove until they awakened; he dared not waste the precious kerosene. He stared hard at the primus stove and the nearly empty five-gallon can of fuel beside it. A wave of concern washed over him. Without the convoys into the Old City, every home was cold this morning for want of fuel. All meals were eaten communally at Tipat Chalev to conserve fuel and ration food supplies. Enough fuel was alloted each week to perhaps brew a kettle of tea or heat enough water to wash or maybe take the chill off in the early morning cold. The responsibility for the quarter weighed heavily on Moshe—not only for these two precious souls in his care, but for all who looked to him for leadership in this desperate time. He knew that the Jewish Agency was doing all that could be done to restore a lifeline with the Old City Jews, but he also knew that no convoys were making it to New City Jerusalem from Tel Aviv. Even if the Arab High Committee and the British allowed a convoy into the New City once a week, would there be any provisions to send to the beleaguered Old City Jewish Quarter? He himself had helped outline the rationing program for the entire city of Jerusalem before he had entered the Old City. He knew how desperately short supplies were everywhere. *What we need now is a miracle*, he prayed silently. He would not tell the rest how urgently the miracle was needed; many in the quarter lived daily on the edge of panic as it was. Only now, in the early morning, when no one was awake to see the worry on his own face, did he let his soul cry out for his people, and for these two who had become his life.

Slowly, he sat down in the rocker. Steamy vapor rose from his lips as he breathed. In the semidarkness he watched and prayed for guidance and wisdom in the face of despair. His thoughts came back to Rachel alone. If there was no one else in all the earth, the depth of his concern for her well-being was enough. Gladly he would lay down his life for her. And for Tikvah, for the sacred stones of Zion and those within her walls. For now, however, he could better serve them by living and working for their protection.

Emotion stung him as he sat in the cold silence and gazed at Rachel's peaceful face on her pillow. To him, she was the beauty that had finally filled the hollow place in his heart, the one that he had always loved and searched for even before he had known her. He wanted to reach out and touch her now, but he was afraid to disturb her. He longed to tell her the joy and fulfillment she had brought into his life, but there were no words deep enough. She had given him hope, but it was a hope that had the spector of fear as its shadow. *It was easier*, he thought, *before I loved. It was so much simpler when it was only me and a cause to die for. Now I want to live. For her sake and the sake of the child I want to live!* In a world of imperfection and cruelty, Rachel had become the one anchor of beauty and tenderness that made his own life feel suddenly precious to him. *It was easier to think of leaving this earth to offer myself for the sake of Zion before I knew her.*

He rose and stood over her for a moment, then took a yellow notepad from the table beside the bed. It was full of figures for rationing and scrawled plans for feeding the occupants of the quarter. For a moment he studied the top page, crammed with his own comments about shortage of grain for bread and the meager supply of beets for making borscht for the next six weeks. First there would be no bread, and soon after there would not be beets enough for even a very thin soup. *Six weeks for the beets. Less than one week for the last of the grain.* He sighed heavily. This morning, with Rachel sleeping so peacefully, it seemed impossible that the time would pass.

He returned to his seat and with the dull stub of a pencil, he began to write the words that filled his heart. "For Rachel," he wrote. "My beloved . . ." He studied the words for a moment, then began again, this time writing in Hebrew.

A dozen times he scratched out phrases and started fresh, sighing in frustration. At last the words seemed to tumble out of his heart and onto the paper. For ten minutes he wrote until he was certain that words could never express the depth of his love for her. He finished his poem and signed it simply, "Your husband." Then he read it over and rolled his eyes at his inadequacy. He closed the notebook, determined that he would try later to say what lingered in his heart. As the sun sent its first certain light over the city, he laid the notebook back on the bed table. He reached out to touch her face; then he bent to kiss her forehead. Her eyes fluttered open and she looked dreamily up into his face.

"Time to wake up, Rachel," he whispered, kissing her lightly.

"You're dressed already?" She tugged on his shirt, pulling him easily down to her side. "All business, I see."

"I will make a fire for you and put the kettle on; then I must—" She kissed him and wrapped her arms around his neck. He yielded easily to the warmth of her lips. She smiled beneath his kisses, then laughed lightly, taking his face in her hands.

"That was only a good morning kiss," she teased. "Soon you will be able to heat the kettle with a touch."

He blinked hard and took a deep breath. Feeling a bit light-headed, he sat up and ran his hand over his face. "What a blessing it would be to have only you to think about," he said.

"I cannot let you be so easily sidetracked, love." Rachel sat up and wrapped her arms around her knees as she looked at him. "Not yet, at any rate. You must finish the tunnels beneath the quarter. Ehud and the others will be looking for you."

"They will know where to find me," he said huskily, reaching for her.

"Later," she said playfully, dodging him and getting out of bed on the opposite side. She shuddered with the cold. "The fire, if you please."

"Aren't you sorry you did that?" Moshe stood and crossed to the primus stove. He poured a small amount of kerosene into the reservoir and fumbled with the matches to light the stove. When he turned, Rachel was back under the covers, watching him with her chin in her hand. "You!" he cried.

"You have work to do." Her tone was matter of fact. "You must save the Jewish Quarter. And I must prepare breakfast for two hundred hungry children, yes? You will thank me later for urging you to do your duty. Now kiss me goodbye and go find Ehud. I'll bring your tea and breakfast."

He shrugged in helpless acquiescence. "Maybe I will thank you." He kissed her again.

"Go," she ordered in mock seriousness. "I will bring you your tallith later. Remember you are to pray with the rabbis."

Moshe clapped his hands to rouse Shaul who stood up and stretched, then shook out his coat and ambled after Moshe. Moshe winked at Rachel "I would rather pray with you." He softly closed the door as he slipped from the apartment into the harsh reality of daylight and the morning air of the quarter. To the east, the sun had just topped the amethyst colored mountains of Moab. Light glinted on the windowpanes of the city, making it suddenly seem all golden and clean. "It is good to be alive," he said softly to God. "On this morning I am glad to be alive."

Shaul had followed on his heels and sat down, looking up at Moshe expectantly. Moshe patted him and rubbed his hand along his bony ribs. "But you, fellow, you will not be alive unless you get some food, eh?" He knelt down and took Shaul's broad head in his hands. "There is not enough here for us to eat and we cannot feed you, do you understand? One of these days some hungry citizen may size you up for a stew pot, Shaul, and Rachel's heart would be broken. And little Yacov's. And mine as well, I admit it. So, you need to go!" he said loudly. He stood and looked at the dog who gazed back at him through amber-colored eyes. Shaul did not move. "I said go!" Moshe commanded. "Find Yacov! Be gone!"

Shaul stood stiffly and looked down the street where Moshe pointed. "Go!" Moshe shouted again. Shaul looked back at Moshe, then tucked his behind and trotted slowly away toward the barricade that led out of the Jewish Quarter and the city.

Far below the plane, the Atlantic gleamed in the light of perpetual dawn, like polished silver. David opened his eyes and stretched lazily. Michael was disheveled, but wide awake and staring moodily out the window at the shining sea.

"Morning," David said quietly.

Michael glanced at him and his face was full of pain. "Morning," he replied. "Did you sleep okay?"

"Better than last night." David frowned as he remembered the night before.

"You said her name." Michael winced and turned back toward the window.

David ran his fingers through his hair and studied Michael's profile. He longed to tell him the truth—that Ellie was safe, that all of this was an act. He opened his mouth to speak, but a small bespectacled man walked past him in the aisle and looked directly at him. David closed his mouth and stared silently at his hands.

Ten minutes passed in silence until Michael spoke at last. His voice was edged with bitterness. "I keep asking myself how all this can happen, Tinman. I was sitting here watching the sun come up like it has for a million years, and I just thought about all the people who have watched it come up, and now they're gone. Like they were never here at all."

David frantically searched his mind for a way to comfort Michael without letting him know the truth of their mission. "Every one of us is going to die someday, Michael. There's no getting away from that."

Michael pursed his lips. "But there's no justice in it. None. And I'm not just talking about what happened to you and Ellie . . ." He gestured helplessly. "The whole reason we're here on this airplane is because the world still hasn't had enough Jewish blood. We're still fighting to survive, and the world is still turning its back. Just like it did when six million children and old people and women were shoved into the ovens. And where's God in all of this? Huh? Where?"

"He's still here," David answered quietly.

"Yeah?" Michael spat. "Then why is all this stuff happening? If there is a God, then why has He allowed it to happen?"

David bit his lip and blinked thoughtfully. Michael was at last talking of more than Ellie's "death." The events of the past few years had caused him to question the very validity of any god who could stand by in silence while millions of innocents died for no other reason than their heritage. Words seemed trite in the face of such a question. "I wonder the same thing myself sometimes, Scarecrow. Honest I do." David cleared his throat and continued. "And I always come back to the belief that God didn't do this terrible thing. Men did. Men who did not acknowledge God. Or accept Him."

"Well, what about all the people who claimed to know God and yet turned their backs while millions were herded into the camps? What about the high and mighty church?"

"The church is an organization. Made up of men. And a whole lot of people hide out there, but it doesn't mean they know the Lord. My dad is a preacher, Michael, and I didn't know the Lord even though I sat in church for years."

Michael stared blankly at him. "And you think you know God now?" His words were almost accusing.

"Yes. I'm sure of it," David answered.

"Nobody can know God," Michael said flatly. "I mean, how can you know something so big and impersonal? I'm not an atheist. I've got eyes. I can see the stars and the oceans and the mountains. Okay, so there's a God. But I just don't *know* Him. He's too big. I'm an agnostic, I guess. I can't figure it out."

David smiled slightly and once again was filled with appreciation for Michael's honesty. "I think that realizing how big God is puts you miles ahead of the people who sit in church every Sunday and cram God into a little box. The Bible agrees with you on that point, that no one can know the mind of God. He's too big for us to figure out."

Michael nodded. "Too big," he agreed. "And too heartless and unjust and cruel."

David shook his head slowly. "No, Michael," he answered quietly. "You're talking about *us* again. About people." He inhaled and searched his heart for what he truly believed. "We are the heartless ones, Scarecrow. I've thought about it a lot lately, and the things my dad said have come back to me, you know?"

"Like what?"

"Well . . ." David frowned thoughtfully. "We all like to pretend that we are made in the image of God. But the Bible says that nobody is righteous. Not one human. Even the good things we do are like a pile of dirty rags. We hide behind self-righteousness, and everybody thinks *he's* right."

"Well, history has proved that the human race is basically rotten all right," Michael agreed dourly.

"So how would you show people your true self if you were God, Michael? I mean, let's say that there are a thousand different religions down here and all of them are saying, 'God is this and He wants you to do this and this to get to Him . . .' How would you show people what you were like and what you wanted them to be like?"

Michael shrugged. "I think I would just wipe them out and start all over."

"Maybe you would. But that's not what a merciful God did. Instead, He came to this earth and lived as a man among us. He healed the sick and raised the dead, and do you know what *we* did to *Him*? We nailed Him to a cross."

"And the Jews have been paying for that one ever since," Michael replied bitterly. "Some God."

"The Jews did not kill Jesus, Michael. Our sin did. The sins of every person on earth were paid for by His death. And He *offered* himself. Nobody killed Him without His consent."

"Then why have we Jews been labeled as Christ-killers? How many of our people have died at the hands of the church and people who are supposed to be Christians?"

"You said the magic word: *people*. Self-righteous hypocrites who would be the first to crucify Christ all over again if He were to show up in Times Square tomorrow." David paused as Michael stared down at the vast ocean beneath them. "But if you want to see what God is really like, Michael, look at Jesus. Look at the Jew from Galilee and study what the prophets said about the coming Messiah. Jesus is the Messiah, the Son of David, the only true image of God we're going to see."

Michel turned back to David. "I can respect what you believe, Tinman; but it's not for me. If it gets you through, that's fine, but I don't even believe in my own religion anymore. I can't."

"You don't want to."

"That's right. I don't want to. Not now. Maybe not ever. If you want to know the truth, I'm just too mad at—" He waved his hand and sighed, unable to finish the thought. Without another word, Michael slouched down in his seat and closed his eyes to silence his anger with a merciful sleep.

Her hair tied back beneath a soft blue scarf, Rachel's eyes glistened like patches of sky shining from between the clouds. She pushed Tikvah's black pram slowly through the streets as though this were a day like any other and Jerusalem were a city at peace. Never mind the heavy iron grates that shielded shop fronts, or the barren shelves in the tiny markets. She inhaled deeply, catching the scent of freshly roasted *poppeetes*, melon, sunflower and pumpkin seeds, all delicately salted. Her mouth watered at the aroma, and she told herself that it was only her imagination.

But she knew better. A scant few blocks away, beyond the barricades, Arab vendors sold them on the streets and in the souks. There, fresh fruit was readily available, along with the Arab version of a bagel, the *ka'ak*, dipped in a cummin seed and salt mixture known as *za'atar*. Moshe had described his breakfasts in his bachelor days as a quick stroll through the souks for freshly squeezed orange juice and even hard-boiled eggs. Little had changed for the Arabs beyond the Jewish sectors of the city. *It is my imagination*, Rachel thought again as her stomach rumbled at the scent of freshly baking ka'ak and bread.

She looked into the pram at the small package of dried matzo bread and a bit of hard cheese, along with a jar of weak coffee, wrapped to keep it warm. Breakfast in the Jewish Quarter was no longer a matter of a simple stroll through the streets. No one had seen an egg in weeks, and although the orange orchards in the countryside hung heavy with fruit, there was no juice on the tables of the Jews in Jerusalem. *Someday*, she thought, *I will fix him cheeze blintzes and apple strudel and all the coffee he wants. And Moshe will smile at me and ask if I remember when I brought him breakfast in Tikvah's pram.*

Little Tikvah yawned and stretched, enjoying the vibration of the pram wheels over the rough cobblestones. As long as Rachel looked at her sweet face and pink cheeks, war and death seemed very far away. As long as she did not think of Ellie and poor David, she could pretend that she was simply out for a walk on a breezy February morning and life was good and normal.

Moshe's tallith lay at the foot of the pram. Rachel had wrapped the blue velvet pouch inside a pillow case for protection. And inside the pouch was one gold coin from her dowry.

This morning, Moshe would pray with the old men, the scholars who had spent a lifetime studying Torah. Their fears for the future were darker than the nightmares of frightened children. To leave their sacred houses of study; to forsake the ink-blotched desks where they had sat through half a century of endless hours of discussion—this would mark the end of their existence. Just as it had meant the end of Jews in Europe. This morning, Moshe would attempt to assuage their fears and enlist them in the army of the Haganah as defenders of their homes. Moshe's argument would come cloaked in a tallith and bearing one golden coin.

The day was still early enough that Rachel could hear footsteps, and she looked up as Yehudit Akiva approached on the shaded side of the street. Yehudit's eyes met hers, then Yehudit glanced quickly down to the street. Her young face seemed even more pale than usual; the finely sewn navy dress she wore was ill-fitting and hung too loosely on her frail body. Rachel stopped and watched, wanting desperately to speak to the tormented young woman, but Yehudit averted her eyes, wildly looking everywhere but at Rachel and the baby. She increased her pace and almost hugged the shop fronts as she passed unavoidably by.

"Good morning, Yehudit," Rachel said kindly, her heart reaching out to the girl. Yehudit did not reply and as she passed, Rachel gently added, "We have missed you."

Yehudit tucked her chin and slowed a bit. "I cannot speak to you," she whispered desperately. "My father—"

"I understand," Rachel said quietly, certain that no one was watching. "I bear no ill will toward either of you."

The girl stopped in her tracks a few feet from Rachel. She looked up into the depth of Rachel's eyes. Sorrow and longing for friendship spoke louder than words. Her brown eyes and thin face looked haunted, like a caged and hopeless animal.

Rachel smiled sadly at her, but she did not smile back. Yehudit opened her mouth to speak; then, as though pursued by the specter of her father's rage, she lowered her eyes again. They stood on opposite sides of the narrow street—Yehudit, half-turning as if she wanted to run away; Rachel, facing her with a heart filled with pity. Neither of them spoke for a long moment; then Rachel said gently, "Tikvah has missed you. She has grown. Would you like to see her?" she asked as she moved a step nearer with the pram.

Yehudit's expression changed to a hesitant hope as she glanced up once again. "How can you speak to me when it was I who betrayed you?" Her voice was barely audible and it shook beneath the weight of her shame.

Rachel came nearer, then stopped. "Yehudit," she urged, "look at me."

Yehudit blinked hard, clenching and unclenching her hands. At last she turned her gaze to Rachel's loving face. The tenderness in Rachel's eyes spoke clearly of forgiveness.

"Please," Yehudit begged, covering her face with her hands. "Do not look at me so tenderly. I betrayed you to my father." She took a step backwards until her back touched the wall behind her. "He sent me to you as a spy. And they tried to take the baby from you because of what I did."

Images of that terrible night at Nissan Bek Synagogue flashed through Rachel's mind. She remembered the judgment of Rabbi Akiva and the tears of Yehudit when she realized what her betrayal had cost. Rachel had forgiven her even then. "Yehudit," she said, extending her hand, "the things you told your father about me were true. From the time I was fourteen I served in a Nazi brothel. I betrayed everything I knew was right because I wanted only to live. Can I then curse you for wanting the approval of your father?"

"But you had no choice," Yehudit said in self-condemnation.

"We all have a choice," Rachel replied sadly. "The prophets have said that each of us has made the choice to turn from God to do what is right in our own eyes. I was justly condemned, Yehudit. I betrayed God and my people and myself. And I found that there are things worse than death."

Yehudit looked up at her in wonder at her words. "You admit this to me?" she asked. "After what I did to you?"

Rachel smiled at her, and peace radiated from her expression. "It was all true. But I have found something much bigger than my sins. My heart was broken with my guilt, Yehudit. And God has said He will not turn away from a broken heart. His love can forgive me the terrible choices I once made. And if God can do that even for me, can I do less than accept it and go on to forgive those who might have wronged me? To live on this earth is to make choices. Right and wrong. Sometimes we make wrong ones. Like I did. Like you did. We take those mistakes to God and ask forgiveness, and then we go on. Maybe a little wiser, yes?"

Rachel reached out to lift Yehudit's chin and lock her eyes in her steady gaze. "I choose to forgive you, dear Yehudit. It is a good choice, and I think it makes God smile."

"But I can never make up to you . . . or God what I have done." Tears flooded her eyes and hung precariously on her bottom lashes.

"Then I will let you in on a secret that will also make God smile," Rachel said. "There is someone very special to Him that *you* must also forgive."

"Tell me who?" Yehudit pleaded.

"Yourself," Rachel said simply. "You must forgive yourself, Yehudit. And then learn from Him to make better choices."

For a long time, the young woman stood staring gratefully into Rachel's clear blue eyes. "What has happened to you?" she asked in wonder. "You are not the same as you were."

Rachel opened her mouth to speak, when the heavy slap of footsteps sounded against the pavement around the corner. Yehudit stepped away from Rachel quickly and wiped her eyes. "Yehudit—" Rachel began.

"I must go." Yehudit looked furtively over her shoulder and hurried away, once again pursued by the shadow of her father.

Moshe and Ehud rounded the corner of the street as Yehudit scurried away like a dry leaf before the wind. Even when Ehud called Rachel's name, she continued to watch Yehudit until she disappeared around a corner.

"What is it?" Moshe asked her, touching her lightly on the shoulder.

Ehud scowled as he recognized Yehudit, "I will tell you!" he snapped. "It isn't a what, it's a *who*! Yehudit Akiva, that slimy, worthless little—"

Rachel turned angrily on Ehud. "You will not speak of her like that again, Ehud!" Her eyes flashed.

"But everyone knows what she—" He tried to protest.

"She is just a girl. Seventeen and alone," Rachel defended.

"A traitor." Ehud drew his chin up, not willing to surrender his position.

"And so was I called a traitor," Rachel replied quietly. "When I was seventeen and alone."

Ehud looked as though she had struck him. His belligerence instantly melted and his brow wrinkled in worried remorse. "But no, Rachel. I did not mean—Moshe, tell her please . . ."

Moshe clapped him on the back and followed Rachel's gaze to where Yehudit darted around the corner. "She knows what you meant, Ehud. And she is right. She is right about that poor creature."

Ehud stood dumbfounded, silenced by the rebuke. He scratched his beard self-consciously, uncertain of what he could say.

Rachel drew in her breath and blew away the grim thoughts, turning with a renewed gentleness to Ehud and Moshe. "I brought your breakfast," she said as though nothing had happened. "Meager though it may be."

Ehud rubbed his belly. "All morning I have been smelling bread baking!" he exclaimed. His stomach rumbled. "Somewhere in the Armenian Quarter people are eating very well."

Rachel took the package from the pram. "Only matzos, I'm afraid." She handed the package to Moshe. "A little cheese and coffee for you both."

"Ah, for a blintz!" sighed Ehud, his complaining stomach speaking louder than his complaints about Yehudit.

Moshe said little, and seemed lost in quiet thought. "I need to hurry," he told her. "I need to wash and go to Hurva in a half hour. Did you bring my tallith?" he asked. "And my phylacteries?"

Rachel nodded and handed them to him. "And the other thing we talked about," she added quietly.

"Well then." Moshe's hand lingered on hers as he took the tallith from her. "Pray for me?" His dark eyes smiled into hers.

Ehud slowly opened the paper-wrapped packet of cheese and grimaced. "Insert in that prayer, if you will please, a little request from Ehud, eh?"

Rachel rolled her eyes in mock exasperation and directed her attention to Ehud, who towered above her. "Well," she asked, "what is it?"

"When we are all praying for manna this morning," he said with amusement in his eyes, "ask God to send mine down in a loaf of challah bread. Warm. Fresh from the oven like I am smelling all morning, eh? And maybe one for little Dov as well. Poor fellow is half mad with the aroma. I told him it is a new device of torture from the mind of the Mufti. Just pray for challah, Rachel." Ehud took a bite of cheese. "And if we get it, I'll share mine with that little Yehudit girl that you think so much of. I swear it!"

167

Rachel shook her head, amused by Ehud's method of dealing with the Eternal for breakfast. "You have a bargain!" she exclaimed.

"Speaking of breakfast," Moshe said quietly, "I want to tell you, Rachel, I sent Shaul back to Yacov this morning."

Her eyes filled with hurt, and she searched Moshe's face for explanation.

He cleared his throat. "He was hungry," he said simply. "He has no chance at all here in the Old City. We cannot feed him. Not even scraps."

Rachel nodded. "I understand," she whispered. "You are right, of course. But I shall miss him."

———

Shafts of sunlight filtered down from the high latticed windows of Hurvah Synagogue and fell in pools of light on the mosaic tiled floor. Leather phylacteries on their foreheads and hands, the rabbis and Moshe swayed as they prayed their morning prayers beneath the shelter of their tallithes.

Moshe's was the only black beard in the group of ten who called him up for an *aliya*, to read the Torah portion. Wizened faces with closed eyes and furrowed brows uttered the prayers and supplications of the morning service.

"Sovereign of all worlds! Not in reliance upon our righteous deeds do we lay our supplications before you, but by reason of your abundant mercies." Each man rocked up on his toes as though reaching for God with his whole being. "What are we? What is our kindness? What is our righteousness? What is our strength and power? What shall we say in your presence, Eternal! our God!" Voices rose on the beams of light, swirling upward among motes of dust. "Are not all heroes as nothing before you? And men of renown as though they had never been; the wise as though void of knowledge? For the multitude of their deeds are mere emptiness, and the days of their lives are a fleeting breath before you . . ." Moshe's heart rose with the chanted words of the Siddur, and his thoughts were woven with this ancient prayer. *We are so small before you, Lord, and so in need of help. In this tiny particle of time we are doing all that we can do. It is not enough. The people you have put into my care will soon be hungry. They are afraid. And so am I. So are all of us who stand before you now and hope for a nation* . . . His eyes fell on the words of the prayer book open before him.

"Verily, you are the first, and you are the last, and besides you, God, there is none. Oh, gather those that hope in you from the four corners of the earth, and cause all the inhabitants of the world to recognize and clearly see that you alone are God over all the realms of the earth." The aged lips moved, speaking the words by rote that had been uttered for thousands of years in the same hope.

Is this the moment of our return, Lord, Moshe questioned. *Or are we fools, acting out a hopeless drama with a final act that will be our deaths? I admit to you and no other, Lord, I am afraid for this remnant. From these old men to tiny Tikvah. And for my Rachel.*

Voices rose, louder with the plea to a heaven that had seemed stone deaf for two thousand years, "Our Father in heaven, show mercy to us; and fulfill that which is written: *At that time I will restore you, then will I assemble you; for I will render you a name and a glory amongst all the peoples of the earth, when I bring back your captives before your eyes, saith the Eternal.*

For a full half hour the prayers continued. It was the same prayer murmured by millions through the centuries, millions who had died without seeing an answer of fulfillment. Silent centuries had come and gone as the actors in the drama had been replaced by others who read the same lines. *Maybe today,* Moshe thought as they closed their prayer books and removed their phylacteries before folding the prayer shawls and sitting down to talk. *Maybe this is the moment when you will return to Zion, Lord, and bring us home.*

Stooped and frail, an ancient rabbi shuffled toward Moshe. His gnarled hands shook and his voice was high and tremulous.

"You are the son of Sachar the butcher," quavered the old man as the others gathered around.

"Yes, Rabbi," Moshe said respectfully as he laid his tallith back in the velvet pouch.

"We have trouble here in the quarter, and yet the young men say you bring unity, nu? You have wed the granddaughter of Rabbi Lebowitz and you do not take her away to safety. Why not?"

"We stay here because we believe that this is where God would have us be. To defend the houses of study and prayer." The sweep of Moshe's hand took in the Great Hall of Hurva Synagogue. "If we do not stay, the Mufti will destroy everything we love most."

The rabbis nodded and murmured agreement. "Ah yes," said the old man again. "I think you are right. Not so very long ago our Muslim brothers gained a reputation of desecrating the things that are holy to us Jews. This is true."

"I am a son of this city. My heart is here, although God has called me to many other places in my lifetime. I believe that this is where we must make our stand."

"Well spoken. Well spoken. We have thought so for some time also. Now, we have asked you here for a purpose." He paused and tapped his fingertips together. "The very young are helping with this cause, nu? And yet you have not included those of us who have white beards in this plan of yours to save the Old City. This is not right. We share what food there is. We have lived here, and many of us have never so much as ventured from these streets. Is this not also our home? May we not also help? Your Jewish Agency pays those young men to fight. Can we not also be a part?"

Relief flooded Moshe's features. He studied the serious and sincere faces of these venerable men. "I have come for the very purpose of asking for your help!" he said enthusiastically. Reaching into the tallith pouch, he pulled out the gold coin Rachel had brought to him. He held it out to the circle of rabbis. "I came to enlist you," he said as their eyes fixed on the shining coin. "We are now in need of a miracle."

"True. True, this is a fact," they all echoed.

"Men cannot work miracles without the hand of the Eternal."

"Well spoken, young man. This is so."

"Thus far, our army has enlisted only men to defend. I will tell you that I believe we need men of God to pray. Every minute of each day we need prayer to go up before God for the sake of His people's return to Zion."

"This is a fact!" cried one very small old man. "Well put, son of Sachar the butcher!"

"The Jewish Agency will pay you one shilling a day—"

"Oy! So much! A shilling, he said? A shilling a day?"

Moshe smiled at these men who had so long lived on the generosity of benefactors who paid them a stipend to study and pray. "Yes. A whole shilling. But you must guarantee that this hall will never be without prayer, eh? Not even a single moment must pass when we are not reading the Psalms and asking God for a miracle."

"A splendid idea! Maybe Messiah will come!"

Moshe nodded. "We will keep looking up," he said gently. "No doubt having a nation to come to would be nice for Him."

"Then we will organize, nu?" said the oldest. "We must have a minyon of ten men at all times."

"And no one should fall asleep," said another resolutely.

"First we should ask God for bread! True? Of course true. And then maybe pray for the strong men who fight for us."

"Gideon had only a few men against thousands, remember. And he won a great victory!"

Lists of names were drawn up and plans laid for those too aged to dig tunnels or man the barricades to use their talents in approaching the Almighty. Priorities were made. First bread. Then weapons for defense of the Holy City. These were the miracles they would pray for. And in all of that was the unspoken understanding that the appearance of the Messiah in Zion was the most important prayer of all.

15   The Vigil

On and off, throughout the long, droning hours of the early morning, Michael slept with his mouth hanging open and his head against the porthole window. David perched uneasily in the uncomfortable seat beside him, drifting in and out of sleep. A perpetual sunrise seemed to hang on the tail of the aircraft like a bright banner until finally the light that pursued them across the Atlantic overcame them.

David had no idea what time it was. He rubbed the heavy stubble on his face and swallowed, his mouth feeling like cotton. Other passengers stirred in their seats, taking loaves of bread from brown paper bags and munching on fruit they had packed the night before for breakfast.

David eyed the top of a stale sandwich that poked out from Michael's pocket. Gingerly he reached over and pulled it out. Michael sat bolt upright and muttered, "What?" Like a drunken man, he smacked his lips together and looked around at the awakening passengers. His hair was sticking up on the side of his head, and his face was dark with stubble.

"Morning," David grinned.

"Oh. Yeah. Is it?" he yawned and stretched.

David handed him a sandwich laden with dripping slices of salami. "Breakfast."

Michael rubbed his eyes and smoothed his hair back over his bald spot. "Great," he said sleepily. "I'm starving."

"Lots of grease and garlic." David took another sandwich from Michael's pocket. "Just the way you like it."

"But kosher, remember!" Michael held up an instructive forefinger, then took an enormous bite.

The two men ate in silence, savoring their meal. For David, this was the first time in days he felt even halfway rested.

Michael licked his fingers delicately, then whispered, "Where's the can?"

Jerking a thumb toward the back of the plane, David stood and let his companion out to stagger down the aisle and wait in a long, bedraggled line. Grateful for the elbow room, David scooted over and peered down at the tops of the sunlit clouds. Below them, he knew, the Atlantic was dark and stormy. The rays of sunlight reflected off the silver fuselage of the plane, and he shielded his eyes against it. He scanned the horizon, noting the extent of the storm front they had entered sometime during the night. The clouds stretched as far as he could see.

Twenty minutes later, Michael returned to reclaim his window seat. He looked out over the clouds and remarked, "They say it's the coldest winter on record. Look at it, will you?"

David rose slowly and stretched away the ache in his body. He scanned the rows of rumpled passengers; the seats were mostly occupied by U.S. servicemen with their shirts unbuttoned and ties askew. Here and there middle-aged businessmen sat reading newspapers, but among the group were only five women. Directly behind him, a thin man in a brown double-breasted suit stared up at him through glasses as thick as bottles. A fedora was perched awkwardly on his head and a pencil-thin moustache twitched nervously above a wide, unsmiling mouth. "Morning," David met his gaze, and the man rustled his Italian newspaper and muttered, "Gute morning." Then he looked quickly away.

When David returned, the little man was staring out the window and chain smoking Players cigarettes.

Moments later, a plump, middle-aged woman in a bright red floral dress joined the man and she, too, began to smoke and talk while the man only grunted an occasional reply.

"How'd you like to have that resting on your shoulder?" Michael whispered and wriggled his eyebrows.

To David's right, across the aisle, a handsome young lieutenant yawned and opened his eyes. He shook the sleepiness away and blinked at David. "Morning," he drawled with a Texas accent. "Ain't I seen you somewhere before?"

"Anything's possible," David replied quietly.

"Well, I ain't one t' forget a face," he said. "It'll come to me."

David smiled and nodded politely, not willing to talk with this personable stranger. He pulled a copy of one of Ellie's Zane Grey novels from his pocket and began to read.

Men walked up and down the narrow aisle as the hours crept by. David traded places with Michael and, after finishing the novel, stared silently out the window.

"Seems t' me I seen that feller someplace," the lieutenant whispered to Michael.

David concealed a smile as he heard Michael's solemn reply. "He just lost his wife. I don't think he wants to talk to anybody, y'know."

After a time, Michael wandered back to a group of men in uniform and sat on the arm of a seat as they all told stories of their months in Europe. Most, Michael learned, had entered the war too late to see any action. Their jobs had been to mop up the mess, and now they were returning home.

When the co-pilot stepped into the cabin from behind a brown curtain, all conversation stopped. He raised his hands and began to speak. "First I'm going to give you the good news," he said.

"The man's a comic, no less," muttered Michael.

The co-pilot continued, "We are less than an hour away from New York." A burst of applause resounded through the cabin. He raised his hand to silence it. "However, we just received word that New York is closed due to snow." A groan filled the cabin. "We are, therefore, going to Washington, which is only a bit more than an hour away. Those of you who had connections to make . . ."

David buried his head in his hands. *Connections, he says, I've got a coffin with no body and cargo full of illegally smuggled artifacts. And no connections in Washington. How, he wondered, am I going to get this stuff to New York?*

". . . we will do our best to see to it that you reach your destination." He bowed slightly as the soldiers raised their voices in a collective *booo.* "Okay, fellas," he said good-naturedly. "I was where you are once. You'll get home." He caught David's eye, and the smile vanished. He walked down the aisle and sat next to him, ignoring the cat calls that still rang out. "You are David Meyer, aren't you?" he asked sympathetically. "I know this is tough on you—"

"Not much you can do about the weather."

"You're going to Los Angeles, aren't you? We can get you a flight out of Washington immediately."

"Well, thanks, but I have business in New York. My wife left some work. A manuscript for an article and I need to—"

"I am sure we can ship the body on ahead and then if you like you can—"

"No!" David snapped loudly, taking the man aback. He lowered his voice. "I mean, no thanks. I want to stay with her, thanks."

The co-pilot frowned and looked at his hands. "Of course. I understand. You want to leave from New York, then? Or maybe you could take a train and make it back to Washington in time to fly out from here in a day or two. I mean, without having to take the coffin all the way to New York."

David felt sick. "There were some people who were going to meet me—"

"By now your friends know where you will be. They'll announce it at the terminal."

"Right," David said grimly. "They'll know what to do, I guess." Suddenly he was seized with the realization of how fragile his mission was. A single snowstorm had thrown every plan into chaos. He had a list of names memorized for his connections in New York. Customs in New York had been notified by the State Department of the nature of the cargo in the coffin. A funeral home was standing by ready to extricate the scrolls from the coffin and then cremate the remains of the "body." David sighed and rubbed a hand over his forehead. Hours of planning were now shot to pieces.

The co-pilot patted David on the arm. "It will be okay. If I can help in any way, Captain Meyer—" He paused. "You were sort of a hero of mine in the war, you know. What a pilot!" He tugged at his white starched collar. "I was sorry to hear about this."

"Thanks," David answered, inwardly cursing the snow. "I guess there's nothing we can do about the weather."

"From the looks of it, this storm isn't about to let up, either. We're in for a few days of heavy weather anyway. Another couple of hours, and even Washington will be shut down tight as a clam. If you decide you want to go on to L.A., I'm afraid you're going to have to do it immediately. Either that, or plan on waiting a couple of days."

David's first inclination was to board the next plane for Los Angeles, just because that would give him a few hours more to figure out what to do. But Washington was a whole lot closer to New York and the people who were prepared to receive his cargo. *And besides, that goat isn't getting any fresher,* he thought.

As the plane descended through the turbulent skies into Washington, David sat tensely in his seat and frowned at the streamers of rain that beat against the shiny wing of the DC-4. When at last the wheels touched the runway, beads of perspiration clung to David's brow and he had the look of a man who did not enjoy being in an airplane. As the attendants in their rain slickers wheeled the ramp to the door, David scanned the crowd of people just inside the terminal. He imagined that every man in a trenchcoat was waiting to cart him off to jail.

Lines of weary travelers formed behind long tables where U.S. Customs officials rummaged through suitcases and duffle bags in search of undeclared contraband from Europe. A tall, grim, stoop-shouldered man wearing a gleaming badge darted among the travelers like a hound dog on the scent of quarry.

David and Michael waited beside the glass doors until the shiny metal coffin was wheeled into the customs area. David left his luggage and walked beside it until the baggage attendants stopped in front of a scuffed double door marked *PRIVATE*. The tall man lifted his head and peered down his nose at the coffin. Then he left a dispute about the cost of a Swiss watch and marched toward David purposefully.

"We'll have to have a look," he said, still fifteen feet from

David. He gestured for two uniformed customs men to assist him.

David's heart sank and he glanced nervously around the room. "But this has been cleared with the State Department already," he protested. "In New York."

"This is Washington, son," the man snapped. "Do you know what's happening over at the Capitol right now, huh? Communists. That's what."

"Look, I'm an American citizen." David drew himself up to his full height and set his jaw in a bluff he hoped would work. "David Meyer is my name. Check my passport if you like."

"I know all about that," said the unrelenting official. "All about it. But I've got my orders. We've got hearings going on this afternoon with a whole gaggle of Commies, and this"—he tapped the lid of the coffin—"this comes from Italy, don't it? They're having Commie elections next month. The whole place is full of them, son. I'm not saying you're doing anything you shouldn't. I know all about who you are and where you're going. But this came from Italy, and there's no telling what could have been slipped in here. No telling."

David narrowed his eyes threateningly. "My wife's coffin was sealed in Palestine, officer. And you are going to rummage through it over my dead—"

Michael hurried to David's aid. With a horrified look on his face, he grasped the officer by his sleeve and pulled him to one side. David heard the whispered words "bombing victim," and "Captain Meyer . . . war ace," but in the end, Michael's pleas for reason in this delicate situation were of no avail.

"I am real sorry about that, young man, but we got ourselves a new kind of war going on. They call it the *Cold War*, and it's going on right here in Washington. What's going to happen if I let this go through and those Italian Commies have smuggled something in to their comrades in there? Stranger things have happened. I assure you we handle cases like this with the utmost discretion. You are welcome to observe if you'd like."

They were beaten. David stepped away from the dolly and held his hand to his forehead. "I can't," he said in a hoarse whisper.

Michael cursed softly and blanched. "I'll . . . go." He half choked on the words. "Sit down, Tinman." Then he looked fiercely at the officious guard. "Somebody is going to hear about this," he menaced.

"Good. I'll get a promotion. I'm only doing my job."

David sat down and waited while the cart was wheeled through the doors. Five minutes passed, and he felt the flutter of raw nerves in the pit of his stomach. The other passengers opened their suitcases, flashed their passports, and shuffled off to find rooms somewhere in the crowded city. He tried not to imagine what was happening behind the doors, and hoped against hope that at least the rubber body bag would remain unopened.

Suddenly the doors banged open and David caught a glimpse of Michael sprawled out on the floor of the room. A sour, unmistakably dead odor drifted out as one of the two attendants rushed to get a paper cup of water. As he pushed the doors open again, David craned his neck to see the tall officer, ashen-faced, fumbling to replace the screws.

The men all looked ill as they emerged from the room. Michael, now conscious, was half-carried, with his arms slung over the shoulders of two equally shaken guards.

The tall man wiped sweat from his forehead and waved his handkerchief a moment before he blew his nose stoutly.

"What a job!" he muttered. "Poor girl." Then he said to David, "Sorry about the little woman, Captain Meyer. What you must be going through!" he exclaimed.

A plump woman in an official uniform half jogged toward David as he took Michael under his arm.

"Are you David Meyer?" she asked in a high squeaky voice.

"Michael," David slapped his friend gently on the cheek. "Are you okay?" Then he answered the woman. "Right. I'm Meyer."

She sniffed and studied Michael with concern. "Does your friend need to lie down?" she asked.

"No. He just hates to fly," he whispered confidentially.

She made a face and sniffed again. "Oh. Well, your friends asked me to tell you that they will be waiting outside and they have an ambulance." She peered at Michael, his face still blanched. "Is the ambulance for him? Nothing serious—"

David motioned toward the doors as the tall officer and his two pale attendants pushed the dolly out into the room. "For that, I imagine."

Michael staggered beside David as they left the customs area and passed through the terminal waiting room. Bored and disgusted, passengers lounged around on long, shiny oak benches.

Only one of the customs officials followed them now, pushing the coffin on the dolly with their luggage heaped on top. Bored expressions came alive with interest as they passed by. Michael, grim and dull with shock, was the recipient of dozens of sympathetic looks. David searched each face among the crowd, hoping for some sign of recognition. *Friends* he thought. *With an ambulance.* No one approached them, and after a few minutes, Michael muttered, "Where's the bathroom?"

David looked at the customs man. "Would you stay here for a minute? I'm afraid he's going to be sick."

The customs man nodded readily, but did not speak. He pursed his lips unhappily as they walked away, no doubt wondering who would want to steal a coffin anyway.

David leaned against the cool tile wall, as Michael retched behind the closed door of a pay toilet. Then he helped his friend wash his face. "What happened in there?" he asked quietly.

"You don't want to know," Michael replied in a pitiful voice. "Don't ask, Tinman."

"Look, Michael." David's words were laden with sympathy. "I need to tell you something—" he began hesitantly, only to be interrupted by the entrance of the thin man in the bottle glasses who had sat behind him on the airplane.

The man nodded an acknowledgment and David clamped his mouth tight. "Forget it," he whispered as the fellow entered a stall. "Let's go."

Michael took a deep breath and left the men's room. Looking at Michael's red-rimmed eyes, David felt a rush of guilt that he had so thoroughly set Michael up as the fall guy in this. Still, Michael had played his part, and now the effect was so complete that no one would doubt that there was indeed a body inside the silver container stretched out on the dolly.

"Look," said the customs man, "I need to get back. I'll call you a skycap to help you with this until your friends come."

Reaching into his pocket, David pulled out a wrinkled dollar bill and handed it to the man. "Thanks. We'll get it."

David had hoped to be inconspicuous in his arrival in the United States. Those hopes were now smashed as he stood in the center of the terminal beside the coffin and gray-faced Michael. He groaned inwardly as a crisp British voice echoed to him from across the wide terminal.

"Captain Meyer?" He and Michael both looked up to see the

178

shapely form of Angela Saint-Martain walking quickly toward them. She wore a gray tweed skirt with a red sweater.

"Ah no," groaned David. "Now the press."

"But you *know* her," Michael waved at her. "She said she was a friend of—of—" he stammered.

"Ellie's," David finished lamely as he gave her a half-smile.

"David!" she exclaimed. "I thought you were booked through New York." She removed her dark glasses and scanned the length of the coffin with a horrified look.

"How did you know where we were booked?" David asked, not feeling even the least receptive or polite.

She smiled patronizingly and looked at Michael, who scratched his head self-consciously. "She said she was a friend."

"And I am." She took David by the arm. "Didn't you tell Michael I helped you find the ring?" Her words were tinged with hurt.

"She did." David felt uncomfortable at her touch.

"And he owes me a cup of coffee."

"Some other time." David shrugged away from her, but she maintained her grip. "You can see we're—"

"Stranded," she finished. "Like everyone else on the East Coast. Well, I just flew in. Lost my baggage and well . . . it's just too strange to be coincidence that I see you fellows here. Can I help in some way?"

"We're waiting for some friends to come. I thought they were here already." David scanned the waiting room again as the loud-speaker announced a list of canceled flights. Through the front doors, he saw a blue and white ambulance pull slowly to the curb. A bald man in a rumpled raincoat stood up and looked directly at David. He crooked his finger and walked out the door past the ambulance. "As a matter of fact here they are." He nodded politely and disengaged his arm from hers.

"Staying in Washington long?" asked Michael, wishing that her arm had been linked with his.

"Just to cover the anti-Communist hearings." Her voice was full of disappointment. "I'm staying at the Mayflower if you're going to be in town a few days—"

"Afraid not." David's tone was brusque and preoccupied as he trundled the coffin toward the door.

"Well, we can have our coffee another time then." She walked beside him.

"If we're around—" Michael began.

"We won't be," David said under his breath. "If we're lucky."

"Well, Mr. Cohen, it sounds as if David can't make it. I am such a stranger here. I would love to hear from you."

"Terrific!" exclaimed Michael, the color returning to his cheeks.

The man in the raincoat pulled his fedora low on his head and turned his back to the wind as they approached. He eyed Angela, then looked past her to David. "Captain Meyer," he said in a soft southern accent. "My name is Nichols. U.S. State Department. We've been expectin' y'all. Thought you might need a little help since the weather threw a wrench in the works."

David blanched. *State Department? What happened to the Jewish Agency?* He coughed into his hand. "Well, I was . . . that is, we were expecting . . . someone."

Two muscular ambulance attendants were already loading the coffin into the back of the van over David's feeble protests.

"Well, let's just say we feel like you're a war hero come home under tryin' circumstances, Captain. We like to lend a hand to our own." He smiled and David noticed his teeth were yellowed.

David gulped, overcome by fear and panic. This was not an eventuality he had considered. But his expression reflected a man too overwhelmed with gratitude to express himself.

Michael was eager to comply with the hospitality of the U.S. State Department. Possibly, he would even have enough time to make a trip to the Mayflower Hotel for coffee with the shapely young woman who stood drinking in every word.

"How kind you gentlemen are," Angela offered. Then she smiled graciously. "Well, I really must be off." She touched Michael lightly on his arm. "And I hope to see you sometime." She turned on her heel and re-entered the terminal as David stammered and stuttered reasons why they did not need any help. The ambulance doors clanged shut and a long, sleek limousine pulled up to the curb behind it.

"Get in, Captain Meyer." The southern accent dropped away. "No more protests. Just get in." The ambulance pulled off. "You are being watched." His voice was a low murmur. "Get in."

David raised his eyebrows and glanced back through the glass doors to the retreating form of the woman. Then he watched as the ambulance sped off toward the highway.

"I don't see that we have a choice," he smiled. "You've got a hostage, after all, don't you?" He climbed into the limo and the bald man closed the door after him and Michael, then slid in on the passenger side next to the uniformed chauffer.

Throughout the drive into the capital, the bald man did not speak, but occasionally David saw the eyes of the driver looking back in the rear-view mirror.

Great heaps of dirty snow lay piled beside the road into the city. The gray sky alternately spit snow and rain, until finally a steady veil of white flakes began to fall, concealing the top of the Washington Monument, blending marble and earth and sky into a glittering white haze.

David stared out the window at the streets of the capital as the limo crept slowly over the slick pavement. He was indeed certain that the airport here would soon be totally shut down, along with most of the other major airports in the East. He grimaced at the thought of being a guest of the State Department for any length of time. It was urgent, he had been told, that the scrolls reach Weizmann in New York. How he would accomplish that now was a question he would apparently have to consider on his own.

He had lost sight of the ambulance several minutes before when the driver had switched on his flashing lights and sped through traffic that parted for him like the Red Sea. The driver of the limo cursed quietly and touched his foot carefully to the brake pedal as the traffic closed ahead of him.

David scanned the row of houses and tightly packed shops of Washington and felt as though he had been out of the country for years instead of months. As the car wound its way through the back streets of Washington and into the shabby slum district that lay almost in the shadow of the Capitol dome, David asked quietly, "Where are we going?"

"The mortuary," the bald man answered. "Don't you have a few items to pick up?"

Unwilling to pursue it, David simply assumed the man was speaking of their luggage, which had been loaded into the ambulance with the casket. He watched as black men and women hurried to unknown destinations through the snow. Coats on the children were ragged and thin; windowpanes were broken and covered by rags and torn blankets. And in the center of this poverty was a sign above an ancient leaning brick building that read BLESSED'S MORTUARY. The ambulance had just pulled away and, with the red light still flashing, was turning back onto a main thoroughfare. The sleek black limousine drew amused looks as it pulled up at the curb in front of Blessed's. The bald man turned around and said, "Your turn, grieving husband. Don't you have a few personal belongings to get?"

David frowned and opened the car door, stepping out onto the slippery sidewalk. He took careful, mincing steps to the entrance of the mortuary, conscious of the open stares he was receiving from the black population. He was greeted at the door by a short, very round black man with a fringe of white hair around his head. "It is mo' blessed to give than to receive," he smiled broadly. "Welcome to Blessed's, suh. Your friends have already done said you'd be a'comin' to take care of arrangements." He ushered David into a small walnut-paneled office warmed by a gas stove. It smelled heavily of stale roses, David noted as he sat down in a worn velvet chair. "I is Mistuh Blessed." The round man offered his hand. "And you is Mistuh Meyer."

David smiled nervously and nodded. "A few of my things were left here, I believe."

"Why, Mistuh Meyer," laughed Blessed. "We bin doin' business a long time and ain't nuthin' ever got away from us." He winked knowingly and David frowned, wondering how much the man knew about what.

"My clothes?" David asked. "My luggage."

"My man puttin' dat into the car right now. Ain't no use you worryin' 'bout somethin' so light as dat." He nodded knowingly. "Day say you gonna want the body cremated. Well, we can do dat an' no extra charge." He pulled out a white sheet of paper and dipped a pen into an inkwell and began to write. "You want a brass urn or a copper? Copper tend to tarnish, but I reckon it big enough t' hold what you got in dat coffin." He laughed again.

David squirmed uncomfortably. "Mr. Blessed," he asked hesitantly, "I . . . I . . ." He almost asked what the little man imagined he was doing there. "I'll take the copper."

Blessed stuck out his lower lip and nodded, scribbling on the paper. "Uh-huh. And does you want it inscribed?"

"No," David answered helplessly. "I don't think so."

The little man wrote the word *no* firmly on his sheet.

"May I see my wife?"

Blessed laughed loudly then, and peered at David like he was a crazy man. "Why you *is* a new one! I bin in business for twenty years and ain't nobody ask't t' see no *body*."

"What exactly is your business, Mr. Blessed?" David asked quietly.

"Ain't polite t' ask." Blessed laughed again. "But ain't no mortuary in town 'cept mine dat'll take an unembalmed body from Europe and turn it t' gold, man! You do go on! What does I do?" he roared with laughter. "You don't need t' play games wif' Mose Blessed. What you got in there? You done robbed King Tut? I seen it all. I seen all of it." He lowered his voice. "Had a Rembrandt come through here last month."

David's eyes grew wide and he wondered who the men in the black limo were. "Artifacts," David said. "Bronze Age. Jewelry."

"I figgered! That mostly what I gets in here from the Middle East. Artifacts." He nodded. "Come on, then. I 'spects you wants t' visit your wife." He howled with laughter and led David down a dark, narrow hallway. Little rooms were on either side of the hallway, and in several of them embalmed bodies lay peacefully in state in their Sunday best. Blessed turned to grin at David's curious stares. "They's jus' for show," he whispered. "A man cain't make a livin' buryin' dead folk in the ghetto, don' you know. Nobody got no money to pay extra for bronze handles on the casket. We jus' buries 'em real simple like. But you ought to see our New York showroom," he said enthusiastically. "Jus' plum full up with real bodies."

"Local folks, I take it?" David asked.

"Oh, lands, yes. Folks is always dyin', an' we gots a reputation for the bes' prices in town. Ain't nobody goes nowheres else for a decent burial. We's legit on dat account."

David scratched his head in fascination. "You ever worry about getting caught? I mean with your other business?

Blessed laughed again. "Ain't no white man gonna come down here t' check on ol' Mose Blessed. Not unless he got business hisself. Twenty years I been dealin' in art an' antiques, you might say, and ain't nobody ever checked a body comin' in from Europe. 'Specially not one dat been green a while, if you knows what I means. 'Course now with dem hearin's goin' on down to the Capitol, folks is gettin' mighty suspicious 'bout other folks, an' a man cain't tell. No sir. A man cain't," he shook his head and the rim of hair looked like a bright halo in the darkness of the corridor.

"How did you know I was coming?" he asked, curious about the identity of the men in the car.

Blessed guffawed. "Why, New York jus' called an' said you wasn't comin' in dere. Said you'd be here. I been paid already. Don't matter to me where you land. But I'll have to charge you extra for the large urn." He opened a door with squeaky hinges and stepped aside, letting David walk into a dark, cold room ahead of him. "Dis here's the embalmin' room." He flicked on a light. The metal coffin sat unopened on the floor, and beside that was a metal table with a large body stretched out beneath a white sheet. David shuddered.

"Local?" he asked.

"Oh yes, man. It be cold as a deep freeze in here," he said. "In the summer I needs lots of ice, but in the winter all I does is turn off the heat. It keeps dem cold enough." He stood over the metal casket. "Well, here's your wife," he said with a twinkle in his eye. "I 'spects you two want to be alone. I'll go get your urn." He walked back toward the door, then turned and winked at David and nodded toward the body on the table. "An' don't worry none 'bout him. He ain't in no shape to bother you none." Then he added, "I tell you what, though, in his time he was one mean junkyard dog." He shut the squeaking door slowly enough that David felt he had wandered onto the set of a Boris Karloff movie. He shuddered again, looking around at the grim display of bottles and rubber tubes, and stopped short at the sight of pliers and a screwdriver on the metal counter below a wall of frightening-looking devices.

He drew his breath in slowly, then knelt to examine the screws that held the casket lid on tightly. A rubber seal protruded between the top and bottom. David understood the reason for the pliers and screwdriver. Quickly, he went to work opening the container, taking a deep breath and holding a kerchief over his nose as he finally pried the lid up. Still, he was totally unprepared for the power of the stench that radiated into the cold room. The rubber body bag remained zipped, and David noticed that the mortician in Palestine had done an excellent job of making the form of the body enclosed appear human. It was no wonder poor Michael had passed out cold. He lifted the body bag slightly, feeling revulsion creep over him as he shoved the rubber liner to one side and felt beneath the white, satin-covered padding for the pouch containing the scrolls. His hands slid from the head of the coffin to nearly the opposite end before he felt the rubber-wrapped leather case bearing the treasure. He tugged on the case, dislodging it from its hiding place. Then, as the door popped and squealed slowly open, he slammed the lid of the coffin shut.

"Whewee!" Blessed exclaimed. "Somebody done picked a ripe one. Ain't no customs man gonna live through dat!" His voice was filled with admiration. "Gonna have to open a window and dat's all there is to it!" He set the large shining urn on the foot of the table bearing the dead man, and he rushed out.

Feeling as if he might gag at any moment, David took the urn from the table and opened it. It stood about two and one half feet tall and was indeed ample space for his precious cargo. Carefully, he slipped the scrolls into it and clamped the lid down tightly. Then he rushed to the door and clicked the light switch off before he staggered, coughing, into the hall.

Mr. Blessed stood before him with his palm out, as David choked and gasped for clear air. "That'll be twenty more for the copper urn," he smiled. David dug deep into his pocket and pulled out the money, making mental notes to get reimbursed by somebody later.

Humming *Onward Christian Soldiers* softly, Mr. Blessed accompanied David to the front door of his establishment. He waved cordially to the men in the limousine and they waved back as though they were old friends of Mose Blessed. Thoughts about strange bedfellows filled David's mind as he carried the urn to the car and slid in out of the cold.

"Okay," he said abruptly. "Come clean. Who are you guys?" he demanded.

16 Rescue

One look into Michael Cohen's seething face told David that the cat, screeching and clawing, was definitely out of the bag. David placed the large urn strategically on the seat between himself and Michael. Still, he could feel the indignant glare burning through the urn and possibly tarnishing the copper he had just paid twenty bucks extra for. He chose to ignore the issue that simmered so near to Michael's boiling point. Yes, Michael had been played for a sucker; a schmuck and a shlock, but they would deal with that later.

"I take it you fellas are not with the State Department?" David asked, feeling a tremendous weight lifted from his shoulders.

"Depends on which state you are referring to," said the bald man. "We have to have faith." He turned around and extended his hand to David. "In spite of the recent happenings in the U.N." He winked. "Michael here is all caught up on everything. Aren't you, Michael?"

Michael grunted and scooted farther into his corner of the car. "The least you could have done is tell me she was alive."

The bald man shrugged. "I thought he knew. Sorry."

Michael's voice grew louder and he talked around the tall urn. "Yeah. I spent the last two days looking out for you! Getting you Coke! Crying and . . . *fainting* and throwing up! What was in there, anyway?"

"A goat," David said apologetically.

"Yeah? Well, I'm the goat. Some friend! Some friend you are!"

"Well, you were great, Michael," David said sincerely. Then he looked into the amused eyes of the chauffer who gazed back at them from the rear-view mirror. "He was great. You should have seen him."

"Fainting!" Michael spat. "And crying! And throwing up! You could have at least told me!"

"You could have fainted and cried like that? I tell you, it was better this way, Scarecrow. You were great."

"I could have pulled it off," Michael said angrily.

"Nah," David shook his head. "You're too honest."

At that, Michael exploded into a sputtering rage, stammering the word *honest* as if it were an incredible insult. "Honest! You call me *honest*! I hang around with you, don't I!"

"Well, at least tell me you're relieved she isn't dead," David said quietly, remorse thick in his voice.

"You bet I am." He shook his head and stared out the window, his anger lessening at the thought of Ellie tucked safely away at the Jewish Agency building. Then he added, "Boy, if she could have seen me cry. Wouldn't she feel good?"

The bald man cleared his throat and said, "You must have done everything right. Both of you. And I think we've had a little help from the man upstairs. You're here—"

"Now, how do we get these things to Weizmann?" David looked up at the falling snow that thickened with every passing minute. As they drove slowly past, the White House looked like a dim shadow behind the curtain that blanketed the city.

The bald man laughed easily and turned around. "Weizmann is here," he said, appraising David's reaction. "Here in Washington."

"But I thought he was supposed to be in New York."

"He was, until last night. We tried to reach you before you left Rome. To reroute you here. Even the railroads are shutting down. I don't think you would have made it in time if the blizzard hadn't forced you to land in Washington."

David leaned forward in his seat. "In time for what?" he asked quietly.

"You haven't heard?" The bald man's face became a mask of consternation. "We were sold out in the U.N. yesterday. I don't know what it was. Maybe the *Post* bombing was the final straw. Anyway, the U.S. Rep stood up in the General Assembly yesterday and announced that the United States is changing its position on Partition."

Michael forgot his injured pride and sat bolt upright. "Not now! We're so close."

"Close to annihilation according to the reports," said the bald man sourly. "Anyway, the U.S. says it will support a United Nations trusteeship in Palestine. Out of the hands of the British Mandate and into the arms of the U.N. The papers are full of it. It topped the Senate hearings and the blizzard on the front pages. Big news, boys. Bad news for us."

"Yeah," Michael said dully, staring down at his hands. "But

what's that got to do with me and David?"

"Weizmann took the first train to Washington to see the President." The bald man thumped the urn. "These little items are some sort of trump card. If you guys had showed up in New York, Weizmann would have been sitting in the Oval Office empty-handed."

David shook his head in wonder at the turn of events. "Where is Mr. Weizmann now?" he asked.

"The Mayflower Hotel," answered the bald man.

The urn at his bedside, David slept for three hours before he showered and shaved in preparation for meeting Chaim Weizmann. Michael, however, had changed immediately and left the tiny room to sit in a conspicuous seat in the lobby of the hotel. He returned, hours later, disappointed at not having bumped into Angela, but he had read the *Washington Post* twice from front to back and was now well-versed in the news for that February day in 1948.

As David pulled on his newly pressed suit, Michael filled him in on the latest communique from Palestine. The Arabs had once again destroyed a Jewish convoy to Jerusalem, stopping it in the pass of Bab el Wad. Several Jews were killed. The British intervened after several hours of fighting and managed to rescue the majority of the Jewish drivers. The cargo had been abandoned to the Arabs. In the U.N., the discussion about a United Nations' trusteeship raged on. No one, it seemed, was eager to enforce peace on the Arabs and Jews at the cost of their own men. Words like "unworkable" and "impractical" dominated the page. Support was rapidly waning. In New York, a cargo ship carrying several tons of TNT, bound for the Jews in Tel Aviv, had been seized by port authorities. The U.S. arms embargo against the Jews in Palestine was still in full effect, regardless of the fact that the English openly sold weapons to the Arab nations. In addition to all of that, the worst blizzard of the century was upon them, postponing the round of parties for the Washington debutants of 1948.

"And you didn't see Angela, huh?" David straightened his tie in the mirror.

"I called her room three times." Michael stretched his legs out and stared at his shoe tops. "Maybe she's still looking for her luggage."

"Watch that dame, will you?" David said, scrutinizing his reflection. "I don't trust her. She's got the look of a newspaper woman. Predatory, you know."

"Listen." Michael spread his hands helplessly. "You're the one who married a journalist. I'm just interested in a little dinner, maybe dancing. We're sort of on leave here." He smiled thoughtfully. "And the lady has legs."

"Yeah," said David sarcastically. "Two of them. The better for chasing down stories with."

"You think if I run she'll follow?" Michael brightened. "Actually I think she likes you."

"I'm a married man."

"She don't know that. She thinks you're a lonely widower in need of comfort." Michael stood and stretched.

"Let her keep thinking that. I'm telling you, Scarecrow"—David tossed Michael his hat—"watch yourself with this dame."

"If she'll give me half a chance." Michael raised his eyebrows and did a Groucho Marx imitation as David shoved him out the door.

The elevator to Chaim Weizmann's hotel room was slow and complaining. David cradled the heavy urn in his arms and leaned against the back corner of the mirrored cubicle as it stopped at nearly every floor. A skinny, uniformed black man manned the elevator controls and announced each floor in a heavy accent. "Seventh flo'!" he called and the doors clanged open.

Michael's face lit up in boyish delight as Angela Saint Martain stepped in. For the first time, she was not wearing sunglasses, and her eyes were brown and wide with surprise. Her mouth formed a little "Oh!" as she took in David and the urn, then Michael secondarily.

"Have you come to take me up on my offer?" she asked David coyly. "Or just for a visit?"

Michael burst in, "We'll be here for a few days, probably. Would you like to have dinner?" His voice was excited and too eager.

"With both of you?" she asked. Then she looked at the urn. "Or possibly all three of you?" She smiled at David and said a bit sarcastically, "Still carrying your torch, I see."

He did not reply, certain that she somehow was on the trail of a story.

"Sixth flo'. Goin' down."

"This is our stop," said David quietly as he stepped around her. "You and Michael go out. I'm not up to it. You understand."

She raised her chin in a gesture that seemed almost defiant. "Not yet I don't," she said. "But it usually doesn't take me long to catch on."

"I'll call you!" called Michael as the doors of the elevator clanged shut. He hurried after David, who strode down the hallway toward Weizmann's room.

"She's on to something," David said in disgust. "I don't know how, but she's got a bead on us."

Michael rubbed his hands together in anticipation. "I don't care. As long as she'll have dinner with me." He took a deep breath. "I'm partial to that accent, too."

"Just make sure you let her do all the talking. Got it?" David frowned and felt the dull throb of a headache begin in the back of his head.

———————

David had never so much as seen a photograph of Weizmann, but had heard of him as the champion of Zionism, the Samson who had spent a lifetime fighting for a Jewish homeland. He was a scientist who made his home in London, weathering political storms abroad, even as David Ben-Gurion had chosen to work for a homeland by planting a vineyard in the barren rocky hills of Palestine. As Ben-Gurion attacked challenges like a lion, Weizmann was a diplomat and an orator. "The 600,000 Arabs who live in Palestine have exactly the same rights to their homes as we have to our National Home."

Weizmann was not a lion. David saw instantly that he was not even the Professor in the Wizard of Oz who made pronouncements from his Emerald City and expected that they be obeyed. Somehow, David had imagined Weizmann as a towering figure with a firm jaw and a voice something akin to Winston Churchill.

David was not prepared for what he saw when the door was opened. Weizmann sat in an overstuffed chair, his feet in a pan of hot water and his head covered by a towel. He looked frail and old and very weary. The sound of the door closing caused him to raise his head and grope for his glasses. Coughing, he slid

190

them on slowly, and even as he peered through the thick lenses, he strained to see David and Michael. The room smelled of menthol and eucalyptus oil.

"Who is that?" he asked, breathing with some difficulty.

The bald man stepped forward. "David Meyer and Michael Cohen, Dr. Weizmann," he answered respectfully.

"Good," he wheezed. "Come in. Sit down." He waved his hand and took off his glasses, then covered his head with the towel again.

The two ambulance drivers played cards at a small table, and the chauffer read the newspaper in the far corner of the room.

David sat down in a chair opposite Weizmann and carefully placed the urn on the floor in front of him. "Ben-Gurion asked me to give you his regards," said David.

"Which one are you?" Weizmann asked.

"David Meyer."

"Ah yes!" Weizmann's voice gained strength. "The pilot. The war hero. Come aboard our team, have you?"

"Yes, sir." The smell of menthol made David's eyes water slightly. "I brought the scrolls."

"Well, when I'm finished here we'll have a look at them. I've been fighting this since I got off the boat from London," he sniffed. "Doctor says I must do this twice a day or perish." There was amusement in his voice. "Imagine! Me dying before we have a state." He breathed deeply. "God forbid."

"Amen," chirped Michael, his hat in his hands.

"Well, we're all agreed," said Weizmann. "So tell me about your trip. And then tell me how things go in Jerusalem."

For twenty minutes, David talked about the desperate conditions in Jerusalem and in all of Palestine. Weizmann listened attentively, nodding and asking questions.

"Unless the arms embargo is lifted, Dr. Weizmann, I don't see how we're going to survive the first wave of attacks in May. The British have not even left yet, and the Arabs have already got Jerusalem corked up. If they knew how underarmed we really are there, I don't think they would wait for the withdrawal. The food situation is bad, of course, but the real need in Jerusalem is for weapons. That hasn't changed."

Weizmann exhaled slowly, then inhaled, sounding a bit clearer. "That's better now I think," he said, dropping the towel and drying his feet as the bald man took the pan of water away.

He put his glasses on and stared resolutely at David. "So why are you working for us?" he asked. "Are you addicted to hopeless causes?"

"No," David answered firmly. "I believe that this is meant to be. A Jewish homeland. I brought the scrolls. They are two thousand years old. As old as the destruction of Jerusalem, yet they hold a promise that hasn't changed in all that time. God promises that He hasn't forgotten. We will have a homeland. I just want to have a hand in helping that promise come true."

Weizmann studied him through the thick lenses of his glasses. "And so you shall, young man," he said softly. "Are you willing to tell these things to others? To other Americans?"

"Of course. Among other things, that's why I'm here."

"Good. Then you shall have a chance." Weizmann put his slippers on and leaned back with a sigh. "Now," he said, "I would very much like to see what you have brought."

"So would I," David said, realizing that he had only seen the photographs of the scrolls. "My wife was the first to see them. She photographed them and then, of course, Moshe Sachar and Professor Moniger recognized their signficance. Both men are hoping these will belong to the Nation of Israel someday."

"Let us just hope that now is the moment of fulfillment for all the promises and dreams, young man."

As the card game was cleared off the table, the men in the room gathered around. David popped the lid off the urn and reverently took the package from inside. He laid it on the table and unrolled the protective rubber covering, at last revealing a cracked leather shepherd's pouch. David felt his pulse quicken as he gently removed a paper-wrapped package from the pouch. Simple twine held the paper, and it looked like a birthday gift that had been wrapped by a child. David untied the twine, then pulled layer after layer of paper from the scrolls. At last, the worn, brown edge of a leather scroll was revealed. Everyone in the room held his breath as five more precious scrolls were revealed one after another.

Weizmann extended a gnarled hand and touched the largest of the scrolls, the Isaiah scroll. The touch was a caress, and in a trembling voice he whispered, "So far you have come; so long you have survived—for this hour, to shout your promise to others, that the world may know God has not forgotten."

A sense of awe touched each man in the room as Weizmann

opened the scroll. David could still see the neat rule lines that had been drawn to justify the precise Hebrew letters. An ink splotch lay near the border, and elsewhere another spot. *Was it a tear?* David wondered.

"Ah," said the aged man as he bent down very close to read the words on the golden leather. He began to read quietly, as David imagined the hand of some other man, long dead, who inscribed the promises without hope of living to see them fulfilled.

> "But Zion said, 'The Lord has forsaken me, the Lord has forgotten me.'
>
> "Can a mother forget the baby at her breast and have no compassion on the child she has borne? Though she may forget, I will not forget you! See, I have engraved you on the palms of my hands; your walls are ever before me. Your sons hasten back and those who laid you waste depart from you. Lift up your eyes and look around; all your sons gather and come to you."

Weizmann stared silently at the words for a long time and then rolled the scroll closed again. Michael walked over to a chest of drawers and pulled open the top one. He held up a Gideon Bible and flipped through the pages, finally turning to Isaiah chapter forty-nine. "Here it is," he said, skimming through the chapter. "It's in the Bible. Isaiah 49. It's all the same." He sat down to read the Bible as David carefully wrapped the scrolls back the way he had found them.

Weizmann clapped his hands together and said, "It seems the Lord has already made up His mind. Now if He will just consult with Harry Truman, eh?"

———

It was nearly six o'clock when the phone rang. Michael had been up for some time and was reading the Bible as though compelled by the very words he read. Though he had read scripture as a child, it seemed all new to him. The bald man picked up the phone and spoke in hushed tones for a moment before handing the receiver to Weizmann.

The expectant look on the old man's face died like a flame in a strong, cold rain. "Did he give you any reason?" he asked, then waited for a reply. His voice was thick with disappointment.

Michael looked up from his reading, and the two card players dropped their hands. "No reason? Did you tell him that I traveled all the way from London?"

David looked at the pouch containing the scrolls. Their trump cards would be no use unless President Truman played the hand. *God,* he prayed, *we've come this far. The rest is up to you.*

Weizmann sighed and closed his eyes. "Yes. Quite. I suppose he has set his mind firmly in this decision, then? Hmmm. Yes. I see. Thank you so much." He set the receiver down and groped for a chair. Suddenly he looked even older, and David thought it was not beyond the possibility that the soft-spoken champion of Zionism would not live to see his dream come to pass.

Weizmann looked up into each frozen face. "The President refuses to see me. He will not consider it. The matter is irrevocably closed."

Michael snapped the Bible shut. "Gee, after all that." He pursed his lips and frowned, searching for something to say, but he found no words of comfort or encouragement. He shrugged and clucked his tongue in sympathy. "I'm going to step out for a bit," he said. "Any of you fellas hungry?" Heads shook in a negative reply and Michael slipped quietly out the door.

"And he seemed like such a sympathetic chap when I met with him in November," Weizmann remarked after a long silence. "We got on splendidly."

The bald man grimaced. "I'll tell you who he isn't fond of," he said loudly. "Rabbi Silver. Silver has put Truman on the defensive. It isn't you. I don't even think it is Zionism. Truman feels like he's been under attack by Silver since Partition was signed. He feels like every Jew in America is gunning for him, and he's just plain mad."

"Have we no one to act as an advocate for us?" asked Weizmann, resting his head in his hands.

"I'm afraid we've been given the answer," said the bald man.

Weizmann looked up, his eyes large and sad through the lenses of his glasses. "Well then, I may as well return to England." He looked directly at David. "I am sorry, young man, that you brought these"—he nodded toward the scrolls—"such a long distance for no purpose."

The ache in David's head vibrated with the disappointment. Somehow he could not believe that everything that had happened was now leading to a dead-end. He rubbed his temples

194

and walked slowly toward the scrolls. "What do we do with these?" he asked. "Mr. Weizmann, I can't take care of them anymore. Could you hold on to them anyway? Even though you can't get in to see the President?"

Weizmann nodded. "It would be an honor."

"Well then," he said, shaking Weizmann's hand, "I think I'm with Michael. A good meal and a long night's sleep."

———————

David was nearly to the elevator when he remembered something that had played in the back of his mind like a vague shadow as Weizmann had asked about an advocate. There was one man in the United States who had immediate access to the private counsel of Harry Truman. Years before, Harry had been business partners with him in a haberdasher's shop in Kansas City. The man's name was Eddie Jacobson. He was still in Kansas City, still selling hats and, by last count, still a Jew.

The elevator doors opened, revealing Michael and Angela standing together. "Sixth flo'. Goin' down."

"No thanks," said David as Michael opened his mouth to speak. David turned on his heel and marched quickly back to the room of Chaim Weizmann. "We may have an advocate, after all," he announced. "Mr. Weizmann, there's a little hat maker in Kansas City . . . can somebody get the long distance operator?"

———————

Four nights later, a softer snow fell on Washington. David pulled the collar of his overcoat up on his neck as, flanked by Chaim Weizmann and Eddie Jacobson, he slipped in through the east gate of the White House. He carried the scrolls in a large padded valise, and as Jacobson and Weizmann entered the Oval Office, he sat nervously outside and waited for nearly forty-five minutes. At last, the double doors opened, and a smiling Jacobson motioned him to bring the valise and enter the office.

Flags flanked the President as he sat behind his large desk. For some reason, David was astonished and relieved that Truman looked exactly like his photographs. He snapped to attention and saluted when Truman glanced up.

"Mr. President."

"At ease, Captain Meyer," he said in a nasal twang. He stood up and extended his hand. "You're a fella I always wanted to meet. How many German planes did you shoot down, son?"

"Well, they were mostly Italian," David said. "ME-109's. Unstable aircraft at best," he said modestly.

"Franklin thought we ought to give you something special for it, anyway," he said.

"You mean Roosevelt?" David asked.

"Who else?" Truman said with characteristic shortness. "But I suppose you got decorated like a Christmas tree and now you've gone off to fly planes in Palestine." He looked at David and cocked an eyebrow. "What's wrong with you, boy? You like being shot at?"

"No, sir," David answered, looking toward Weizmann who was smiling broadly. *Things are going well*, thought David.

"Well, sit down." Truman nodded toward a chair and pressed his fingertips together. He looked at Jacobson, "Well, Eddie, you always were a better businessman than I. What do you think about this proposition?"

"I don't think you could ask for more secure collateral." Jacobson eyed the valise. "I saw them, Harry. They are magnificent."

Truman squinted and stared above their heads in deep thought. "What are you flying, son?" Truman asked David.

David shifted in uneasy embarrassment. "Piper Cubs, sir. And one Stinson."

"And your men"—he looked at Weizmann—"are fighting with the jawbone of an ass. Bluff. That's all you are. Bluff. The way I see it, the Smithsonian would be more than happy to display these." He nodded toward the valise. "But I'd feel a whole lot better if you could redeem them someday as a free nation."

"That is gracious of you," Weizmann nodded. "That would make one old man very happy, at any rate."

"The Almighty might agree to that as well." Truman's words rattled like machine-gun fire. "And I could stand to be in good with the Almighty." He paused and reached for the phone. "Pipers, huh? How much allowance did they give you to play with, son?" he asked David.

"Forty-five thousand."

"That ought to get you about one wing of a DC-4, I'd estimate. Still, we have a few planes left over from the war you helped us win. We might be able to stretch your dollar a bit. Now mind you, I'm not saying this is lifting the arms embargo. No, sir, I can't do that, and if you tie my name up in anything I'll call you all liars. Understood?"

Weizmann nodded, and so did David. "Yes, sir," he said again in awe.

"And you'll have to come up with your own pilots and mechanics, but there's nothing wrong; nothing in the law that says a young veteran can't start his own airline and fly wherever he wants to fly. Let me see," he said thoughtfully rubbing his hand across his lips. "Most of them are in Burbank, I think. A couple of C-47's and some Constellations ought to do for a start." He looked sternly at David. "But if you're going to do anything like fly weapons to Palestine, you'd better start from somewhere outside the country. Mexico maybe. Or Brazil. That's strictly illegal here. Absolutely. You'll lose your citizenship, and the press would get hold of it. It is illegal to run guns. Now, machine parts are something else. Farming equipment. You can haul all of that you want."

———

Thirty minutes later, David stood on the sidewalk outside the White House. Harry Truman himself had picked up the valise and deposited it in a closet just inside the office. The scrolls were collateral for a loan of equipment. The payment he required was a nation; the nation of Israel that would survive the onslaught of five well-armed Arab nations. For the first time in months, David had a glimmer of hope that survival was indeed a possibility.

17 Revelation

Michael sat across from Angela in the coffee shop of the Mayflower Hotel. She looked into his eyes and stirred her cup of tea languidly.

"But *why* do you have to go, Michael?" she asked in a pleading little-girl voice. "We've had only a week together, but you know what I feel for you."

"You keep looking at me that way and I won't be able to remember why I'm going," he said, taking her hand in his. "What is it with you reporter-type women and us flyers?" he asked. "David is absolutely nuts about Ellie . . ."

The coyness dropped from Angela's face and her voice suddenly hardened. "You mean he *was* crazy about her."

Michael blanched, "Yes. Sure. I mean he was. Before uh . . . you know."

"I don't think he much likes me," she pouted, pulling her hand away and fiddling with the scarf that matched her blue silk blouse.

"Don't let it get to you," Michael said. "David's a funny guy. Takes a while to get to know him."

"How long did it take Ellie?" she asked.

"I don't know. Two or three years, I guess. Now me, on the other hand, I'm easy to know. What you see is all there is."

She smiled and studied his face. "I think you're right, Michael," she sighed and took a sip of tea. "So tell me, they were only married one night, right?" She asked, setting her cup down.

"That's it. One night." He buttered his toast, not at all happy with the thread of the conversation.

"The radio said she was killed when the darkroom walls collapsed on her."

"I guess that's right," he shrugged.

"You know I found her ring?"

"Hey, Angela, this is not the most appetizing type breakfast conversation, you know?"

"Sorry," she apologized, sipping her tea again. "It must be the reporter in me. I'm curious about everything. I was curious that first morning when I walked into the darkroom and the walls were still standing."

Michael began to cough, choking more on her words than on the toast. She had hit very close to something, she was certain of that, and after he gulped some water she began again.

"I'll bet you didn't know about the darkroom, did you?" she pried.

He cleared his throat and looked around to see if anyone was listening. "No, I didn't," he hissed.

"When did David get around to telling you she was really alive?"

He felt all color drain from his cheeks and he looked furtively around the room. "Shhh! Angela!" he demanded.

A smirk of satisfaction crossed her face. She put her elbows on the table and rested her chin in her hands. "I thought so," she said with finality. "Where is she, then?"

"Angela!" he said through clenched teeth as though she were inflicting intense pain on him. "Somebody might be listening. You don't know how serious this is."

She laughed and blotted her mouth. "It must be, for you not to tell even me. And after what we have come to mean to each other. After the last few nights, especially."

Michael looked down at his hands. He was ashamed and embarrassed. David had been right; he reeked of honesty! "You gotta promise me this isn't going to get in any newspaper," he said in a low voice.

"Michael," she pouted, "what do you take me for? I am just curious, that's all. She is a friend of mine, too. This is an awful trick—brutal to play on people who really like Ellie."

He raised his eyebrows in agreement and drew a deep breath. "You're right about that. I cried all the way from Palestine to here. And I fainted when they opened the coffin in customs. It was awful."

She pulled out her compact and powdered her nose. "You looked terrible that night," she agreed. "Pale as a ghost. That's why I didn't pay any attention to you." She looked him in the eyes. "I should have known better," she winked.

"I had you spotted right off," said Michael. "When you showed up at the mortuary, I said to myself, 'Now this girl has definite possibilities'—and boy was I right!"

She held him with her gaze for a moment, then asked, "So what *was* in the coffin, anyway? I mean, if Ellie is still in Jerusalem—where is she?"

"They've got her at the Jewish Agency building," Michael whispered. He put a finger to his lips. "They think maybe she might have been the target the night of the *Palestine Post* bombing."

"How flattering. They think the Arabs blew up an entire building just to kill her? There are easier ways of killing someone I should think."

"Well, some guy had been trailing her and . . ."

Angela rummaged in her purse and pulled out a tin of Players cigarettes. "So what was in the casket?" She held the cigarette up for Michael to light. He patted his pockets in search of a matchbook and came up empty-handed.

"Papers and stuff," he said. "I don't know what all. Good grief, Angela, you are nosy."

"Well, this is quite a story, even if it has to remain top secret. I had most of it figured out, anyway. I knew she wasn't really dead."

"You're good," he said with admiration. "How'd you figure it out so fast?"

"I just watched. You and David. It was not so very difficult really. And it's fairly obvious something important came over in the casket. No one would go to that much trouble without cause." She studied the Players for a moment, then began to paw through her handbag in search of a lighter. "It doesn't matter. I can keep a secret." She smiled softly at him. "You know, Michael, I'm going to be in Hollywood in another week. There is so much hubbub in the movie industry about this Communist business. Black lists and all that. Michael, darling, could I join you out there? I think Burbank is right next door."

Michael's face lit up. He rubbed his bald spot and gazed back at her with obvious affection. "You know, I can't think of anything that would make me happier." He reached out and took the silver lighter from her hand and touched its flame to her cigarette. "I'll call you from there, hon."

———

At the head of his men, Captain Stewart marched through the labyrinth of Old City streets in the Jewish Quarter. Hostile, angry Jewish eyes stared out at him from behind shuttered windows of empty shops. Haganah men scurried behind the domes of rooftops and quickly secreted their weapons in prearranged hiding places.

Stewart returned their looks of hatred and mistrust. His eyes devoured every sight, marking the most insolent of the stares from the onlookers who watched him pass. He had filled the shoes of Captain Luke Thomas scarcely two months before, and his duty as a British officer in the Old City had been fraught with trouble and bitter incidents. *And now the Yids have put their children up to stealing bullets from my men,* he thought angrily. *As if they think I will not do my duty as an officer even if the offender is a child . . .*

Jewish heads leaned close together to whisper questions and

speculate as to the destination of Captain Stewart. They had seen little of him since the terrible night two of their number were arrested and turned loose in the center of an angry Arab mob. Captain Thomas, on the other hand, had walked the alleyways at will without an escort before he had been replaced by this stern, vengeful young Englishman. Only with ten men as escorts could he move safely through the Jewish Quarter. Some turned their backs as he passed. Others lifted their chins and narrowed their eyes, holding their breath lest they shout the thoughts that raged inside. *Murderer! The Tuevel in the flesh! Nazi! Goyim filth!* But only silence followed him and the ten men who held their sten guns ready if even one stone was hurled. Captain Stewart believed it was fear that kept the hatred in these streets at bay, but the citizens knew better. Only common sense and self-control dammed up the current of anger.

"See," whispered some, "they march toward Chaim Street. They will go to arrest the men at the Warsaw Compound."

"No," said others, "he carries a leather portfolio under his arm. He goes to speak to Rabbi Akiva for terms of evacuation. You will see!"

As the soldiers marched up the twisted Street of the Stairs and past the armed camp that was the Warsaw Yeshiva and synagogue, those who watched from the rooftops called down to the merchants and housewives who gossiped in the streets. "They stand before the gate of Rabbi Akiva! He has come to speak with the mayor!"

Heads nodded in comprehension, and shook from side to side at the obvious answer. Akiva was one of the few within the Jewish Quarter who still had any dealings at all with the English. He and his small group of followers were the last who believed that a peace could be negotiated with the Arabs who surrounded them. *Of course! It had to be the mayor's house! He is the only one who will not be taken to prison for his politics, nu?*

Captain Stewart rapped sharply on the gate with the sterling silver knob of his riding crop. Within a few moments, the gate opened and he strode inside as his men stood watchfully in the street.

Curious murmurs filled the quarter as everyone guessed the nature of this bold visit.

Yehudit Akiva, her eyes downcast, led Captain Stewart through the dark hallway to where her father brooded in his study. Yehudit had become merely a shadow that flitted around the house seeking refuge from the rabbi's anger and disapproval. She had spoken kindly of the woman Rachel Lubetkin, and thus shamed him in her support of this one who disputed his authority. Now the rabbi's daughter lived under the constant threat of her father's disapproval and abuse.

Yehudit tapped lightly on the dark wooden door and waited for the gruff reply: "Enter."

Rabbi Akiva bore the newly acquired disfavor of his people heavily. Black circles hung beneath his dark eyes. His bushy black eyebrows were locked in a continuous frown, and his thick lips curled in a scowl behind his beard. He was in a bad humor, that was evident. She ushered the captain in, then slipped out, closing the door behind her without a word.

"Welcome, Captain Stewart." Akiva stood up from behind his massive desk and extended his hand.

Stewart nodded, "Good afternoon, Mayor Akiva." He tucked his cap under his arm and stood for a moment, as he debated which of two wing-backed leather chairs he would sit in.

Akiva raised his eyebrows, "Is it?" he indicated the left chair closest to the towering, cluttered bookshelf and Stewart sat down, crossing his legs and balancing his leather portfolio and hat across his knees.

"I suppose it is not." Stewart did not like this obsequious Jew. He reminded him of a pawnbroker or a moneylender who dickered over every detail until the terms were without compromise and exactly as he wished. But today, Stewart knew, he had this man where he wanted him. "Things are not going well here in the Old City, I suppose." He tapped his riding crop on the arm of the chair.

Akiva crossed his hands on the desk in front of him. "Not since the deaths of the two men you arrested. No. I would say things have not gone well. You made a sacrifice, Captain Stewart, of the men who opposed me and my policies of conciliation. You gave them martyrs. Reasons to fight. Reasons to defend. You made that woman, Rachel Lubetkin, a prophetess among us. They all flocked to her cause. I had proof of what she was, and you gave them martyrs." His voice was sullen and angry. His face grew red as he spoke and the veins stood out above his white collar.

Stewart cleared his throat loudly, and bile rose in his throat at the reprimand of this arrogant Jew. "The incident was beyond my control. The lives of my men were threatened. Our policy, as you know, is to protect the lives of our own first. We are not here to enforce the peace at the risk of our lives. Partition is no longer a British problem. It belongs to the United Nations."

Akiva smiled a sarcastic smile. "Nevertheless, you have made our position here more difficult."

"You mean your own position as mayor of the Old City, do you not?" Stewart stroked the crop and studied the face of Akiva.

Akiva adjusted his glasses. "Until these Haganah people came, I tended to believe that my position was that of all the people here in the Old City. The deaths of two innocent men at the hands of a mob have changed everything."

"Innocent!" Stewart barked. "According to the laws of the Mandatory Government, these fellows were far from innocent. They had weapons in their possession—"

Yehudit interrupted with a knock, and Captain Stewart fell silent as she entered with a steaming tray of tea and small pastries. Wordlessly, she set the tray on the edge of Akiva's desk, then slipped out, leaving him to pour the tea into delicate china cups, too dainty for Akiva's fingers, it seemed.

Stewart nodded curtly and bit into the flaky crust of a pastry laced with honey and almonds. "Even without the help of British convoys into the Old City, it seems the house of Akiva is not going hungry," he said appreciatively. "Very good."

"We were wiser than most," Akiva said. "Our cellars are full. We have enough for quite a long time with just the two of us here now. My other daughter is gone to stay with relatives in Haifa. She cares for an elderly aunt, so you see we have enough. Yehudit cooks for me."

"And the rest of the Jews are hungry?" He queried.

"And angry."

"And uncooperative," Stewart replied, savoring the aroma of his tea.

"They are uncooperative to me as well," Akiva said. "Because of your mistake. A point we have already discussed."

Stewart looked as though he might defend himself for an instant; then he thought better of it and took yet another bite. "And how do you propose we rectify that?" he asked.

"I would suggest that you restore the convoys into the Old City."

"Under your direct supervision, of course?" Stewart smiled with understanding.

"Of course."

"Ah! A wise plan. That would restore you to power among your people, and put you in a position to assist us when the United Nations revokes Partition as unworkable and Palestine is once again in the control of the British Mandatory Government? Quite brilliant, Mayor Akiva."

Akiva lifted his cup to his lips and smiled fleetingly. "And you are quite astute, young man. You see, of course, that a Jewish homeland is the worst possible thing that can happen to those of us here in the Old City. We are quite comfortable with things the way they have been. The Zionists would give us a homeland without the Messiah. Ben-Gurion and his Jewish Gentiles. They do not believe in God! They have no intention of—"

Stewart raised his hand to interrupt. "These are matters that have nothing to do with what we are trying to achieve here. If you Jews want to fight among yourselves—well then, that's your business, isn't it?" he smiled. "I want to know what you can give me in return if I give you the convoys."

Akiva mused for a moment; then a gleam lit his eye. "A Jewish terrorist, perhaps? The leader of the soldiers here in the Old City?"

Stewart sat forward in his chair. "You know who he is? And where?"

Akiva looked down his nose at Stewart and said threateningly. "We can have no more martyrs here. Do you understand me? No more unnecessary deaths."

"You have my word as a gentleman, Mayor Akiva." Stewart's eyes lit up.

"It must not appear that I have had anything whatsoever to do with it when you take him, nu? And we must have it known that I have negotiated with the British for food convoys to resume into the quarter. That I have done this alone."

"Of course. That is a point in fact, is it not? You see, Mayor, I, too, believe that the Partition proposal will fail and that we will go back to things as they were before. I am for preserving the status quo of the Old City. I believe we might, indeed, keep the Jewish Quarter intact."

Sighing with satisfaction, Akiva smiled broadly at Captain Stewart. "You truly are an astute young man. Perhaps with an eye for your political future, eh? The young Englishman who saves the Old City from the Zionist terrorists, eh? My own future is at stake here, as well you know. So we must cooperate. Hand in glove."

He stared into the liquid in his cup. "My grandmother met a gypsy once who read tea leaves. She told her a grandson would one day rise to great importance . . ." He laughed out loud, for the first time in over a month. "So. First you must reestablish the distribution of the food through me. Then I will tell you when you may take the man we spoke about. By that time no one will care if he is here. They are hungry enough to listen to reason. They are hungry enough to listen to me again."

The sound of Captain Stewart's chair scraping across the floor signaled Yehudit that his conversation with her father was at an end. Quickly, she moved away from the door where she had knelt and listened for the last half hour. She looked to the floor guiltily as Captain Stewart flung the door wide and walked out, followed by her now smiling father. For the first time in a long time, the rage of Rabbi Akiva did not simmer beneath the surface, causing her to cringe inwardly. But there was something about this new face that was even more sinister than the brooding look and gruff manner.

"Get the captain's coat," he ordered impatiently when he noticed her framed in the doorway of the parlor. Then he looked at Stewart apologetically. "She is slow and a stupid girl. I could not trust her to go to Haifa in place of my other daughter or I would have sent her." He then turned on Yehudit like an angry dog. "I said get the captain's coat!" he shouted as she stood mute and humiliated before them.

"But, Father—" she began. He raised his hand as if to strike.

"I have no coat," the captain protested. "I . . ." his words trailed off as Akiva's glower once again turned into a noxious smile.

"Well, then," he shrugged. "Yehudit, show the captain out."

Her cheeks red with shame, she led the captain out into the courtyard and then to the gate where his men waited. He paused for a moment, then in a gesture of kindness that was uncommon to him in dealing with Jews, he turned to the girl. "How old are you, girl?"

She did not answer, but blinked hard as she stared at the flag stones at his feet.

He repeated more gently, "How old are you? Can you speak?"

"I am seventeen," she whispered.

"And did you bake the pastries we ate today?"

She nodded quickly.

"They were very good. Quite good," he said. Then, unable to think of anything further to say, he pulled the gate open and walked out with his eyes straight ahead.

David Ben-Gurion paced the length of the tiny cubicle of Ellie's room, and back again. He held in his hand a slip of notepaper with a message that had been intercepted by the Mossad in Beirut.

"It is from someone named Montgomery," he said grimly. "Security has cracked somewhere along the line. They not only know you are alive; they know precisely where you are. The message was not even sent in code. Just, 'Ellie Warne is alive and in residence at the Jewish Agency in Jerusalem.' Then this Montgomery signature. We don't know what to make of it unless they just want to let us know they are aware of every move we make."

Ellie looked pale and tired after two weeks in the bowels of the Agency. "David is all right, isn't he?" she asked in a quiet voice.

"Certainly. He made a stop at your publishers in New York, and then he and Michael Cohen flew out to California. Every indication is that they are doing well. It is going smoothly. But this"—he slapped his hand against the paper—"this has us all baffled."

Ellie pursed her lips thoughtfully. "A million people could know I'm alive. Anyone at *LIFE* editorial. Maybe someone at home. My parents might have mentioned it to a friend, and it just might have gotten to the wrong people."

"Well, we think you had better leave Jerusalem. I will be moving headquarters to Tel Aviv. You must come along."

Ellie shook her head as if she were dreaming. "You mean you're letting me out of jail?" she asked incredulously. "Well, hurray! I'm ready."

Ben-Gurion looked at her affectionately. "A little fresh sea air might do you some good at that." He patted her cheek. "I will send word to Howard."

18   The Armenian Baker

Moshe followed Ehud and two Yeshiva students up the ladder of Hannah Cohen's basement. Blinking against the bright afternoon sunlight, they stepped up into her parlor and were greeted with a cup of steaming tea.

"Moshe!" she exclaimed happily as Moshe emerged from the semidarkness. "Oy! So filthy you all are!" She looked them over from the top of their dust-colored hair to their boots. "It's been a long time since anyone was down in the cellar. Not since my husband Mendel died, God rest his soul; he was a good man, but he never cleaned the cellar!"

Moshe smiled and gratefully took the tea, slurping it down in one gulp. He almost laughed out loud at the sight of Ehud standing among the dainty Victorian parlor chairs like a giant uncleaned artifact holding a tiny flowered teacup in his great bear paw. Cobwebs clung to the top of his hair, and he was so completely covered with dust that only his eyes appeared lifelike. Hannah Cohen had called the captain a strong and handsome man on several occasions, and Moshe wondered if she was not hoping to find a replacement husband to clean her cellar.

Ehud stood mute and uneasy in the presence of this plump, vivacious dowager who warned them all not to sit on the furniture, but invited them to come back when they had made a visit to the mikvah to get clean. She was delighted that the corner location of her home made it the most ideal location for an intersection of the tunnel passages that now linked the Jewish Quarter from basement to basement underground.

"And did it go well?" she asked Moshe, clapping her hands together. "All day you're down there hammering and pounding away like large termites. Are you finished?"

Moshe swallowed the last drop of tea and nodded. "We now have a complete subway system, Hannah. Like in London. Only we have no trains to run through your cellar. Only men." He patted the map in his pocket.

"Only men!" she exclaimed demurely.

"And we will happily put the trapdoor back for you," Ehud

quickly interjected, setting down his cup. "So!" He wrestled the heavy wooden trapdoor over the opening to the basement. "And with your carpet over it you will never know we are beneath you! Ha! Just the scramble of little mice down there, nu?" He busied himself concealing the basement opening as though he wished to also hide himself from the fluttering lashes of Hannah Cohen.

"Now, Captain," she looked at him coyly. "You must promise that you will be more than just a little mouse in my basement. After all, I have tunnels running off all directions from my cellar. Surely you will be here often. If you would like a cup of tea or perhaps a blintz."

Ehud eyed her suspiciously from beneath his dust. "A blintz? How can you make a blintz in a famine?"

"Well, we do still have a few special things, you know. Everyone is saving something for Passover next month and I perhaps will have a little something, too. So if ever you think you just can't live without a blintz . . ." Hannah patted his arm and a cloud rose above him.

"Can I bring these fellows with me?" he squinted and raised his chin slightly like a fox examining ways to get the bait without entering the trap.

"Well, we shall all have tiny portions . . ." Her smile faded a bit as the eager expressions of the silent Yeshiva students brightened at the thought of such a treat. "But we are at war, nu?" She turned to Moshe. "I don't suppose you got permission to tunnel through the basement of Rabbi Akiva? Now, there is a man who could have blueberry blintzes every morning if he wished." She lowered her voice. "They say he has enough in his cellar to feed the whole Jewish Quarter for a week. He certainly has more on one shelf than I have in my whole market! Oh well, perhaps someday there will again be food to sell. In the meantime, if I tried to sell candles, the sun would shine twenty-four hours a day."

"It was good of you to donate the food in your market for rations, Hannah," Moshe replied sympathetically.

"So? Am I going to eat it all? All alone? And there isn't enough money in the quarter to buy food when food is scarce. Better I share it with my neighbors then wake up one morning and have it all stolen by God knows who, nu? I just saved a little something special. For blintzes, like I said."

"Keep account of all of it, Hannah, and I'll see to it you are

208

reimbursed by the Agency." Moshe put down his cup.

"The Agency!" Hannah rolled her eyes. "The Agency might as well be on the other side of the moon. Besides"—she jerked her head toward the window to where a small ragged group of Ehud's Torah schoolboys played stick ball in the street—"skin and bones they are, anyway. To see them eat is payment enough for my conscience. I can spare a few pounds to give them," she laughed and patted her ample hips.

Ehud looked toward the ceiling and cleared his throat noisily. "Yes," he said, his voice a bit higher as he tried not to notice Hannah's hips. "They are hungry little fellows. But brave, eh?"

The shouts and laughter of the boys penetrated the window-pane. "And they play stickball like they play against the Mufti himself," said one of the dusty Yeshiva scholars quietly. As he spoke, the leather-covered ball was socked hard by the largest of the two Krepske brothers. It soared high in the air, bouncing off one roof to yet another, where it ricocheted off a wall and finally bounced over the sandbag barricade that marked the border between the Jewish Quarter and the now-deserted Armenian Quarter. A collective groan rose from the players and everyone in Hannah Cohen's parlor joined in their dismay.

As the younger of the two Krepske brothers lowered his head to charge his brother, Ehud sighed heavily. "Well, that is that. There will be no more stickball for a while. That was the only ball . . ." His voice trailed off as, tall and lanky, red-haired Joseph marched resolutely past the battling Krepske brothers.

"Momzer! Schmuck! Idiot!" Shouts were interspersed with blows.

"Well, stop them!" Hannah insisted. "You fellows go stop those boys!"

"Let them fight," Ehud said flatly, still watching Joseph.

"I will not!" Hannah darted out the door and into the street, parting the shouting onlookers like a ship through the waves.

Moshe watched with amusement as she waded into the center of the fray and snatched up the brothers by their collars. She scolded them loudly like a jaybird while they flapped and swung at the end of her arms.

At the end of the street, Joseph stood on tiptoe, looking over the barrier into no-man's-land. Ehud did not speak, but scratched his head and moved toward the door as if compelled by some foreboding. "Joseph!" he called as he stepped onto the cobblestones. No one except Ehud had noticed the slender boy. "Joseph!" he called again.

The boy took a quick look over his shoulder, then bolted over the sandbags and disappeared over the side.

Moshe's attention had been drawn away from the spectacle of Hannah and the Krepske brothers just in time to see Joseph disappear over the barricade. "Dear God!" he muttered, bolting from the door after Ehud, who steamrolled down the street to see what had become of Joseph. They reached the sandbag wall at almost the same instant. Ehud clambered up and cautiously peered over the top into the deserted street and the Arab barricade beyond. He could see movement on the other side of the Arab barricade. He glanced up to see the concerned and angry Haganah guards that watched Joseph from the rooftops. He could not see Joseph.

"He's a momzer, that boy!" Ehud spat. "But brave. Last week he came back with an entire bandolier of bullets. But to get shot over a ball!"

"I can't see him," Moshe said quietly. He glanced up toward a Haganah guard who mouthed the word *gone*. Then he pointed to a large building near the center of no-man's-land. The door was slightly ajar, and the sign above the boarded window read, *D. Agajanian. Baker.* "He must have gone in there," Moshe said.

Behind them, Hannah still scolded and the Krepskes raged at one another and cried while the other boys looked on, unaware that Joseph had crossed over the line into danger.

Ehud cursed under his breath as the Arab guards at the far end of the street both turned to look in their direction. "Foolish boy!" he said angrily.

"There is the ball." Moshe's tone was puzzled as he spotted the battered ball beneath the window of a shop across the street from the baker's. "What is he *doing*? His question was full of anguish.

"If he lives," Ehud menaced, "I will personally kill him."

"There he is," Moshe cried as Joseph poked his bright red head out the door. He saw them and waved happily; then he peered furtively up and down the street and fixed his gaze on the ball. "Don't go after it, you fool," Moshe said softly. "Get back here." The Arab guards gazed long at the street, no doubt watching Moshe and Ehud.

Joseph charged from the door and dashed across the street.

Arab guards leaped to action as the boy scooped up the ball and ran zigzagging down the narrow street toward Moshe and Ehud waiting at the wall. Catching a glint of sunlight on the barrels of Arab guns, Ehud clambered up to the top of the sandbags and exposed himself to their fire. "Run!" shouted Ehud, waving his arms. "Run, Joseph, run!"

The crack of rifle fire was followed by the high whine of a bullet and screams of the boys as they pressed themselves against the stones of the street. Joseph bore down, running harder for the barricade, dropping the precious leather ball. He stumbled as yet another bullet tore the air, narrowly missing him. He fell to the street, sliding painfully against a building. He jumped to his feet again, a bit unsteady.

"Get down, Ehud!" Moshe shouted as yet a third Arab joined his companions and drew a bead on the captain who cheered at the top of the barrier.

"Run, Joseph!" Ehud shouted, halfway down the other side of the barricade now. He extended his great hand to help the boy as a bullet whistled by and plowed into the sandbags only inches from his left ear. "Come on, boy!" Ehud reached out to grab his hand, throwing him high into the air and over the top of the barricade as his feet still churned in flight. Yet another bullet slammed into the wall, catching the fabric of Ehud's dusty trousers as he vaulted up and over into safety.

Joseph lay skinned and bleeding from his fall, his breath coming in short, panting gasps. Ehud landed beside him, still furious, pale with fright beneath his dusty mask. He blended in well with the color of the sandbags—a fact which had certainly saved his life moments before.

"*You!*" he roared, grabbing the wide-eyed boy by his shirt front. "You could have been killed! You nearly were killed!" he shouted. "And I was nearly killed with you!"

"I—I—" the boy stammered. His yarmulke was lost and red sidelocks tumbled about his face.

"You—you—for a ball!" Ehud shouted, shaking Joseph. "And where is the ball? Eh? Where is it? Still over the wall!"

The younger boys had picked themselves up from the street and stood huddled around Hannah, watching fearfully as Ehud shoved Joseph back against the sandbags. He raised his hand as if he might strike the boy, and Moshe stepped between them.

"No, Ehud. That's enough," he said quietly. "The boy has had

211

enough. He is not harmed. Enough."

Ehud lowered his hand and his eyes. He was still angry at Joseph's foolishness, but ashamed of his outburst.

Joseph covered his face with his hand and wept softly. "I could have made it," he said. "I have done it before."

"*Before*?" Moshe asked incredulously. "You mean you have gone into the Armenian Quarter before? You have crossed the barricades?"

Joseph nodded and wiped his tears with his sleeve. "Yes. It was not the silly ball I was after. It was—" He looked past Moshe and Ehud to the group of boys. Then he fell silent and looked away.

Ehud pulled a kerchief from his pocket and thrust it toward Joseph. "Take it, boy," he said gruffly.

"Come on." Moshe put an arm around the boy's shoulder and led him toward the open door of Hannah Cohen's house. The eyes of the younger boys followed them as they entered and Ehud shut the door softly behind them.

Hannah frowned momentarily, then whisked the stickball team reluctantly away. "Go on. Go on home," she ordered. "And stay away from that barricade, or the Arabs will look tame compared to me!" She clapped her hands as they shuffled off around the corner; then she strode purposefully into her house.

The boy sat shamefaced on the edge of a dainty round-backed chair while Moshe and Ehud towered above him.

". . . and so it was not the ball you were after?" Moshe asked sternly.

Joseph shook his head slowly from side to side. "No. Mr. Agajanian has been a friend. A close friend." He looked up toward Ehud. "That is where I got the bandolier of bullets."

"From the Christian baker?" Ehud frowned and tugged his beard.

"Yes. And other things. He is a good man. His son George is a good friend of mine. He is also my age, you see. And he has a daughter as well. Sylvia. She is also . . ." He paused. ". . . my friend."

Moshe sighed deeply as memories of his own brother and the young Arab girl he had loved flooded his mind. "But surely," he said gently, "George and Sylvia have gone. They are not in the Armenian Quarter any longer, Joseph."

"No," he said dully. "Mr. Agajanian sent them to Beirut where they will be safe. He has stayed behind these months. I go to visit him. And he gets me . . . things."

"Like the bullets?" Ehud asked.

"Yes," Joseph answered sadly. He dug into the pocket of his trousers and pulled out a long iron key and a soiled piece of notepaper. "And this." He handed the key to Moshe. "He is leaving tonight. He can no longer stay. It is too dangerous, you see. So he asked me to give this to the leader of the quarter. I did not think I should give it to Rabbi Akiva." The note hung limply from his fingertips. Moshe took it but did not open it, waiting for Joseph to finish. "He is going to Beirut also. And he told me he wants to help. To do what he can, you see?" Joseph's voice seemed almost pleading for understanding. "George was our Shabbes Goy. He lit the lamps for us on Shabbat. I wanted to say goodbye to Mr. Agajanian. I will certainly never see him again. And I wanted to give him letters to George and one for Sylvia."

Ehud put his hand on the boy's shoulder. "Do you know what you risked?"

"Only what is inevitable if we stay here," Joseph answered quietly. "If we stay and fight we will die, will we not?"

Moshe and Ehud exchanged glances. "Perhaps not," Ehud said gently. "Not when we have such brave soldiers as you to fight beside us."

Hannah returned from the kitchen with a small tray holding a cup of tea and three small almond cookies. "I have kept these for something special," she said kindly as Moshe read the note. "You were a brave boy, Joseph. Foolish also, but brave. And so were you foolish and brave, Ehud. You have a hole in the leg of your trousers from a bullet. One cookie for each of you, nu?"

Joseph smiled for the first time since the incident, and Ehud bowed curtly to Hannah and carefully selected a cookie as Moshe read the letter from Mr. Agajanian.

This is the key to my bakery. Locks may make little difference when I am gone; however, my Jewish friends are welcome to what I have left behind. Men of the Mufti have taken all that was to see. In my basement is a tall cupboard, and behind that a door. You must take what you find there to help you in your struggle. It is my hope that you may defeat this wicked one and that I might return home someday also. God be with you. Come at night as soon as possible. Be cautious also of the Englishmen. They pass by each hour two times. I have timed them at a quarter until the hour and a quarter past. It was not so very long ago a million of our own people died at the hands of the Turks who ruled here before the English. I leave this here for you in their memory. May God grant you victory. Your servant, D. Agajanian.

Moshe read the words aloud, then folded the letter carefully and handed it to Hannah. "You must burn this," he instructed. "No one must know of this, or Joseph's friend would be in grave danger." He looked solemnly at the boy, who savored his cookie. "Did he give you any indication of what was in his basement?"

Joseph wiped his lips with the back of his hand. "No. He only embraced me and told me I should not come with you or come over the barrier again. The danger was too great."

"He is right. From now on . . ." Ehud warned as Hannah struck a match and the note yellowed then dissolved in a flame which she tossed into the sink.

"Is this man someone you trust, Joseph?" Moshe searched the boy's face. "He would not trick us for the sake of his own safety?"

"Oh no! He is a great patriot. A soldier himself before he became a baker. He fought the Turks with the British, you see. He has a large picture of an Armenian general that hangs in his house and he often told us stories. He is a true and honest man. When we heard the Jews had died in Poland and all over Europe, he told us how the Turks had murdered a million of his people while the world stood silent. He will do what he can do to help."

"He gave the boy the bandolier of bullets, did he not?" Ehud interjected.

Moshe clapped Joseph on his back. "You have done well, son. It is important that you not mention this to anyone. As far as you are concerned you went over the barrier to fetch the ball, eh? And we have scolded you and shamed you for your foolishness."

Joseph nodded jerkily and stood up. He ran his hand over his head. "And I lost my yarmulke and bloodied my knees in just punishment." He smiled, then bowed slightly to Hannah. "I will not tell them about the cookie, either," he promised.

Hannah hugged him and showed him out, leaving Moshe and Ehud to ponder the contents of the unexpected note. They were even uncertain how many men they should take with them on their foray into the Armenian Quarter tonight. "Perhaps we should bathe when we come back," Ehud mused, playing with the hole in his pant leg. "We seem to be wearing the perfect camouflage, nu?"

Moshe wrapped up his cookie in a clean napkin and carefully put it in his shirt pocket. "Four men, I think. We will go with Dov, who is small and quiet, and also with Rabbi Vultch."

"We may need a rabbi before this night is over," Ehud agreed grimly, as he stared out the window toward the barricade.

19   Bread and Bullets

Moshe led the way through the subterranean passageway that now connected the quarter from one basement to another. With the Hurva Synagogue at its hub, the passages reached out to the far corners of the quarter's boundaries and Haganah men now moved in relative safety beneath the streets.

Ehud had to wriggle through some of the smaller openings, and he complained that only small men had supervised the linking of the cellars. Dov and Rabbi Vultch moved through without difficulty, and Moshe stooped slightly as he walked, once knocking his head against a low beam. His entry into the Old City by way of ancient tunnels had given him the idea of linking the strategic points of their little outpost. So far, it seemed to be effective. Even children from the more exposed points of the quarter now traveled to Torah School below ground. *Soon*, Moshe thought, *we may need road signs*. Arab snipers had been frustrated for lack of Jewish quarry, and the residents all breathed a bit easier. As the Christian Arabs and Armenians had evacuated their quarters, Moshe had pushed the Jewish perimeter farther out, and had hacked yet new tunnels to the edges of the barricades. Now, he was only half a block from the Armenian bakery. If the note and the invitation to the hidden wealth inside the baker's basement was a trap, he and his men would not have far to run in order to disappear down a hole and scatter like mice in separate directions. Three individual tunnels fanned out from Hannah's house, and each of those ran beneath a hundred more houses that would provide an exit to the streets above. Here and there, meager weapons had been hidden, but only a privileged few among the 100 Haganah defenders now in the city knew their exact whereabouts. There would be time enough for weapons when the British left.

The passages themselves twisted and turned, following the ragged course of the houses and alleyways above. There was little rubble that remained, nothing left to trip over, but every third doorway into the next cellar had been shored up loosely. If the support beam were shoved hard enough, the bricks above it would collapse on any would-be pursuer. The bricks and soil that had been hacked away had been hauled up and bagged for use at the roadblocks and barricades. With the exception of a pitiful lack of weapons and food supplies, the Jewish Quarter had built a defense network that was not only sound but hopefully baffling to the thousands of Arab militiamen who waited eagerly for the evacuation of the English troops. *If we had food enough*, thought Moshe, *it would take them weeks to ferret us out.* Hope had sprung up in the hearts and minds of the defenders. *After all,* it was whispered, *only a few starving Jews in Warsaw held the entire German Army at bay. Only a few men and women held them fast until Warsaw was no more. This army of Jihad Moquades are children with toy guns compared to Nazi Panzer divisions and tanks! And we held them there until Warsaw was only a heap of stones.*

By the dim glow of the candle, Moshe could see the narrow ladder that led up into Hannah Cohen's parlor. It was nearly midnight, but Moshe had no doubt that she would be waiting for them to urge them on and wish them safety. Wordlessly Ehud mounted the ladder and climbed up to the top, putting his shoulder to the heavy trapdoor and heaving it open. Hannah's worried face peered down at them from the softly lit parlor. One by one they climbed up and she patted each man on the shoulder and whispered, "Shalom." Shutters were drawn tight and Moshe scanned the room quickly, noting the lamp on a small round table near the door.

"Hannah, put the lamp out," he whispered. "Then go to bed, will you?"

"And you think I could sleep with you out there dodging the English patrol and the Arab snipers? So go on and get out there, already, so you can get back and I can get to bed, nu?" she scolded them, then blew out the lamp.

"We must be very quiet," Moshe told the men. "The baker said that the English will pass at half-hour intervals—"

"The baker said, the baker said," Dov sighed. "And you think we can trust him?"

"Why didn't he tell us what's behind the cupboard?" Rabbi Vultch wondered aloud. "It's some kind of trap, I tell you. He was a good baker to be sure, but he has been paid off by someone."

"Look, if you want to stay here—" Ehud frowned in disgust.

"Go, already!" Hannah urged. "Agajanian was a good neighbor. A kind Goy. And not a friend of the Mufti and his hoodlums. Hurry! Soon the patrol will be passing!"

The men stood silent in the darkness for a long moment; then Moshe spoke in a low voice. "If you wish to stay," he said, "I understand. But I think maybe this man Agajanian wished to help us somehow."

"Remember the bullets he sent with Joseph?" Ehud nudged Dov.

"Old bullets," said Dov. "And we have no guns which they will fit, nu? I say this is a trap."

"Then stay here," Moshe said. "I will think none the worse of you."

"I will!" Ehud raised his voice. "Come along, you little rat. You've come this far, and I know you to be a brave man. If someone tries to get you, they will have to go through me, at any rate." He nudged Dov again, and Dov laughed nervously.

"I have always been a coward," Dov replied. "That is why I fought so hard to stay alive in the war."

"And here we are again," Rabbi Vultch said. "Hannah is right. The baker was a kind man. Kind to Jews. And a good baker besides."

"Go. I will have tea for you when you come back." Hannah herded them all toward the door. "And don't get hurt!" she demanded as Moshe opened the door and peered out.

He stepped out into the cold night air and slipped silently along the faces of the buildings. He did not look back to see if the three others followed him. He pressed on now as though he were alone, the warm iron key in his pocket. Haganah guards posted on the rooftops had been warned that they would steal out of the quarter tonight. As he clambered over the sandbags, he thought he heard a whispered, "Mazel Tov! Good luck!"

He dropped to the other side of the wall, and darted toward

217

the shadows of a deserted doorway a few yards beyond. Scrambling footsteps followed him as he made his way toward the dark bakery of D. Agajanian. For an instant he thought he smelled the aroma of freshly baked bread, and his mouth watered as it had a thousand times when he had walked down this street as a boy. Shuttered windows stared down at the four shadows who floated down the crooked street. The sound of voices, Arabic and British, wafted on the breeze, and laughter echoed high in the night. In the distance, Moshe saw the orange glow of a cigarette. Above them, in a narrow strip between the buildings, a million stars glistened like diamonds on the black velvet of a jeweler's showcase.

Suddenly the crack of a rifle split the night. Moshe froze and pressed himself tight against the wall. The others threw themselves against the pavement or crouched where they stood. Again the high screech of laughter drifted from the Arab barricade. "What a waste!" whispered Ehud. "See how they waste bullets in fun." His voice was heavy with disgust and envy at the ready availability of ammunition for Arab guns.

"Shhh!" Moshe warned; then he moved out across the street to the door of the bakery. The breath of his three companions was hot on his neck as he fumbled with the key in the key hole.

"I have gone mad," hissed Dov. "I smell bread baking."

"I too," said the rabbi.

Then the sound of marching footsteps echoed down the otherwise abandoned street. Their voices hushed and even breath was locked inside their lungs as the sound of the British patrol clicked off seconds in time and narrowed the margin of their safety.

The rusty key jammed, and Moshe worked it back and forth while his men pressed nearer. He prayed and pulled the key from the lock, then jammed it in again. Instantly the lock sprang open and with one movement, Moshe pushed open the door and slipped in. The others followed on his heels and as if by prearranged plan, Ehud shut the door and clicked the inside bolt, then dropped to the clean tile floor. Outside, the sound of soldiers' footsteps grew louder then stopped as they halted on command before the door of the bakery. A firm hand jiggled the door latch and heaved a shoulder against the door.

"Secure, sir," a voice filtered thinly through the door; then boot heels clicked against the cobblestones on to the next abandoned business.

The aroma of fresh bread was almost intoxicating as the four men waited for the patrol to distance itself from them.

"The baker," whispered Dov. "He has brought us here to tantalize us. To murder us with the sweet scent of challah when we live on only borscht and crackers!"

Ehud moaned softly as Rabbi Vultch and Moshe inhaled.

"My mouth is watering," said Dov. "I shall drool upon these clean tiles."

"Good," Moshe raised himself slowly from the floor. "Then the British guards will slip when they chase us. Hurry!" his words had an urgency to them now.

"Do we dare light a candle?" asked Ehud.

"Not here. The shutters may not keep all the light from escaping." Moshe felt his way through the darkness around a cold counter. As his hands groped for an opening to the back part of the bakery, he touched something warm and soft on the countertop. At nearly the same instant, Rabbi Vultch cried out with a small restrained call of delight.

"He has left us bread! He has baked us bread! Stacks and stacks."

Moshe felt the heap of loaves before him on the countertop. Counting the stack that reached higher than his head, he estimated three dozen loaves in his pile alone.

"Somebody light a match!" cried Ehud.

Moshe struck a match, guarding its feeble light with his cupped hand. There in the flickering shadows stood row upon row of fresh baked challah, the braided white bread of the Shabbat meal.

"He was a good baker," said Dov in awe, staring at the bread. The match burned Moshe's finger and he dropped it quickly and struck another.

"Enough to feed an army," he chuckled.

"And it will take an army to carry it." Dov had the look of a little boy in a candy store. He hefted a loaf and tore off a crust. "A *good* baker!" he exclaimed with his mouth full.

Moshe spotted a note beside the first stack on the counter. *"Shabbat Shalom to my friends and neighbors. D. Agajanian."*

"When this is over he will certainly have my business," said the rabbi, likewise tasting a piece from Dov's ragged loaf.

Moshe grinned and struck another match; then he walked quickly past the still-warm brick ovens to the back of the shop.

A clean metal door with a broken handle was ajar slightly as though someone had left it open to show the way. As the others stumbled after him through heaps and mounds of bread that lined their way, Moshe pushed the door gingerly and stepped onto a dark stairway. As the cellar door was shut behind them Moshe struck a match and pulled a candle from his pocket. Lighting the stub, he held it high. The floor of the wide basement was totally empty. As Agajanian had written, the Mufti's men had taken all that was visible. *How, then, had he found the flour to bake such mountains of bread before he left?* Moshe pondered as he walked carefully down the steps.

"There is the cupboard," said Ehud in his deep voice. The words echoed from the empty vaults of the ceiling and the clean-swept floor.

The dark wooden cupboard on the far wall was easily twelve feet high and seemed to be securely attached to the bricks with deep screws that had long since rusted into the walls. The men examined it by candlelight, noting that the anchors that held the cupboard upright had certainly remained untouched since the day they had been placed there. The inner shelves were barren. Small dusty rings showed where canned goods had sat in neat rows until they had been taken.

Dov tapped on the walls of the heavy wooden cupboard while Ehud turned a slow circle in the center of the room.

"Well, boys," he boomed. "It's enough the fellow left us bread to feed the quarter for at least a week. The cupboard nonsense is—"

Moshe pulled hard on the shelves themselves, noting that they slid easily from their brackets. One after another he pulled them out in rapid succession as Ehud fell silent and Rabbi Vultch held the candle and Dov stacked the shelves neatly to the side. "Bring the candle nearer," Moshe instructed. Its light reflected on the lenses of Dov's and the Rabbi's spectacles as it illuminated the interior of the cupboard. Moshe ran his hands along the joints in the back, finally giving a delighted cry. "That's it!" Slowly he pulled the wooden back panel to the side. It slid open reluctantly at first, then more easily, revealing a doorway about five feet in height behind it.

Ehud gave a low whistle. "This Armenian should have been Jew!" he exclaimed.

"A clever fellow," agreed Dov, stooping to peer into the room.

Holding the candle before him, Moshe entered the chamber. The air inside was easily ten degrees cooler than in the cellar. The room was fifteen feet high to the crown of an old Byzantine archway, and nearly twenty-five feet long. Twelve feet wide, it was stacked to the height of Moshe's head with sacks, and propped up against the front of the sacks was a large oil portrait of a dark-eyed man sporting a thick moustache and wearing a gaudy medal-bedecked uniform.

Rabbi Vultch gasped, "Stalin! This fellow Agajanian is a Communist!"

Moshe laughed and moved closer with the candle. "It does bear a striking resemblance to Stalin, but I think this is Mr. Agajanian's Armenian general. Standing watch over our treasure, no doubt."

Ehud tore the corner of a bag open slightly and reached his hand in. He pulled it out and sniffed it, then smiled with satisfaction. "Grain," he said simply. "The baker has left us grain with which to fight the war."

"Right now as important as bullets." Moshe patted the wall of grain sacks. "If these are one hundred pound bags . . ."

Ehud hefted one. "At least."

"Well then, that is twenty to a ton," Moshe figured, mentally calculating the number of bags in the chamber. "I guess two hundred bags anyway, eh?"

"Praise be to the Eternal who feeds us manna in the wilderness." The rabbi raised his hands in blessing. "Ten tons of grain."

Ehud pulled some bags from the front of yet another cupboard and opened the doors. "And a little wine!" he exclaimed. "For Passover. You see, it is even Kosher!" He held up a bottle, then gasped as he searched the back of the cupboard. "And also"—he reached in "a little something to fit those bullets of Joseph!" He triumphantly pulled out two old rifles. "Now, this was a baker!" He laughed loudly.

Moshe scratched his head and stood in awe before the treasure trove. "They are World War One vintage weapons," he said. "I think Mr. Agajanian must have thought he would have to fight the Germans again. He was ready if they swept into Palestine. So. He has left us a legacy. The Turks and the Germans murdered a million Armenians, and then six million Jews. But our little baker was ready for them if they came again." He looked at his watch. "Nearly a quarter after." He put a finger to his lips. "The British patrol will be passing by again." He blew out the candle, unwilling that even a glimmer of light might escape up the stairs and out the shutters of the bakery. For several long minutes they stood in silence in the utter blackness until the faraway rattle of the door latch was heard. Moshe waited another two minutes before he lit the candle stub again and sighed. "Now, how do we get this home?"

Ehud was already stuffing his pockets and waistband with wine bottles. "Dov is right. It will take an army!"

"We will carry back what we can tonight and come for the rest later," Moshe said quietly.

"The bread," suggested the rabbi. "First we should carry the bread, nu?"

"No, we should each carry a bag of grain. Then if we could not make it back for the rest, the grain would stretch farther than just a few loaves of bread," said Dov. Moshe wondered how such a little fellow would ever manage even one sack of grain.

"Dov is right," agreed Ehud.

"Then it is settled." Moshe shouldered one of the grain sacks as Ehud wrestled two onto his shoulders and set them outside. Panting and sweating, Dov and the rabbi also hefted their burdens. Moshe took a slow look around, feeling suddenly wealthy. He saluted the Armenian general and stepped out of the secret room. Ehud and Dov were already poised to put the cupboard back as they had found it; sliding the back panel into place, and carefully fitting the shelves back onto their brackets. Only then did Moshe notice that the dust on the shelves was a permanent fixture; no doubt applied to the stain on the cupboard to make it appear an untouched and a grimy sentinel in an otherwise spotless establishment.

Each man groaned softly under the weight of their burdens. Ehud, however, carried his two bags with the ease of a fisherman used to hauling in heavy nets.

They leaned their grain sacks against the wall and sat down to wait for the British patrol to pass. *Like stevedores on a coffee break,* Moshe mused.

Dov raised his chin and inhaled the aroma of bread that escaped from the shop above. "We may never taste such bread again as that Armenian has made for us." He pushed his eyeglasses up on his nose, then rose and walked calmly up the steps and out the door. Momentarily he returned and pausing on the landing, he held up four golden loaves of challah.

"Good man," said Ehud, tugging at his waistband to show that he had indeed lost inches from his expansive belly since he entered the Old City.

Dov had little weight to lose. Small and fragile looking beneath his long black, baggy coat, Moshe knew that the serious face behind the beard was still thin and pinched; yet unrecovered from years of starvation and want. Moshe studied the thin shadow of a man who moved toward them with an offering of bread that was surely as valuable to Dov as gold to any other man. There was no light on his face. He seldom smiled, and his eyes were as somber as the clothes he wore. *Dov has called himself a coward*, thought Moshe, *and yet he is as brave a man as ever was born*.

Dov tossed the loaves to each of his companions, then sat down on his sack of grain and tore off a hunk of bread.

"There have been times in my life when I dreamed of having a loaf of bread all to myself. The way a man dreams about women," Dov said as he stuffed his mouth and savored the taste of the bread. "In Warsaw there was a very brave Christian fellow who threw a sack of bread over the wall of the ghetto once a week. People fought for that bread. Some died for a taste of it, you know? We heard later that the Gestapo caught the man and shot him for giving bread to Jews. Bread was very expensive in those days." He stroked his loaf. "Later, after the ghetto fell and a few of us escaped through the sewers and into the woods to join the Partisans, sometimes we got a crust from farmers. Chaim was bigger than I." Dov's voice grew tender when he mentioned the name of his friend. "He needed more to feed his body, I think, but there was never enough. I was grateful to be small. I could eat less. Hide better. I made a much more difficult target." He paused and Moshe thought he saw a half smile. "Chaim would have liked to taste this bread. Since he is gone I will remember him kindly when I eat for both of us."

No one replied, but somehow the memories of weeks without bread made the challah taste better than any meal. Rabbi Vultch chewed slowly, tearing off one small bite at a time. He did not look up and the wide brim of his black hat hid his expression from Moshe. "When I was a young man here in the Old City, the Muslims would bring us bread at the end of a fast. And we would do the same for them at the end of theirs. I cannot remember what it was that first stirred them up. There was a terrible massacre in Safed when I was nineteen years old. We all became very cautious after that. But even so we said to ourselves and our Arab neighbors, 'It can't happen here. Not among us. We will always be friends.' In the thirties we had terrible riots here. Our friend the Mufti began the slaughter with his words. He stirred the people to a Jihad, and there was killing in the streets. Murder of innocents and violation of our women. Do you know why? Can you imagine what issue would cause such grief?"

He did not wait for a reply, but shook his head slowly as if he still could not believe the answer. "We Jews wanted to put up a partition to divide the Wailing Wall into a place for women to pray that was separate from men. Imagine! Only to separate men from women—a little screen, a small partition it was and the whole world fell apart because of it. In the end many thousands of us and them were killed. And now!" He tore off a piece of bread, and then tore that in two. "Now the United Nations has put up a little Partition in Palestine, eh? To divide Arabs and Jews . . ." He held the two chunks of bread up to the light. "One or the other of us will be swallowed. I pray to God it will not be the Jews again." He popped a piece of bread into his mouth just as the sound of British boot heels marched to the door. The morsel remained uneaten as the door latch rattled loudly; then the footfalls echoed and were gone.

Each man breathed a sigh of relief, then, tucking bread into their pockets, they shouldered the burdens and moved quickly up the rickety stairs and toward the front door.

Backs bent beneath their heavy burdens, they could not move stealthily back toward the Jewish barricade. Dim starlight illuminated them as they shuffled over the uneven stones like creatures of the darkness. Their breath, heavy and panting, chugged and steamed like the smoke from a locomotive. Retreating around a corner, they could still hear the footsteps of the British. Moshe prayed that their own movement was undetected.

A dozen yards from the barricade, Dov stumbled and fell beneath the weight of the bag. Ehud hurried on and, dumping his two sacks against the sandbags, turned back to help Dov. The little man's glasses hung lop-sided on his face as he scrambled up. Ehud shouldered the cargo easily and linked his large arm with Dov's, half-dragging him the rest of the way to safety.

"Who goes there?" a Haganah guard called down from his rooftop post.

"Shalom!" Moshe hissed. "Come down. Give us a hand."

The sound of scrambling broke the silence that had clung to the quarter like a mist. In hushed tones, Moshe explained the situation to two young, lean Haganah men.

"There is bread. Enough to feed everyone, perhaps for a week. But we will need sacks to stuff it in and haul it."

"In the basement of Tipat Chalev," volunteered Dov. "The women have been stitching sacks for sandbags. We will need to hurry, though. Only twenty minutes and the British patrol . . ."

Leaving one man as a guard, the others lugged the grain three blocks to Tipat Chalev. The door was unlocked, but there was no light in the main dining room. Ehud staggered in first, barking his shins against a wooden bench. Dov dropped his sack to the floor and dragged it toward the basement. As they opened the basement door, a wash of light stung their eyes. Below them, the women of the quarter worked and talked. Some sewed, others separated bullets from beans. Surprised and worried faces all turned toward them as they crept carefully down the stairs. Moshe waved and smiled back at Rachel's upturned face. As he moved toward them with the grain sack on his shoulder, she turned Tikvah toward him and said, "There's Papa." The baby sat propped in her lap taking in the hubbub in the basement.

At the foot of the stairs, the men let their precious cargo slide to the floor. "We have a gift from God," Moshe announced. "Bread! Lots of bread!" A delighted murmur rippled through the room. Moshe went quickly to Rachel's side as Ehud explained about the need for sacks. "Shouldn't you two be in bed?" Moshe said quietly to Rachel as he reached out to take Tikvah's waving hand in his own.

"That is what I was going to ask you." Rachel kissed him lightly. "We have done a lot tonight. This is the best time to work. And with the tunnels, now most of us can go home without the British patrols ever suspecting. You know I have married a genius."

"We will have more tunnels to dig," he said. "Under the Armenian Quarter. But tonight we need to pick up a gift." He pulled a piece of bread from the pocket of his coat.

"Oh, it's beautiful!" cried Rachel. "Ehud's manna. I will remind him of his promise to share it with Yehudit."

"Just in time for Shabbat." He stood up and held the bread high. "We need you to help us," he said loudly. "The wisest thing we can do is form a chain from our barricade to the home of Hannah Cohen." Hannah waved and Moshe noticed her hands were full of cloth. She had chosen to work while she awaited their return. "Six of us can fill the bags with bread and then run it back to our border. We can store it at Hannah's and then bring it here through the tunnels." He pointed to several of the younger, more agile women. "You, please. And you and you." Rachel started to stand up. "No, you stay here with Tikvah. I'll be back soon." He patted her cheek, and with a train of willing helpers behind, entered a tunnel behind a movable panel and traveled the three blocks to Hannah's house underground.

It was almost exactly a quarter past two when they stood huddled in Hannah's front parlor with their arms full of empty sacks. The British would soon pass the bakery, then go on to prowl the rest of the quarter. As they huddled together in the pitch black of the parlor, Moshe struck a match and checked his watch, counting off the seconds that would provide their margin of safety. At last he whispered urgently, "Now!" He and Ehud, Dov, Rabbi Vultch moved quickly toward the barricade. In their arms they carried dozens of sacks. Moshe fingered the key in his pocket; then he slipped over the sandbags and sprinted up the deserted street to D. Agajanian's.

In a mad scramble he threw open the door and began to stuff bread into his sacks as the others followed. When he had filled half a dozen, he sprinted back to the barricade and passed the bread over the wall into the waiting hands of a woman who then passed it hand over hand through a living chain to Hannah's house. The only sound was the slap of feet on the cobblestones and an occasional whisper, "Here I am," as arms reached upward to receive the gift.

Moshe passed Ehud and the rabbi three times as they ran the relay. Dov remained inside the bakery, stuffing sacks and propping them against the door for the others to pick up and carry away. Not confident that he could guess the time, Moshe crouched behind the counter and lit a match to check his watch.

"Four minutes," he whispered hoarsely.

"Halfway through, do you think?" Ehud glanced around him.

"There's more still," said Dov. "A whole room next to the ovens. A bit stale. He must have baked for days."

"May the Eternal bless him," intoned Rabbi Vultch, opening a bag and inhaling the sweet aroma.

"All right, take what we have. This time cross the barricade and we will wait until they pass." Moshe whispered, shouldering another load.

"Give me the key," said Dov. "I'll lock up."

Moshe passed the key to Dov, then followed Ehud and the rabbi quickly back to safety, slipping easily over the barricade. Seconds ticked past and Dov did not appear.

"Where is the little rat?" Ehud peered over the sandbags into the darkness.

"He said he was going to get a load for himself," said the rabbi as the sound of the guard approached in the distance.

Feeling a surge of fear for the safety of Dov, Moshe put a finger to his lips and a short burst of "shhh" passed down through the line as the British neared the bakery.

Laying his sacks of bread on the street, Dov jammed the key into the stubborn lock for the fifth time. Sweat poured from his brow and made the palms of his hands slick and cold. Again and again he wriggled the key and tested the latch as the thump of shoulders against other doors moved nearer, and the words, "Secure, sir," rang out clearly.

Dov's breath came in heavy vapor, steaming his glasses. The rush of his own blood filled his ears until the sounds that struck through the black night seemed like hollow echoes from the bottom of a barrel. Still the lock did not catch. He gathered his sacks of bread and slipped back into the bakery, closing the door and shoving the inside bolt into place just as the guard passed the front window of D. Agajanian's bakery. He fell on top of the soft bags of challah, and lay his cheek against them like a pillow as the room seemed to spin around him.

The door latch rattled from the outside. "Secure, sir!" Then, a silence fell and voices mingled together in one exultant cry of discovery.

From where he huddled behind the barricade, Moshe heard an English voice shout clearly, "It's a bag of bread, sir! Cap'n Stewart, here's a big stack of fresh baked bread!"

Moshe turned quickly and whispered urgently to the helpers, "Scatter! Go home! Pass it on." Quietly the word filtered back through the ranks and the scramble of footsteps rang out as a short burst of sten gunfire flamed briefly, illuminating the patrol of a dozen soldiers and fracturing the lock of the bakery shop. A flashlight beam cracked the black street, searching out the corners and passing briefly over a small, round leather ball near the barricade. Moshe pressed himself against the sandbags and listened as the guards kicked the broken door open and shouted as they entered the shop. Another short burst of machine-gun fire exploded; then Moshe turned and followed the others, running toward Hannah Cohen's house and the safe, black obscurity of the tunnels.

———

Mindlessly clutching a bag of bread that thumped on the basement steps behind him, Dov groped his way toward the cupboards as the shouts of the British filled the shop above him. He had only moments, he knew, before they would find the basement door and follow him. Stumbling across the cold stone floor, he reached out like a blind man and touched the rough hewn wall.

"There!" an English voice shouted. "A door!" The thump of footsteps crashed across the floor.

As the door swung open and a single beam of light splashed across the void, Dov touched the cupboard. He opened the doors and slid his lean body between the shelves, closing the cupboard after him as three guards scrambled down the steps into the empty basement. Dov hugged the bread to himself and felt the back panel of the cupboard for the groove that Moshe had grasped to pull the back open. His breath was louder than their voices.

"Nothin' down 'ere, Cap'n!"

"Well, watch yourself!"

"'E could be 'iding in the cupboard there!"

The light fanned the dark doors, slipping through the crack and showing the grain of the wood and the indentation of a slender handhold. Dov grasped it firmly and pulled it silently to one side, revealing a black hole just big enough for him to slip through into the secret storage chamber.

"Stand back, Tommy!" a cautious voice warned in front of the cupboard. "Keep your gun on it."

"Come out!" came the command.

"Put a bullet or two through it, Tommy." A burst of machine-gun fire raked the huge sentinel that hid Dov from the men of the patrol. Splinters of wood flew everywhere and Dov heard the soft rush of grain escaping from sacks penetrated by the shells.

The guards threw the doors open and laughed "Blimey! Nothin' in 'ere, Cap'n Stewart." Then a muttered, " 'Ad me scared out of me wits, you did."

Light filtered through several holes in the back panels. Dov touched his face and noticed that his glasses had fallen off somewhere during his flight. Then the lights blinked away and the men climbed the steps back to the shop while they teased one another about the execution of the huge basement cupboard.

Still not daring to move, Dov clutched his sack of challah to him. It would not matter about his glasses, he thought. For a while, anyway, he was confined to a dark and solitary cell. He smiled to himself and remembered old dreams. He had in his hands the fulfillment of a prayer. He was totally alone in the dark with his own bag of Shabbat challah and no one with whom he had to share it.

20   Betrayal

Captain Stewart toyed with the earpiece of Dov's broken glasses and carefully considered his words. "It occurred to me that perhaps you have been holding out on us, Rabbi Akiva?" he questioned the brooding rabbi who sat sullenly across from him in the darkly lit study. "If your people have had access to a bakery full of fresh bread, why should you need a British convoy of food—food transported by British soldiers, for British troops, at a risk of British lives?"

"I know nothing of this!" Akiva snapped. "No one in the quarter has eaten challah for weeks."

Stewart reached down and took a paper-wrapped package from beside his chair. "Then they, and you, will appreciate a gift from the British Mandatory Government." He placed the package on Akiva's desk and unwrapped it ceremoniously. It contained a golden loaf of challah. "For your Sabbath meal." He smiled and narrowed his eyes, appraising Akiva's reaction. "We are here to protect not only the Jewish Quarter but the Armenian Quarter and the Muslim Quarter and the Christian as well. Since the Armenians have had the good sense to evacuate, considerable stores of perishable food items have been impounded by my authority."

Akiva raised his thick eyebrows. "Food for my people is still food. Whether it comes on a British truck or some other way."

"There is enough for everyone in the Jewish Quarter to have a good Sabbath meal. Perhaps enough for a week." Stewart shrugged. "It simplifies things. A convoy will be difficult to arrange now. But this"—he tapped the loaf with the eyeglasses—"if you keep your end of the bargain, I can have this delivered into your hands immediately."

"I told you what I can do for you," Akiva replied. "I am a man of my word."

"I am certain your people will realize that when you feed them. My men will need a little cash on the side, as well, but perhaps we can arrange a bit more food once I have the criminals I want."

"One man. I promised only one. The leader of the defenders alone." Akiva leaned forward and clenched his fist. "And I will have no more martyrs. He is to be removed from the Old City, and that is all. No more martyrs, or there will be no hope of my people coming to their senses. You will lose. And I will lose."

"I am a man of my word also. We will take him for questioning. If there are others with him and there is evidence—"

"I simply want him out of the quarter. He has usurped my authority and there is no one left here that you can deal with reasonably but me." Akiva justified his actions easily beneath the guise of helping his people.

"Of course. That is why I am here. These men are terrorists. Hoodlums by nature, we know that. The government has no quarrel with the Jewish people as a whole. We simply want to eliminate the troublemakers so that we can get on with the business of keeping the peace. Eventually people will see the reason in this." His words seemed to soothe Akiva. Stewart paused and cleared his throat, allowing the rabbi to consider what was certainly the only course of action. "Someday, history will reflect on your choices and consider you a wise man. We have assurances from the Arab High Committee that if they can deal directly with you once again, perhaps a compromise can be reached. The Jewish Quarter may remain intact."

Akiva nodded and stared at the challah. "I had hoped for more to bargain with than just one cartload of bread. You promised me two convoys of food, under my distribution, before you took him."

"There will be more, I assure you. We want you to regain the confidence of your people as much as you do. You seem to be one of the few reasonable Jews left in Palestine," Stewart remarked with casual assurance.

"There are still a few of us left." Akiva relaxed with the flattering words of Stewart. "Most here in my quarter are reasonable men. Most believe that Zionism is blasphemy without the Messiah. If the bonds of this siege could be loosened, you would see them hand over these Haganah fellows to a man. My people are afraid now. Simply afraid. They shield these men because they fear for their own safety."

"Rabbi Akiva"—Stewart's words were patronizing now, as though he were speaking to a child—"haven't we always assisted the Jews in dealing with their Arab neighbors? It has been English lives that have been sacrificed in keeping the peace."

"This has all gotten out of hand, to be sure," Akiva agreed, dropping his guard and in so doing, dropping the price in the bargain for the arrest of Moshe Sachar. "I am sure my people will appreciate bread for their Shabbat meal. Along with your promise that there will be more. We are sensible people. Not difficult to deal with. Once the criminal element among us is removed—"

"Then you will give me names?" Stewart said with satisfaction.

"After Shabbat. After we have the bread in our hands you may take him. Only one name in exchange for the bread. And you must take him after Shabbat."

Stewart nodded and leaned forward, pressing his fingertips together. "Agreed."

"He is a tall, handsome fellow. He was born of a good family here in the Old City and is well liked, though he is an *aprokosim*, an apostate. He is a renowned archaeologist, and I warn you, if he is injured as those two others you took—"

Stewart waved his hand in dismissal of the thought. "I gave you my word. No martyrs."

"He has a wife and child. They are loved by the people. They must not be touched."

"We are not in the business of hurting women and children. What is the man's name?"

"He is of the house of Sachar. Moshe. Moshe Sachar."

Stewart's eyes widened. He sat up rigidly in his chair. "Sachar? He is here? In the Old City?"

"You know of him, then?" Akiva asked in a puzzled tone.

Stewart shook his head in wonder, calculating the windfall that this would bring to his career. "Don't you know, man? The fellow has been implicated in the Jaffa Gate bombing. He was with the Jewish Agency dealing with convoys and distribution and the like, and someone saw him, recognized him at Jaffa Gate immediately after the bombing. We've had a warrant out for his arrest since Tuesday. He was positively identified by three people who were there. His photograph—"

"A terrorist," Akiva said with grim satisfaction.

"Rabbi Akiva, you are fully justified in giving us this information. To have done less would make you a criminal also. We will make sure his acts are common knowledge after his arrest. That way, if there is any criticism of you—" A flush of excitement climbed to Stewart's cheeks. "Even Zionists claim to abhor what was done at Jaffa Gate. After all, it was that action that stopped the convoys into your quarter."

"Then he is to blame for our situation."

"Exactly." Stewart rose and pocketed the broken eyeglasses. "And no doubt there are others of his persuasion about him." He smiled a tight-lipped smile of determination. "We will handle the matter. He is considered armed and dangerous, of course."

Akiva silently considered his good fortune. His rival was not, after all, a man of valor and honor, but a criminal of the meanest sort. How appropriately were the words of the psalmist applied to Moshe Sachar, soon to be taken to his just end! "Let the wicked fall into their own snare," mused Akiva, taking the loaf of challah and extending his hand in a pact with Stewart.

Yehudit Akiva stood in the center of the large kitchen and stared upward at the wrought iron lamp that hung from the domed ceiling. She trembled with the memory of the words she had heard at the keyhole of her father's study. The English officer would not wait until after Shabbat to arrest Moshe Sachar, Rachel's husband. Today he would take him to the prison in the New City. This afternoon, while the bread was distributed to the people of the quarter and they smiled gratefully into the face of her father, the husband of Rachel would be taken. *It is just,* she thought. *If it was he who helped to murder those at Jaffa Gate, then he is a dangerous man and it is just that he be taken. But he has done so much for the quarter, they say. And the people love him. Rachel Lubetkin loves him.*

Yehudit turned her eyes toward the door that led to the courtyard and out. *If he is guilty, then he must be taken. But if he is innocent, then he must be warned. Choices. I must make a choice.* She could slip out and find Moshe Sachar, perhaps. But if her father knew. . . *And how can I know if he is guilty?* She hugged her shawl tightly around her and remembered the face of Rachel in the street, her eyes full of kindness and light. She remembered the face of Rachel thrown to the floor of Nissan Bek, judged and condemned by the rabbis who followed her father. *Choices.*

She fixed her gaze on the door latch and imagined herself crossing the courtyard and running down the street and pounding on the door of Rachel's apartment. *Tell your husband he must hide himself from the English officer!*

Still Yehudit did not move. *Is it wrong for me to know and say nothing? Or should I risk disobedience to my father and tell the husband of Rachel that he must hide?*

Sweat formed on her brow, and yet she was cold inside. Her stomach felt sick and she wished she had not listened to the words of her father and the Englishman as they plotted. She took a step toward the door, then looked back over her shoulder as though she expected her father to hear her thoughts and storm into the kitchen with his fists doubled and his face a mask of rage. *He cannot hear my thoughts,* she told herself, taking yet another step toward the door.

"Yehudit!" the voice of Rabbi Akiva bellowed from his study. She gasped and shuddered, then wheeled around as his voice again searched her out. "Yehudit! Where is my water for washing?"

Her voice shook as she called weakly back to him, "Coming, Father!" She threw her shawl from her shoulders and rushed to fill his basin of wash water. She would not go to Moshe or Rachel. She could not.

233

Throughout the morning, as the British loaded the bread onto handcarts, Moshe and his men continued to work to tunnel beneath the Armenian Quarter toward the basement storage chamber of D. Agajanian. Dov had escaped somehow, Moshe was certain of that. His body had not been carried from the bakery, and a house-to-house search by British troops and Arab militiamen had turned up nothing. If it was possible, Dov would return to the Jewish Quarter after nightfall.

Loaded handcarts were covered by canvas tarps and trundled off to an unknown destination as a few Jews gathered at the barricade to watch. In the meantime, nearly eight hundred loaves of rescued challah had been whisked away down the tunnels and stacked in neat piles for distribution at Tipat Chalev.

Old rabbis patted Moshe on the back as he passed them in the street, "The Eternal has heard our prayer, young man! You see, the money has not gone to waste, nu? The Eternal has sent us manna, true? Of course true! So, you do your job and we will do ours!"

Smiles decorated the faces of even those who had been the most skeptical. It was a small miracle, to be sure; half the bread had not been rescued, but nevertheless it was a good sign that God was watching.

Moshe did not tell the others of the enormous store of grain that still awaited retrieval beneath the bakery. He would wait until it was safely in their possession so that hopes would not be dashed in the event that they were unable to rescue it. This small delight, this gift for the Shabbat table, was all that was needed to lift morale today. And when morale was low again, the grain would be in their possession and yet another, more dramatic miracle would sustain them. Only a few knew of the treasure that waited half a block away.

Moshe raised his face to the warm sunlight that streamed down between the buildings. He breathed a prayer of thankfulness as he walked briskly toward home. A stooped rabbi in a long ragged coat, with shoes as scuffed and as cracked as his ancient face, shuffled slowly toward Moshe. His gnarled hand raised a cane in greeting, and he cracked a toothless grin behind his snowy white beard.

Moshe did not recognize the old man, but he stopped and

nodded respectfully. "Shabbat shalom, Rabbi," he said when the old man did not take his eyes from him.

"You!" the voice quavered with age. "You are the young fellow!" His hand was still raised. "Praise be to the Eternal. They told me about the challah and I have come to see it for myself. They say you pay a shilling a day for the old ones to pray," he said.

"Yes, Rabbi," Moshe answered in the way he would talk to a child. "Prayer is a good defense."

"A wise fellow you are indeed," the rabbi lisped, for lack of his teeth. "I am the oldest among us." He raised his cane. "I am ninety-nine years old, and only once in my life have I been out from behind these walls, nu? When I was ten and they began to build the houses outside the walls, I went to see. But I came back the same day, and have lived here ever since."

Moshe answered politely, "Yes, Rabbi."

"These old eyes have seen much," he said, pointing to the clouded eyes that hid behind slits of leathery skin. "We here in the quarter are in need of a miracle. I rose from my bed to see the challah. And I will pray also for miracles, whether you pay me a shilling or no."

"A very important thing to do, Rabbi." Moshe patted him gently on his bony shoulder.

"And I would like very much if you will join me to make a minyon and pray this afternoon, nu?" He smiled again. "If I should live so long. And together we will pray for our Messiah to come. I would like to live so long to see Him here. Then maybe we will have a nation. True, young man? Of course true! Together we shall pray in yet another Shabbat at least. Young and old, nu? Four o'clock then. It is agreed. Four o'clock at the Sephardic Synagogue. If you can pay the Ashkenazim to pray, then we Sephardim can pray also."

Moshe glanced at his wristwatch. "At four then, Rabbi. It will be a great honor."

"And we will pray up yet another miracle," said the old man, leaning heavily on his cane. "Such as this almost makes a man feel eighty again!" There was a twinkle in his eyes and Moshe laughed out loud as the rabbi shuffled on toward Tipat Chalev to view the miracle.

"Shabbat shalom. Until four o'clock." Moshe stood and watched the old man creep slowly away, waving his hand in farewell. *For such as these, Lord,* Moshe prayed, *we must preserve the quarter.* To evacuate most of the aged residents would be tantamount to a death sentence. There were many more besides this ancient Sephardic rabbi who had seldom, if ever, set foot outside the gates of the Old City. Their lives had been lived in pursuit of knowledge of the one true God. Moshe stared after him. *If only they could know our Messiah,* he thought sadly. *Then their questions would be answered. What a wealth their knowledge of Torah would bring to the world! What richness would be shared with those who know Jesus and yet do not know the heritage from which He came.* Moshe sighed. For now it was not yet to be. There was only mistrust and fear of Christians by those who sought to know God and live righteously, without knowing the Righteous King of Israel. And those who knew the King did not know His people. *Come soon, Yeshua,* Moshe prayed as the old rabbi tottered away. *Reveal yourself to those who seek you but do not know that it is you they look for.* He looked beyond the Jewish Quarter to the spires and domes of the churches that packed the city of Jerusalem. There was bitterness and division between those who worshiped beneath those roofs, Moshe knew. And the truth of the identity of the Messiah had been obscured and mutilated by hatred, bickering, and corruption. "All our righteousness is as filthy rags," Moshe muttered aloud, remembering the words of Isaiah. "And yet you love us still." Church spires and mosques and synagogues beckoned men to prayer, and yet their hearts were hardened against the God they worshiped and against one another. Moshe shook his head slowly, feeling grief not only for the millions of his own people who had died but for those who had stood by as it happened and those who had planned it—for all of mankind who stood before God as a fractured mockery of righteousness. *And each man does what is right in his own eyes. What was it you called us? White-washed tombs, full of dead men's bones.*

As he stood in the street, the voice of Ehud erupted behind him. "Moshe!" he was out of breath. "I have been looking all over for you!"

Moshe turned to see a red-faced Ehud covered with dust and grime from the tunnels. His first thought was that a wall had collapsed or someone had been injured. "Ehud?"

Ehud took him by the arm and pulled him into an archway of a door. He wiped sweat from his face and looked to the right and left to see if they might be overheard. "Akiva has called a public meeting. At four o'clock at Nissan Bek. He says he has negotiated some great deal with the British, Moshe. He is up to something." He lowered his voice. "Something is amiss. I feel it here." He thumped his great chest.

Moshe frowned, thoughts of the tragedy of division still fresh in his mind. "We should maybe give him a chance to be heard," he replied quietly. "If there is something he has done to help . . . well we can't refuse it just because it comes from the hand of Akiva."

"I can! The man is a devil in Hassidic disguise! You can't tell me you trust him?" Ehud grimaced in disapproval.

"No, I can't say that." Moshe patted him on the back.

"I say that any deal he makes with that Captain Stewart is to betray us."

"Captain Stewart? How do you know—"

"Amos saw Stewart and his men leave Akiva's house. They made no secret of it," Ehud said matter-of-factly. "Remember what Stewart's men did to Shimon and Chaim over one small detonator!" He drew his finger across his throat. "You didn't see it. I did! I tell you this is a man who hates Jews. Some bargain has been struck, so says Akiva. In the marketplace when a bargain has been struck, one pays a price for something the other has, eh?"

"Go to the meeting, Ehud. I am going home for a while to rest. I have not slept since the night before last. At four o'clock I have to meet with the Sephardic rabbis. We can talk after that."

Ehud stuck out his lower lip and studied the weary face of Moshe. Dark circles hung beneath his eyes. "Go home," he said finally. "Sleep. I will keep my eyes and ears open."

Moshe opened the door quietly, aware that Tikvah was most likely asleep. The shutters of the little room were closed, and it was dark except for a tiny stub of a candle that glowed on the table. Dressed in her white camisole and a long, dark blue skirt, Rachel was leaning over a washbasin, her hair dripping sudsy water.

Moshe did not speak for a moment, but stood watching her as she hummed softly, unaware of his presence. For an instant he saw her again as she had been that first night on the *Ave Ma-*

ria—bitter, ashamed, longing for death but afraid to die. Yet even then her beauty had stirred him. He smiled. *So much more beautiful now. Can this be the same Rachel? Vulnerable. Innocent. Able to trust me with her heart as if it had never been betrayed.* There were no more wounds to make her fearful of his touch. There was only the miracle of their love. *Thank you, God, for giving her back her life.*

He drank in this image of her, determined that if times ever seemed hopeless, he would call up this memory. "Rachel," he said softly.

Water dripping down her face, she peered at him out of one eye. "Oh! You are back too soon, Moshe!"

He laughed out loud and remained in the center of the room with his arms crossed. "Just in time, I would say. You are a vision." He glanced at her bare feet and laughed again as she rung the water from her hair. A pink blush crept up her shoulders and then to her neck and into her cheeks.

"Moshe, please!" she begged, clearly embarrassed. "Go away until I am finished!"

"I will not." He tossed his jacket onto the bed. "This is the best view I have had all day." Walking to her, he leaned over to kiss her shoulder.

"Please," she said again. "It isn't proper for you to see me like this. My hair wet and my feet bare . . ."

"Are you finished?" He brushed away her objections and bent down to smile into her wet face.

"No! I just started and the water will get cold if I don't . . ."

Handing her a towel, Moshe pulled a chair over to where she stood. "Then I will help you," he said softly.

She blotted her face and hesitated, looking at him curiously. "What?"

"Come on." He nudged her into the chair and placed the basin on the floor behind her. Gently, he caressed her face in his strong hands. "You know how I love to run my fingers through your hair. Now lay your head back."

A soft light filled her eyes and she obeyed him, feeling her body relax as warm water coursed through her hair and Moshe massaged the back of her neck and head. She sighed with contentment and closed her eyes as the gentle warmth of his touch flowed through her.

Moshe studied her expression, and again, the familiar, exquisite ache of his love for her filled his heart.

She let her head fall back into his hands. "Where did you learn such a thing?" she whispered.

"I am a man of many talents," he replied as he stroked the back of her neck.

"I never heard of a man washing his wife's hair," she said after a long pause. Her words were soft and drowsy with relaxation.

"Oh? Well it is written in the Talmud, Little One." He stroked her cheek. "It is a well-known mitzvah. Babba Moshe twenty."

"Yes?" she opened her eyes, half-believing what he said. He smiled down at her, then kissed her softly on the mouth.

"Yes," he teased. "Now close your eyes." He slowly poured the steamy water over her thick, black hair. Then he rubbed flakes of soap together in his hands and began to massage again.

"Oh, Moshe," she breathed. "I will not be able to stand."

"Then I must be doing something right."

Rachel gazed up into his face and his eyes seemed to speak to her soul. She parted her lips in a smile. "And what else does the Talmud say of a husband's duty to his wife?" she asked as he rinsed the suds away one final time.

"That he is to love her and care for her as himself." He blotted her face and hair with a towel, then pulled her easily to her feet. "And there are other things. Secret things." Moshe held her close and felt her softness against him. "We speak of them only in silent devotions. But I can teach you if you like."

She raised her face to his and he kissed her, taking her breath away. "Teach me then," she whispered, "learned rabbi."

21 Shabbat Sacrifice

The sweet aroma of simmering borscht filled the little apartment as Rachel spread the clean white tablecloth over the table. She had picked up the ration of soup at Tipat Chalev for Moshe and herself and an extra portion for Ehud who would share the Shabbat meal with them tonight. She had heard murmurs among the women in the kitchens that even the miracle of the challah would not be enough to sustain them for long. Very soon there would not even be beets for soup.

Rachel looked at the golden loaf of challah that rested on the counter beside the candlesticks. Somehow, that one loaf was reassuring to her that God was also keeping accounts of the rationing. The Old City Jewish Quarter was not lost yet. When the beets were gone and the last of the challah eaten, somehow enough would be provided. Some among them celebrated the arrival of the bread; others shook their heads and complained, *Not enough. How long can we live on this? It is not enough.* Rachel had answered quietly, "It is enough for tonight. For this Shabbat." But the women still cast an eye toward the dwindling supply of beets, and Rachel understood their fears. They had watched the English soldiers empty Agajanian's bakery of more bread than they had stacked on the tables of Tipat Chalev, and they had felt cheated of what was theirs.

"God," Rachel prayed as she set the shining plates on the table, "if you can provide a little for us, can you also not provide a lot? Or at least enough for each day at a time? *Enough* is as good as a feast, Papa used to say."

She glanced at the clock. It was nearly four. Moshe had gone to pray at the Sephardic complex while the others had gone to hear what Mayor Akiva promised would provide the answers to all their problems.

Rachel felt skeptical, even a bit angry at the thought of Akiva, this jealous and devious man, drawing the confidence of so many after what he had done. She held the silver blade of a knife up and looked at her own reflection, "He feels the same way about you and Moshe, you know," she told herself. She shuddered and put the knife down. Soon it would be Shabbat, and she did not want to begin the evening with a heart that was not at peace.

She went to Leah's old crank phonograph and picked out a thick black record. "Mozart Konzert für Horn und Orchester nr. 3," she read, remembering how music had filled the room as she and Leah had laughed and talked and prepared for that last Shabbat two months before. *How I have changed since then!* she thought. *My soul was so hungry—even a feast was not enough to fill me.* She smoothed her hair back as the sweet strains of the French horn swirled around her. *Now I have Moshe and Tikvah, and for all my life they will be enough.*

A hesitant rapping sounded at the door. Rachel frowned, wondering who had come, since most of the residents of the quarter had gone to Nissan Bek to hear Akiva speak. She opened the door a crack to see the red face of Joseph as he stood panting and out of breath on the landing.

"Mrs. Sachar," he began. "I am looking for Captain Ehud."

"Yes?" She felt a twinge of concern. Fear showed on the young man's face. "Either Ehud is working on the tunnel, or perhaps he has gone to Nissan Bek to hear what Mayor Akiva has to say. I am not certain. He will be here later though, for Shabbat meal."

Joseph clutched his throat. "May I have a glass of water?" he asked.

Rachel stood to one side and let him in as she quickly poured him water from an earthen pitcher. He nodded and gulped it down without a word.

"What is it?" Rachel asked. "What is wrong?"

"If he is at Nissan Bek, he will know." Joseph wiped his lips on the back of his hand.

"Tell me." Rachel took the glass from him, her heart beating faster and a sense of dread filling her.

"Look," he said, crossing to the window and pulling back the corner of the curtains. "They are everywhere."

Rachel followed his finger to the street, gasping as she saw two English soldiers standing together on a corner. "But *why*? Stewart's men have not come here since Chaim and Shimon were murdered by the Arab mob two months ago. At least not many of them, or for very long."

"I will tell you why," he said flatly, his voice carrying the intonation of a war-weary adult. "All the loaves we couldn't get last night? All the loaves Agajanian left for us? Well, the English have brought them into the quarter. To Nissan Bek for Akiva to hand out. Challah is piled high like promises, and word is that maybe they will start the convoys again."

"Why, Joseph!" Rachel exclaimed. "That is good news!"

The boy did not reply for a moment; then he added. "Most of our fellows have gone underground, into the tunnels, until they see what Akiva and the captain are up to. There are soldiers all over the quarter; surely this bread has cost us something."

Rachel put her hand against her cheek and leaned against the counter in deep thought. "Go get Ehud," she said quietly.

"And together, go to Moshe. Maybe this is nothing. Maybe the convoys are going to begin again and Akiva has done something good for us. There must be no trouble on our part, if that is the case. Ehud and Moshe will know what to do." She took him by the shoulders. "But hurry, Joseph," she tried not to let her own fears show themselves in her voice. "Hurry and find them; then come back and tell me what they say."

———————

The day that had begun so bright and cloudless grew gray and threatening. Four o'clock. Handcarts piled high with challah surrounded the bimah in the center of Nissan Bek Synagogue where Rabbi Akiva stood with his hands outstretched over the people who jammed the auditorium. He smiled benevolently at them as they eyed the great mounds of bread and murmured among themselves.

"My friends," he began, "I have called you here—" The murmur of the crowd died down and eyes looked expectantly up to where Akiva stood.

Ehud glowered from the back of the room. His face was a reflection of the disapproval he felt for the people who gulped the words of Akiva with the same eagerness with which they would soon devour Akiva's offering of challah.

". . . For some time I have been negotiating with the English in hopes of acquiring bread for our quarter. Last night a good bit of the bread was stolen."

The people talked excitedly among themselves as Akiva paused for effect. ". . . by some among us who are of the criminal element and believe that violence is the only way to achieve our goals . . ."

Ehud crossed his arms angrily and wished that he had the note from D. Agajanian to show the assembly. But it was burned to ashes now, and there was no hope of calling Akiva a liar. His loaves far outnumbered those at Tipat Chalev. Ehud would report these words of deception to Moshe and together they would decide what best to do. He looked up at the murals of Moses smashing the tablets of law, and wondered what the Law-Giver would have said in answer to the sweet, deceitful words of Rabbi Akiva. *So, God, Akiva takes the credit for delivering this bread to the quarter, eh? Smite him with your right arm. That is your challah. The*

Armenian baked it and you delivered it into our hand. True? Of course true.

"The very fellow who is responsible for the Jaffa Gate bombing, the end of the convoys, and the death of two of our citizens moves among us like a wolf among the sheep . . ."

"Who does he speak of?" Ehud muttered aloud and stood erect at the sound of his words.

A small nudge in his ribs caused him to look down at his left elbow. Covered by her shawl, Yehudit Akiva stood slightly behind him. "You are a friend of the husband of Rachel," she whispered in a barely audible voice. "You must warn him. Go now, if you know where he is."

Ehud stared at her, dumbfounded as she moved quickly through the crowd and away from him. Then he looked at Akiva; the smile on his face. "So!" he said as Akiva spoke.

". . . and we have the assurance from the English captain that if and when this fellow is gone from our midst, then the convoys will resume. We will not go hungry! We will not have to leave our homes!"

As the crowd applauded, Ehud dashed out the door of Nissan Bek into the street. A quick glance told him that, indeed, the British had exacted a price for the challah that was heaped in Nissan Bek. On every corner an armed soldier stood, scanning the streets and the rooftops. Ehud pulled the collar of his coat up and strolled easily down the broad steps into the street. His pace was slow and deliberate, even though his heart raced with the thoughts that Moshe was to be betrayed at any moment. Was he, too, marked for arrest?

"Ehud!" a young voice called to him. He turned to see the worried face of red-haired Joseph hurrying toward him.

"Why, Joseph!" he hailed the young man as though there were nothing wrong.

Joseph lowered his voice. "All the soldiers. What is it?" he asked as Ehud clapped him on the back.

"Well, it looks as though we will have our challah for Shabbat, my boy!" he said loudly; then he covered his lips as he wiped his hand across his beard. "Go now, quickly. Moshe prays with the Sephardim in their synagogue. Be calm, boy! Tell him to hide in the tunnels. *Now!*"

Applause echoed from inside the Nissan Bek. Joseph asked no questions; instead, he walked quickly away from Ehud. Ehud yawned and stretched, then sauntered after the boy in the same direction. He nodded pleasantly at the British soldiers who stood with their sten guns on their hips. They were not there to guard the Jews from harm, of that much Ehud was certain.

Ahead of him, Ehud could see Joseph duck into the shop of a tin smith. *Smart lad,* thought Ehud, aware that the tunnel from the cellar of the shop ran in a direct line toward the Sephardic Synagogues.

Ehud nodded pleasantly at a grim-faced young soldier, who stared at him with blank disinterest as he passed. He quickened his pace and turned a corner as Joseph emerged from the shoe-maker's shop across the street. Half a block away, he could see the low rooftops of the synagogues that were below ground, down a narrow flight of stairs.

Several soldiers stood in the square surrounding the Sephardic complex. Joseph walked quickly past them without looking up as Ehud still strolled nonchalantly behind him. "Hurry, boy," he muttered, hearing the march of footsteps behind him. He inwardly cheered as Joseph's bright hair disappeared down the stairway.

Ehud browsed for a moment through the window of the half-empty shoemaker's store. Clasping his hands behind his back, he rocked on his toes and studied the display of shoes. Then he lifted up his foot and looked at the sole of his shoe. He could see the entrance to the synagogue in the reflection of the window-pane. Seconds passed like long minutes and Moshe did not emerge with the boy. When he did, Ehud knew, it would only be a few steps into the nearest shop to the safety of the tunnels. *What are they doing?* he fretted, feeling his hands grow damp with sweat.

He counted six British uniforms in the square. All seemed to be watching the synagogue. No one even glanced in his direction. As the sound of boots against the paving stones grew nearer, Ehud turned and slowly moved toward the steps where he knew Moshe had gone. He touched the yarmulke on his head and walked down the dark stairway toward the massive wooden doors. There was no sound in the shadows and he reached out toward the latch. Behind him he heard the certain click of a pistol cocking to ready.

"You may stop where you are," said a menacing voice. "Ehud Schiff, is it?"

Ehud stood with his hand poised on the latch. "What do you want?" he asked quietly as the sound of running echoed in the street above.

"Turn around, please," said the crisp English voice.

Captain Stewart stood in the shadows beside the stair, his hand covering Joseph's mouth as he held the boy in a hammer-lock. "What do you want?" Ehud asked again.

"Why, Captain Schiff. What a silly question. You know very well why we are here. We have cornered our prey quite easily, don't you think? While he prays."

Ehud narrowed his eyes threateningly. "Let the boy go," he growled.

"So he can bring the rest of your men down on us? We are trying very hard to avoid an ugly incident, you see. That's why we are waiting out here for your friend." He motioned with his gun for Ehud to stand away from the door. Ehud did not move. "We will take you with us, of course," said Stewart. "As an ac-complice. Were you also part of the Jaffa Gate bombing?" he asked.

Ehud snorted in disgust. "You are a fool, Englishman." He moved a step closer. "Let the boy go."

"You are a fool, Schiff, if you think I won't shoot you where you stand." He pulled Joseph tighter against him and the boy tried to shout from beneath Stewart's firmly clamped hand.

"I am no fool, Englishman," Ehud muttered.

"We will do our best, of course, to avoid giving you Jews any additional martyrs." Shadows of soldiers circled the landing above them.

Ehud glanced upward at the same time as Joseph. The boy squirmed and kicked out at the captain; then, finally opening his mouth wide enough, he clamped his teeth around the captain's fingers.

Stewart yelled and hit the boy hard, throwing him across the bottom step as three more soldiers rushed down. In an instant, Ehud lunged toward the door and flung it open, bellowing into the quiet hall, "Moshe, run!"

Confusion filled the entrance of the synagogue. Ehud saw Moshe standing in the center of the hall in his silk tallith, his mouth open and his prayer book in his hands. Wide-eyed old men stood beside him as the guards charged through the door, slamming Ehud in the back of the head with the butt of a sten gun. Joseph cried out as the rattle of gunfire raked the plaster dome of the synagogue, and the old rabbis covered their heads and cried out to God. Moshe stood still and unresisting as they charged, and yet Stewart tore the tallith from his head and threw it to the ground as his men hit him hard in the stomach and searched him for weapons. There was no hope of escape; Moshe had seen that in the first moment they had opened the door.

"He's clean, Captain!" shouted the soldier who searched him. "No weapons."

Stewart grabbed Moshe by the hair and pulled his head back, placing the muzzle of his gun at Moshe's throat. "No funny business, Sachar. We have orders to shoot to kill you on sight. No questions asked. Behave yourself. We are going out of the city in peace. Do you understand?"

A strong young man with a neck like a bull kicked Ehud in the back and pulled him to his feet. "And that goes for you as well."

———

It was nearly sunset before Joseph, clutching Moshe's torn Tallith, stumbled up the Street of the Stairs. The alleyways of the quarter were totally deserted and silent except for the heavy panting of the boy as he hurried toward Rachel's apartment. The British soldiers were gone now. Surrounding Moshe and Ehud, they had vanished from the Old City before the people emerged from Nissan Bek with their arms laden with bread and their hearts lifted by the promise of food convoys under the direction of Rabbi Akiva. They had all gone home for their Shabbat meals, unaware that Moshe was the one Akiva had meant when he spoke of the criminal among them. They would pass a quiet Shabbat, ignorant of the fate that had befallen the courageous young man who had worked so hard in their midst.

Tears streamed freely down Joseph's ruddy cheeks. He had a bruise on his left cheek and a cut above his eyes where the boot of an English soldier had kicked him. He did not remember much after that. When he had come to, only Moshe's tallith lay where it had fallen and a very old rabbi had sat alone on a bench and wept as he told of the arrest of Moshe and Ehud.

Through windows above him he could see the soft glow of Shabbat candles being lit. Wives and mothers encircled the flames with their arms and pronounced the blessings of the Tahina. Each, no doubt, remembered to thank God for the loaves that now rested on their shining tables.

Joseph ran harder, trying to beat the sunset to the door of Rachel Sachar. He jogged beneath the dark vault that covered the street and the echo of his own footsteps seemed to pursue him with the horror of the price the quarter had paid for the loaves of Mr. Agajanian's Shabbat bread.

Finally he reached the foot of Rachel's stairs. He leaned heavily against the banister, not at all certain that he had the strength to climb to her door. When he looked up to the landing, she stood there, her eyes wide with understanding and her skin pale with grief. She did not look into Joseph's face, but kept her gaze steadily on the torn tallith in his grip. Slowly, her arms at her sides, she walked down the steps. She stopped and stood in silence on the step above him, then she reached out and he placed the tallith into her hands. He bit his lip in grief for her as she laid her cheek against the silk and said the name, "Moshe."

"He is not dead," Joseph's voice trembled. "They have taken him. Him and Ehud. The old rabbi told me they are arrested for the Jaffa Gate bombing." The words came in a rush.

She did not respond, but closed her eyes and said again, "Moshe." After a long time of silence, she turned and, still holding the tallith to her cheek, ascended up the steps and closed the door quietly behind her.

Joseph sat down heavily on the bottom step. He cradled his head in his hands and wept openly—not for Rachel or for himself or Moshe or Ehud, but for the people who were bought so easily for a loaf of challah and a promise of more.

———

Never had there been a night so dark. Even the faint glow of the moonlight lay veiled behind a thick layer of black clouds. Sunlight had slipped away, bringing Shabbat on its heels, and Rachel had not lit the candles in time. It was too late—too late to light them unless she violated the injunction against work.

So she fed Tikvah in the dark. And rocked her in the dark. When the child slept against her shoulder, she laid her in the cradle and sat alone, clutching Moshe's tallith in the dark. And she knew that the night was not half so black as the hole that ripped her soul wide open and left her to bleed without comfort. Unlit Shabbat candles. Uneaten soup and bread. Clean plates and silverware. Goblets still waiting for the wine. Her life was suddenly, once again, all of those things. And hope was crushed like a dying ember within her heart.

She could find no words to utter except the name of Moshe. And the God who had seemed so very present not long ago now seemed, once again, unreachable and distant. The English had taken Moshe—like they had taken Chaim and Shimon; like they had forbidden her family entrance into Palestine and pursued the *Ave Maria* with their gunboats. Those same people now had her Moshe. She played out each scene again and again in her mind and the blackness of the night was the backdrop as she sat silently in the rocking chair and remembered. The clock ticked. Hours passed and she wished for footsteps on the stair that would come to take her away, too. She listened to the soft breathing of the baby and to the beating of her own heart, and she wished that it would all end.

Think of good things, she told herself. And she remembered Moshe's touch and the look of his face and his gentle smile until she felt near to madness. These few weeks in the shelter of his love had been a feast. But it was not enough now that he was taken. *Can you leave me so alone, God? Now that I have known him, can I live without him? Like the challah you sent to us this time; this little moment of our love is not enough. If my heart is to keep beating and my mind to stay sane, God, I will need more than memories to feed on. If I am to live without him, God, you must feed me with your love, for I have no reason to wish that the sun will rise again in the morning.*

She wept into the tallith that had hung so proudly over his broad shoulders. And she was certain of nothing anymore except that, yes, in all of this, God was still God. In the darkness she whispered the words that Job had once uttered, "For I know that my Redeemer lives and that in the latter days he will stand upon the earth." Moshe had told her that someday that same Redeemer would dry all her tears forever. She would believe that. But for now, there was no hand to hold in the darkness but her own.

PART 3

The Deed
Mid-March through
April 9, 1948

*"At times you think that things have come
to their end, that you are no longer
capable of doing anything. You are
mistaken if you think so. Do not let
apathy and despair overpower you, or
even influence you. Harness yourself to
hard, intensive work; work as hard as
you can. . . ."*

Published in a Jewish underground paper in Warsaw during
the Nazi occupation

22   For the Peace of Jerusalem

The skies over southern California were crystal clear and bright. A soft March wind swept through groves of oranges and carried the first scent of blossoms over the Burbank airport.

David pried up the dirty window of his office and took a deep breath. A whiff of aviation fuel blended with the smell of orange blossoms. He smiled with satisfaction and turned to Michael, who was perched on the edge of the scarred desk sipping a cup of cold coffee. "Now, that's what I call air," he said.

Just a few dozen yards away, mechanics shouted at one another and cursed as a tray of tools clattered to the pavement below the wing of a large, rather shopworn, Lockheed Constellation. It was one of three in front of the rented hangar that bore the logo of *Service Airways*. David was listed on the registration as president and Michael as vice-president. Two out of ten C-47 transport planes sat next to the Connies, and the others waited at Ontario airport to be ferried to the field in Burbank.

Mechanics scrambled over the wings of the distinctive, three-tailed Constellations as David shook his head in amazement at the scene. Each of the planes had cost the government a quarter of a million dollars to build. Each had been sold to David and Service Airways for a paltry fifteen thousand dollars, on seven hundred dollars down payment. Even as the planes were being reconditioned, Golda Meir was traveling around the nation speaking on behalf of the embryonic State of Israel and raising millions of dollars with which to equip it. Publicly, the President was still favoring an arms embargo, but privately, David and a handful of others knew he felt differently. Funds raised for defense were being laundered through various organizations and fictitious companies until they trickled slowly into the account of Service Airways. Not only was David able to purchase a fleet of aircraft, he was currently paying top wages to mechanics who had been lured away from Lockheed, TWA, and Douglas Aircraft.

"Some supervisor from Lockheed called." Michael sipped his

251

coffee laconically. "The guy was mad. I mean we're talking maniac here. Said we stole half his best mechanics. Nobody can compete with a buck seventy-five an hour."

David nodded and inhaled deeply. "He's right. What did you say?"

Michael grinned. "I hired the guy. Sam Baker. Nobody knows Connies like him. What he knows ain't in the books, you know?"

David gave a short burst of laughter. "I always thought you were short on brains, Scarecrow. Now I find I got myself a pure genius for a vice-president."

Michael nodded in agreement. "You're right. He'll be here after lunch. So. Now we got mechanics by the dozen and enough planes to compete with the Air Force. All we need is pilots. And co-pilots. And flight engineers. We can pay them—if we can find them."

David's stomach growled. He had skipped breakfast, and it was nearly eleven o'clock. "Got any suggestions? The only guys we knew to ask are already in Palestine—Bobby Milkin and those guys." He glanced out the window and spotted the shapely form of Angela walking briskly toward the office. Grease-smeared mechanics stopped their work and turned their heads toward her. Here and there a wolf whistle careened off the top of a plane and pursued her as she moved past them with total disregard. David grimaced. The sight of Angela rarely gave him any pleasure. And the fact that she had moved into an adjoining room next to Michael at the Hollywood Roosevelt Hotel made him extremely uncomfortable. "Here's your girl," he said dully as he moved aside and Michael stepped up to the window.

Michael took a quick glance at Angela, dressed in a blue sweater and matching skirt. She wore dark glasses and carried a sheaf of papers in her hand. "Hey, you got it!" Michael shouted; then he charged out the door and met her just beneath the wing tip of a Constellation. She wrapped her arms around his neck and kissed him as the wolf whistles and catcalls increased in volume. David grunted, then sat down in the chair behind his desk. He put his hands behind his head and fixed a polite smile on his face as Michael banged the door open and entered with Angela. He waved her papers above his head excitedly.

"Now here's the genius!" Michael put his arm around Angela. "Pure genius, boy! I'm tellin' you!"

"Hello, Angela," David said without enthusiasm. "Good to see you."

Her face hardened a bit as she studied his expression. "Is it?" she asked in an injured tone.

"Look at this." Michael laid the sheets reverently in front of David. "Look!"

David sniffed and pursed his lips, then looked down at what appeared to be lists of names. "Yeah? What is it?"

"I'm telling you, the girl's a genius!" Michael rubbed his hands together and kissed her on the cheek.

"I don't think David is interested in my help," Angela said flatly.

"David!" Michael cried. "Look at the lists, will you? She's gotten us the complete list of veteran pilots from the V.A.! Names, addresses, phone numbers! Take a look!"

David cleared his throat uncomfortably and picked up the papers on his desk. The cynicism so firmly etched on his face began to fade as he studied the alphabetical listings of names.

"Not just pilots," Angela said quietly. "Co-pilots, flight engineers, and navigators as well."

Dumbfounded, David stared in disbelief at the names and former occupations of the men who had fought the airwar over Europe and the Pacific. "But how?" he asked, feeling suddenly ashamed of his suspicion and dislike of Angela.

"She's a genius, that's how!" Michael bubbled.

"I don't know what to say." David frowned and looked up into her face.

She pulled her sunglasses off and her brown eyes seemed to radiate hurt and disappointment. "You could try 'Thank you.' "

"Yes." David stood slowly. "I guess I could. Uh. Thank you. Thank you, Angela. Really, this is great." He laughed uneasily. "Michael's right. You're a genius."

Michael dragged a wobbly chair across the concrete floor for Angela. She sat down and crossed her legs. "Great," Michael said. "Now we all agree. So tell me, how do we get in touch with these guys?"

Angela did not take her eyes from David, who gazed back at her with a mix of admiration and remorse. "I thought perhaps we might ring them up?"

"Ring them up!" Michael exclaimed. "Hey, Tinman, don't you just love her accent? Sure. We'll just call all the ones that look like they got Jewish names, huh? Easy. Didn't I tell you she was great?"

"Yep," David said softly. "You did. I guess you're a good judge of character, Scarecrow."

"Scarecrow had a heart, did he not?" Angela said. "It was the other one, the tinman, who had no heart."

"Ah, come on, Angela," Michael joked. "He's got a heart. And a great big one, too. You just have to get to know him—ain't that right, Tinman? How about let's all be friends now?"

David blew his breath out slowly. "Well, I guess I'm willing," he said. "I'm afraid I misjudged you." He tucked his chin. "You've just saved us a couple years of hard work, you know."

"Apology accepted," she said after a moment of hesitation. "David."

Armed with two hundred dollars in nickels, Angela and Michael manned the phone booths in the lobby of the Hollywood Roosevelt Hotel while David worked alongside the mechanics and the surly new Lockheed supervisor who joined the team after a small squabble about wages. David grudgingly paid the man the princely sum of three dollars an hour, fully aware that this was, indeed, the fellow who had almost written the book on Lockheed Constellations.

His head beneath the metal cowling of an engine, David failed to notice the figure who stood quietly at the foot of his ladder. At the sound of a deep, throaty cough, David raised up and looked down at the concrete runway below him. A gray-haired man in a blue, four-button suit shaded his eyes and stared back at David. He had the look of a government man; the carriage of one who would do his duty, no matter how minute, at any cost or personal sacrifice. He was, David thought, the masculine version of an old maid librarian who raised a finger to her lips in a *shhh* at the slightest provocation. David muttered an involuntary "uh-oh," and ducked beneath the cowling to stare at the engine again in hopes the man would go away.

"I say there!" The fellow called up. "Are you David Meyer?"

David pretended to ignore him.

"Mr. Meyer? Captain Meyer?" the man called again.

David did not raise his head. "Meyer ain't here," he said loudly.

"Captain Meyer!" the fellow insisted. "All these mechanics cannot be mistaken about the man who pays them such generous wages. My name is Samuel Alexander. I am with the CAA. Civil Aeronautics. . . ? You have heard of us, I assume?"

David grimaced and stared hard at the Pratt and Whitney engine of the Connie. He sighed in resignation and glanced down at the granite-faced federal official. He had been hoping to complete work without government interference. "I'm your man," he grinned and descended the ladder. He stayed on the bottom rung and extended his hand. The man's handshake was limp and unfriendly. He peered up past David at the aircraft.

"Your *airline*"—he said the word with disdain—"is in violation of several regulations of the CAA," he commented caustically.

"Yeah? How's that? We just took delivery on the ships. My partner and I only ferried over two of the gooney-birds this morning from Ontario. How can we be in violation?"

"As a federally registered airline, you are required to equip all planes for civilian use. *Civilian!*" he emphasized. "These gooney-birds, as you call the C-47 transports, are obviously still equipped for military use. Troop and heavy equipment transportation. All this"—he motioned broadly with his hand—"must be removed before you can fly them commercially *anywhere* in the U.S."

"But—but—that will take months of work! Thousands and thousands of dollars!"

The man raised his eyebrows. "Well, if that is a problem for you, you should have thought of that before you decided to start an airline. Shouldn't you?" He smiled, then pulled the smile away in a moment. His expression was grim and officious as he handed David a list of requirements for renovating military planes for civilian use. "Failure to comply will result in the grounding of all your planes and a loss of your CAA license."

David scanned the page in dismay. Seats had to be replaced, equipment ramps removed and modified, radio equipment replaced, and even toilets installed for men and women. "Months!" he muttered as the CAA official walked away in satisfaction after a warning that he would return to check on progress. "Thousands of dollars." David felt a sinking feeling in the pit of his stomach as he read the words *Impounded aircraft for violation of codes* on the bottom of the paper. "And the Old Man wants everything done and in Palestine yesterday!"

As the funds raised by Golda Meir were quietly passed along through channels in the United States and Europe, surplus weapons were being purchased and assembled at various points for these very planes to carry on to Palestine. This hitch would delay their plans at least until May. Possibly longer. And, David knew, any longer would certainly prove fatal to the hopes of a homeland.

David stalked to his cluttered desk and picked up a cable that had arrived through an unnamed messenger the night before. It read simply; SERVICE AIRWAYS. YOUR AIRPLANES DO US NO SERVICE IN BURBANK AMERICA. MOST URGENT YOU RETURN TO ROME WITH BIRDS AND DRIVERS TO AWAIT FURTHER ACTION. BG

As for David, he wanted nothing more than to return to his Palestine milkrun with a flock of new birds and drivers. Mostly he wanted to see Ellie's face and hear her voice once again. Even if his mechanics were miracle workers and finished before May 14, David still did not have the crews he needed to fly the planes. He sat down heavily in the dilapidated desk chair. Angrily he scrawled out a simple reply, easily passed in code through channels to Ben-Gurion's new headquarters in Tel Aviv. The wire read, *Working for miracles. May one. DM*

It was nearly sundown before David climbed wearily into the 1936 Chevy convertible that he had locked in the garage of a friend before he left for Palestine six months before. He pulled to the shoulder along a nearly deserted two-lane road to tug the cloth top down so he could get the full effect of the orange groves in bloom.

He stood for a moment in the waning light and stared at the ragged horsehair seats and the broken speedometer of his old, familiar car. Memories of picnics with Ellie and trips to the beach and quiet nights alone with her in his arms returned with a force that made him nearly reel with missing her. The car was the same; the orange groves and sleepy villages of California were unchanged. The warm spring breeze and first gleaming stars were just as they had been on a thousand other spring nights. But everything was different, somehow. *He* had changed. Things mattered now that had never mattered before, and the peace of this place and this moment took on an unreality that almost frightened him. More real to him now was the scent of smoke and death and the constant staccato popping of gunfire in the streets of Jerusalem. Recent events, and the peril of those he had come to love in faraway Palestine, shattered an innocence he had carried with him even as a pilot fighting the Nazis over Europe. At least then the American people had been behind what he was doing. They were at war here, too. Shoulder to shoulder they worked, and even here, in the middle of scented orange groves, there had been no feeling of peace for this country.

That had been some comfort to him and the rest of the fighting men. *Now,* he thought angrily, *every other guy is working nine to five and coming home to a nice little wife and slippers and a pipe and Edgar Bergen on the radio, and here I am. Dear Lord, I wish I didn't know about this mess. I wish I had never heard of it except in the newspapers.* It was one thing to be in the middle of a dogfight over Germany; it was quite another to live with people for whom the war had never ended, to see their faces and know their stories. Rachel, Moshe, Ben-Gurion, Yacov and Grandfather—their faces were as vivid before him as Ellie's sweet smile. God had called him to this impossible task, David knew, and he was willing to work, even though he would have rather been counted among the millions of GIs who came home believing that their world was once again safe and at peace. "I resent this a little, God," he said aloud. "I guess you know that? Well, I'm here anyway, aren't I? You made me care about these people of yours. So now you're going to have to figure out a way to make this whole thing pull together. Because frankly, I'm stumped. Just when I think we got it figured out, some government monkey comes along and throws a wrench in the gears."

David leaned against the car door and crossed his arms as he stared up into the darkening heavens as though he were expecting an immediate and audible answer. But there was none. Dim stars brightened and the sweet aroma of blossoms surrounded him, but he could not find the solution to the refitting requirement the CAA had just used to ground his planes. "Somebody's got one lousy sense of timing, Lord. I hope it isn't you." David glanced at his watch and noted the time. He had left it set on Palestine time just so he could know in a moment what Ellie was doing. Tomorrow's sun was just now coming up. David tried to imagine her at the new Tel Aviv headquarters as she lifted her tousled head from her pillow. *Good morning, David.* But all he could bring to his mind was that last afternoon in the basement of the Jewish Agency building when they had danced in the candlelight beneath the banner that read, *Honeymoon Suite, King David's Hotel.* Ellie had laid her head against his shoulder and whispered, "Anywhere you are is the City of David."

Tonight, his brow creased with worry, he answered her, "You're right about that, Ellie. And I brought the whole war right back home with me." He looked up helplessly at the sky. "Now the question is, how do we get it back to Palestine where it belongs before it's too late?"

———

Looking up toward the sea wall where massive breakers slammed against the stones, Ellie walked slowly along the beach of Tel Aviv. Huge ships of the Royal Navy were at anchor, none daring to brave the storm that raged over the Mediterranean. Only the most foolhardy of smugglers would attempt to run contraband to the shore of Palestine in weather like this, anyway. Nature herself had blockaded the shore from refugee boats and boats whose holds contained weapons or equipment that might aid the Yishuv in its struggle against the violence of the Arabs and the apathy of the world.

Tucked in the pocket of her yellow rain slicker was a damp copy of this morning's issue of the *Palestine Post. Moshe Sachar, Professor of Archaeology Hebrew University, Implicated in Bombing.*

Ellie looked back over her shoulder to the little red house where Ben-Gurion and his wife Paula had taken up residence, giving Ellie a spare bedroom. For the first time in weeks food was plentiful since their arrival in Tel Aviv. But Ellie and the others who had shared in the hunger of Jewish Jerusalem found themselves eating with a sense of anguish for those they had left behind. Far from being good for her, the fresh sea air of Tel Aviv had deepened her grief for Jerusalem, for dear Rachel, and for Moshe and Ehud as they languished behind the bars of the dank Central Prison. A feeling of helplessness settled in on her as she passed the days in Tel Aviv in relative safety. It was easier to face the sunrise when she was among those who were in danger. Now, her every thought was spent on seemingly futile hopes for the salvation of the Holy City. Yacov, Grandfather, Uncle Howard— all of them suffered, while she was sentenced to walk along the beach and wish for an assignment to take her into the thick of the fray once again.

At least news had been encouraging from the States and David. The scrolls were in the proper hands and had provided collateral for David's air force. And he too, was doing something. *Doing* something; while she did nothing but pray. Those in Jerusalem were doing something. They were hanging on. And here she was, eating well, sleeping in a comfortable bed—and waiting. Doing *nothing*.

The cold salt air stung her nostrils and numbed her cheeks. The distant crash of the surf echoed as sea gulls circled and called above her. The sea and the birds, it seemed, continued on as they always had. When the Romans had landed on this shore—and the Crusaders and the Turks and the British—the sea birds had followed ships and called the same, unchanging plaintive cry: *Peace! Peace! Peace!* But there was no peace on the shores of Palestine. Nor would there ever be, Ellie knew, until the One they waited for returned to Zion.

Ellie lifted her chin and inhaled deeply of the aroma of the seashore. "It smells like Santa Monica," she said aloud to the birds. "Are you sure we aren't in Santa Monica and all of this has been a dream?"

Peace! Peace! Peace, the gulls replied. Ellie remembered the flock that had circled high above the *Ave Maria* as she had chugged out to rendezvous with a freighter filled with refugees. She turned her eyes to the gray hulks of British gunboats. *No, that wasn't a dream.* A homeland; that was the dream that had called men to deeds so hopeless, yet so brave, that Ellie's own heart had nearly burst with admiration for these who were God's chosen. Moshe, Rachel, Yacov, Ehud, Howard, Luke, even her own dear David . . . whether they were simply holding a thin line against the Arab threats, or building the little air force, each one of them was working for the Return. "And so am I, Lord," she whispered. "Standing here on the beach praying for the peace of Jerusalem. Like your sea gulls, I guess I *am* doing something too."

———

His jaw set with uncharacteristic anger, Michael Cohen paced back and forth in front of the window of David's room. A floor lamp with a dark green shade was the only light, and the dimness of the room at midnight made the darkness of their moods seem even more intense. David lay in bed with his hands under his head and watched Michael bounce back and forth like a ping-pong ball.

"And I thought we were going to be all set!" he exclaimed. "A couple of weeks at the most." He cursed and kicked over a wooden chair at the bedside. "Can they do that? Ground us until we get everything just the way they want it?"

"They did it," David said in a rusty and tired voice. "I sent the Old Man a wire in Tel Aviv. Explained the situation. Told him to get Ellie up there taking pictures of the new air strips at least so we will know what we're flying into when we do get these babies in the air."

"But May first! David, they need the stuff *now*! Angela and I went to a movie and you should have seen the newsreels! Jerusalem is bottled up like a bug in a jar. And that buddy of yours . . . Moshe Sachar?"

David sat bolt upright. "What about him?"

"The British hauled him out of the Old City in chains. Got him on trial for the Jaffa Gate bombing."

"Are you sure?" David felt a familiar sick hopelessness overtake him. "Are you sure about the name?"

"I'm sure about the face. The guy looked pretty beat up, though. They got him and some other fella at the Central Prison. It don't look good, Tinman. The news reports made it sound like he was really guilty."

David groaned and put his head in his hands. "Poor Rachel," he muttered.

"Poor everybody if we don't get those planes off the ground and get a few supplies to the men who need them." He stopped and pulled the slats of the venetian blinds down to look out at the imposing edifice of Graumann's Chinese Theater across the street. "Do you suppose somebody blew the whistle on us with the CAA? You think maybe somebody tipped them off? I mean, that we are headed for Palestine? It's just one more thing to hold us up. And here we got a whole list of flyers coming here tomorrow to interview. I thought we were . . ." He paused and his voice trailed off as the neon of the theater marquee blinked eerily on his face.

"I've thought of all that," David said miserably. "But I don't know anybody but us who knows enough of the details to fill anybody in. As far as the mechanics are concerned we're a legitimate operation." David looked up at Michael's intense profile.

Michael squinted and continued to stare down to where tourists matched their hands and feet to the handprints and footprints of movie stars set in the concrete in front of the theater. "What's up?" David asked again.

"I dunno." Michael's voice was almost a whisper. "I mean, all night, me and Angela kept seeing this guy. A little guy with thick glasses. At dinner and then behind us at the movie. And I think I've seen him somewhere before tonight. And he's down there now. Looking up here."

David was out of bed, standing beside Michael in his shorts and undershirt. He peeked out the window following Michael's gaze. "There's fifty people down there prowling around." David's voice betrayed irritation.

"Look," Michael pointed. "The little guy there in the rumpled blue suit. Under the poster on the right."

David saw the small, disheveled-looking man with glasses so thick that even his large nose seemed as though it would not support them. The man lit a cigarette and stared openly up toward their window. "Yeah. Yeah," David nodded. "I think I've seen him somewhere before, too. But where? Maybe he's not looking up here at all. How many rooms are in this hotel, anyway?"

"Looks harmless enough," Michael frowned. "Like an accountant. Hold it a minute. See what he does when I switch off the light."

David continued to watch the man while Michael flicked off the light switch. "Well, will you look at that!" The man looked away as the light blinked off; then he shifted his weight, threw down his cigarette butt and crossed the street toward the hotel. "Looks like we got ourselves a shadow, Scarecrow," he whispered.

The man dodged traffic and scurried onto the sidewalk directly below their rooms. "Angela noticed him first," Michael said quietly. "You know, I wouldn't have noticed the guy if he'd reared up and asked me for a light. She's good at noticing. Spots everything. Could you believe that list she brought in today?"

David did not reply for a long moment, but continued watching as the man disappeared beneath the blue canvas awning of the hotel entrance. "She's okay, Scarecrow. I guess I misjudged her by a mile. I figured she was just another newspaper reporter on the make for a story, but she has really come through for us. She's okay."

"Glad to hear you admit it," Michael said smugly as he switched the light back on. "I've gotten kind of attached to her, if you know what I mean. What I'm saying is . . ." He stumbled for words and blushed. "I'm thinking about getting hitched, y'know. I mean, uh, if she'll have me."

David grinned at Michael, still feeling a sense of uneasiness about his words. But he submerged any objections and said, "Well now, that's great, Scarecrow. Really great."

" 'Course, I ain't asked her yet. You know, she's so intelligent and gorgeous. I still can't figure out what she sees in a guy like me."

"Well, you're gorgeous too, Scarecrow." David slugged him playfully on the arm. "Since she knows Ellie, maybe we can make a foursome at pinochle some time."

"Well, I ain't asked her yet; but, David, I think she really loves me, you know. I mean . . ." He rolled his eyes with enthusiasm and gave a low whistle. "And is she ever smart. Figured out what was going on with us, and I never said a word to her. And now we got all the flyboys in the world coming over to apply for jobs in the morning." He cleared his throat uncomfortably. "I know you weren't exactly thrilled about the way things developed here . . ." Scarecrow finished lamely.

"I just didn't want to see you get in over your head. Slow down a little, Scarecrow. I mean, life is kind of up in the air for us now."

"Look who's talking." Michael threw his head back in a laugh. "Mister one-night-stand honeymooner himself."

David rubbed a hand wearily across his face. "You're right. And you're a big boy. You're going to do what you want anyway, so . . ." David raised his hands in surrender and climbed back into bed. "Be careful, will ya?"

"I'm ready for anything," Michael said. "Including the book-keeper downstairs." He pulled back his jacket to reveal a .38 caliber revolver tucked in his waistband.

David grinned and reached under his pillow. He pulled out an enormous .45 with a long, dull black barrel. "Me, too."

23   A Time for Risk

Sunlight streamed through the dusty venetian blinds of David's drab room at the Hollywood Roosevelt Hotel. Michael stood at the door with a clipboard and David sat at the chipped wooden desk with a sheaf of applications. Pilots on the right, co-pilots on the left, and flight engineers in the center.

In a red and black flannel shirt and Levis, David did not look like the budding young executive of a brand new airline, but his casual attire did not seem to make any difference to the unemployed airmen who flocked to be interviewed.

A baby-faced young man with black hair and round-rimmed glasses stood fidgeting in front of David. David studiously considered the application before him.

"Mick Grady?" David asked, noting the Irish name of the applicant. "Navigator."

Mick Grady held his hat in his hands and twirled it around on his finger. "That's right. Thirty-seven missions over Deutschland, and I got us there every time. *Uber alles*," he said with a cocky confidence. "And I can do it without a compass. Celestial navigation. I can do it."

David squinted down at the name. *How,* he wondered, *had a name like Grady gotten on a list of Steinbergs and Rosewalds and Goldsteins and Levys?* "Mick *Grady*?" He cleared his throat. "Irish name, isn't it?"

Mick nodded and rubbed his hand across a pink cheek. "Last time I checked," he said. "Of course, I changed my name. When I came to Hollywood. You can't get a job in Hollywood with a strange last name. Gable changed his, and did you know John Wayne's first name was *Marion*!"

David sighed with relief. "Okay, what *was* your name?"

"Last time I had it changed . . . the time before this, it was Daugherty. Irish names are big in Hollywood. Producers like Irish names. My *real* name is Mick Feinsteinel, though; nobody wants an actor named Feinsteinel, so I changed it to Daugherty first."

David scratched his head. "That's Irish, too. So why did you change it to Grady?"

Mick shifted slightly and peered at David like he had missed the entire point. "Simple. *Everybody* in Hollywood changes their names, right? So when somebody asked me what my name was before Grady, I wanted to say Daugherty. See? You think I want anyone to know my name was Feinsteinel?"

David frowned and traced the logic of the boyish young navigator who stood grinning at his own genius. "Well, then." David cleared his throat again and did not comment at Mick's backward reasoning. After all, it did make a kind of sense. "Navigator, huh? Thirty-seven missions."

"Yep. There and back again." Mick cocked his head to the side. "Now level with me." He lowered his voice and leaned forward conspiratorially. "Are you guys legit? Is this airline stuff on the up and up?"

David drew himself up and in his best executive tone said, "What a question, Feinsteinel. You come in here off the street . . ." His voice was indignant.

"C'mon, I ain't stupid," the pink-cheeked young man said. "You are David Meyer, American War Ace. You returned from Palestine a month ago with lots of dough and bought up three Constellations and ten C-47's, not to mention a couple C-46's thrown in for good measure. You're paying top wages to a hundred mechanics and now you're hiring ex-flyboys with names like Levy and Goldstein and—"

". . . and Mick Feinsteinel," David interrupted, extending his hand. "Sounds like you know as much about the operation as I do."

Mick hesitated a moment, then grasped David's hand firmly. "I make it my business to know where I'm headed," he grinned. "Where do I sign up, and when do I begin?"

"Sign here." David handed him a pen. "We'll be leaving the States by May first, anyway. As soon as the planes are ready. We have to rip out everything that even remotely resembles military use and replace it all with materials for civilian use."

"That's a shame." Mick handed him the pen and stood erect. "Considering where we're going."

"Can't get around it. The federal regulations are strict about it, and if we're going to fly at all . . ."

"Well, I still say it's a shame. Too bad you can't change your name. From American to another nationality."

"Too bad," David agreed. He stood and stretched. It had been a long morning with over two dozen interviews, and the afternoon ahead would be full as well. "Michael will give you a call in about a week. We'll be assigning crews to work together then. And if you've got any leads, you know, guys who might be interested in getting in on the ground floor of a new airline . . ."

"Planning on any bombing runs over Cairo?" Mick grinned. He slapped his hat on his head and the brown fedora gave him the appearance of a boy trying to look older in his father's clothes. David studied him a moment and decided that Mick Feinsteinel, Daugherty, Grady really did have a boyish, Mickey Rooney appeal to him. He would have made a great extra in the Andy Hardy films. It was hard to picture him in a B-17 bomber dropping a load of bombs over Heidelberg. Or Cairo, for that matter.

"Thirty-seven missions, huh?" David said quietly. "So what name do you want to go by—Grady? Daugherty? Fein. . . ?"

"Mick is okay." He adjusted his hat over his eyes. "Just plain Mick."

The afternoon dragged on with an odd mix of experienced flyers and fresh-faced hopefuls marching past the hotel maid in endless succession to David's "office." A few believed the story that David was starting up an airline to fly refugees out of Europe in a fleet of war surplus planes. That was, after all, a common story after the war. All were dissatisfied with civilian life on the ground and longed to get back into the sky where they belonged. Car salesmen and clerks, firemen and dishwashers—they had one common bond: a mutual disdain for the law of gravity. Married, single, divorced and married again, they paraded through the halls of the Hollywood Roosevelt Hotel in search of reawakened adventure. Most, like Mick, suspected that they were throwing in their lot with something much bigger than just another airline. Many were certain of it. But those that asked too many questions were immediately shown the way out without hope of reentry. There was, after all, no use opening the door to one who wanted to know the minute details of the operation. Gossip was buzzing like a swarm of flies, anyway.

Only two planes remained without pilots at the end of the four days of interviews. As Michael opened the door and admitted the next applicant, David grinned broadly and stretched out his hand to the man he recognized as the co-pilot of the trans-

Atlantic flight that had carried the casket to America a few weeks before.

"You!" David said with surprise. "How did you. . . ?"

"You should have called me earlier." The co-pilot shook David's hand and sat down on the edge of his chair. "I heard you were in town."

"You know I never did get your name, I'm afraid." David ran his fingers through his hair.

"Feinsteinel. Martin Feinsteinel," the dark-haired young co-pilot said.

"Any relation to Mick Grady?" David narrowed his eyes and scanned Martin's face for resemblance. The clear hazel eyes and boyish face did indeed look something like Mick. The wide, easy grin was almost identical.

"My younger brother. One great navigator, I can tell you. I tried to get him on with the airline, but he was too young or too short—or too *Jewish*, maybe. That's why I'm here. My supervisor let me know it will be a cold day in July before he lets a Jew be a pilot. I flew over fifty bombing missions in Europe, and that's what I came home to. I'm not bitter, mind you. I mean, at least it's a job. Better than what most other fly-boys get. But the attitude surprises me, you know?"

David nodded, thinking he should have recruited the co-pilot the minute he offered to help three weeks ago on the plane. "Small world, isn't it?"

"Yeah. Too small. Getting smaller all the time for Jews, I think. If you guys are up to what Mick said you were up to, I'd like to come on board. I'd like to help, Captain Meyer. I told you that on the plane before we landed in Washington, and I meant it."

"That's one I don't have to think twice about." He shook his head in awe at the coincidence. "But call me David, okay?"

Martin handed David his application. Everything was filled out in neat and precise printing. Age: 29. Height: 5'10". Weight: 160 lbs. Marital status: divorced. Children: one. Education: thru Junior year at University of Southern California. Enlisted Air Corps 1941. Pilot B-17. Fifty-three missions over Germany.

In each of those fifty-three missions, David knew, was a story. He had on occasion accompanied a flock of Flying Fortresses over hostile territory. ME-109's had been as thick as mosquitos, hungry to plunge and sting. Through flak and machine-gun fire, the Fortresses had flown on, never desperate to reach a destination, just steady and certain of their purpose and target. At times an end had come suddenly in an explosion of armed bombs that shattered the aircraft and split the sky with twice the force of thunder. Other times, the end had come slowly when first one engine died and then another, and the unrelenting force of earth had pulled the giant wounded bird downward until it was left a twisted heap of smoldering metal.

David had watched tiny specks, men like himself, bail out and pray as their parachutes popped open, then pray that they would fall more quickly to earth as enemy bullets sprayed the sky around them. Fifty-three missions Martin had flown, and yet he returned home to work only as co-pilot in an airline that flew docile passengers through calm skies. *When Nazi flak at last died away,* David thought, *so did the brotherhood that let all men battle the enemy as equals. Black men were taken from the front lines to ride on the back of the bus again. Jewish doctors who saved lives of battle-torn soldiers came home to America, still denied rooms at hotels and membership in clubs. Red men with silver stars were looked on with suspicion and not welcome away from their reservations. Fifty-three bombing missions were still only worth the job of an assistant pilot in a major airline.*

"I thought you must be Jewish, Captain Meyer—"

"David."

"David, then. With a name like Meyer, you know. But they never mentioned it in the newspapers. Never said you were Jewish."

"Well, I never thought of myself as Jewish," David shrugged. "My grandfather Meyer married a lady named Broadhurst, and I guess the buck stopped there."

"Well, one-quarter Jewish would have been enough for the Führer. He didn't care if a person was a converted Christian, a doctor, a scientist. As long as at least one of the grandparents was Jewish. That was enough."

"So I heard." David was thoughtful. "Hey, Feinsteinel, didn't you ever worry about getting shot down over Germany with a name like that on your dog tags? I sure did."

"Naw. I carried a spare. In Germany I would have gone by the name Grady. Have you heard that before? I told Mick if he thinks Hollywood is tough—" He laughed and gave a low whistle.

"I'm hoping Palestine will be a little easier than the last war," David said quietly as he scanned the list of Jewish names on the roster. "I don't think our Arab friends are too big on taking prisoners either, from what I hear. And you know it's real likely that we're going to lose our citizenship and our passports. Not to mention our GI benefits. You sure you want to do this? You and your brother?"

"I would like for there to be at least one place in the world where it is an advantage to have a Jewish name, Captain . . . *David.*" He said slowly. "The only place it never mattered was a mile over Berlin with the bomb bay doors opened. It would be nice if maybe there could be a place in the world that was peaceful where we could land and still have a little respect as a person. I meant what I said to you. I hoped you were not throwing away what you had done in Palestine because of the death of your wife."

David coughed into his hand and leaned forward. He screwed up his face and searched for words. "Well, then, uh, welcome aboard. And now a little something about that casket—" David stopped midsentence; the sudden memory of the flight cleared in his mind. As though someone had held a photograph before his eyes, he remembered where he had seen the man from Graumann's, the man who had been on their trail for days. "He was the guy who sat behind me on the airplane," he said quietly.

Martin wrinkled his brow in confusion. "Wha—"

"There was a little guy on the airplane. Sat right behind me and Michael. He was with a heavyset woman . . . or at least beside her. And he couldn't speak English. Then he followed Michael and me into the men's room at the airport in Washington. He showed up here the other night following Michael and Angela." David's face was thoughtful.

"You're being followed?"

"Yeah. I thought the guy was maybe one of the Feds at first—until now. Neither Scarecrow nor I could place him. But he's *not* American. Which leaves only one solution to the question. He's an Arab agent."

Martin narrowed his eyes and smiled a knowing smile. "Why don't we get a few guys together and beat the tar out of him? Teach him a little lesson?"

"Great idea. I was a little hesitant in case he was American, a government man. But this changes things."

"So? What are we waiting for?" Martin was ready and eager

to get his hands on his first Jihad Moquade.

"We haven't seen him for a couple of days. Angela has. Michael's girlfriend," he explained. "She said he's followed her twice. Got her pretty shook and Michael is ready to tear the guy apart. But he's just sort of vanished."

"He was on my plane?" Martin mulled it over.

"Sitting right behind us."

"Well, if you can give me a couple of days I can track it down. At least find out what his name is. You remember what your seat number was?"

David rummaged through his bureau drawer in search of his airline ticket, holding it up in triumph. "Kind of a pack rat," he remarked. "But sometimes it pays off." He glanced at the stub. "Row four seat B."

———

Never in the history of Palestine could anyone remember a March so cold. The month had come in like a lion and remained fierce and unrelenting with temperatures hovering just above zero, and soldiers on both sides of the barricades shivering without relief in the sleet and hail that pelted Jerusalem. Haj Amin had vowed to strangle Jewish Jerusalem, and with the aid of nature, he had nearly done so. Even the tiny plane that carried Ellie and Ben-Gurion to Tel Aviv and freedom was now hopelessly grounded. Kerosene had dwindled and finally disappeared. Women cooked meager rations on fires made from lighter fluid and DDT. Necessity, it seemed, had become the mother of many an invention.

From a makeshift office in a small red house in Tel Aviv, David Ben-Gurion pored over the charts and rationing plans that had been drawn up by Moshe for the salvation of Jerusalem before he entered the Old City. He had listed twenty-one staple items in the warehouses of Jerusalem. What remained on March 9, 1948, was a pathetic reminder of how near to annihilation Jerusalem was.

Ben-Gurion's face seemed locked in a permanent scowl as he read through the list. "There is no fresh meat, fruit or vegetables left in the markets. Ration for members of the Haganah is four slices of bread, a bowl of soup, a can of sardines, and two potatoes. And these are the best-fed men in the city." The old man slapped the papers down on his desk and ran his hand through his tousled hair.

Ben-Gurion scowled at the half-dozen men who gathered around him in a conference to decide what might be done to aid the besieged city. A plump, soft-looking man with a balding dome and thick glasses spoke up hesitantly. "Avriel has been successful purchasing arms in Czechoslovakia. We can at least look on this as a bright spot. And, of course, there is the success of David Meyer in America. The planes will be a wonderful aid in airlifting supplies when the time comes—"

The Old Man slammed his fist on his desk. He roared in a voice that set each of the commanders in his small Tel Aviv study back in their seats. "The weapons will not save Jerusalem in Prague! As of this minute, not one shipment has reached us! Not one! And these planes that might lift the weapons over the British blockade? Where are they? On an airfield in Burbank, America! Small use to us there! We eat in Tel Aviv, but what of our brothers in Jerusalem? And if food supplies are becoming desperate, what of ammunition and weapons?"

The room fell silent beneath his withering gaze. Each man felt stunned and helpless against the tide that rose near to engulf Jerusalem and their hopes of a homeland. Unless the tide turned, the Yishuv faced certain annihilation. The threats of the Mufti were becoming a reality. Ben-Gurion spoke again: "Our population is centered in three places . . ." He swiveled his chair around and thumped the large map of Palestine that hung behind him. "Here in Tel Aviv. Halifa, and here . . ." He tapped the red circle that was Jerusalem. "The Holy City itself. We could survive if we lost one of the other cities, but not if Jerusalem was lost. It would break the backbone and the spirit of the Yishuv. The Mufti knows this, even if we do not. It will do us no good to be overcome by the Arabs and then say, 'Well, we had weapons in Prague and planes in America.' "

A tall, slender man dressed in the green corduroy of a Haganah commander stared sullenly at the narrow gorge that led to Jerusalem. "The Arab buzzards have roosted in Kastel, overlooking the pass. Like the Romans did. And the Crusaders. And the Turks."

The soft, bespectacled man spoke up again. "The British High Commissioner gave us his solemn pledge that he would keep the road open from here to Jerusalem."

Ben-Gurion narrowed his eyes. "And he has not kept his word. May 14 will be too late."

The certain truth of his words settled in on the men in the room. "Then what are we to do?" asked one. "When will the planes bring us the weapons we need?"

The Old Man flipped the edge of a cable he had received earlier in the day. "May first is the soonest, it seems. The planes are being refitted to meet the standards of the federal government in the United States. Since the airline is registered there, it must comply. Captain Meyer assures us that his men are working day and night. The pilots and flight crews have been chosen, but the federal inspectors are making modifications as difficult and time-consuming as possible. Delay is their game." He sighed and turned his eyes upward toward a shadowed corner of the ceiling. "Delay is one thing we cannot withstand. We cannot wait any longer." He fixed his eyes on the tall, slender man in green. "Aluf Levy, how many men can you draw from the defense of Tel Aviv?"

"Perhaps fifty who are armed," the man answered after a moment's thought. "And those would not have more than four rounds of ammunition each. Not enough."

Ben-Gurion brushed the last comment aside. "And how many trucks can we find tonight for a convoy?"

The plump, bespectacled man pinched the bridge of his nose and shifted his weight wearily. "By tonight? Maybe forty. More or less."

"Done!" Ben-Gurion clapped his hands together. "Fifty guards and forty trucks. One driver and one guard. Two guards every fourth truck in the convoy."

"But the weather!" Protested the plump man.

"The weather will be our friend, because it is the enemy of the Mufti's men." The Old Man leaned forward in his chair and stared down the protest. "And the darkness will provide additional cover." His voice was edged with desperation. "We must get this convoy through to Jerusalem. We must let the people see that they are not cut off from the rest of the Yishuv. It is time, gentlemen, that we take risks."

24   Captive Hope

The March winds moaned around the corners of the Central Prison on St. George Street in the British-held area of Jerusalem called Bevingrad. Rolls of barbed wire protected the area, piled high against the walls and watchtowers like tumbleweeds in a desert dust storm. The masses of wire surrounding the buildings created an effect much like the brambles that had covered the walls of Sleeping Beauty's castle in the old fairy tale. But now, there was no prince to do battle against the dragon that held the entire city in its claws.

Like the barbed wire that surrounded the Central Prison, and the bars that held Moshe and Ehud captive, all of Jewish Jerusalem was now besieged by the surrounding strength of Haj Amin and his warriors. The dark specter of hunger cast its shadow over the 100,000 Jews who remained behind the brambles that climbed the slopes and choked the road from Jerusalem to Tel Aviv. From his cell deep in the bowels of the Central Prison, Moshe knew that without help, Jerusalem would fall to Haj Amin's forces long before the British evacuated in May.

Moshe sat on the edge of his cot and stared out at the whitewashed stone walls beyond the rusty bars of his cell. Somewhere, in another cell another prisoner was racked by a cough that echoed through the hallway. In the tiny cell next to his, Ehud snored peacefully as water dripped from the ceiling into a tin bucket. The cell on the other side of Moshe was empty, it's walls pocked and marred from the explosion of a smuggled hand grenade when two condemned Jewish fighters had taken their own lives rather than die at the end of a British rope. Since then, Moshe knew, the British preferred to hang their prisoners at Acre Prison rather than risk the wrath of Jews in Jerusalem. He and Ehud had been scheduled to be transferred to Acre within the next few days. "When the weather cleared a bit," the Commandant had said. They were to be executed quickly to placate the angry Arab mobs who cried out for blood in answer to the Jaffa Gate bombing.

Their trial had been swift. The witnesses had made certain

identification of Moshe Sachar as being present at the site of the bombing. He had been dressed as a priest. He had helped load the convoy that day, and he had been present when the police van was stolen. His replies that he had been attempting to enter the Jewish Quarter of the Old City in disguise had been useless. He was obviously an accomplice. The indignant cries of the Jewish Agency on his behalf had been to no avail. The evidence was too great. Moshe Sachar had been found guilty. Ehud Schiff had been likewise convicted of smuggling and carrying a weapon. The punishment for both men was the same as it had been for other Jews in the long history of the Mandatory Government. To carry a weapon, even for self-defense, was punishable by death. Of that crime, Moshe mused, they were indeed both guilty.

It did not seem to matter that an Arab woman had testified that she had seen Moshe moving from one wounded person to another, giving aid to them after the bombing. It did not matter that she had seen him weep as he had covered the body of a young boy with his coat, or stopped the flow of blood from a severed artery and thus saved the life of an unconscious man. He was Haganah; he was a man of two identities. That was proven. He had defied the laws of the government for years. All proven. The judges had come to a swift decision. Not even prominent archaeologists were above the law.

Moshe's request for a Bible had been granted immediately. His request to have a rabbi in attendance had been denied. *To bring a Jewish rabbi into the compound could prove fatal to him,* they had explained. *There are Arab snipers everywhere.*

The irony that Moshe sat in prison while there were Arab snipers everywhere had somehow escaped the logic of the surly and taciturn guard. Moshe had nodded in understanding.

"Maybe at Acre," he had answered.

The guard had smiled a tight-lipped smile of sarcasm. "Aye. You'll be in need of a rabbi then, won't you?" he spat. "But you'll not get the blood off your hands that way."

Ehud had risen up in indignation when he overheard the guard's words. He cursed loudly and shouted, "It's your white paper that is stained with the blood of innocents! It's fellows like you that kept my wife and children out of Palestine! It is the blood of six million now that cover you and your land and all the world that stood silent. There is no blood on him! No blood on the hands of Moshe Sachar! He saved thousands while you turned

273

millions away from this land—!" Ehud had broken into sobs then, and Moshe had tried in vain to comfort him as he sank onto his bed and the red-faced guard strode away from the echoing accusations. Other prisoners had taken up the cry and tin cups had banged against the bars in protest. The meager supper had been denied to the prisoners, and a cloud of despair had once again settled on the cells of Central Prison.

That had been two days ago. Ehud had said little since then. His rage had dissipated, and now he spent the hours of endless prison twilight in a sleep brought on by emotional exhaustion.

Moshe lay back on his cot and stared at the ceiling. For all those days, it seemed, he had been able to think of nothing but Rachel. When he slept brief minutes, he could almost smell her sweet skin. Her voice called to him; a hundred times each night he woke to find she was not there. Each moment of waking seemed more difficult than the last. He remembered the poem he had written to her; it seemed small and inadequate, but he prayed now that she would find it among his papers and *know* . . . "Kocham cie, Rachel," he whispered in Polish. "I love you." Then he sighed and turned his face into his pillow. *Take that message to her, God, he prayed. Kocham cie! Tell her. Tell her that love is stronger than even death. Tell her for me. Hold her for me.* He rubbed his hands over his face as if to wipe away reality. *I have always known this moment would come. I thought I would face the gallows bravely, not afraid to die because I had made my choice to risk my life for what I believe. But now, Lord, I will tell you. I long to live! If it is the time you have chosen, Zion will come even if I am not here to see it. I am very small in the scope of so many who have died for this dream. But I matter very much to one person. I am her nation. I am her home. I am her dream. And for her sake I want to live. We need a small miracle here, Lord. A little personal miracle. Not for me, but for Rachel. I know you can make a little miracle for her even if it is not your will that I be alive to see it. In the meantime, please say to her for me, Kocham cie!*

The slow footsteps of guards checking the sleeping prisoners intruded on Moshe's thoughts. He squeezed his eyes tightly shut against the bare light bulb that shone from a socket opposite his cell. Rachel stood before him, her hair soaking wet and her feet bare. ". . . it isn't proper," she protested, and Moshe laughed aloud as the guard's shadow fell over him.

In the black night, through sheets of rain, the young Arab boy ran through the streets of his village.

"Wake up!" he cried. "Wake up! A Jewish convoy approaches the pass! Commander Kadar has sent me! Wake up and gather at Kastel!"

Lights blinked on as Arab Irregulars sprang from warm beds and dressed hurriedly. Vintage weapons and ammunition were slung over shoulders of young and old alike. The battle cry, "Allah Akbar!" filled the night, and women wrapped themselves and stepped out into the muddy streets for one last fleeting glimpse of husbands and sons who swarmed to meet the call of Commander Kadar.

On the rock-strewn slopes below Kastel, they gathered to wait in the cover of the boulders and washes for the convoy of forty trucks that slipped and groaned toward Jerusalem.

Kadar was among them, soaked and bent in the force of the storm. He shouted instructions and commands above the roar of the wind that cut through his coat and tore the warmth from his skin. Only a few yards from the rutted road, Gerhardt and Yassar crouched expectantly with slick, cold fingers on the handle of a plunger wired to a string of land mines in the road.

"They come! They come!" A shout rose up from the stones and ravines. "Allah Akbar! Allah is great!"

Kadar shielded his eyes with his hand as he peered through the gale and spotted forty pairs of lights that stared out at the darkness like narrow swollen eyes behind their shields. "Allah Akbar!" The cry arose and mingled with the moan of engines and the wail of the wind. "He has delivered them into our hands!"

———

Sergeant Hamilton, Smiley Hitchcock, and young Bill Harney stood in a solemn line before Luke's desk. Ham tossed the daily edition of the *Palestine Post* on Luke's desk blotter and said quietly, "We wanted y' t' know we're as angry as the next man about your friend the professor goin' t' be 'anged."

Smiley cleared his throat, "A pure miscarriage o' justice, sir, make no mistake about it. An' me an' the lads was talkin' about it an' wanted y' t' know 'ow we was feelin'."

"It were brave of y' t' testify for 'im, sir," offered Harney. "An' though y' might be gettin' a bit o' flak over it, we fellows wanted y' t' know we're behind what y' did for the professor."

Luke nodded in acknowledgment of their concern. "Well, I thank you for that. I don't suppose there's a man under my command that isn't of a tender heart for these people. You are the best."

"Aye!" spat Ham. "An' that's why the High Commission transferred us all 'ere to ordnance an' put that Cap'n Stewart an' 'is bunch in the Old City in our stead."

"Aye!" agreed Smiley. "Remember the day Stewart was with us at Zion Gate an' I mentioned the bombing of King David Hotel? I didn't know Stewart's brother 'ad died there." He wiped his brow at the memory.

"Well, Stewart is evening the score now, ain't 'e?" offered pink-cheeked Harney.

"An' now there's nothin' t' be done for Professor Sachar, is there, Cap'n?" asked Smiley.

"No." Luke shook his head slowly and stared at the headline that stained the integrity of justice itself. "I am afraid all that can be done for Moshe Sachar has been done."

"Well, naught but two weeks an' you'll be bound for 'ome, Cap'n Thomas," said Ham. "An all this will be over for y'. Over an' done."

Luke smiled sadly. "I don't know that this will ever be finished for me, Ham. For twenty years I have served King and country. And now I am afraid I am leaving for England with a sense of defeat so profound—" He did not finish, but fixed his gaze on the large artillery shell that had contained the scrolls. On its head was scratched the names of those who had been with him through the battles of North Africa. Only these three men remained of those names. All the others had returned to England and the peace of private life. Soon it was to be Luke's turn. He met the gaze of each man in his office. "We have been through a lot together, haven't we, lads?" He smiled, but his eyes were full of sadness.

"Aye," agreed Ham. "An' we want y' t' know we'd still follow y' anywhere, Cap'n. You say the word and we're behind y', sir!"

"Aye! That's a fact!" chimed in the other two.

"In two weeks, lads," Luke said, "I'll be a private citizen, collecting a pension. But I won't forget you. Not any of you." He gazed out the window. "And I won't forget this place, either." He

sat silently for a moment; then he sighed heavily. "Our one con-
solation is that we have done everything that could be done to
help. And we are only men, after all."

Ham turned and tapped the pointed cone of the large shell.
"Ain't none of us ever forgot the day this come in after us, Cap'n.
You shouted for us t' duck, and duck we did! There wasn't a thing
else t' do! But, sir, it was God 'imself that stopped this shell from
killin' everyone of us. We 'ad done everything there was left t' do
t' protect ourselves an' it wasn't enough, now was it lads?"

Smiley and Harney agreed as they looked at the shell. "Not
a thing."

Ham continued. "Well, sir, t' get t' the point. I suppose there
comes a time when a fellow just 'as t' say everything 'as been
done that can be done. And then leave the rest up t' God."

"You're a wise man, Hamilton," Luke said quietly.

"Well, Cap'n," Ham looked surprised, "it was you yourself that
taught us that one."

"Now, the trick is," said Luke, "knowing when you have truly
done everything there is to do, eh?"

———

Rachel sat in the rocking chair and stared at the still-made
bed. She had not slept all night, but had sat up with Leah's Bible
open across her knees and searched for some word of comfort
among the pages. For the first times since she had heard from
Moshe about the depth of God's love for her in Yeshua, the Messiah, all the phrases seemed to fall flat; her prayers sounded hollow and unacknowledged. She stood accused by her own past
once again, and the voices of the night whispered to her that
Moshe's arrest was only one more punishment for her great sin.
You are not forgiven, the darkness seemed to say. *And for the rest
of your life you will pay for what you have done. And those who
know you will suffer, too, because of you.*

Again and again she flipped the pages to stories of God's anger and vengeance against sin. God's love seemed as cold and
distant as the stars, and once again she felt fear for little Tikvah
as the child lay softly breathing in her cradle. Near to panic, convicted once again in her own mind, Rachel pushed against the
dark clouds of confusion and doubt that covered her. *Do not pun-
ish me, God,* she prayed, *by harming this child. Do not take
Moshe's brave and noble life because you wish to repay me for my*

wrongs! Instead, let me die. Or make me live far away from them, for that alone is the worst punishment. But do not harm them, Lord.

With the sunlight, came the familiar wave of nausea that had overcome her since Moshe had been arrested. The smell of food made her stomach turn and sent her groping for a cold cloth. Weight seemed to drop away from her already slender frame, and daily she had begun to weaken. *Perhaps God has heard my prayers,* she thought, *and will let me sicken and die but allow Moshe and Tikvah to go on living without me.*

Tikvah stirred and Rachel forced herself to attend to the little one. As she mixed the dwindling supply of milk, another attack of nausea assailed her and sent her to her knees over the washbasin. Long minutes passed as Rachel slumped to the floor and lay there quietly watching the ceiling tilt and circle above her. *Let me die now, God,* she prayed. *Hannah and Shoshanna will find Tikvah. If only you will take me instead of Moshe.* But God did not answer even her offer of sacrifice. Old ghosts and memories gathered in the little apartment to accuse her until the days of joy with Moshe dimmed in her memory. Tikvah wailed a hungry request for breakfast that finally roused Rachel from where she lay near the kitchen table. She rose slowly, grateful that the reeling sense of sickness had diminished somewhat, but disappointed that God had not chosen that moment to take her. Perhaps He wanted her to suffer longer. She changed and fed the little one, then held her in her arms and told her how much better off she would be if Rachel were to simply go far away. And for a while, the worst doubts surged against her like a high tide bent on drowning her in the depths of self-pity. *If Moshe really knew what I have lived, he would not truly love me,* she thought. *He has only deceived himself. He only thinks he knows who I am.*

This morning when she bathed the baby, she did not sing or speak out loud. Silent tears fell, unnumbered like the doubts that finally had overtaken her hope and smashed it into dust. If ever God had seen her, she reasoned, He had turned His back and looked away. And that, too, was her fault.

When Shoshanna knocked at the door, Rachel did not answer it, making the old woman believe that she had gone on to Tipat Chalev for a small breakfast ration. She rocked Tikvah silently until the child slept again; then she laid her in the cradle and opened the small chest of drawers to stare for the hundredth time at Moshe's tallith. It was torn, shredded like all her hopes and dreams. She had been a fool to think that she could ever find happiness.

On the night table, Moshe's notepad lay unopened where he had placed it. Clutching the tallith to her, she ran her fingers over the cramped handwriting that read *PLANS* on the cover. She opened it slowly and wept again at his notes. Lists of supplies contained phrases like, "God willing, if we can ration the beets until . . ."

"Oh, Moshe!" she cried. "What use was any of it? What good is it to us now?"

Her tears dropped on the page, diluting the ink. Unwilling to mar even one letter of his handwriting, she blotted the page and wiped her eyes, determined to find the control she needed to read on. As she flipped through the pages, she gasped at the discovery of a poem that was scratched and scribbled and rewritten. She drew her breath in sharply and made her way to the edge of the bed where she lowered herself slowly.

"My dearest wife, Rachel,

Forgive my pitiful attempt to write you a poem, but this morning as you lay sleeping . . ." she laid the notepad against her breast and cried out, "Moshe!" She closed her eyes and for a moment felt that he was very near to her once again. She read his words silently then, imagining his voice speaking to her:

. . . as you lay sleeping here before me, I thought I have never seen one so beautiful as you. My heart overflows with love for you and gratitude to God for bringing me such a gift. So I will try to speak with a measure of eloquence, although I am a linguist, not a poet.

There are pools that do not reflect the sky
　　There are stars that are not diamonds
　　There are sunsets that do not inflame the imagination
　　But there is no look deep into your eyes
　　　　That does not make my heart beat faster
　　　　And my breath come quicker.

There are drinks that do not quench thirst
　　There are meals that are not feasts
　　There is sleep that does not refresh
　　But there is no embracing you, no touch
　　　　From you that does not fill my heart

With love, my soul with peace.

There are songs that strike no responsive chord
There are poems with images that fail
There are love stories whose partners
    find no counterpart in us.
But there is no "all-surrounding,"
    "lost without you," LOVE
    in all the world for me . . .
                    but yours.

Her broken heart seemed to swell and break once again as
she read the final lines of his note to her:

> This is not enough, my love, to say how true and real my
> love is for you. There is no language, ancient or modern, that
> can speak the words that my heart speaks when I am with
> you. But I will try again and again to say it: Kocham Cie,
> Rachel. I love you forever, Moshe.

Rachel tenderly traced the writing on the page as though she
were touching Moshe's face. She wiped her eyes and reread the
words again and again. "Thank you, Moshe," she said to him as
though he were there in the room with her. "And I love you forever—" She could not finish, as words seemed to freeze in a
throat that was tight with tears. When she found the breath to
continue, her words became a plea and a prayer, "Dear Lord, I
am surrounded by clouds of doubt and fear and confusion. Are
you still there, Lord? Have you written me a hidden love letter
too? I want to believe, God, but I will need you to help me believe!" She buried her face in her hands. "Are you still there,
God?"

25　The Informers

Yassar bowed elaborately before his cousin, the Mufti; then,
gathering his robes over his arm, he sat down in one of two chairs
beside the ornately carved desk.

"Kadar reports that you have done well in our service at the pass of Bab el Wad." Haj Amin lifted the corner of his mouth slightly in a gesture of pleasure.

"It is not to my own honor, but for that of the people of Palestine and the house of Husseini." Yassar blinked in the glare of the lamp. "We stopped them just after the pumping station," he said excitedly. "Forty Jewish trucks. Gerhardt and I were but fifteen feet from the barricade. The lead car tried to ram through when I detonated the mine. The fools!" He clapped his hands together happily. "They drove their trucks upon one another, inching in, closing in, until we had only one long target! We could hear them shout to one another over their wireless radios. Commander Kadar ordered that our men rush to the attack and force the Jews' armored car windows closed. How the Jews must have suffocated in there! The dead ones we found after the battle had stripped to their shorts. Some escaped into the Hillman of the Jewish commander. He was a brave fellow indeed, even for a Jewish devil. He rescued many, and then was himself killed when a land mine struck his vehicle and he overturned."

"How many Jewish trucks escaped?" Haj Amin narrowed his eyes in anticipation.

"Only half. A bit more than half. Twenty-one out of forty. They were turned back and the rest of the trucks were abandoned to us. Sacks of flour! Cases of meat and sardines! Oranges! The villagers of Beit Masir, Saris and Kastel came and carried it all away. Almost all. A small amount we have brought here, as you requested."

"A full truckload?" Haj Amin lifted his chin and tapped his fingers against his desktop.

"Not so much as that. Perhaps a few days' ration for the Old City Jews. Only a bit."

Haj Amin cleared his throat. "I do have a promise to keep to Captain Stewart, it seems. And the British Mandatory Government. It will be enough to foster the belief in our generosity. A few days' ration for the old rabbis, eh?" he chuckled. "You have done well, cousin. You are learning well, and we are pleased with our kinsman."

Yassar bowed his head in acceptance of the pleasure of Haj Amin. "And now there is something else. Something even bigger that will please you, Haj Amin. I have found the man who will help us destroy the Jewish Agency."

The Mufti sat up and leaned attentively on his arm. He fixed his gaze on Yassar. "Someone inside the Agency?"

"Close enough to get inside," Yassar replied cryptically. "He is an Embassy driver for the United States. He has been in their service for years and wishes to wed my sister. He does not have the 600 pounds required by my father for the payment, and so . . ." Yassar shrugged and grinned.

"And so . . ." Haj Amin nodded his head in understanding. "It is well known that I am a man in favor of suitable marriages. What, then, is this fellow's proposal?"

"He has spoken with the guards, the Haganah at the Agency. They do not suspect him of anything. He drives the Ambassador to and fro without question." He swept his hand broadly and raised his eyebrows in the infallibility of the plan. "He has even told these fellows how much he is in need of the 600 pounds for the *mohar* required to purchase my sister."

"And have they offered to help him acquire it in some way?" Haj Amin leaned back against his chair and appraised his thick-lipped cousin.

"Indeed! You are a man with wisdom, Haj Amin!" Yassar clapped his hands together again, and the Mufti noted that his young cousin's enthusiasm was annoying. "He has offered to sell them Bren guns! He may drive through the Jewish barricades without question. He will park the car in front of the building and give them the guns. Then he will cross the street to buy a pack of cigarettes and when he disappears"—He raised his hands and brought them together in one final explosive blast—"so shall the Jewish Agency disappear as well!"

Haj Amin rubbed his chin and smiled a tight-lipped smile of approval. "I hope the Jews will find their guns worth the price they pay." His ice-blue eyes twinkled with delight. "A brilliant plan, Cousin." He paused and sighed with satisfaction. "And we are making good our promise to the world and the Jews that we will strangle Jerusalem. What better proof then to destroy the seat of Jewish government beneath their very noses? And you, Yassar. Have you learned enough from our Commander Gerhardt to embark on this task alone?"

Yassar frowned and looked down at his scuffed shoes. "Alas, he lacks generosity in sharing many of his secret skills. I fear for the sake of the plan that it must be he who creates the bomb."

"You are an honest man, Yassar, to admit your skills are still not fully developed. Most would not wish to share such glory with another, even at the risk of failure." He raised his hand in a gesture of blessing. "Allah will reward you, and it is my promise that if you succeed in this, your glory shall one day outstrip that of Gerhardt and Kadar as well."

"You are most gracious, Haj Amin. It is my hope one day to bring great glory for the house of Husseini in our fight against the Zionists."

"See to it, then." Haj Amin picked a loose thread from his brocade sleeve. "Tell your friend that Haj Amin Husseini will be happy to provide him with the 600 pounds required to marry a daughter of the house of Husseini. And more, besides. He will undoubtedly be looking for a different kind of employment after this. Perhaps we shall find him a post within our government when Jerusalem is the capital of the Arab nation of Palestine. Tell him that, will you? Tell him he hastens the day when there will be no more Zionists in his nation. He will one day be considered a great patriot. As will you be as well, Yassar, my cousin." Haj Amin laid aside the use of the royal *our*, and in a gesture of absolute familiarity called Yassar "*my* cousin."

Recognizing the great honor, Yassar flushed and lowered his eyes, determined to live up to the confidence of this great man. "Tomorrow, then, should be soon enough for me to speak with him. I will sup with him and we will settle the bargain before he has a moment to reconsider what he does. I will tell him to ask the Jews for much money for the Bren guns; then he will have enough to begin life with my sister in some comfort."

"And the United States will be our unwitting accomplices. The plan is indeed faultless, Yassar." His face was amused. "It is humorous that perhaps this young woman American journalist may indeed find herself the victim of her own charade." He looked up at Yassar's bewildered face. "Did we not inform you? Our servant Montgomery reported from America that the girl was not dead at all. She resides at the Jewish Agency building as some part of an elaborate hoax."

"But her casket . . . the newspapers carried such glowing obituaries. Why?"

"Perhaps to pull the authorities off the scent of her lover, the American flyer. We cannot tell. However, even though he announced to the world that he is no longer working with the Zionists, he is this very minute purchasing and refurbishing planes.

For an airline, so he says. Montgomery tells us that he stayed at the same hotel in Washington with Dr. Weizmann, the Zionist criminal himself."

Yassar gasped at the news. "Yes? Why, then, does Montgomery simply not kill this Meyer fellow?"

"Our servant is more clever than any of us in matters of intrigue, Yassar," he commented patronizingly. "It was, after all, Montgomery who provided the Reich with information on the British command in North Africa. I have long since learned that this one moves easily and well in the darkness and in the end finds the light of information that is invaluable to us. The answers are not yet known in their entirety. After all, if Meyer were killed now, the Jews would simply send another to replace him and we would have sacrificed the one connection we need to gather information about Jewish operations."

"But what of these planes? Could they not bring the weapons the Jews need over the British blockade?" Yassar frowned.

"That, too, has been taken care of. The American government is choked with rules and regulations. Our friend Montgomery has discovered that this propensity for regulating every detail works to our advantage. Minor officials are the most conscientious in carrying out every minute detail that the laws demand, it seems. A call was placed to the proper department, notifying them that these planes of Meyer's are not up to regulations for commercial flying. It was also intimated that perhaps they were purchased for illegal purposes . . . such as gun-running to the Middle East." He laughed a short, hard burst of laughter. "The planes have been grounded until they meet the tiniest details of the government code. I do not think we need trouble ourselves with thoughts of Captain Meyer's airplanes. They surely cannot be ready in time to provide us with any threat whatsoever. As the fat, rich Jews of America give their money to Golda Meir in a hopeless cause, the reality is that nothing they do will be done quickly enough to save Jerusalem, or Palestine, from what is already fact. Both the city and the countryside are in our grasp. Now they must simply struggle against bonds that will not be broken."

Yassar bowed his head briefly in acknowledgment of his cousin's words. "Your confidence strengthens me, Haj Amin. Your trust in the will of Allah for our people gives me courage to fight until the last Zionist is no more in Palestine."

"Tonight I leave for Damascus." Haj Amin pressed his finger-tips together and studied the large golden ring that adorned his index finger. He saw his own reflection in the crescent moon. "We will meet with the Arab League there to discuss arms, and we think it best if our presence be elsewhere when the Jewish Agency is destroyed. As ever, it must look as though this act is uninspired, except by the patriotism of common people in the countryside. It is best if I be absent and be called to return in victory when the time is right."

"Of course." Yassar stood, anxious to proceed with the plans for the next step in the crushing of Jewish opposition. "We will speak by radio with you when it is accomplished."

Haj Amin dismissed Yassar with a blessing from Allah; then he took out a British-made fountain pen and scrawled a letter to Kadar, who served him so faithfully in the pass of Bab el Wad and the village of Kastel . . .

> Trusted Servant Ram Kadar: As commander of the forces that hold the pass from the grip of the Zionists, we feel per-haps your presence at the meeting of the Arab League in Da-mascus will be of much value. If it is true as you believe that the Jews will undertake one major offensive against the pass, your testimony may be important in acquiring the artillery and equipment we need to destroy them totally . . . Come, then, to Damascus and leave the pass in the hands of Ger-hardt for a short time until our purpose is met . . .

The flock of C-47 gooney birds rested row on row in front of the Service Airways' hangar at Burbank airport. Martin, David and Michael had ferried the remaining eight over from Ontario airport the afternoon before, and now well over one hundred mechanics swarmed over them like ants at a picnic. The clank of tools on metal and voices laughing or cursing filled the air as benches that once carried paratroopers were ripped out and tossed in heaps on the runway. Twice more the official from the CAA had dropped by to inspect the progress of the renovation. He had made no secret of his curiosity about the origins and goals of Service Airways. His questions were open and probing, ripe with suspicion. David had watched him prowl among the aircraft and had considered the possibility of a bribe; but instinc-tively, he knew that this was a fellow who prized duty over money and regulations over practicality. After all, hadn't the President of the United States declined to become involved with bending the CAA rules even a little bit for the sake of Service Airways? To bribe this petty official would simply provide ammunition for the cannons of the press. They would find out, somehow, just as the CAA had somehow obviously gotten a tip that these planes were Palestine bound, and had done everything in its power to delay departure until mid-May, when the British would be leaving.

Just inside the opening of the hangar, a welder worked over the blue flame of his torch, fabricating spare fuel tanks that would be placed into the C-47 aircraft. David was hoping that the extra tanks would make a refueling stop unnecessary in the long, slow Atlantic crossing ahead of them. There was, he felt, no use risking a stop on an airfield that could ultimately prove un-friendly to their mission. They would simply go it alone, even if the world's support was hostile to their efforts.

Looking tanned and fit, Martin strode through the raft of planes. He cheered each worker on, calling many of them by name, and asking questions about the progress of the work. David liked this affable man and admired his business sense. *It was no accident,* he thought, *that Martin was on that plane, was it? No coincidence where you sit, is there, Lord?* Martin Feinsteinel was just exactly the man David had needed to help him steer through the barrage of paper work that came with the Service Airways territory.

Martin looked to where David was standing and hailed him, waving a slip of blue notepaper in his hand. "Hey, David," he called, "I think I got your man."

David studied the name on the paper while Martin got an orange Nehi soda out of an ice chest by the desk.

"Abraham Rosovsky?" David wrinkled his brow. "Sounds Rus-sian or something, doesn't it?"

"I don't know from Russian," Martin popped the cap and slugged down a long drink of soda. He wiped his lips on the back of his hand. "I thought it sounded Jewish myself. I knew a kid named Rosovsky in our congregation when I was a kid."

"What kind of an Arab would have a name like that?"

"Well, I wouldn't worry about it. The guy is probably another Mick. Probably has a dozen passports and fifteen names. Maybe even Grady, who knows. Anyway, Rosovsky is the name he used for the flight. Apparently he was no relation to the lady who sat next to him."

David sighed in frustration. "Yeah. Thanks." He sifted through a stack of part orders and receipts on his desk until he came up with another slip of paper with a scrawled message on it. "The Mossad," he said slowly, "believes we are being watched. *Infiltrated* is the word the Mossad used. They've got an agent trying to figure out who it is. But they say practically every move we make is being relayed to the Arab High Committee by someone named Montgomery. They think this thing with the CAA really is the work of an informer. They want us to watch our step. Be careful." He frowned and watched Martin take another swig. "I'd like to get my hands on that little Rosovsky creep and wring the truth out of him."

"David." Martin's voice was solemn. "You know, so far all that's happened is we've been delayed. But have you seen the newsreels? I mean, if this guy is who we think his is, he's got himself a cannon in his pocket. I don't know about you, but I'm going to—"

"I already did," David grinned. "I got myself a .45 at a pawnshop. I'm not worried about meeting the guy head-on . . ." His voice trailed off. "I worry more now that we've lost track of him, you know?" He scratched his head and gazed at Martin with concern. "I'm glad you and Mick are on board. Just cover your flanks, both of you. I think it really might be a good idea if you carried a gun. I am sure of one thing . . . if we do get past the CAA and get these babies up in the air where they are supposed to be, the Arabs aren't going to play by any rules but their own."

26   Purim

Under the watchful eye of Captain Stewart and his men, the captured Jewish convoy truck was unloaded at Zion Gate, and its contents trundled through the Armenian Quarter to the hungry Jewish Quarter.

Rachel cradled Tikvah in her arms as she stood beside Hannah and watched the loaded handcarts arrive at the barricade at the end of the street. No words were spoken as Yeshiva students took the handcarts and Rabbi Akiva inspected the contents with a nod of approval.

From a darkened window, Dov and Rabbi Vultch and seven other members of the Haganah watched. This meager offering would not last the quarter long, that much was certain. The tunnel into the storage room of D. Agajanian had long since been finished, but as Dov had emerged blinking into the daylight, it had been decided that not a word would be mentioned until the day when the Mufti's paltry gifts stopped coming altogether. That day would come, but there would still be the grain to help them survive.

In the meantime, the citizens of the quarter were fed handfuls at a time from the remains of Jewish convoys that had been destroyed and looted in the pass of Bab el Wad.

Today was the fourteenth of Adar, known as *Tanit Esther*. This was a fast day, the day before the holiday of Purim. On this day in the fifth century B.C., Queen Esther and her uncle Mordecai effected the deliverance of the Jews of Persia from massacre at the hand of Haman. The food had come from the Mufti under the pretext of a gift for the holiday. Tonight, Rachel knew, the scroll of Esther would be read in the synagogue; then the food would be passed out to the grateful residents and the fast would be broken. *How ironic*, she thought as she watched a handcart of canned sardines roll by, *that this holiday remembers deliverance from Haman, a man who plotted to destroy all the Jews, and this year we are fed by a man who lives for the same purpose. The Mufti is like Haman. He seeks our lives just as Haman did and yet some still trust that he would spare them when the English leave. He strangles us with one hand and convinces the world of his good intentions by offering us crumbs with the other hand.*

As the last of the carts rolled by, Akiva spoke quietly to Captain Stewart and signed a paper on a clipboard. He pushed his glasses up on the bridge of his nose and raised his eyes to look directly at Rachel. Then he turned his gaze away from her and spoke quietly to Stewart again. Stewart looked over his shoulder to where Rachel stood. He raised his eyebrows as he appraised her, then spoke again to Akiva. *Yes*, thought Rachel, *I belong to Moshe Sachar. I am the young woman you took him from; and this is his child. Take us too, for you have taken our lives already.* She wondered if Stewart sensed her pain and anger as she stared back at him defiantly. He tipped his hat briefly to Akiva. The rabbi turned abruptly on his heel and followed after the handcarts toward Nissan Bek. His eyes focused straight ahead, and his face carried the look of a proud and self-satisfied man. He was once again in control of his people and his quarter.

"He is a puppet," hissed Hannah as he turned a corner and disappeared. "A puppet in the hand of that *Haman*, the Mufti. If he is not careful he will hang us all on the Arab gallows."

Rachel's brow furrowed deeply at her words. First on the gallows, she knew, would be Moshe. Word of his conviction had come over the radio hidden in the darkness of a cellar. Rabbi Vultch had come to her and quietly spoken the words she had heard in her heart from the moment Moshe had been taken. *He is to die. He and Ehud together.* She had not wept at the news. Too many tears had already fallen in the darkness of night as she buried her face against his jacket and cried out to the Lord. This word from the rabbi had only been confirmation. So Moshe would walk before her and take with him a hope that she had held since their marriage. *If we cannot live together on this earth*, she had whispered to him, *then I will pray that God in His mercy will let us walk hand in hand into His kingdom together. I could not bear one moment of life or breathe one more breath if you were not here on this earth with me.*

But for now, she knew, Moshe still lived. He was safe in some dark cell at the Central Prison in Jerusalem. He was safe from the rage of mobs who tore and slashed and destroyed without ever questioning the truth of guilt or innocence. For this moment he was alive, and so she could go on breathing for another day, one hour at a time. And perhaps he could hear the words she whispered to him as she lay alone on their bed. A hundred times a night she dreamed she heard him and prayed that she would not waken. And when the morning sunlight took him from her, she prayed that perhaps an Arab sniper would see her in the Old City streets and help her sleep in Moshe's arms again—this time, forever.

Tonight is the eve of Purim, she prayed, *when Esther saved her people from the gallows. If once you saved your people, God, could you not save just one life? Could you not give Moshe back to us? To Tikvah and me?*

The shadow of the gallows had always fallen dark over the

ghettos. The world was full of Hamans, but there were always too few Esthers, and even fewer days when deliverance was celebrated.

Hannah studied her intently as she gazed after the stern, dark figure of Akiva. "You are as gray as ash, child," Hannah said gently, putting a hand on Rachel's arm. "And you have grown even more thin." She clucked her tongue in concern. "Are you not eating what ration you receive? You must eat it; little though it may be, you should not lose weight so quickly."

Rachel did not tell Hannah that grief for Moshe had driven her appetite away; that each morning she rose to a wave of nausea that caused the room to spin around her. "I am eating," Rachel replied quietly.

Hannah searched Rachel's face and frowned at the high, delicate cheekbones, now too pronounced in the beautiful face of the young woman, "And are you well?" she asked.

Rachel nodded curtly, not returning Hannah's look. "I am," she replied simply. Tikvah's robust and healthy appearance was a sharp contrast to Rachel. "I am having some difficulty sleeping at night," she answered uncomfortably when Hannah continued to stare at the dark circles under her eyes.

"You must try, Rachel, not to think of it. You have a child in your care now and you must remain healthy for her sake. When my own dear husband went, God rest his soul, I thought I perhaps would not live. I did not wish to live. But here I am still . . ."

Rachel clouded up at her words. "Please. Please, Hannah. Thank you for caring, but . . ." Rachel met her gaze with tormented eyes.

"You are a young woman. You will not be alone for long, my dear." Hannah's words meant to comfort, but they ripped at Rachel's very soul. She wanted to cry out, to shout her outrage at the suggestion that she could ever share her life with anyone but Moshe. Instead, she lowered her eyes to a puddle on the cobblestones before her. "There are pools that don't reflect the sky," she whispered as she remembered Moshe's clear, loving gaze. She saw her own reflection and the clouds in the water. *I want you to look at me, love,* Moshe had once said, *and tell me what you see.* Then she had seen her own face in his eyes and he had told her, *Love is the only mirror we must use to judge ourselves and others. If I, who am just a man, can love you so very much, when you look into the mirror of God's love, Rachel, you will see hope, and joy and mercy.* For a long moment, Rachel pondered his words and watched the pool as reflected clouds drifted behind the serious young face that gazed back at her. A sense of understanding came to her as it had that first day in the Old City with Moshe. A slight smile played on her lips and once again she looked into the mirror of God's love for her and Moshe and Tikvah. "Hannah," she whispered, "dear Hannah, I am not alone. Even now with Moshe in prison and condemned to die, I am not alone. Nor shall I ever be again."

Hannah looked at the baby in Rachel's arms, believing that Rachel had found her comfort in the child. "A child is a good thing," she said without understanding. "But perhaps there will be a young man for you again someday."

Rachel listened to the words of Hannah, this time without anger. Those words that had cut into her heart like a dagger had been spoken with the intention to comfort her. Rachel smiled sadly as she saw Hannah through the mirror of God's love. "While Moshe still lives," she replied kindly, "I can only hope and pray that someday he will once again be the man who shares my life."

"Of course," Hannah assured, patting her on the shoulder. "Of course you may hope that. It is only natural right now." She raised her eyes toward the heavens. "God should only let us live so long to have such a great *simcha*, nu? Such a great pleasure and day of rejoicing! To save Moshe and that big ape, Ehud! That day we should declare a holiday like Purim!" She pursed her lips and looked away. "Unfortunately, God has run short of miracles for His people, I think."

"Why, Hannah!" Rachel chided. "Grandfather has said that God's greatest pleasure is making miracles from the dust of our despair. I will hope." She looked at the pool again. "And I will pray even as they stand at the gallows. And if they are laid in the grave, then I will still believe the most wonderful miracle of all—that God has a place for us in His kingdom. That we will be together always and forever."

"Ah yes. Life is short and full of pain . . ." Hannah agreed.

Rachel raised her chin and looked up past the large gray thunderheads that gathered above them. One small, bright blue window of sky glistened in the midst of the threatening clouds. "But *Love* is forever, Hannah, and full of beauty. These clouds will pass and we will see someday that the sky is still there. Blue and clean. That it was always there—the same, unchanging sky, only hidden behind the clouds for a while. Like God, eh? He still likes miracles, I think."

Hannah appraised her with an uncomprehending stare. She shrugged and put her fingertips on her lips as she tried to understand the words Rachel had just spoken. "Well, child," she said at last. "This is the Holiday of Purim. Even if God forgets His miracles, we Jews certainly make every excuse to celebrate them, nu?" She put her hand on the door latch. "Would you care to come in for tea? Here we stand in the street solving all God's riddles for Him."

Rachel shook her head. She wanted to have some time alone to think on the things that God had whispered to her this afternoon. "No thank you," she said. "I have things to do before the service tonight."

"Well, bring your basket to pick up your rations!" Hannah instructed. "You are too thin, Rachel. Too thin!"

Rachel nodded, then looked up with surprise to see that Captain Stewart still stood beside the barricade staring at her. She met his gaze; then, as Hannah gasped at her action, she walked toward him. She stroked Tikvah's head and said quietly, "Hush now, little one," as the child wriggled and squirmed against the tension in Rachel's body.

For a moment, Stewart looked as though he might turn and run from her approach, but her eyes held him rooted in the road.

A few paces from him she stopped and stared silently at him. "What do you want?" he snapped when the accusation in her eyes became unbearable.

Rachel spoke haltingly, carefully choosing her English words. "I saw you . . . the night you gave Chaim and Shimon to the mob," she said quietly.

He raised his chin defiantly. "I don't know what you are talking about."

"I was there," Rachel said, pointing to a rooftop on the border between the two quarters. "Shimon was the father," she said with difficulty, "of this child."

Stewart did not look at Tikvah. "You were his wife? I was just doing my duty. Your husband—"

"No," Rachel interrupted. "The wife of Shimon is dead. She died in childbirth that same night. It was she that you shoved to the ground."

Stewart's face went blank for a moment as the memory of the

292

pregnant woman crying out swept over him. He looked at the baby for an instant, then turned his eyes away quickly. "I . . . I am . . ." He did not finish.

"Tikvah is my child now," she said softly, searching his face. "And the child of my husband, Moshe Sachar, whom you have also taken away."

Her words seemed to sting Stewart. "I am doing my duty as a soldier in difficult times, madam." He said loudly, lifting his chin as though the flag of England were passing by.

"You are flesh and blood." She studied his face. "Yes, you are human, as are we. But somewhere you have lost your soul, Captain Stewart. And mine is the higher duty to take pity, then, and pray for one so empty and bitter as yourself. May God have mercy on you."

Stewart flashed her a look that contorted his face in rage. "I don't need the prayers of a Jewess! And a filthy whore at that. Yes! Akiva told me all about you, woman. Hitler had the right idea as far as I'm concerned. Five long years we fought to liberate you Jews and the rest of Europe. Five years my brother fought against Hitler; then he comes to Palestine and gets himself killed when a handful of Jews blow up the King David Hotel! And for what? For your ragged lot. For people like you! Whores and money-grubbing Jews." Stewart spat on the street in front of Rachel; then he turned on his heel and strode angrily out of the quarter.

Hannah came quickly to her side and put a hand on her shoulder. "What a terrible man. Half-human. Come, Rachel; come along now."

"We must be careful not to hate even men like him, Hannah," Rachel whispered. "Or we could become like him." Tears filled her eyes and she knew that this man who had murdered Shimon and taken Moshe was a creature chained by his own bitter, unreasoning hatred. "I will pray for this man; perhaps there is still something left of a human soul inside."

In the synagogue that evening, the story of Esther was read, and the children of the quarter booed and stamped their feet at the mention of the name of evil Haman. Spirits were lifted among the residents as the ancient story of God's salvation through the deeds of one woman was recounted. *Could not the God who saved the people of Esther also somehow save us?* The message of Akiva, following a play performed by the children, spoke of conciliation and the fact that in the days of Queen Esther no army had been necessary to defend the Jews of Persia against the plotting of Haman. In his words, the small band of Haganah who stood on the fringes of the crowd was accused of usurping the power of God to defend His people in time of crisis.

Akiva motioned broadly with his hand. ". . . God used men of peace to bring about His plan! Men like Mordecai! What, then, might have happened to God's people if rabble had come among them to stir them to violence?" He paused and focused his gaze on Dov, who stood at the back of the hall. "The accusations of Haman would have been justified! Think of the slaughter that would have come upon our people if they had not waited in silence for deliverance . . ."

A murmur of approval rippled through the crowds. Akiva pointed to the stack of food at the back of the room. "See what patience has brought to us?"

Dov's jaw was set, and his black eyes blinked angrily at the words of Akiva. As agreement with Akiva passed from one to another of those gathered there, Dov finally could remain silent no longer.

"Patience has brought death to our millions!" He shouted above the whispers of the citizens. "Were you there? Were any of you there in Warsaw with me?" He stepped forward and the crowd parted for him. The hush of shame settled over the room as the small, dark-eyed man strode toward the bimah. He turned to face the people, and Rachel saw that, despite his small structure, Dov lived up to his name, *Bear*. He looked fierce and brave and wise in his fierceness. "Silent witnesses," he cried toward heaven, "speak to us now that we may hear the truth!" He scanned the faces before him as Akiva sputtered angry protests behind his back. "Queen Esther did not wait in silence. She acted!"

"You! You interrupt the service of Purim! Return to your place or you will be removed!"

"As Moshe Sachar was removed?" Dov spun around to face Akiva. Akiva fell silent as he looked down at Dov. "I was in Warsaw!" Dov's voice shook. "I tell you I have heard the words of appeasement—these very words—spoken before. As we offered 10,000 of our own people to satisfy the Nazi demand for blood,

294

these words were spoken! When only 5,000 were demanded to come to the square a day later, these words were spoken. Peace! Our leaders begged for peace. While young and old were gathered and crammed into cattle cars and stripped and starved and gassed and burned, our people cried for peace! Our leaders cried for appeasement and sacrificed only a few more to the Nazi god Molech! I saw it all!" The people stood in stunned silence. Akiva stepped back and glared with eyes that smoldered with hatred. "I watched from a rooftop while my own father stood waiting for the trucks in the ghetto square. He, too, was a rabbi, and he said to those who waited to die with him, 'Jews! Do not be downcast! For today we go to see the Messiah! We should drink a toast!'"

Dov's voice broke. "And he took those five thousand bravely, and they died together. But even their sacrifice was not enough. And I tell you that on that day I and others with me decided to serve God by *living*! By fighting so that others might live! Believe me when I say the sacrifice of Moshe Sachar on the gallows will not appease false gods who offer false peace, any more than the deaths of a mere 5,000 satisfied the hunger of the Nazis for Jewish blood. One life will not save the one thousand of the quarter against the Arabs. Five thousand did not save six million in Europe. All perished together as we will, and this quarter will, and our way of life will unless we defend ourselves!"

Beads of sweat stood out on little Dov's brow. Rachel stood almost rigid as he spoke. She felt his every word as though it were her own. Shame closed every mouth as other members of the Haganah made their way through the crush to stand beside Dov in the center of the hall. "We are those who seek to protect you. We are the line that stands between you all and the kind of slow death that comes of supping on empty promises!"

Akiva bellowed loudly, "The promises are not empty! You see we have food here! Food!"

"Stolen from a Jewish convoy!" Dov retorted. "Ambushed in the pass of Bab el Wad! The Mufti has vowed to strangle the city, and he is doing just that! You eat crumbs bought with Jewish blood! As surely as Jewish blood bought a stay of execution in Warsaw! But if you do not come together as one, you too will be sacrificed on the Mufti's altar of Jihad!"

"It is you who should be offered!" Akiva shouted, gripping the rail of the bimah until his knuckles turned white. "You dare deny the power of God! On this holiday of Purim, when we remember the miracle of salvation—"

"God saved His people through the lives of others who were willing to die in their defense! Haven't the rabbis of old spoken of how Queen Esther could have been killed by the king when she came to him so boldly? Did it not take courage for her to offer her life in order to save her people? She did not bargain with the devil, Haman. No! She laid her own safety before God, and then acted on what she knew was right, even though she knew she might die for it!" Dov turned toward the people. "And there is a miracle of God! That one small person can change history by acting on what is right; by finding the courage to stand up against evil and *fight*! Our Holy Scriptures are full of such people as these. David against Goliath! Gideon against the Midianites; Moses himself; Joshua! Each one of the prophets! And, yes, some died, but the most wonderful miracle of all is that we are still a people in a world that has hated us! And this miracle has been made to happen by those who have believed God and had the courage to stand and fight!"

Rachel closed her eyes in prayer for Dov as he spoke. From the four corners of the room, other young men began to move forward toward Dov. Rachel smiled as she looked down to see the faces of young boys—the Krepske brothers and Joseph—among the group. Two elderly rabbis stepped out from the citizens and joined men who now numbered nearly two hundred. One white-bearded old man raised a shaking voice and said loudly, "Moshe Sachar offered us payment for prayer. I will offer my prayers of defense and salvation for the Old City and for these men who are willing to die for what is right. That is all that I can do, but I will do it!"

Akiva raised his chin angrily and glared down at the old rabbi. "And I say to you, that if we join with these men, we will lose everything!"

"And what good is everything, Rebbe Akiva," said the old rabbi, "if it is gained by sacrificing what is clearly right? I am with Queen Esther!" he cried. "I will lay my case before the King of Heaven and if I lose this life, at least I will have done what I might do for the sake of righteousness!"

Rachel felt the eyes of the women in the women's section of the synagogue. Each one looked to her as though she, too, might speak. But she did not. It was enough that Dov had spoken up.

God has not forgotten His promises to Israel, she thought. *He must be pleased that there are those here who are willing to offer their lives for that promise. Like Esther. Like Moshe.* She closed her eyes for an instant as the words in Leah's Bible came back to her. *What good is it for a man to gain the whole world if he loses his own soul?* She listened as argument filled the hall like volleys of gunfire.

"I say negotiation is the only path—!"

"The only certain path to death is appeasement! You negotiate with a friend of Hitler!"

I was so young, Lord. I did not know I bought each heartbeat with a piece of my soul. How you must weep when you see how little it takes for your enemy to buy us! Your own Son was betrayed for thirty pieces of silver. Moshe was traded for bread. Will your City now be sold for empty promises of peace? You have not forgotten your promises to gather us once again in this place as a nation. But still we doubt, and many of us have forgotten that you have said it will happen. I believe you, Lord, but help the part of me that does not believe. Give me the courage it takes to trust that you are still there behind the clouds of doubt.

That night the assembly left the great hall divided. Men still stood in small cliques and shouted arguments on the steps as Rachel hurried home with Tikvah and a small basket of rations. She burst into the lonely apartment, and after she had changed the baby and put her to bed, she went to the top bureau drawer and took out Moshe's torn tallith. She studied the jagged wound that had nearly ripped the tallith in half. "I will trust you, Lord," she said aloud. "I will trust that this nation will be as you promised."

By candlelight, she took out her sewing basket and worked throughout the night, remembering how the tallith had covered her and Moshe as a wedding canopy, and then again, how proudly he had worn it as he prayed, lifting his heart to an unchanging God.

And as she worked, she remembered how Moshe's face had shone as he had read to her from the Scriptures a passage that she had been unable to find later when she was alone: *"Who can separate us from the love of our Messiah? Shall tribulation or distress, or persecution, or famine, or nakedness, or peril, or sword? As it is written, For thy sake we are killed all the day long; we are counted like sheep for the slaughter. No, in all these things we are*

more than conquerors through him that loved us. For I am con-
vinced, that neither death, nor life, nor angels, nor demons, nor
any powers, neither height nor depth, nor anything in all creation,
will be able to separate us from the love of God that is in Messiah
Yeshua, our Lord."

Again and again those words returned to her, and for the first time since Moshe had been taken, she saw herself clearly reflected in the pool of God's love. And she knew for herself the truth of what Moshe had told her, *Oh, God, your love is stronger even than death. It is bigger than my loneliness and someday you truly will wipe away my tears.*

27 Deliverance

Bundled up against the chilly wind that blew in across San Francisco Bay, David and Martin sat on the huge posts that jutted up from the dock at Fisherman's Wharf. The fleet of fishing trawlers bobbed where they were moored, and whitecaps flashed on the gray water of the bay. David counted the seconds it took for the white light atop Alcatraz Prison to circle in its warning for mariners. Every ten seconds it swirled around like an angry eye looking for a foolish seaman who might venture out beneath the Golden Gate Bridge to the turbulent Pacific.

A light sprinkling of rain began to fall, beading up in Martin's hair and clinging to their jackets. A sea gull perched on the end of the dock and cocked its head as it appraised David and Martin. Then it shuddered and took off slowly, circling as it searched for a warm place to sit out the approaching storm.

"Are you sure he'll come?" David asked Martin.

"He'll be here." Martin crossed his arms and tucked his chin against the cold. "He's a good man."

David glanced up at the group of four muscled stevedores who unloaded crates from a trawler at the far end of the dock. Occasionally one would glance toward David and Martin as if to ask what reason these strangers had to sit on these pilings. Across the street, a portly man in a bloodied apron stared suspiciously out the window of his fish market. David stared back frankly, envying the steaming cup of coffee in the fish merchant's hand.

"I could do with some coffee," David muttered. "I give your colonel five more minutes, and then we leave, Martin. I'm freezing."

Martin nodded. "Colonel Brannon is a good man," he repeated. "He'll be here."

David glanced at his wristwatch. *Five thirty-five a.m.* The normally bustling wharf was seemingly in hibernation this morning. "Probably he overslept," David said sourly as he imagined the warmth of his bed. They had driven all night long to meet with Martin's friend, retired Air Force Colonel Charles Brannon, and now Brannon was late. Granted, he was only five minutes late, but in this weather, it was enough to put David on edge. Had a storm not been raging only a few miles out, the wharf would have been teaming with fishermen unloading their catch, and David and Martin would have been unnoticed by anyone. Now, even the furtive glances of the stevedores and the suspicious fish merchant made David nervous. He found himself glancing over his shoulder; half-expecting to see the bespectacled weasel of a man who had been trailing them across Los Angeles. Still, from the glowing reports that Martin had passed along about the colonel, this was a fellow worth waiting for, worth recruiting, if possible. Up until now, no one over the rank of captain had joined the ragtag little group of flyers in Burbank.

David closed his eyes and shuddered; then he looked up the deserted street to where a small man in a gray overcoat walked briskly toward them. His face was concealed beneath a black umbrella and he walked around puddles on the warped sidewalk. "Someone's coming," David said quietly. "Is that him?"

Martin shook himself awake and followed David's gaze. "Nope," he replied; then he looked back at the splintered boards of the dock. "Brannon is a big guy. Big."

David shifted uneasily, still studying the small figure that approached. He wished that he could see the man's face. His eyes narrowed as he stared at the black umbrella and he stood slowly, tempted to tear away the thing that hid the man's face from view. He imagined himself tackling this early-morning pedestrian to reveal the obsequious little spy who had become the thorn in their flesh. David took a hesitant step; then the man stepped from the sidewalk and crossed the street to enter the shop of the fish merchant. David rubbed a hand across his mouth and frowned. "I'm getting paranoid," he said to no one in particular.

"What?" Martin smiled at him.

"I said, I need a cup of coffee," David answered. Then, without waiting, he strolled across the street toward the fish market. The hair on the back of his neck bristled as he fixed his gaze on the door.

Martin called after him. "Bring me a cup, will you?"

David raised his hand in silent acknowledgment.

"I might bring you more than that," he muttered, convinced that the slight man in the trench coat was indeed the man who had been on their tail. Through the clear glass door, he could see the dripping umbrella hanging on a wooden coat rack. He quickened his pace and leaped over the curb as his pulse quickened. The man stood with his back to the window as he talked with the merchant. David grasped the doorknob and lunged through the door as a tiny bell above him jingled and the merchant and his customer turned expectantly to face David. Beneath the pedestrian's brown fedora, warm brown eyes stared questioningly out from behind tortoise-shell glasses. A thin moustache wriggled slightly beneath a bulbous nose as David stood in the open doorway and cold air blew in.

The merchant spoke in heavy Italian, "You leava th' door open. You lika to come in?"

Wrong man. You're a fool, Meyer. David closed the door awkwardly behind him and stood stupidly staring at the two men. "Me and my friend would like some coffee," he stated.

"Coffee?" asked the fish merchant. "You wanna have coffee only?"

David blinked dumbly, ashamed that he was ready to tackle a perfectly innocent man out for a stroll. "Well . . . uh . . . maybe a pound of salmon." He began to dig through his pockets for change as the merchant smiled broadly.

"Of coursea we got salmon. Whadda you like? Smoked or fresh?"

"Smoked," said David, suddenly hungry. He waited a few minutes while the first man was attended to, then laid his bills on the counter and slipped a paper-wrapped package of salmon into his pocket as the merchant poured two steaming mugs of coffee. David promised to return the mugs shortly; then he

300

slipped out the door and back across the street to where Martin now waited with a large jovial man with a red face and a sprinkling of gray in his thick dark hair.

"Charlie Brannon," said Martin proudly, and David offered the seemingly good-natured colonel his own cup of coffee. "Told you he'd be here."

Colonel Brannon shook David's hand warmly. "Pleased to shake the hand of a legend," he said to David. "I'd have come out to meet you no matter what the weather."

"Thanks," David said. "But you're the fellow we're here to see."

Brannon's face turned instantly serious and he pulled a folded newspaper from beneath his arm. "Martin told me all 'bout that, Captain Meyer. And I was seriously thinking of accepting your offer—"

"Was?" David asked.

"Have you seen this?" Brannon tapped the paper. David took it gingerly and studied the columns on the front page. There in large type were the words: ARMS BOYCOTT TO MIDEAST TIGHTENS. And below that a smaller headline read: U.S. SERVICEMEN LOSE CITIZENSHIP, BENEFITS. David scanned the columns, then looked up at Brannon. "This is not news to us," David said quietly. "The CAA is threatening to revoke our license unless we meet their code. It's harassment, that's all."

"It's a little bit more than harassment when they start taking away a man's benefits. I'm retired. A twenty-year man. I've got a wife and three kids. Two in college. I can't afford to lose my retirement, fellas. Much as I'd like to help—"

"We're all facing threats, Colonel Brannon. You've got a reputation as one of the best squadron commanders in the war. We could use a man like you."

Brannon sipped his coffee. He looked out past the row of trawlers, his gray eyes matching the sea. Slowly he shook his head from side to side. "When Martin called, I thought that maybe this was something I needed to do. I wanted to meet you. Talk this over. But this . . ." He motioned toward the newspaper. "So what if the CAA revokes your license? You can always register your planes somewhere else. Most of the ships here are registered in Panama or Ecuador . . . But if they take my citizenship, boys, I'm a goner. I happen to like being an American. I can't register my life and my loyalty in any other country—" Brannon stopped short, gazing curiously at the smile that played across David's lips.

"What did you say?" David asked in wonder.

"I said I'd like to help, but if I lose my citizenship I can't—"

David slapped the colonel on his back, spilling his coffee. "No! The stuff about registering the planes in another country? That's it! Panama!" David looked out at the row of ships and grinned broadly. "I don't know why we didn't think of it before!"

Brannon and Martin exchanged glances as David laughed loudly and sat down on the piling.

Early the next morning, David placed a long-distance call to the Mayflower Hotel in Washington and explained the workings of government bureaucracy and his hopes to register the airline in Panama.

For the trip to Panama City, David chartered a small, four-passenger private plane. He left Michael in Burbank to supervise the installation of extra fuel tanks inside the C-47 transports. Martin Feinsteinel sat beside him as they passed over the arid land of Mexico and down into Central America, finally landing on a huge, empty concrete runway on the Pacific side of the Isthmus of Panama.

Grass grew tall in the cracks of the tarmack, and as they stood in the sweltering sun, Martin gave an enthusiastic nod of approval. Panama had only two DC-4 aircraft and virtually no air traffic to compete with the fleet of Constellations and C-47 transports that they hoped would be the foundation of an air force and the salvation of an infant nation.

Scores of empty hangars lined the runway. The windows of vacant offices were a reminder of the wartime flurry that had created the airport only a few years before.

Three small, private planes huddled near the flat-roofed terminal building where a tired-looking man with brown skin stepped out of a swinging door to shade his eyes against the sun and ponder the arrival of these gringo strangers.

"On first glance," said Martin as he wiped the sweat from his brow, "I'd say your idea has led us . . ."

"Down the yellow brick road to Oz," David finished with a grin. "Can you believe it? And I was worried that there wouldn't be enough runway here to land a gooney bird on."

"Well, I know you fighter pilots are used to touching down on postage stamps, but I want to tell you, even for a big baby this is plenty of room. As my mother would say, Oy gevalt! Is this ever a *shiddach!*"

David laughed. "A marriage match?" he asked.

"Sure! They got the airport but no planes, right? We got the planes and no runway! You bet; this is a real shiddach, buddy!"

The dark-skinned man at the door of the terminal beckoned them to come in. It was too hot in the middle of the afternoon for him to traipse out to see what they wanted, after all.

The man wore stained trousers and a soiled white shirt that was open at the collar. He spoke with a heavy Latin accent but had some command of the English language. ". . . and you want what, señors?" he had asked in amazement when they explained their purpose. "You want to bring your airplanes here? To Panama? Ai!" He touched his finger to his temple.

"How far is it to Panama City?" David ignored his open-mouth stare.

"Oh," the man said, "that depend."

"On what?" Martin asked with irritation.

"Well, if you walk, it take you all day. Ten miles, no? If you take the bus, it take maybe an hour. But there no bus here no more. A taxi take you ten minute."

"Where're the taxis?" David scanned the squalid little building, staring out the window to the parking lot where weeds grew high.

"There no taxis, neither." The man sat down in a wooden chair and put his feet up on a packing crate. "Will you like a glass of tequila, maybe?"

"Well . . . how. . ." David sputtered. "How do people get into the city?"

"Nobody come here no more, señor," he said through a yawn. "Not since the war end, see?"

"How do *you* get home, then?" David wiped his dripping brow and coughed into his hand at the reek of sweat that emanated from the smiling man before him.

"Oh, I don't live in Panama City," the fellow said, pouring himself a glass of tequila. "I live over there." He pointed vaguely across the runway. "But maybe I could get you a taxi," he grinned, revealing teeth that were badly in need of brushing.

Martin turned his back on the man and whispered to David, "I think he is telling us we need to bribe him."

David raised an eyebrow and reached into his pocket and

pulled out a sweat-drenched dollar bill. "Call us a taxi, then, will you?"

The man shrugged and looked disdainfully at the dollar bill. "Taxis cost much more than that, señor," he said.

Curbing his impulse to grab the man by his collar and swing him around a few times, David rummaged for a five-dollar bill and dangled it in front of the fellow.

"No, señor," he said. "Taxis are more like a dollar a mile."

The price had been established and was paid. David now had a precedent as to how business in Panama was to be conducted—*Cash. Under the table.* Somehow, he felt that they had indeed stumbled onto the perfect place to use as the base of their operations.

Two hours after the phone call, a battered taxi clattered up in front of the terminal. A complaining driver, who also reeked of days without soap and water, made his fares wait while Spanish words flew back and forth. The terminal attendant and the cabbie discussed fare, destination, and the fact that David and Martin were suckers in the first degree.

"He say you gotta pay him twenty American dollars because he had to come all the way out here and you interrupt his siesta."

David nodded reluctantly and pulled a twenty from his pocket. "Yeah. Okay."

"In advance," said the man.

"When we get there," David insisted, climbing into the backseat. Springs poked up threateningly, and a blanket covered large gouges in the upholstery. "Hey, what kind of taxi is this, anyway?" he demanded.

"The driver say the goats get in last week and eat the seats," explained the man as he slammed the door. "Good luck, señors!" he called. "I will watch over your airplane for you while you are gone!"

"For a price, I am sure," David mumbled.

The rutted road to Panama City had some remnants of asphalt, but mostly it was covered by thick, choking dust. Grass huts and hovels lined the way; pigs grunted and rooted along the ramshackle fences, and old dogs slept in the shade beside their masters.

The Department of Commerce was a low, whitewashed adobe-brick building in a town that was obviously in siesta. There was virtually no one on the sidewalk, and the hot afternoon sun beat down on a shaded park littered with sleeping bodies. As David and Martin stepped from the taxi and paid the unsmiling driver his ransom, suddenly the street was filled with ragged children with hands out for small change. In nearly perfect English, they offered the two men merchandise and services that ranged from shoeshines to pretty señoritas to keep them company.

As they climbed the concrete steps and broke through the wall of children into the interior of the commerce building, David breathed a sigh of relief. The air was filled with the busy clacking of typewriters as a fan swirled the stagnant air above. A pleasant-faced receptionist sat behind a long wooden counter. She looked up and greeted them in perfect English.

"May I help you, gentlemen?"

"I don't know," David grinned and leaned on the counter. "I have found that every time I say *yes*, it costs me something."

Her brown eyes sparkled. "That is not the case here," she answered. "If you're looking for the office that administrates the Canal, you have come to the right place."

"Well, actually, we've come to talk with someone about setting up an airline here in Panama," David replied.

Her eyes grew wide. She stood and looked at them with what seemed like awe. "Oh, my!" she said. "We weren't expecting you so soon. We meant to have a welcoming committee at the airport."

"Well, uh . . ." David looked over his shoulder to see if someone had stepped in behind him. "I don't think anyone knew we were coming," David said weakly. "Did they, Martin?"

"Oh yes! You must be David Meyer and you are . . ." She checked a notepad, and David noticed that all the typists had stopped to stare at them. ". . . Martin Feinsteinel? You were with TWA." She looked at Martin. "And you are *the* David Meyer. We got a call, you see. From the U.S. State Department. You are a personal friend of the President's."

"The President?" David's voice squeaked.

"President Truman? We were told to expect a call from you. My goodness." She was flustered. "I'll have to call President Arias about this!"

———

Two days later, a sleek, black limousine pulled up in front of the Panama air terminal, escorted by four other vehicles, one of which contained the President of Panama and the Minister of Transportation. Yes, indeed, Panama would be more than pleased to have a new airline based on the Isthmus. Papers were filled out and signed. Processing would take no more than a week or two at the most; then the airfields and hotels of Panama would be ready to welcome the mechanics and crew of Service Airways. *It pays*, the President of Panama confided in David, *to have friends in high places, does it not?*

David still had not figured out how the wheels of fortune had turned so certainly their way, but he raised his eyes to the bright blue sky over Panama and thanked his Father for working out the details. *A week or two at most, Lord,* he prayed. *Thank you.*

28   The Bomb

Just inside the Damascus Gate, behind the shop of an Arab tinsmith, the sleek, black car of the American Consulate was parked out of view of the marketplace.

All four doors and the trunk were open like the wings of a beetle ready for flight, and Gerhardt worked deftly inside the door panels, taping the explosives onto the metal frame. Yassar watched the hands of the master-craftsman of death as fuses were wired to a timer that fed to the odometer behind the dash.

Shaking and sweating, the Arab driver of the consulate car cradled a brown burlap bag in his arms. In the bag were two Bren guns and ammunition that would cost the Jewish Agency a price higher than anyone could imagine—600 pounds for an Arab girl's *mohar*, and the lives of those who staffed the heavily guarded stone building on King George Avenue. And finally, it was hoped, it would cost the Zionists their illusions that anywhere in Jerusalem was safe.

Yassar held a door panel in place as Gerhardt silently replaced the screws. Every hollow place; every inch of the official vehicle was crammed with deadly explosives that made its metal shell alive with the force to tear down stone walls to heaps of gravel.

Proud of his undetectable handiwork, Gerhardt walked around the vehicle, slamming each door in turn as the driver looked on with apprehension.

"What if something goes wrong?" the driver asked in a trembling voice.

Gerhardt appraised him with hard, cold eyes. "Then you are a dead man." He smiled a thin-lipped smile. "If you do not reach the Jewish Agency in time, you are a dead man because the car will explode." His amusement faded and he stared threateningly at the frightened man. "And if you change your mind, if you run away or abandon the car, you are still a dead man." He took a step toward the driver and his jaw twitched with fury. "Because I myself will kill you—with great pleasure. Do you understand?"

The driver wiped his mouth with his hand. His eyes were wide and Yassar thought he looked as though he might collapse before the plan could be carried out. "Yes," the man said at last. "Yes."

Gerhardt rubbed his hands together. "Good. Then we have all done our part for the Mufti and the cause of a United Palestine," he laughed cruelly, as if to mock his own words.

"I—I—" the driver stammered. "I will do my duty in the hope that Allah will bless me and our leader."

Gerhardt smiled cruelly, "Yassar tells me you do this not for the Mufti or for Palestine but for a woman, eh?" he sneered.

The driver lowered his eyes and nodded. "I hope to marry."

Gerhardt laughed loudly and shook his head. "Ah yes! He hopes to marry!" He turned his eyes full on the driver. "What we men will do for a woman, eh? Today you will murder men who have trusted you. For the sake of a woman's soft body." His face became wild as he spoke. "Today men who trust you will be blown to bits. Heads and arms severed, eyes torn out—not because of your great fervor for Palestine or Haj Amin, but for the sake of the pleasure you will reap with a woman."

The driver blinked with horror at Gerhardt's words. "But what I do is also for the sake of—"

Gerhardt shook his head in disagreement. "For the sake of Palestine? Listen to the liar, Yassar," he said, tormenting the driver. "What you do, liar, is for your sake alone. You will remember their faces when you lie down beside her. I promise you that. And the sweet perfume of her skin will smell like death. Someday our people may hail you and me as heroes, yes? But we will know the truth . . . we will know . . ."

"Gerhardt!" Yassar shouted as Gerhardt's words flowed down a demented course into the pool of his own guilt and insanity. "That is enough!"

"NO!" Gerhardt shouted. "Death says there is never enough flesh to feed his appetite! Death says that someday even the sweet soft body of his woman will grow old and die and rot and—"

The driver covered his ears with his hands. "Stop!" he shouted. "Stop! I will do what I must!"

Yassar stepped between the two men and faced Gerhardt with a resolution that caused Gerhardt to laugh hysterically again. He wiped gleeful tears from his eyes. "Did you see my woman, Yassar? Did you see her? She cost me everything—"

"Stop now, Gerhardt!" Yassar pleaded.

"Yes! And I killed for her. And she is a Jew! And now the English will kill the man who has her! They will hang him for me! Hang him for the sake of Fredrich Gerhardt! When I am the master of death, someone else will have the pleasure . . ."

Yassar turned and took the horrified driver firmly by his arm. "You must speak of this to no one," he said quietly. "Now go! Do what you must, and you will have my sister. But do not fail."

As he slipped behind the wheel of the consulate car, the driver kept his eyes riveted on the maniacal face of Gerhardt. "I . . . I . . . do what I do also for the sake of Palestine," he said in a choking voice to Yassar.

Yassar nodded and touched him on the arm. "Then Allah will bless you," he said as Gerhardt raved on in the background. "Allah akbar! May he be with you!" Then he turned and watched as Gerhardt, great captain and servant of Haj Amin Husseini, dissolved into tears like a woman.

Kadar sat to the right of Haj Amin during the second session of the Arab League in Damascus.

Ismail Pasha, the dark-eyed Iraqi chosen by the league to head joint military operations against the Zionists in Palestine, cleaned his nails in profound disinterest as Kadar carefully explained the military situation that existed in the pass of Bab el Wad.

". . . if the Zionists can break through to Jerusalem—"

"But they have not," said Pasha cooly. "Your men seem to be doing a splendid job—"

"Yes! With scraps of camel dung you pass along to us from the Western Desert! Where are the field guns you have promised us? Where are the modern weapons?"

"The men of Palestine, *your* men, do not have the training to handle artillery. What if the Jews overran your positions and captured such weapons? Then we, the forces of the Arab League, would have to win them back again at a greater cost to our own men."

The muscle in Haj Amin's cheek twitched with silent rage at these words. It was evident that the League was quietly deciding that an Arab Palestine would not, after all, be an independent Arab Palestine. Haj Amin's voice was calm as he spoke. "In other words, our men who now sacrifice their lives for the nation of Palestine do so simply to clear the road for your forces? Where are the additional weapons you have promised to take Jerusalem and Haifa and Jaffa? Artillery and tanks?"

"Those items are in our arsenal. You have all you need for the time being, and your guerilla tactics are most effective. Besides, we of the League will take Haifa and Jaffa and Tel Aviv and Jerusalem after the British leave. We will take them in a matter of days after they are gone."

Kadar jumped to his feet. His face was a mask of rage. "You are a traitor!" he shouted, stepping forward.

"And you are a fool," countered Pasha. "The Jews are done for. They are finished already. The war is won! Have you not heard that the United States proposes a U.N. trusteeship for Jerusalem? The Jews do not oppose this. They are beaten. Why should we give you more money and weapons? We have done enough for now. Later it will be for us to finish this matter!"

"And I tell you this," Haj Amin said in a low, threatening voice. "Our servant in America watches while the Jews buy aircraft and prepare an air force that you will face if we do not finish them now!"

"You speak of Montgomery." A smile curved Pasha's lips. "Montgomery believes also that the Jews shall mount a major offensive soon to open the road to Jerusalem. Is this not so?"

Haj Amin nodded. "In the pass of Bab el Wad."

"With what shall these Jews fight? Those aircraft that make

you tremble are all in America, unable to fly because of the American arms embargo. The Jews have no weapons to speak of, Haj Amin. What you have is far superior. Perhaps you wish us to supply you with artillery and tanks so that you may also hold your brothers of the Arab League from the borders of Palestine?"

With those words, Haj Amin rose slowly and stood beside Kadar to face the other members of the League. "You betray us. You seek our nation to divide among you like jackals squabbling over the carcass of an antelope. But I tell you now that the house of Husseini will stand alone for the liberation of Palestine from Britain and the Zionists if we must. If our only weapon is terror, then the world will scream for relief from the agony we will bring . . . until there is one Palestine within our rule."

From the British Officer's Club on Julian's Way, the Montefiore windmill was plainly visible across a rock-strewn field. Beyond that was the tall tower of David's tomb and the jagged slope that dropped down into the Valley of Hinnom. The walls of the Old City wound from Jaffa Gate to Zion Gate, and as Luke looked out the window of the officer's mess hall, he could see tiny, ant-like men standing watch along the ramparts. They had cheered as the Jewish Agency disintegrated in smoke and rubble this morning.

The music of Jimmy Dorsey played in the background as weary officers carried their trays to vacant round tables and sat down to eat. Food was not hard to come by for the members of the British armed forces in Jerusalem. Unlike the Jews of the city, they were able to purchase fresh meat and vegetables among the Arab Souks that did a thriving business selling to the Jihad Moquades and Arab Irregulars who had flocked to the city to fight the Zionists. After meals, scraps and leftovers were distributed among ragged Jewish children who clustered around the back door of the kitchen. Three days earlier, a Jewish woman was wounded and her child killed by a sniper who had climbed to the top of Montefiore windmill in search of prey. Luke had headed the seven soldiers who dynamited the domed roof of the windmill. Still, he worried for the children, Yacov among them, who came each day for whatever food there was. When he was able, he purchased food at exorbitant prices on the black market, and slipped it to Yacov as he darted around the building across Julian and into Rehavia. The lad had carried home a small hunk of lamb for stewing and half a loaf of bread the day before. Luke wondered if Yacov would come out today. Word had come that Moshe and Ehud were to be transferred to Acre, and the bombing had driven Jews indoors.

Drunken, raucous laughter filled the room as Stewart and three other junior officers banged through the doors. Stewart met Luke's gaze from across the hall. Stewart's broad smile faded to a smirk as he motioned toward Luke; then he laughed loudly again. Luke turned away, studying the lengthening shadows of the Old City walls. He did not respond to the sound of approaching footsteps or the sarcastic call of his name.

"Well, if it isn't Captain Luke-the-Jew Thomas," the biting voice of Stewart hailed. "Did you hear your comrade Sachar the Zionist-Socialist-Terrorist is due to be hanged Wednesday? Quite!" Stewart's voice was cheery with victory. "Did you see the Jewish Agency, Thomas? The Arabs are evening the score a bit, eh? Jaffa Gate. The King David Hotel." Luke still did not reply as silence fell over the room. Not even the rattle of forks on plates was heard as the dinner music played on in a strange counterpoint to Stewart's jeering voice. "Now your friend the archaeologist will be executed in two days for the Jaffa Gate bombing, Thomas! What do you think of that?"

Luke continued to gaze out the window, but felt a hot flush of anger rise to his cheeks. Stewart came nearer and Luke caught the heavy scent of whiskey on his breath. Stewart put his hand on Luke's shoulder and whirled him around. "I am speaking to you, Captain Jew-Lover!"

Luke removed Stewart's hand slowly, with the care of a man brushing a black widow spider from his sleeve. "That will make one more innocent man executed for a crime he did not commit, won't it? How many have you personally fed to the Arab mob in the Old City already?"

With a roar, Stewart lunged at him. Luke stepped aside as the intoxicated captain stumbled and fell to the floor. "Jew-Lover!" Stewart screamed. A tall, stately major stood up.

"Now see here, Stewart! This is not the time or the place!"

"He is obviously drunk," Luke said loud enough that the major could hear him. Then he smiled thinly at Stewart who struggled to regain his footing. "A bottle of Glennlivet is not the way to ease your conscience, Stewart. Or even numb it. Not unless you plan on drowning in it. You and the entire Mandatory court system with you."

"You!" Stewart lunged toward him again and Luke stepped aside like a matador fighting a blood-crazed bull. Stewart rammed into the table, sending a shocked group of junior officers scurrying out of the way.

"How many members of the Arab High Committee were there to act as his judges?" Luke asked as Stewart pulled himself up from the table and turned unsteadily to face him.

"He was guilty! It was proven!"

"Guilty of what? How many lives did he save because he was there? You heard the testimony. Stewart, you're still trying to wreak revenge on the men who killed your brother at the King David two years ago. Moshe Sachar is innocent of wrongdoing."

"We have laws! He has broken them!"

"There are higher laws that he has obeyed instead."

Stewart stood panting before him. His eyes were red and sweat poured from his brow. "He is guilty!"

Luke appraised him with pity. He shook his head slowly from side to side. "Stewart, if a man like Moshe Sachar is guilty of death, then God help us all. For our own laws condemn us before a greater Judge."

Stewart stood clenching and unclenching his fists. He grimmaced at Luke's words as though he had been hit. He ran his hands through his hair and staggered back against the table. Lowering his eyes to the floor, he did not watch as Luke walked past him through the silent room, then out into the cold evening air. He had left his coat inside, but it did not matter; the bite of the wind was a welcome distraction from the searing heat of his anger toward Stewart. Luke leaned against the metal pipe that supported the awning above the entrance to the building. He looked westward toward Rehavia District and then bowed his head briefly in a prayer for Howard and Yacov and Grandfather. In only one week he would be leaving Palestine and Jerusalem to the defeat that would surely come. And yet, he had no longing to return to England, to private life. His heart was here. With Moshe and Rachel Lubetkin; with Howard Moniger and his red-haired niece. The thought of a peaceful life at home seemed suddenly the worst kind of farce. How could he have peace in his heart while others suffered so cruelly and unjustly? Had that not been what he had spent his life fighting against?

There is a higher law, isn't there, Lord? And you have called me to fight for that as well. He slammed his hand against the support in anguish. *But what am I to do? I am only one man. What difference can I make?*

The doors squeaked on their hinges behind him. He continued to gaze toward the horizon, afraid that if he showed his face to any man at that moment, his thought would be revealed.

A voice, lightly flavored with a touch of Scottish brogue, spoke his name quietly, "Cap'n Thomas, is it?"

Luke nodded, "Yes."

"My name is Fergus Dugan. An' I wanted you t' know I understand wha' you're feelin'. Me an' my lads spent the day down at the Jewish Agency building tryin' t' help, an' I think we're feelin' the same sort o' thin' as you." His warm brown eyes were full of concern. "They haven't found the driver from the American Consulate yet, but I'll wager no one will be roundin' up any Arab professors or doctors and puttin' them on trial for the deed as we've done with Professor Sachar." He shook his head. "I knew Stewart before his brother was murdered. He was not a bad sort. But he's gone mad for revenge. Like a lot of others. They aren't just hangin' Moshe Sachar, you know. They are hangin' the whole of Zionism."

"And I'm afraid they have won," Luke replied, looking down Julian's Way toward where the Agency building lay in rubble. "They have broken the morale. Broken the spine of the Zionist dream, Captain Dugan."

Neither man spoke for a long time as two other officers passed quietly by, their eyes downcast. Fergus settled his beret on his curly red hair and sighed. "Aye," he agreed at last. "Jerusalem is finished. Between the arms embargo against the Jews an' our own heavy-handed treatment of the Haganah, Partition is a joke." He smiled sadly, "An' the strange thin' about it is, our own government is rejoicing in its end. Like Stewart exulting in the hangin' of an innocent man. Ah," he frowned and shook his head. "The pride of men can be an ugly beast. The glory of Britain fades . . . we lost India to Ghandi, and when the wee little man was murdered, there was secret rejoicin' in the clubs of London. And there will be rejoicin' when these Jews go under for the final time, mark m' words."

Luke said little in reply to Fergus Dugan's words, but he agreed down the line on every point. It was good to know he was not alone in his sentiments. "And I was just standing here wondering if there was anything that I could do to help . . ." Luke knew his words were near to admitting treason.

"Aye? Were you thinkin' that, Cap'n Thomas?" Dugan's brogue became a little thicker. "If you're figgerin' on cooperatin' wi' your conscience, weel, I'll tell ye, I'm all fer throwin' m' lot in wi' ye!" His eyes had the look of a conspiratorial clansman, ready to defend the Highlands from England's invading hordes.

Luke laughed in spite of the seriousness of the conversation. "It's no wonder England had such difficulty conquering the Scots," he said.

"Cap'n Thomas," Dugan said, all humor now gone from his voice, "I know a few others who feel the same as I. I believe that if we do not do what we can to help, we have poked God himself in the eye. For these people are truly in the center of His love."

For the first time since Ellie had known him, David Ben-Gurion had the look of a defeated man. His eyes were red from tears that he had shed at the news of the Jewish Agency bombing. Thirteen dead. Thirteen dear friends who were more than mere names and faces; with them the Old Man had shared the first dreams of Statehood.

The shades were up on the window of his study and the gray sea and British gunboats were plainly visible in the harbor. Ben-Gurion stared out at them as the sunlight glistened on the water. Before him was a folder of Ellie's aerial photographs and a story she had written describing the plight of Jerusalem.

Still gazing at the harbors, he cleared his throat and said quietly, "It is an excellent story. Except that you forgot to mention that there is only food enough left to feed the people in Jerusalem for four days. Did you know that, Ellie?" he asked wearily. "Four days. And then all the reserves are gone."

"I knew it was bad," Ellie relied, shaking her head. She did not finish her sentence.

"But not so desperate, eh?" He swiveled his chair around to face her; his characteristic brusqueness returning. "Your photographs of the convoys speak louder than words. I think the American public will get some small idea of what we are up against. But one must live through a siege . . . or die in one . . . to truly know the effects of hunger."

He put his chin on his hand and stared past her to his book-shelf to a leather-bound copy of the works of Flavius Josephus, the first-century historian. "Jerusalem has been besieged dozens of times. Perhaps the worst was in the year A.D. 70 when Titus surrounded Jerusalem and trapped an estimated two million people within the walls at Passover. Nearly all of those perished and the rest were carried away as slaves when the city finally fell. And I suppose that was the beginning of all this . . ." He waved his hand across the room and toward the sea. "That was the beginning of our Passover prayer, *Next Year in Jerusalem*."

His voice broke for an instant, and he swallowed hard and then continued. "There are only one hundred thousand of our people in Jerusalem now. It is almost Passover again. You would think somehow we could find a way to get food and ammunition to a mere one hundred thousand!" A faint smile played across his lips. "I had hoped perhaps your husband would help us; the ancient proverb says, *Salvation Comes from the Sky*. But four days is all we have left until hope runs out with the food."

"Shall I send the story in as it stands?" Ellie replied after a full minute of heavy silence.

"I would like you to add one thought." The Old Man rubbed his hand across his lips as if to loosen his words. "Mention that members of the Jewish Agency have fully conceded that the city of Jerusalem must be an international city run and governed by the United Nations." He looked her straight in the eyes as if to capture any dismay that might flicker across her face.

Ellie showed no response. She knew what these words meant to David Ben-Gurion. Jerusalem was lost. There was no hope for her to stand against the Arab onslaught. The only hope now for the Jews of the city was a truce and a government directed by the nations of the world. In his words, a dream had died. If there was to be a nation of Israel, it would have to be without Jerusalem as its capital. "Anything else?" she asked.

"You could mention the four days of remaining rations," he frowned. "That people are hungry and the British do nothing to help us supply them. Of course," he added, "by the time this is published I suppose the four days of food will be gone."

Ellie scribbled a few notes, then closed her notepad. "Mr. Ben-Gurion," she said hesitantly, "my father used to say to me that as long as there is life, there is still hope."

He chuckled softly and said to her, "A very good and very old saying. No doubt first written by a Jew hoping to return. Next year in Jerusalem!"

"You're probably right." She felt embarrassed and trite in her attempt to comfort.

"And, of course, it isn't Passover yet. We still have four days of food left." The Old Man looked down at his desk blotter. "There is something else I need to discuss with you. I wanted you to hear it from me," he said gently.

Ellie sat up rigidly, suddenly filled with fear for David. "What is it? Has David been hurt?"

Ben-Gurion's face was grim. "David is fine. It isn't David. I wanted you to know that we did everything that could be done for Moshe."

"Moshe?" her face fell. "Why? What has happened?"

"We have done everything through diplomatic channels. I didn't think it would come to this, even with his conviction. I suppose the Mandatory Government is simply flexing its muscles one last time . . ." His words held an air of helplessness. "They are not interested in justice—only in quiet and appeasement of the Arab High Committee . . ." Ellie stared at him blankly, asking him to say what he dreaded speaking. "What I am trying to tell you Ellie is that there is nothing left for us to do. Moshe and Ehud both are being transferred to Acre."

"To be murdered," she said flatly. "In the name of justice. How can it be?" she cried. "Tell me how?"

The Old Man pressed his hand against his forehead. "We have done everything there was to do"—he shook his head in defeat—"and it is not enough."

29 The Shadow

In the front row balcony seat of Graumann's Chinese Theater, David held an uneaten box of popcorn in his shaking hand. The newsreel splashed the grim reality of the Jewish Agency bombing before his eyes. Angela, Michael, and the Feinsteinel brothers watched in horror as the tragedy was recounted. The blackened, scarred face of the building revealed the force of the blast, and even without the words of the narrator, David sickened at the sight. *Thirteen members of the Jewish Agency were killed in a blast that destroyed one-third of the Jewish Agency building in Jerusalem. . . .*

David searched the faces of the survivors who staggered from the wreckage. The blood on their faces and clothes was a dark gray on the black and white film of the newsreel, but David saw it all again, thick and bright and red in puddles beneath the dying. As a young woman covered her face with her hands and knelt beside the body of a friend, David muttered, "That could have been Ellie. It could have . . ."

Angela put her hand softly on his arm and looked at him with eyes filled with empathy. Then, she looked back at the screen and a corner of her mouth curved in a slight smile.

The tortured face of David Ben-Gurion filled the screen.

From his headquarters in Tel Aviv, Ben-Gurion called the act a dastardly example of senseless murder. He requested that the U.N. call for a truce in the Holy City and that for the safety of its Jewish occupants, Jerusalem be placed under the authority of the United Nations. This is the first indication of capitulation on the part of Zionists in Jerusalem.

Proud and sinister, the shadowed form of Haj Amin Husseini was shown as he moved through a crowd of well-wishers in the city of Damascus. *The Mufti of Jerusalem has ignored Jewish and U.N. pleas for a truce. Like Ben-Gurion, he has moved his headquarters away from Jerusalem and directs actions from Damascus. He has vowed that the Holy City of Jerusalem will be liberated from the Jewish Zionists at all costs and that he will destroy all who resist.*

David studied the man in the brocade robes. His pointed beard and fair skin and hair gave him the appearance of a man of Nordic ancestry who had dressed for a costume ball. Around his neck hung the crescent moon medallion worn by those in his service. David had never seen so much as a photograph of the Mufti before. He stared in amazement that the form before him was human—like any other man. "I expected to see a monster," he commented quietly, and again, Angela touched his arm lightly and leaned to whisper in his ear.

"There is a little humanity in every monster," she said. "That is why humanity is so easily deceived, David."

He frowned and nodded as the scene switched to the blackened hulks of still-smoking transport trucks beside the road in Bab el Wad. Then lines of gaunt-faced children and thin, weary women flashed across the screen. *Jerusalem . . . hungry.*

Memories of refugees in Poland and France and Italy flashed through David's mind. Hungry men and women and children, waiting with hope when there seemed to be no hope left for the Jews of the city.

A final sequence of pictures flashed across the screen as the words *Arab retaliation . . . Jaffa Gate Bombing* were repeated forcefully. David leaned forward in his seat as the thin, downcast face of Moshe Sachar was seen. He was dirty and disheveled. His cheek was bloodied and he was in manacles. Another image of Moshe appeared. This time he emerged from the heavy walnut doors of a courtroom and the narrator droned on . . . *Prominent archaeologist convicted and sentenced to hang for his role in the despicable crime of the Jaffa Gate Bombing . . .*

With a flare of music, the newsreel came to an end.

"We can't wait to hear from Panama." David's voice was choked and dazed. "The Old Man was right. We're not going to do anybody any good sitting on our duffs here in the States."

"But you can't do anything yet," Angela protested weakly. "David, your planes and men aren't ready. You can't possibly leave the States now. Not until—"

"Feinsteinel!" David hissed over Angela's protest. "Have the guys got those extra fuel tanks installed on the first two gooney birds yet?"

Martin nodded in the flickering light of the movie credits. "This morning," he mouthed. "What's up?"

"Can you handle things for us for a few days?" David whispered loud enough that from the two rows behind them came a chorus of "shhh!"

David stood suddenly, no longer able to sit in the theater. He stared at the screen for a moment as the cavalry rode across the rim of a high bluff and the music played the notes to *She Wore a Yellow Ribbon.*

"Hey, buddy, sit down!" an angry voice called behind him.

David hesitated a moment, then said loudly, "Come on. Let's get out of here."

The others stood and followed after him as he made his way down the steps and through the ornate lobby, then outside to where hand prints and footprints of stars were set in concrete slabs in front of the theater. David still held the full box of popcorn in his hand as he strode out to the sidewalk, then crossed the street to the Hollywood Roosevelt Hotel without looking back. The three men and Angela raced after him, their faces a mix of determination and confusion.

"What is it, Michael?" Angela clutched Michael's arm and struggled to keep up.

"Go on to the room," Michael said in a hushed voice. "I think we're leaving tonight. I'll be along in a while."

"Oh, Michael!" she cried as they hurried across the lobby to the elevator. "I want to come with you."

Michael stopped as the others surged ahead. He took Angela in his arms and gazed pitifully into her eyes. "Ah, babe. You gotta stay here for this one. You gotta." He kissed her forehead and brushed a tear from her cheek. "Now, go on up. I'll come on after a while."

She squared her shoulders and turned away from him as he followed David and the Feinsteinel brothers into the lobby bar. She glanced around the almost deserted lobby for the face of the small bespectacled man who had followed her nearly every day since she had arrived at the Hollywood Roosevelt Hotel. He was nowhere to be seen. She touched her finger to the elevator button and waited impatiently for the doors to open. *Somehow,* she thought, *I will go with them. I must.*

The long, dark hallway was even more deserted than usual. Here and there, Angela could hear the sound of a radio playing behind a closed door, but it seemed almost as though she were alone in the entire building. Again she glanced over her shoulder. She felt a sense of desperation as all her plans came crashing down around her because of David's impetuosity. *I must go with them!*

She turned the key and opened the door into her room. Drawers were emptied onto the floor. Sheets were torn from the bed, and the mattresses were sliced open.

Before she could cry out, a firm hand clamped over her mouth and yanked her into the room; then the door slammed forcefully behind her, and she was shoved onto a heap of clothing on the floor.

The bathroom light was on. Framed in the doorway was the small bespectacled man who had trailed her patiently for days and watched for her to make even one mistake. His thick glasses perched low on the bridge of his nose, his face pocked and scarred from acne. In one hand, he held a medallion—a sliver of crescent moon, sprinkled thick with diamonds. In his other hand he held a heavy revolver that he pointed into her terrified face.

"Please do not scream, Miss St. Martain." His thin lips curved into a smile. "Or I will shoot you before we have the truth from you."

"Who are you?" she cried, putting her hand to her mouth.

"Come now." He leaned against the wall. "You are not so innocent as all that. You know perfectly well who I am." The medallion swung in his hand, its shadow crossing her face like a pendulum. "And I know who you are."

She raised her chin defiantly, her eyes falling on the sparkling ornament at his fingertips. "I don't know what you are talking about," she spat.

"Well, I will admit you are much better at what you do than I am," the man said.

"You are insane!" she cried. "Let me go! I don't know what it is you want. I am a friend of theirs . . . that is all!"

"And Michael Cohen's lover? No doubt you would be David Meyer's lover also, if he would have you." He chuckled, showing a row of yellowed teeth. "Oh yes, indeed, you are much better at what you do than I could ever be. But I am persistent. I was sent to watch. Them and you. You almost had me fooled, *Miss St. Martain*." He pronounced the name with a thick sarcasm.

"I am a reporter!" she shouted.

"That you are," he chuckled. "No doubt the Mufti knows the very words Michael Cohen mutters before he goes to sleep at night."

She did not answer, but her jaw twitched in anger at his words. "What do you want from me?" she asked at last. "I don't know what you are accusing me of."

"Yes, you are good." He motioned with the barrel of the gun. "If I hadn't gone through your drawers and found the clothes; men's clothes—"

"They are Michael's."

"They are yours," he said firmly. "Along with the makeup."

"Is it wrong for a woman to have makeup?"

"Theatrical makeup?" he smiled again. "Are you planning on

playing King Lear or Juliet? You may certainly play either part, male or female, at will. I was fascinated the day they interviewed the pilots—to see you scurry about the hallway in a maid's uniform. And yet still I was not sure. I was not at all certain of who you were until I found *this* tonight." He held the crescent medallion higher. "*You* are Montgomery. Isabel Montgomery, treasured servant of Haj Amin Husseini."

At those words, her eyes became dulled and hard as the steel on the barrel of his gun. Her lip curved in a smile that radiated hatred. "And who are you, my little Jewish bookkeeper? Who are you that you would know such a thing?"

"My name, dear lady, is of no consequence to you. It is enough to say that I am a member of Jewish Mossad . . ."

"Zionist intelligence."

"Yes. Intelligence can also be an effective weapon. Your wires have been bold and quite straightforward. You became too courageous, and I think there was your mistake."

She shifted slightly on the heap of clothes. "I don't make mistakes, Jew." She moved her hands to straighten her hair. And as she brought her arms down again, a small flame erupted from her fingers with a crack that sounded like a cap gun. The thick glass of the man's spectacles shattered into a thousand fragments as the bullet punctured his left eye. He had not even had time to be surprised; in seconds he was dead.

Montgomery rose slowly and went to rummage through his pockets while his fingers still quivered and his legs jerked spasmodically. She pulled his passport and identification papers from his suit pocket. She shredded each possible lead to his identity and flushed the papers down the toilet. Then, she carefully tore her own blouse open at the front, sending buttons scattering around the room. She glanced in the mirror, confident that she looked the part of a cruelly abused and frightened woman. Then she smiled and picked up the phone.

"Please ring the bar," she said quietly. She closed her eyes in concentration and brought a well of tears and a voice that shook in terror as she waited. "Michael Cohen, please," she said. "It is urgent." A moment more passed until she wept into the phone. "Oh, Michael! Come quickly, darling! Please, the *man*! That horrid man was waiting for me in the room!"

Michael held the sobbing Angela in his arms as David lightly touched the carotid artery in the neck of the still, little man. He winced at the bloody face and turned away. "Dead, Angela. Good grief. I've been toting around a .45, and you did this with a .22 caliber pop gun."

Angela wailed and buried her face deeper against Michael's chest. Michael sighed. "What a mess. Look at this, Tinman! And in *her* room! We can't leave her here!"

"David! Michael! What can I do? Please don't leave me here alone! Please take me with you!" Angela begged through her tears.

David ran his hand over his face. A headache throbbed in his right temple as he surveyed the devastation around him. "What did the guy hope to find in her room?" he muttered as he washed his hands in the bathroom. He looked into the mirror and noticed dark circles under his eyes. *You're looking old, buddy,* he said to himself.

"We can't leave her here to face this alone," Michael called in to him.

"It's a clear case of self-defense," David said. "Robbery, attempted rape. She'll be out and free again by morning."

"You!" Angela spat. "You *are* heartless!" She leaned heavily against Michael and her shoulders shook with sobs.

Michael glared angrily at him as he emerged from the bathroom and stepped over the body. "She's right." His voice was hard and cold. "You bet it's self-defense. Look at this place! And you think once Angela gets that straightened out with the cops that the Mufti won't be sending along some other weasel to finish her off for good?" He cursed at David. "If this were Ellie you'd have her on the plane with us and under your arm all the way back to Palestine."

"This is different!" David raised his voice angrily, even though he knew he was beaten. The last thing they needed was a woman along on this flight.

"Different for who? I love Angela! And I'm not going anywhere without her. Not now, after this."

David groaned at Michael's words. He stared at the dead body of the little man and shook his head in resignation. "I figured," he said. "This is the last thing in the world we need. Yeah. Okay. She can come." There was only one redeeming circumstance in the entire situation. The body was in Angela's room. Maybe the police would not link the death of the Arab spy with David and Michael. They could hope for the best, at any rate. "All right. Let's move it. Martin and Mick ought to have the spare fuel tanks on the gooney bird full by now. They can wait here until the papers arrive from Panama and then organize the mass migration south. And there won't be a thing the CAA can say about it." He rolled his eyes. "You know, I came back to this country a hero in '45, and I'm leaving it like a fugitive. It'll be a miracle if the CAA ever issues another pilot's license to me when this thing is over," he mumbled.

"Who says it's going to get over?" Michael still patted Angela softly on her shoulders. "Hon," he whispered quietly, "it's gonna be okay. You're going with me. Nobody's gonna hurt you now. You need to get some warm clothes together. It's gonna be cold up there, okay, hon?"

Angela wiped her eyes and nodded. Her face was a mask of grief and horror as she pawed through a heap of clothing on the floor. She rescued a pair of wool trousers and a heavy turtleneck sweater from the clutter; then she found a pair of field boots in the small closet and tucked them under her arm. "I don't want anything else," she whispered hoarsely. "The blood . . . *his* blood."

David nodded. "As long as you know we aren't stopping in Rome for a shopping trip."

Angela shot him an angry look, then walked out the door that joined her room to Michael's.

"Go easy on her, Tinman." Michael's jaw was tense and his eyes burned threateningly. "I mean it." He followed after her, leaving David standing beside the dead man.

"I don't know what you were doing in here, pal," David muttered. "But you sure picked a rotten time to get yourself killed."

Careful to lock the door behind him, David left the room. For Angela's sake, he hoped the body would not be found by the hotel maid until they were well on their way.

30   The Kidnapping

Tikvah's cough woke Rachel from a fitful sleep. Rachel blinked in the darkness and sat up, listening to the deep rasp of the tiny child's breathing. With shaking hands, she groped for the candle and the matches as Tikvah coughed once again.

The room was ice cold; there was no more kerosene for fire, and Rachel jumped from bed in her nightgown and held the light over the baby. Tikvah twisted her head unhappily against the light, but she was too ill to give more than a feeble cry. Her eyes were swollen and her face red with fever. Her little nose was so stuffed that she breathed in unhappy gasps through her mouth. As she picked up the child, Rachel realized that her worst nightmare had come true. Tikvah was suddenly gravely ill, and there was no one, no doctor to help.

She laid her cheek against the baby's and gasped at the searing heat of her skin. Tikvah coughed again as Rachel wrapped her snugly in yet another blanket and took her back to bed with her. She plumped the pillows behind her and laid the little one against her chest, patting her gently on the back and trying to soothe her. "Mama is here, Tikvah, little Jewel," she crooned as the baby tensed and coughed again. The rattle in her chest was ominous and frightening to Rachel. "God of my Fathers," prayed Rachel aloud, as tears coursed down her face, "did you not give this child into my care? If I am unworthy, please do not take her life because of my unworthiness. Oh, God, she is so tiny and so helpless."

Rachel wanted to run down the steps and call for Shoshanna to help but she did not dare leave Tikvah even for a minute. As long as she held her up, against her chest, breath seemed to come a little easier. But when she laid her down, the deep convulsive cough shook the tiny body until Rachel cried out in near panic.

And so, through the night, Rachel sat up with her, singing softly the songs her own mother had sung to her. And she watched alone and prayed for the morning light, for surely in the daylight things would grow easier.

The distinction between night and day had long been lost in the endless twilight of the prison. Moshe slept restlessly and dreamed of Rachel running from Gerhardt in the depths of the earth, while Moshe lay bound and helpless on an altar of stone. Sweat poured from him and he tried to cry out but could not. Then the heavy slap of boots echoed faraway in his mind and the rattle of keys sounded with a voice that called his name. "Moshe! Moshe Sachar!" With a start, Moshe turned on his cot to face a row of soldiers who stood in front of his cell.

"What is it?" he asked, reluctant to leave the dream unfinished. He sat up and cradled his head in his hands. At the next cell, he heard the name of Ehud being called.

"Wake up. We are here to take you to Acre Prison!" said a gruff guard whose face was concealed in a shadow. "Stand up and face the wall!"

Moshe obeyed slowly, putting his hands above his head on the cold stone wall. The door clanged open and, holding their guns on Moshe, two soldiers entered and roughly searched him. He heard Ehud curse the men who repeated the scene in the next cell. "Do you think I have grown horns since I have been here?" the captain bellowed. Moshe almost laughed at the absurdity of such a search, but he knew that since the deaths of two other Jewish prisoners by a smuggled grenade, this search had become routine.

"Get your shoes on!" came the demand. Wearily, Moshe slipped his boots on. The laces had been taken to prevent suicide, and the tongue of his boots flopped out. He had a sudden urge to ask if he might have his laces back since they were going to hang him in the morning. But he remained silent, keeping the humiliation to himself.

"May I have my Bible?" he asked.

"Oh-ho! The Jaffa Gate bomber reads the Bible!" scoffed one of the escorts.

"Keep it to yourself," his officer snapped, reaching for the small black volume beside Moshe's cot. He swept through the pages with his thumb, as though searching even there for weapons. A white envelope fell out and flitted to the floor.

"That is a letter," Moshe said quietly. "My last letter to my wife."

The officer retrieved it and held it up to the dim light. He read the address out loud. "Rachel Sachar, care of Howard Moniger. Rehavia District, Jerusalem."

"If one of you could see that it reaches Professor Moniger for me . . ." Moshe asked.

"Of course." The captain's voice softened a bit as he slipped the letter into the pocket of his tunic.

"And my watch as well, please," Moshe asked. "I am afraid I came here with little else, but I am certain she would like to have my watch."

"What time is it?" Ehud demanded.

The officer glanced at his wristwatch. "Nearly half-past one."

"Afternoon or morning?" Ehud returned.

"Morning."

"You come here and wake a man out of a sound sleep to carry him off and hang him!" Ehud shouted as they snapped handcuffs onto his wrists. "At least a man should die after a good night's sleep!"

Moshe felt the weight of chains that bound his ankles. The soldier snapped the cuffs onto his wrists, purposefully making them so tight that Moshe cried out. The commanding officer mumbled, "Stand aside," and then readjusted them himself and pocketed the key.

Clumsy in the manacles that bound them, Moshe and Ehud walked, surrounded by guards, past filled cells. Other prisoners grasped the bars and shouted words of farewell and encouragement to the two. Behind them, the words of the Shema began from the lips of one man and grew from his voice to that of many, "Hear, O Israel! The Lord our God, the Lord is One! And thou shalt love the Lord thy God . . ."

Black on white, their prison uniforms blended into the bars of their cells . . . "Shalom! Shalom, Moshe Sachar! Shalom, Ehud! God go with you! Next year in Jerusalem, remember!"

They marched past the unused execution room and then past a small, dimly lit guard office, stopping before the massive iron gate bearing a sign on a blue background that announced in three languages, *Central Prison Jerusalem*. Outside the gates, endless strands of barbed wire lined the road, and the large concrete cones, once set to stop the tanks of the Germans, now separated Jews and Arabs.

The chill night air cut through Moshe's thin prison coat and he shuddered in the blackness of the night. He heard Ehud inhale the fresh air deeply and breathe a sigh of relief to be out of the closeness of the prison atmosphere. But immediately they were led to the back of a steel-plated van and lifted into its dark interior by strong, unfriendly hands.

They sat opposite each other on hard wooden benches and the doors were slammed shut, leaving them in nearly absolute darkness.

"Will they take us to Acre by way of Ramallah and Nablus, do you think?" asked Ehud as the sound of the drivers echoed through the steel plate beside them. The engine roared to life and as the headlights came on, faint light filtered through tiny slits near the roof of the van.

"That is the more direct route," said Moshe. "And it is all Arab territory. Probably they will think it is safer to go north that way."

"Safer for who?" Ehud scoffed. "If the Arabs got hold of us, the English would be denied the pleasure of seeing us hang, that is certain. And I will tell you this—I would rather die at the end of a rope than inch by inch at the point of an Arab knife."

The van lurched into motion, moaning as the driver ground the stubborn gears. Moshe closed his eyes and leaned back against the armored shell as he counted turns and mentally plotted the route that took them out of the city. *And here we should be passing onto St. George Road. American Colony to the right. Sheikh Jarrah and the Arab stronghold straight ahead. Here the road up to Hebrew University forks off. How many times in happier days did I drive this road in the morning sunlight? And now we turn onto Nablus Road. Yes, I feel the ruts. If I could look back over my shoulder, I could see Hadassah Hospital . . ."* With difficulty, Moshe stood, swaying as the vehicle proceeded slowly up an incline. He struggled to pull himself up to the tiny slit window above his head. There, glittering in the night, was the tall, brightly lit menorah, the seven-branched candlestick, that adorned the top of the hospital. Moshe kept his eyes on the lights for a long time, recognizing the shadowed shapes of Hebrew University just beyond. "Farewell," he said at last, certain that he would never again see the sight that had been so much a part of his life.

The jostling of the van caused him to nearly lose his footing, and he sat down with a clang as the metal of his chains bumped against the armor of the vehicle.

"Do you know what I regret most, my friend?" Ehud's voice

became tender. "I regret that we shall not be here to see the end of the story, eh? I would not mind so much dying if I only knew that it was for some purpose . . ."

Moshe did not answer. His own thoughts were still watching the Old City Walls, resting beside Rachel. He was grateful that the utter darkness concealed his tears from Ehud. *To never in this life see her face again . . .*

"Are you sleeping?" Ehud asked.

Moshe did not reply, but spent the moments recounting words and looks and the touch of Rachel's hand, as the road narrowed to a twisting, contorted one-lane path.

Nearly an hour was spent in silence, until the deep breathing of Ehud told Moshe that he had fallen asleep. The rolling motion of the van lulled Moshe himself into an almost dreamlike state. Slowly, he relaxed as they passed through the Arab town of Ramallah and on through Samaria toward Nablus. A few miles beyond Ramallah, the banks of the road fell away steeply at either side and the road became so narrow that mere inches marked the difference between safety and disaster. The vehicle shifted into its lowest gear and Moshe felt the pull of the engine.

Suddenly, the van lurched violently and squealed to a dead stop, knocking Moshe and Ehud to the floor. Ehud cursed and bellowed, "A gale!" The sound of angry Arab voices filtered into them through the walls.

A rattle of gunfire was heard as the British driver and guard shouted loudly, "Get out of the way! Move!"

Moshe sat up and banged on the sliding metal partition that separated them from the front seat. "What is going on?" he shouted.

The panel slid open with a clang and the face of the driver peered at them through metal mesh. "A camel. Down in the road! A band of Bedouins are out there. Say they can't get the beast to move. Albert tried to frighten it with gunfire but—" His smiling face froze with horror and behind him, Moshe heard a rasping voice say in distinct Arabic, "Your prisoners please, or you will die."

The driver raised his hands to his head and shouted in terror, "Don't shoot!"

Ehud clasped Moshe's hands in his own and said as the driver was dragged from behind the wheel and the cruel barrel of a sten gun aimed in at them from the mesh, "It is finished then, my friend. Shalom!"

Behind them, a blast of gunfire broke the locks of the van and to a chorus of "Allah akbar!" the doors were flung open and they were dragged out by dark-skinned men in keffiyahs, their faces well concealed by the night.

"Don't kill us! Don't shoot us," the British guard screamed from the front of the truck. Moshe felt his arms grasped fiercely by men who propelled him and Ehud toward the edge of the bank. Rifle butts and gun barrels nudged them onward. "We have them!" A voice shouted in Arabic. "They are delivered into our hands!"

The driver wailed again. "You want them, not us!"

In broken English, another of the robed shadows shouted, "Do not kill the English! Allah has given us the Zionist criminal Sachar and his companion! They are ours to execute!" A shrill cry of exultation split the night. Moshe was kicked hard and sent plummeting over the bank. His last view was of the driver and the guard clambering into the van and slamming the doors. Gun barrels pointed toward Moshe.

"Shalom! Ehud!" he cried as gunfire popped in what Moshe was certain was Ehud's death.

A scream rose loud and long as the engine of the van raced in the driver's haste to run away. Then the gun barrel at Moshe's throat was raised high into the air and a burst of gunfire pursued the truck as the broken doors banged wildly in the back. Moshe closed his eyes and prayed as he prepared for the jolt that would come to claim his life in an instant.

The hems of Arab garments gathered around him in a tight circle. He heard Ehud's voice raised in a curse against the men of the Mufti. *He is not dead yet,* Moshe thought; *they will kill us slowly.*

For a long, tortuous moment not one word was uttered; then a crisp, clean British accent called down from the road. "'E's gone, lads! And 'e's stripped all the gears along the way." A howl of laughter rose and a checkered keffiyah was tossed into Moshe's face.

"Sorry to scare the pants off you, old chap," said the amused voice of Luke Thomas. "There didn't seem to be any other way. Now we'll have to get these chains off you in a hurry. No doubt they'll be sending out a patrol to look for your bodies. We'd best head back cross-country to Tel Aviv. . ."

31   Escape

Its spare fuel tank filled to capacity, the huge, empty hulk of the C-47 gooney bird perched ready for flight at the edge of the Burbank runway.

David clutched a bundle of maps in his fist as the small group hurried across the field to the dark shadow of the bird. "I'm not filing a flight plan," David said to Martin. "As far as anyone knows, I took off on an instrument check and didn't come back, get it?"

Martin nodded, then jerked his thumb back to where Angela breathlessly jogged beside Michael. He lowered his voice and said, "You sure you want to take a dame along on this flight?"

"No choice, what with the dead guy back there. It's that or Michael bailing out on us." David dismissed the subject. "Listen, as soon as you hear from Panama, get the guys out of here. Just pick up and go, got it? Looks like the other team is starting to play dirty, Martin—" He ducked under the wing of the plane. "In the meantime, play by CAA rules. I left a letter giving you the authority you need if anything comes up. Get word to our contacts in L.A. Tell them to notify Rome we'll be arriving about twenty-four hours from now. That's midmorning day after tomorrow. Tell them to have the fuel truck ready and have them get in touch with the men in Prague. I don't want to end up chasing all over Czechoslovakia after stuff we've already paid for. I want trucks at the airfield in Prague, ready to load."

Mick and Michael opened the door to the cargo bay and helped Angela up as Martin extended his hand to David, "Mazel Tov, buddy," Martin said softly. "And keep your eye on the fuel gauge, will you?"

With a firm grip, David returned the handshake, then turned to swing up into the plane. "If we don't make it, you know," David said cheerfully, "you and Mick are going to inherit the air force of a nonexistent country!"

"Just watch yourself, pal," Martin called up. "I don't need the headaches!"

The cumbersome door to the cargo area swung shut and was locked securely by a lever on the inside. Angela stood against the empty shell of the plane and blinked at the darkness. She put her hand to her waist and felt the small, flat leather holster concealed beneath her loosely fitting sweater.

"You better sit down," David said as he passed her on his way to the cockpit. "It's going to be a long haul."

"Sit down where?" she asked in disdain.

"Anywhere. This is a cargo plane, not an ocean liner. We gotta make the best of it." He settled himself in front of the instrument panel and checked off with Michael as the engines whined, then sputtered to a start one after another.

As they taxied down the runway, David talked briefly to the tower and received an okay for takeoff.

"How long will we be?" Angela called from behind the two men.

"We're headed toward tomorrow." David replied between snatches of instruction from the tower.

"Yeah," Michael smiled over his shoulder. "You've heard of slow boats to China? These babies are as slow as they get to still stay in the air. One hundred ninety miles an hour. Which means we'll watch the sun come up over the Atlantic, right? One stop in Cuba to refuel, and that's it all the way to Rome." He frowned. "Did anyone remember to bring sandwiches?" His voice squeaked as the great bird lumbered down the runway and lifted slowly into the air. The sound of the hydraulics lifting the landing gear caused Angela to start.

"What was that?" she cried.

"Nothing much," David replied. "We just snagged a couple orange trees on the way up." He laughed out loud and nudged Michael, who laughed with him.

In the darkness behind them, they could not see the brooding face of the Mufti's servant. She stared at the back of their heads and planned each move she would make in order to bring them and their cargo into the grateful hands of Haj Amin.

Moshe and Ehud stripped to their shorts, tossing the prison uniforms into a deep ravine. They donned time-worn Bedouin robes that had both the look and smell of an authentic camel driver's garb.

"Wonderful!" exclaimed Fergus as he extended his hand and introduced himself. "As m' dear mother would say, ye smell like Lazarus dead four days!"

Moshe felt instantly as though he needed to scratch, but Ehud raised his chin and remarked that the clothes smelled fine to him and would be better once he wiped a few fish guts on them.

Introductions complete all around, Moshe noted Ehud's look of distrust at the British accents and surnames of the small group of nine who had rescued them. "Not a Jew among them," he whispered.

When Hamilton and Smiley and Harney slapped him on the back and reminded him of the night of the Zion Gate bus wreck and their role in escorting him and Rachel into the Old City, his spirits lifted. He was, he felt, among old friends after all, even if they were not Jewish.

"An what ever 'appened t' the pretty lady who was with y'?" asked Smiley as Moshe and Ehud wrapped their laceless boot tops with strips of torn fabric.

"She married Moshe last month," Ehud said in a loud whisper as he pulled a keffiyah onto his head. "And they have a beautiful baby girl." He left the British soldier to ponder such a miracle; then he strode to where Luke stood atop a rock to watch with him as the taillights of the van wound on toward the next small village.

"No time to waste," said Luke with apprehension in his voice. "I give them no more than an hour, and this hillside will be covered with soldiers looking for your bodies."

Moshe said quietly, "They'll be looking for you as well. You know you have put yourselves under sentence of death by this act."

Luke did not reply; the reality of what he had just sacrificed was too near. Home, country, career, a life's work—all was gone in an instant for him, as it was for these others who had come. "It was right," he said simply. Then he raised his eyes as if to search the darkness for a path that would lead them over the rocky, dangerous terrain toward Tel Aviv.

Ehud raised his nose and inhaled; then he said loudly, "The sea is this way, fellows. I can smell her plainly."

By the light of one small flashlight, the men clambered down the slopes that led to the Valley of Ayalon. Dogs howled from Arab settlements along the way. Here and there the lamps of

332

some small house would be lit, and the men would lie still and breathless against the hard cold earth as the feyadeen would throw a cloak over his robes and step out to search the blackness for some sign of movement.

The skin on Moshe's ankles chafed as the boots rubbed against them. Far in the distance, a faint halo of light glowed against the clouds. "Tel Aviv," he said as they topped a rise and scrambled down an embankment to see the lights wink back at them.

Far behind them on the hillside, Moshe saw the first of the lanterns of British who fanned out to follow their tracks. A mile to their right, headlights of four vehicles pulled to the side of the road.

"Turn off that torch!" hissed Luke as they slipped into an irrigation ditch and stumbled in the darkness. Moshe raised his head to see a dozen lights moving toward them. Snatches of conversation drifted on the wind. ". . . over . . . this way . . . saw something . . ."

"Keep moving, lads," urged Ham as he slung his sten gun over his shoulder and herded the other men like a sheepdog. "Stay down! Shhh!" he warned as someone whispered to his comrade.

Searchlights fanned the stony slopes they had just descended, and the hounds of the countryside raised their voices in a loud chorus of protest. Lights in every farmhouse came on and farmers who had only raised their heads to sniff the air in suspicion now turned out to search their land in earnest.

Moshe could not help but think that the prison at Acre would have more to hang than just him and Ehud if they were found.

Bent almost double, they hurried through the mire of the ditch. Mud sucked at Moshe's boots and oozed between his cold toes. Two hundred yards away, the door of a tiny shack flung wide, and a small fierce dog ran screaming across the unplowed field toward them. Louder and louder it barked as it raced toward them, then perched above them on the edge of the ditch as they crept past. Back and forth it ran, pointing out their location like an arrow on a map. Searchlights that had scanned the earth five hundred yards to the north of them now shifted direction to the homing signal of the little dog. Moshe peered over the rim of the ditch to the farmer who stood in his robes outside his door.

"Camad!" he shouted to the dog in Arabic. "Who is there?"

In desperation, Moshe called quietly back in flawless Arabic, "Brother, in the name of Allah! Call your dog away. The English hunt us!"

"Camad!" shouted the farmer. "Camad! They are Jihad! Leave them! Camad!"

The fierce little beast whined, then turned and ran back to his master. The farmer jogged quickly to a small pen made of brush and kicked open the gate, releasing about twenty bleating, confused sheep into the countryside. "Camad!" he shouted again as the dog moved the noisy animals with precision. Then the man called out to the ditch, "Stupid English will think Camad has barked at sheep. Allah bless you, brothers!"

Moshe did not answer as they moved ahead, but he wondered if the others in their group had sweated like he had. "And Allah bless Camad," he whispered as the British soldiers met the sheep head-on and were directed back to the north by the obliging feyadeen.

———

Somewhere over Texas, David looked down at his watch and yawned. It was nearly dawn in Palestine, according to what he called *Ellie time*. She would just be waking up, imagining him in peaceful sleep back in Southern California. *When I come back, I'm bringing her with me,* he decided. *Here I am, hauling a dame clear across the world with me. It might as well be Ellie.*

Michael and Angela slept soundly back on the floor of the cargo bay. In an hour, he would wake Michael and take his turn at some much-needed rest.

A brisk tailwind aided their journey across the southern border of America. Ahead, David could see the blinking lights of Dallas, and he thanked God that they were making such good time. By now, he was certain, people back in Burbank would be getting worried. After all, a pilot didn't take a plane up for an instrument check and then just disappear without causing a little stir. *Yep,* he thought, *this is going to cost me my license. This had better make some difference to what happens in Palestine, or I'm going to be a man without a country.*

He wondered if the little Arab who lay dead on the floor of Angela's room had a backup, someone who might send word to the wrong people that David had taken off in a cargo plane for parts unknown. He was relieved they hadn't filed a flight plan.

He did not relish the thought of being greeted in Cuba by the Mufti's henchmen.

The roar of the engines lulled him to a mental heaviness that made him wish for conversation to keep him awake. He yawned deeply and tried to focus his thoughts on Ellie and their little suite at the Jewish Agency. He wondered if that, too, was destroyed in the blast, and a sudden surge of anger wakened him a bit. Behind him, close in his ear, a woman's soft voice said his name, "David?" Angela put her hands on his shoulders and began to rub his tense muscles with an expertise that made him sigh. "You're so tense," she said, and her voice carried in it a seductive tone that made him instantly ill at ease.

"I need to be a little tense." He reached up to take her hand away. "You're going to put me to sleep, and we'll all wake up in Bolivia or Alaska or someplace."

She slipped into the seat beside him and gazed at the red and green lights of the instrument panel. "All the gauges," she said in flattering wonder. "How do you remember what they're all for?"

"Maybe Michael will get around to teaching you someday," David replied, sorry now that he had wished for company. "Why don't you go wake Michael up and give me a break?"

Michael appeared a few moments later and yawned sleepily. "Yeah, Tinman?" he rubbed a hand across his eyes. "My turn, huh?"

"Yeah." David felt embarrassed for Michael's sake as well as his own. What kind of woman was this who had so totally taken Michael by storm?

"Well, go on back and get yourself forty winks then."

David slid over to the co-pilot's seat. "I'll just stay here, if you don't mind." He wadded up a blanket and leaned against the wall of the cockpit to sleep in cramped discomfort.

32 Yehudit's Plan

Shoshanna clucked her tongue and touched the baby's forehead once again. "Oy!" said the old woman in alarm, then again, "Oy!"

Rachel's brow was furrowed with worry and she held her hands to her cheeks. "What can we do for her, Shoshanna?" she begged.

"Here? In the Jewish Quarter? Dear child, we do not have even one doctor among us, let alone any medicines that will treat such a bad case. I am an old woman, and I have seen this many times with children and with the aged. It is the Angel of Death, child."

"No!" Rachel cried out as though she had been struck a blow to the stomach.

"Perhaps it is the will of God that she be gathered into Abraham's bosom with her father and her dear mother," Shoshanna said quietly. "Here in the Old City there is nothing to do but sit Shiva for seven days and say the mourners' Kaddish."

"Oh, God!" Rachel dropped to her knees at the child's cradle. "Please, take my life instead. Take me and not my baby!"

Shoshanna sighed again and touched Rachel on her shoulder. "And for you, it must be God's will that you live alone and suffer. I will call Rabbi Vultch."

Rachel did not reply. Through tear-filled eyes she gazed down on this precious Jewel who had given her such a will to live when there was no other joy in her life. She touched her hand to Tikvah's cheek and choked as she sang the words of a childhood song;

"Spirit and flesh are thine,
O Heavenly Shepherd mine;
My hopes—"

She sobbed and then caught herself, continuing the melody that seemed to soothe Tikvah.

"My hopes, my thoughts, my fears, Thou seest all;

Thou measurest my path, my steps dost know.
When thou upholdest, who can make me fall?"

Shoshanna slipped out the door and returned a few minutes later with a deeply concerned Rabbi Vultch. Dov followed on his heels, and young Joseph with them. Rachel sat in grim resignation on the floor and held the rapidly weakening child in her arms. The rabbi knelt beside her and touched Tikvah gently, feeling the fever that racked her body. His liquid brown eyes studied Rachel with the compassion of a man who had seen the death of a child before. "When did this come upon her?" he asked in hushed tones as Dov and Joseph stood anxiously beside the door.

"Last night, Rabbi. In the middle of the night. She had a little sniffle before, and then last night—" Her voice was a pitiful cry for understanding.

"There is little that we can do for her here, Rachel. There is nothing to be done here . . ."

"I told her this," Shoshanna said in a quavering voice. "Oy, such tragedy!"

The baby coughed and Rachel held her closer and rocked her back and forth.

Joseph cleared his throat and spoke hesitantly. "This is pneumonia," he said. "My own brother had it last year and nearly died. My own small baby brother Aaron. But Mama took him to Hadassah, and there they have a miracle. It is a new thing called penicillin, and this they gave to Aaron and he lived. You have seen him yourself in Tipat Chalev."

Everyone turned to stare at Joseph, and Rachel bowed her head, afraid to hope for any miracle. Joseph met their gazes defiantly and said, "This is true!"

"How can I leave the quarter?" Rachel whispered. "Tell me how I can get her to Hadassah?"

"There is only one man that I know who might help. It is in his power to help, but I do not believe that he will. That is Akiva. He alone could speak to the English Captain Stewart who hates us with such bitterness." Rabbi Vultch replied, touching the baby again. "But I cannot imagine that Akiva would want to help you, Rachel. He has pronounced you dead and anathema in the congregation. To help you would be to admit your existence."

"Then do not beg him for my sake, but for the sake of this

child," she pleaded. "Please—Please hurry."

———————

By the time they reached the outskirts of Tel Aviv, twenty miles away, Moshe's ankles were nearly bloody from the chafing of his untied boots. The British soldiers under Luke Thomas's command stripped from their Arab garb along the beach just to the north of the still sleeping city. Each of the nine men concealed their precious weapons in a cache beneath the sand, and looked to Moshe for the guidance that would protect them from what would most certainly be death by a British firing squad if they were discovered. Moshe recognized Ham, Smiley, and Harney. The others were new faces and had come simply because they had a finely developed sense of justice and had seen enough of injustice to turn their stomachs.

"We are fugitives now," Luke said quietly to Moshe as they stood on the wind-blown beach and watched the sun lighten the sky over the Mediterranean. "Will you take us in the service of your country?"

"These shores have been a home for the homeless," Moshe scanned each man's face. "Because we have believed that, we have all become condemned men. I cannot offer you safety, but I can offer you a homeland to fight for if you will."

Each man extended his hand to the center of the tight circle, and as the sun cracked the dark horizon, they pledged their loyalty to a nation yet to be born.

"Well then, fellows," said Luke, "while I was with the British armed forces, I was ranking officer. But now I think that Moshe is the fellow we need to listen to." He turned and saluted Moshe smartly and the others followed suit. Moshe returned the honor, then pointed down the beach to where the lights of the city dimmed and faded away.

Forty-five minutes later, exhausted and hungry, they knocked on the door of Fanny Goldblatt, an old friend of Ehud and Moshe. After a full minute, a timid voice called from behind the bright green door of the tiny beachfront house.

"Who is there?"

Ehud cleared his throat and said loudly, "I have come for breakfast, my darling Fanny. And I have brought friends along!"

Nearly as broad as the kitchen doorway, Fanny bustled back and forth from her stove to the crowded table, asking questions as the men devoured a breakfast of blintzes and guzzled coffee as fast as she was able to brew it. Moshe answered her barrage of questions and patted her happily when throughout the course of the meal she embraced him with her pudgy arms and exclaimed, "Like one returned from the grave! So happy your mother would be, God rest her soul, to see you alive and wed to that lovely Rachel Lubetkin! Oy! And the last I heard on the radio this morning was that you had been kidnapped and killed by a band of Arabs!"

"Not Arabs, Fanny."

Smiley, Ham, and Harney smiled cheerfully up at their hostess.

"And not Jews, either." She patted Fergus on his curly red hair. "But *good* boys, all the same, nu?"

"Can you put them up for a day or so?" Moshe asked as he savored the taste of cheese and blueberries.

"As long as you like," she said, pouring more coffee to a chorus of thanks and compliments. "And will Ehud be staying also?" She batted her eyelashes at Ehud who growled and stuck out his cup.

"I need to call the red house," Moshe said. "Get in touch with someone who can get hold of Ben-Gurion in Jerusalem."

"Jerusalem!" she exclaimed. "Why, the Boss has been right here in Tel Aviv for weeks. You have been out of touch, dear boy. And the Jewish Agency was destroyed two days ago. Did they not tell you?"

Nine heads raised to stare blankly at one another. "The Jewish Agency?" Moshe asked. "Destroyed?"

Luke swallowed hard and blinked at Moshe. "I never imagined you hadn't heard about it, old man," he said quietly. "Thirteen killed. But luckily Ben-Gurion and Ellie . . ."

The forks of both Moshe and Ehud clattered onto their plates. "Ellie Warne?" Moshe asked in disbelief. "She is alive?"

"Why did no one tell us this?" demanded Ehud, suddenly angry. "We have only been in prison, not on the moon!"

"I am sorry," Luke said. "I thought you knew something of what had happened after you entered the Old City."

Fanny banged back through the doors and returned with another tray of blintzes as Luke explained the happenings of the previous weeks. "David Meyer is in America now trying to get the air force off the ground, if you will pardon the pun. But he seems to be having very little luck, and frankly, if my opinion can be of any value, you—*we*—cannot wait for his airplanes or weapons. Something must be done immediately for the sake of Jerusalem. All reports have indicated that the Jewish sectors of the city are on the brink of starvation. Ben-Gurion has asked for a U.N. truce."

Moshe sighed, suddenly no longer able to eat. "We were only a few hundred yards away, and yet it seems as though we might as well have been on the other side of the moon. Our rations in the Old City were nearly exhausted when I was taken. We did have a small ace up our sleeve; things must by now be desperate there as well . . . But for us to give up Jerusalem!"

"The Old City residents are, on occasion, receiving some crumbs of goodwill; always from captured Jewish convoys," Luke explained.

"Administered by Akiva?" Ehud spat.

Luke nodded slowly. "I am sorry, Moshe, I have heard nothing else about what goes on behind the walls. Nothing about Rachel. I haven't wanted to draw attention to her by asking."

Moshe nodded, then rose slowly from the table. He picked up the telephone and dialed the number of the red house. A distant voice replied on the other end of the line. "Let me talk to the Boss, please," he said in serious tones. The voice querried him, then paused. "Yes. Tell him it's Moshe Sachar, please. Tell him I'm in Tel Aviv."

————

Rabbi Vultch stood before the broad desk of Rabbi Akiva. His features were etched with pain and compassion for Rachel as Akiva motioned broadly with his hand and said calmly, "Yes. Her husband was killed last night as well. By Arabs, it is said. And you say the child became ill in the middle of the night?"

Vultch nodded, absorbing the news of Moshe's death and imagining the grief it would bring to Rachel. "Yes."

"Well, then, you see, Rabbi, as anyone would see; this can only be the judgment of God against the wickedness of this woman, nu? Of course her husband was a terrorist and due to be hanged anyway, but to have the husband and the child struck down at the same hour . . . it is the judgment of the Almighty."

Rabbi Vultch lowered his head in disbelief at Akiva's words. "You are saying you will not help Rachel Sachar get her child safely to medical care in the New City?" His tone was steady but hard with anger. "You will not speak to the English?"

"I am saying I cannot fight against God's will. If this person is escorted out, the child will die anyway, and then I will have imposed on the captain for no purpose. His men will have risked their lives to escort a prostitute and a dead child out through the Arab Quarter to safety. Can I do that in good conscience?"

"The child is not dead yet. In the New City there is medicine that might save her—"

"There is no medicine in the New City either." Akiva sounded gruff and impatient. "And even if there were, it is the will of the Almighty that the child not live in the care of such a woman."

Rabbi Vultch stared fiercely at Akiva until at last the portly, grizzled mayor of the Old City knit his brows together. "Enough of this," he said. "I have duties of administration to attend to. You can see yourself out, I am certain." He picked up a stack of papers and searched through them as Rabbi Vultch turned on his heel and left, slamming the door behind him. He put his hand to his forehead in an attempt to control the rage he felt. His hands shook and he swayed as he stood in the shadow of the foyer.

A soft, hesitant hand touched his elbow. "Rabbi Vultch?" Yehudit Akiva whispered hoarsely. "Please?" she crooked her finger and led him down the long hallway into the big kitchen. She put a finger to her lips and shut the door behind him. "The baby is ill?" she whispered. "Tikvah?" Her young, pinched face was lined with concern. "I want to help you, please."

He watched as she pointed to a telephone that hung on the wall. "How can you help, Yehudit?"

"Please," she said. "This is a direct line to the British headquarters. You call. You will be the voice of my father and tell them to hurry. Tell them about the child. And tell them that you wish to send your daughter . . . me . . . out of the Old City under escort with Rachel. *Please*," she begged, glancing over her shoulder. "Hurry. Before he finds out!" She picked up the receiver and handed it to him as the phone on the other end of the line buzzed insistently.

"Yes?" a brisk British voice said.

Vultch hesitated, then looked into Yehudit's pleading face. *There is no other way!* "This is Rabbi Akiva. May I have a word with Captain Stewart, please . . ."

33 Up from the Grave

Moshe showered and shaved, donning the clothes he had kept at Fanny's for his forays on the *Ave Maria*. In his dark blue wool trousers and cable-knit sweater, he looked every bit the part of a sardine fisherman on the waterfront of Tel Aviv with a few members of his crew. While the others slept, Moshe, Ehud, Luke, and Fergus strolled down the boardwalk toward the red house. Luke wore an extra set of Moshe's clothes and Fergus covered his civilian dress with a slicker. Ehud was home again in baggy trousers, a heavy pea coat, and his fisherman's cap. He was, however, missing one thing that had been with him throughout the years Moshe had known him. Ehud Schiff now walked along the waterfront of his home port without anyone recognizing him. At Moshe's insistence, he had shaved the grizzled beard that had long been his trademark.

"Better Jew without a beard," he had sadly agreed, "than a beard without a Jew!"

Now, he reached up to touch his nicked and hairless cheeks, and muttered about his nakedness. As the four men passed a news rack, however, he was suddenly grateful for Moshe's advice. Photographs of both of them in heavy beards adorned the front page of the *Post*, describing their kidnapping and murder.

Ehud pulled his cap low over his eyes, and altered the tone of his voice as he stopped to purchase a paper from a small near-sighted man who had been selling papers on the same corner for years. "A shame about these fellows," he said to the vendor as Moshe and the others kept on walking.

"Ah, yes!" exclaimed the newsman as he made change. "Tragic. Professor Sachar was a wonderful fellow. This Ehud Schiff was a bag of wind, God rest his soul, but I suppose his heart was in the right place."

Ehud stared at him fiercely and snatched the paper from him. "How can you speak ill of the dead like that?"

"So, who's speaking ill?" asked the man. "Ehud Schiff, it is said, caused half the gales on the Mediterranean by opening his mouth!"

"Ha! I will remember you said that," Ehud stalked away.

Moshe looked at Ehud sideways. "It is a comfort to know you are going to be missed, isn't it?" He submerged a laugh as Ehud grumbled the last three blocks to the red house.

Moshe had only raised his hand to knock when the door was flung open and Ellie tearfully embraced him. "Oh, Moshe!" she cried, tugging him inside and closing the door. "Moshe!" She wrapped her arms around him and laid a damp cheek against his. "We all thought you were killed last night! The news reports said . . ."

Filled with happiness at seeing her again, Moshe stroked her hair and kissed her lightly on the top of her head. "Yes . . . the news reports also said that you had been killed at the *Post* last month. Rachel and I—"

She saw Luke then and directed her tearful happiness to him, "And *you*," she said, lovingly embracing the proud, straight captain. "You and your men rescued Moshe, they said. God bless you, Luke. God bless you for what you've done . . ."

He patted her awkwardly and chuckled a bit nervously. "Well now," he said in a flush of embarrassment, "we just all have done what we needed to do . . ." He cleared his throat as Ellie stepped back and wiped her eyes.

"Excuse me," she said. "It's just that . . ." Her voice choked up again.

Moshe patted her head as if she were his kid sister. "It is all right, little shiksa," he said quietly. "I myself shed tears when I heard you were alive and safe. Ehud and I only heard this morning, and when I left my Rachel, she still grieved for you."

"It's nice to know I was missed," she smiled through her tears, then laughed. "Where is that old smelly bear of a captain, anyway?" she asked, looking directly at Ehud and Fergus with a polite smile.

Ehud snorted and reached his hand to tug a beard that was now gone. "Well, I am here!" he exclaimed. "It is I, little shiksa! Also returned from the grave!"

With a happy cry, Ellie embraced Ehud and the tears flowed freely again.

Ehud patted her gently on the back and stuck out his lower lip. "Ah yes," he said with a contented sigh. "It is nice to know that one would be missed."

Moshe frowned at the words and said in a quiet voice, "Little sister, Rachel is left in such terrible grief. I was with her when the news came that you were dead, and now the papers report that I am missing, taken by Arab raiders in the night. Before another word is spoken I must go to the radio room. Word must be sent to her in code so that she will know that we are both alive. I know her heart, and at this moment I feel such grief for her . . ."

Ellie touched the face of this sensitive and loving man, then took him by the hand, leading him down the steps of a dark cellar to a tiny bathroom where the radio was safely tucked away.

———

The joy of reunion was quickly replaced by profound weariness as Moshe stared at the map of Palestine and listened with the others to the words of David Ben-Gurion.

"Since the Mufti and his Arab High Committee have rejected the U.N. offer of truce, that means only one thing—"

"Why should he accept a truce when he is so clearly winning the battle for Jerusalem?" asked Luke solemnly. "He does not want the city to be governed by the nations of the world. He wants it for his own."

Moshe finished the logical progression of thought. "And so the Jews of the city will be driven out, or starved out, or simply annihilated."

Ben-Gurion nodded, looking very old, Moshe thought, as he handed the ration lists to Moshe. "Since you compiled these," Ben-Gurion said, "we have been totally unable to resupply the reserves."

Moshe grimly scanned the lists. "No food has gotten through in all the time I have been in the Old City?"

Ben-Gurion raised his eyebrows and shook his head. "We have drawn up some alternate plans for evacuation of our people. Tomorrow it will be submitted to the U.N. Security Council. It will take U.N. troops to help with withdrawal." His words were tinged with the bitterness of defeat.

Fergus stared at the map, focusing on the red circle around Kastel and the blood-red line that marked Bab el Wad. "To have an Israel without Jerusalem," he said quietly, "without Zion."

"Well, gentlemen, we seem to have no alternative at this point. There are one hundred thousand Jewish lives to think of. Not so many when you consider the six million we lost so recently, but they are one hundred thousand that remain . . ." Ben-

Gurion scowled. "The battle for Jerusalem is over. Over."

Luke lifted his chin and narrowed his eyes in consideration of the Old Man's words. Finally, he asked, "How many men do you have in the Haganah?"

"Throughout the entire Yishuv, counting old men and boys and women in the homeguard, perhaps ten thousand." The Old Man smiled a hard smile. "The reality is, of course, that only a fraction of those are armed."

Luke dug a little deeper. "How many are armed and could fight if they had to? I mean, how many could you pull together, say, tomorrow night, and still leave some protection for the rest of the settlement?"

"With weapons and a few rounds of ammunition . . ." He thought, then looked at yet another list. "We can spare no one from the kibbutzim," Ben-Gurion said. "Possibly two hundred from Haifa. Another two or three hundred from Tel Aviv. And then there are the fellows in Jerusalem itself, but ammunition is so short." He reached into his desk and removed Ellie's aerial photographs. "Take a look at this." He passed the stack of photos to Luke. "There are at least two thousand Arabs holding Bab el Wad. And this was last week. Pull a picture out from the bottom of the stack," he instructed.

As Moshe and Fergus leaned in, Luke found an enlarged picture of a dozen Arabs around the body of a dead Jew on the road. In the hands of each Jihad Moquade was a weapon.

The Old Man waited for the detail of the photo to sink in. "Automatic rifles," he said simply. "And bandoliers of bullets around their chests. For our fellows to make a difference, every bullet we have would have to find its mark. Each bullet from a dozen different kinds of antique rifles we have managed to glean from the countryside." He paused for effect. "Of course, some new weapons have come into our hands. Like the two Bren guns brought by the American Consulate driver to the Jewish Agency." His voice was ripe with sarcasm. "No, I am afraid that we have to save what we can. Save every bullet and every man for the day the British leave. And then we will fight and hope and pray and wait for the planes that will bring our salvation."

Moshe straightened the photographs and placed them neatly on the corner of the Old Man's desk. "So we withdraw from Jerusalem," he said hoarsely.

The Old Man nodded, and the room was blanketed in a heavy,

thoughtful silence. A sharp knock sounded on the door and, without waiting for a reply, the door opened and a young eager lad of about twenty poked his head into the study. He had a pair of glasses shoved up on his head and was carrying a slip of paper. "Pardon me, Boss," he said. "This just came in from Rome. It isn't typed, but I thought you would want to see it immediately."

The Old Man scowled at the interruption, but motioned to the young man with his hand. He took the paper from him and spat, "And it isn't decoded either!"

The young man took the paper and read aloud, "Balaam floating Latin Detroit Ford Caleb Delilah jawbone vodka." He glanced up and smiled as though the message was as plain as could be.

"Well?" The Old Man slapped the desk. "What does it mean?"

"Simple. Balaam is David Meyer. Floating is flying. Latin Detroit is Latin America. Ford is a C-47 cargo plane. Caleb is Michael Cohen and Delilah is a woman. Jawbone is weapons, like the jawbone of an ass. . . ?"

The Old Man resisted the urge to comment on this last, and instead sat considering the words. "Go on."

"And vodka is Czechoslovakia. So all together this says that David Meyer is flying from someplace in Latin America in a C-47 to pick up weapons in Czechoslovakia." The young man's eyes and voice were bright. "I thought you would want to know."

The Old Man sat bolt upright. "*When*?" He demanded. "When is this miracle taking place?"

The young man frowned. "Well, right now, I guess, Boss. They wouldn't send the wire if he wasn't on his way."

———

Hours passed in bustling activity as plans were drawn for the relief of Jerusalem.

"If we could get three thousand tons of food into the warehouses of Jerusalem, we could feel safe," Moshe said as he reviewed his figures.

"Three thousand tons?" asked a harried assistant to the Old Man. "How many trucks will we need to haul so much?"

"At least three hundred," Moshe said after only a moment's hesitation.

"Impossible." The man shook his head. "We do not have more than sixty available."

Ehud sat at a cluttered desk opposite them and munched a kosher salami sandwich. "Not *available*?" He boomed. "Where is your sense of priority, man? Have you not heard of piracy? Of hijacking? Of Shanghai? Give me men and we will go into the streets of Tel Aviv! Jerusalem shall have her trucks and drivers too whether they like it or not! Ha!" he scoffed. "Three hundred or five hundred, Jerusalem shall have them!"

Silence fell over the planning room as each of a dozen men looked at the massive figure of Ehud standing in their midst.

"How many Haganah recruits do you need?" the Old Man asked at last.

"Twenty," sniffed Ehud with a defiant air.

"You are saying we should kidnap trucks and drivers?" protested the assistant.

"A captain can find vessel and crew easy enough if he has the stuff pirates are made of." He thumped his huge barrel chest. "Moshe and I have proved that long since." He glanced around the room. "I need twenty men. As big as myself, if you please. As strong and mean as stevedores, eh?"

By unanimous decision, Ehud was given authority to draft the men and trucks of Tel Aviv into the service of the Haganah. With the help of Hamilton and Smiley, twenty of the largest Haganah recruits were armed and sent onto the main boulevard of the city. Promise of compensation was offered to the drivers of privately owned trucks, but if all else failed, the angry drivers found themselves staring down the barrel of a pistol. One by one the convoy gathered on a playing field, and then was moved to an army base the English had already deserted on the outskirts of the city.

Luke and Fergus clustered around maps with Moshe and three other Haganah commanders while the strategy of diversion was discussed and decided upon.

Luke studied the narrow corridor that led from Tel Aviv through Arab territory past Kastel and then Jerusalem. "A thousand soldiers should do it, provided David arrives with more than pop guns. I believe that we overestimate the firing power of the Arabs. They have rifles, but nowhere in all the reconnaissance photos did I see any field artillery. Look." He spread the photos out across the table. Small stone villages dotted the barren hills while broken fences terraced the bleak countryside on either side of the road to Jerusalem. "The strength of the siege lies in these tiny villages along the corridor. The villagers themselves guard the road. They have no telephones, so messages are sent on foot or horseback and they come to fight in Kastel where the gorge is deepest and the road most treacherous." He searched the faces of those who gathered around him. "If we attack all out, here in Ramle, just outside Jewish territory, what do you suppose will happen?"

A rush of excitement rippled through the room as Moshe answered, in awe at the simplicity of the plan. "If we attack at Ramle, word will be sent to all the villages, even Kastel."

"And then?" Luke asked with a twinkle in his eyes.

"It will happen as it always does," said a Haganah commander. "The Arab Jihads will run to defend."

"Exactly!" Luke pointed to Kastel, high in the pass. "And then even Kastel will remain defenseless and open to a smaller force of our fellows, who will take it and open the pass."

Moshe nodded at the sensible logistics of the plan. His eyes met those of Ben-Gurion and saw the old fire rekindled. "Then once we take Kastel, Ehud runs the convoys up the pass to Jerusalem."

"And the Red Sea is parted," said Ben-Gurion with quiet hope. "We will call this plan after the first brave Hebrew who walked into the Red Sea as its waters parted . . . *Operation Naschon*." He looked up to where the young radio operator stood open-mouthed at the daring plan. "Send a wire to Weizmann in America," he instructed. "Tell him to hold off on submitting that plan for evacuation of Jerusalem to the Security Council. Tell him instead that we plan to hold on to Jerusalem with our teeth." He smiled and wiped beads of sweat from his brow. "In the meantime, we assemble our forces and wait. We wait for word from that crazy American of Ellie's, eh?"

"It would be helpful if we had more detailed photos of the terrain around Ramle," suggested Luke. "Fences, terracing, olive groves, and the like." He sifted through the photos of Kastel. "These pictures of the area around Kastel are fairly comprehensive." He handed them to Moshe.

The Old Man said quietly to his assistant. "Get Ellie out of the kitchen, will you? And tell Bobby Milkin we need a pilot."

———

The afternoon sun had burned off the morning haze, and visibility stretched to the horizon of the Mediterranean as the little

Piper Cub circled and climbed above Tel Aviv.

As Bobby Milkin muttered and chewed his green cigar, Ellie looked to the north over the sea, hoping to catch a glimpse of David's plane.

"You say he will come from that direction?" she asked Bobby over the roar of the engine.

"Yeah. North. But he ain't comin' this early. He and Cohen probably ain't even landed in Rome yet, so don't strain your eyes."

Ellie still had not gotten used to Bobby's gruff manner, but she smiled and nodded, still keeping her eyes on the horizon in hope.

Only a few minutes passed before Bobby banked the plane over the tiny stone huts of Ramle. The largest buildings in the village were the mosque and the house of the Muhktar. Ellie raised her camera and snapped the shutter again and again as Bobby flew a few hundred feet above the heads of curious villagers.

Ellie could distinctly see the veiled faces of the women who lowered water jugs from their heads and stared up at the plane. Sheep bleated and ran in confusion around their pens as angry farmers shook their fists at the noisy Piper, and ran quickly to their houses to get their rifles.

As the first shot was fired from the ground, Ellie took the last of two dozen photos. She could not hear the pop of the rifle below, but a bullet hit the wing of the plane with a crack, causing Bobby to curse loudly and pull the plane upward and out of range.

Orchards and stone fences were clearly visible, and even her untrained eye could see that the terrain would provide excellent cover and difficult fighting for both sides.

Stretched across the plain for about six miles, nearly a dozen small villages lined the road, and as they passed overhead, villagers swarmed out to look up and shake their fists in fury at the Jewish plane.

"Do you think this will be as simple as Moshe says?" Ellie asked, looking out at the bullet hole in the wing.

Bobby worked the stub of his cigar and gave a short, sarcastic laugh. "Believe me, sweetheart," he said, "when there's people dyin', nuthin' is ever easy!"

He made one more low pass over the villages, letting the lo-

349

cal military population know that "something was definitely brewing," as he said to Ellie. Several more bullets lodged in the fuselage, and Bobby shook his head in disgust as they turned back toward Tel Aviv. "Them holes," he said loudly, "is there because they want us to know their intentions is serious." He puffed a haze of smoke around his head. "No, this ain't going to be easy."

Rabbi Vultch hurried through the rapidly darkening streets of the Old City to where Rachel waited. He glanced over his shoulder, then bounded up the steps. He knocked, then slipped in without waiting for reply.

Ashen-faced, her eyes haunted, Rachel cradled the baby and glanced up expectantly toward him.

"Stewart is coming into the quarter for you. For you and the baby and Yehudit Akiva," he said in a rush.

She cried out in relief, "Thank God!"

"But, Rachel, he cannot come until tomorrow night."

"Tomorrow! It may be too late!" She held the rasping baby closer to her.

"There is some kind of alert. Something happening. He wouldn't say. But he cannot come until after dark tomorrow."

The baby coughed and gasped with difficulty. "Another night," Rachel said with resignation. "She is so small and frail and . . . how will she live another night?"

Rabbi Vultch closed his eyes. He had done everything he could do. There was nothing left. "I do not know, child. I am sorry."

Yet another knock sounded on the door. He opened it only a crack and peered out onto the dark step. "Yehudit?" he whispered.

Her hushed and frightened voice filtered in to Rachel. "I brought this. For Tikvah. I must go now. I must . . ."

The sound of her footsteps retreated down the steps as the rabbi stooped to retrieve a basket from the landing. He brought it in and opened it slowly. "Kerosene," he said, holding up a glass jar. "And eucalyptus leaves and camphor oil. Enough here to help the child breathe a bit easier until we can get her out. I will fetch Shoshanna," he said. "We must not yet despair."

34   Montgomery

David munched listlessly on a tortilla, purchased with cheese and a case of Coca-Cola when they had stopped to refuel in Havana. The long, tedious hours stretched as slowly as their flight in the lumbering gooney bird.

"We should have taken a Connie," Michael said, staring down at the blank face of the Atlantic.

"Not ready yet," David answered, swallowing a swig of Coke.

"We should at least have brought some take-out Chinese food along." Michael examined his tortilla with distaste.

"Wrong part of the world, Scarecrow," David answered dully. He studied the gauges, and then the *National Geographic* map that lay across his knees like a large napkin. Brushing crumbs away, he frowned, then turned back to where Angela stared dourly out the window. "Hey, Angela," he called. "You want to hear something exciting?"

She threw a disinterested look his way and shrugged.

"Well, I was just looking at the map here, and we aren't going to make it to Rome. Not enough fuel." She did not reply, and he added, "Can you swim?"

Disinterest dissolved into bored disgust as Michael took the map from David. After a few moments, Michael said quietly, "You're right. Looks like we're going to run out of fuel this side of Morocco."

"Too bad," David said with disappointment. "I wanted to stop off in Casablanca and refuel."

"I am not an idiot," Angela said in a voice devoid of humor. "We can't be more than a hundred miles from the Canary Islands." She tapped the map. "Las Palmas has a lovely airport. I have been there several times."

"Now if this were Ellie," David grinned, "she'd be hanging from the ceiling by her fingernails. Angela's a sharp one, Michael. Better watch her."

"I told you," Michael agreed as he pulled Angela forward and pointed out the cockpit window. There, shimmering in the late afternoon sun like a cloud on the sea, stood the snowcapped

351

peak of Pico de Teide on the Canary Islands.

Angela's eyes still reflected boredom as she spoke in tones without warmth or excitement. "The ancient mariners used to think that Teide marked the end of the world, that if they passed beyond it they would find themselves in the claws of some great monster. From the sea, one can see it from one hundred miles out and imagine the dread the sailors felt . . . Beyond this point is the beginning of death for unwary travelers."

David laughed at her words, "Really, Angela, you ought to write for radio. Join Orson Wells for *War of the Worlds* . . ." He turned to her, but she had slipped back into the cargo bay to study the peak of the mountain without additional commentary from David Meyer. She had grown to hate him intensely over the past few weeks. She hated his flippant manner and his high sense of duty that he hid beneath a grin and shrug. And Michael she simply despised for his stupidity and the ease with which he had succumbed to her, while David had remained aloof. *Soon,* she mused silently. *Past the Pico de Tiede, they will find themselves at the end of the world. I will ask Haj Amin and Kadar to plan something very special for David. Michael will die like the dull, uninteresting lout that he is. But David . . . we shall see how high and noble he is when we are finished.*

David circled the island, gazing down at the Port of Las Palmas. The docks were crowded with ships that had stopped to refuel on voyages from North Africa. Green volcanic slopes rose up into the clouds and made the Canary Islands a beautiful haven for tourists as well.

The C-47 touched down gently on the runway, and after instructions from the tower in heavily accented English, they taxied past several other planes to a hangar across the runway. Angela had already unlatched the cargo door, even before the propellers stopped spinning. As David and Michael followed her to solid ground, David realized that this was the first time in nearly twelve hours that the roar of engines did not fill his ears. He shook his head, grateful for the silence, however brief it might be. But still his head seemed to ring with exhaustion.

Angela stretched and looked toward the white, low-roofed terminal building a hundred yards from where they stood. "I'm going to find the ladies' room," she said as David and Michael haggled with a mechanic about the price of fuel purchased with American dollars.

"Half-hour, babe!" Michael called to her. "Don't be long; and see if you can pick up some real food."

She raised her hand in acknowledgment, but did not look back as she passed under two palm trees, then into the brightly lit building. The lobby was crowded with tourists, most unmistakably Spanish, who had come south to escape the still-brutal winter weather that held most of Europe in its grip. *How easy it would be*, she thought, *to simply slip away into the crowd and disappear! How wonderful to avoid another fourteen hours in the same plane with those two!* She would, however, stay with them to the end of the road when she delivered their precious cargo to Haj Amin. She would make the Mufti pay double what the Jews had paid in Prague.

Looking around the lobby, she spotted a newsstand with a rack of cigarettes. It had been weeks since she had been able to purchase a tin of Players. She removed half a pack of American Lucky Strikes from her purse and tossed them into a garbage can.

Speaking in flawless Spanish, Angela ordered two tins of Players and, after taking out a cigarette, shoved them into her handbag. Pulling a silver lighter from a zippered pocket, she held it up to the light and read the words inscribed beneath a gold inlaid lightning bolt: *For Loyalty and Valor to the Reich. Isabel Montgomery from Your Grateful Führer.*

The lighter had been offered as a compliment to one who had thoroughly aided the Lightning War, but also as a jest. Although born in England of Austrian parents, it was often said of her that the only thing truly British about her was her fondness for Players cigarettes. She ran her finger over the words and thought, *The war is not over yet.* Innumerable times, for the sake of the Reich, she had given herself to men who were not of pure Aryan blood. Always she had followed the words of her pledge and sacrificed "with obedience even unto death."

She lit the Players, put the lighter away, and turned suddenly to the small gray-haired man behind the tobacco stand. "Is there somewhere nearby where I might send a telegram, señor?" she asked brightly.

He pointed across the lobby to a closed door upon which the logo of Western Union was plainly visible. Inside the office, one frail woman worked silently at a wide wooden desk piled high with forms. Messages from ships at sea and aircraft were also passed through the office, and the woman had a harried, unpleasant look about her.

"I wish to send a message to Damascus tonight," Angela said.

Barely glancing up, the clerk passed her a form and indicated a jar of pencils on the desk.

She did not write the words of her message in Aramaic, but rather in German, which Haj Amin understood perfectly.

Isabel Montgomery. Sicherheitsdienst.
Haj Amin el Husseini. El Raji der Prophete Damascus Syria.

She knew that the message that followed would bring rejoicing to the private offices of the Grand Mufti of Jerusalem, as her arrival in Damascus in a scant fourteen hours would bring celebration to the streets of the city. There would come a time, very soon, when the words of Himmler would be on the lips of every man who fought for the liberation of Palestine from the "Jewish swine": *Pitilessly we shall be a merciless executioner's sword for all those Jewish forces whose existence and doings we know . . . whether it be today, or in decades, or in centuries.*

Angela finished her wire and passed it to the clerk, who counted the letters but did not understand the message. She smiled gently, as though she had sent a wire to her aged mother telling her not to wait up. The sum of six dollars American was paid, and two dollars additional to guarantee that the message would be sent immediately, ahead of all the others.

"Now," the smile of Angela St. Martain reappeared as the reality of Montgomery submerged again, "is there somewhere nearby where I might purchase food for my friends and myself?"

Twenty-five minutes later, she returned to the refueled plane with a basket laden with food. Her face was serene and refreshed as Michael greeted her with a kiss and helped her back onto the plane. They were, she knew, on the final leg of their journey. She was required to spend only a few more hours with these Jews, and then . . . Damascus.

———

It was well after midnight in Damascus when the cable arrived from Montgomery.

In his dressing gown, Haj Amin sat beside the lamp in the dark, oppressive Victorian-style room of his hotel. Black Sudanese bodyguards stood with their arms crossed in front of the walnut-stained doors as their leader read the cable with an uncharacteristic exhibition of glee.

AM EN ROUTE TO PRAGUE TO PICK UP JEWISH PURCHASES OF ARMS, AMMUNITION AND FIELD ARTILLERY STOP ALL WOULD DOUBTLESS BE USED IN JEWISH PUSH TO TAKE BAB EL WAD STOP HOWEVER, I WILL DELIVER PLANE, CARGO AND CREW TO DAMASCUS TOMMOROW NIGHT MIDNIGHT STOP ALLAH AKBAR, AND IN THE MEMORY OF OUR FÜHRER STOP MONTGOMERY

Within minutes, an exhausted Kadar was shaken from heavy sleep and summoned to the bedside of Haj Amin. He bowed slightly before the exultant Haj, who held up the cable between his fingers. Rarely had Kadar seen Haj Amin with such an expression of delight on his face.

"We have received our answer, Kadar!" said Haj Amin with a laugh. He waved the cable. "This woman, this demon who shares your bed! She is sent from Allah to serve us!"

Kadar took the cable from the Mufti and smiled as he read the confident words. "She will do what she says she will do." He looked up with shining eyes. "Never has she failed." He frowned then as he reread the words. "I should return, then. If the Jews attempt to break through as she predicts, I should be present at my command at Kastel."

Haj Amin shook his head in disagreement. "They will not try. Not when their weapons are in our hands. Stay here. Greet your Isabel as you have in past days. Linger. Rest in the sight of the Arab League. Then take all she has brought to us back to Palestine and crush the Zionists once and for all. Crush them as a loyal Palestinian."

———————

The C-47 arrived in Rome shortly before daybreak. Claudio and Irving, whom David had met before at the airstrip outside Rome, greeted them warmly and brought out the fuel truck that had been standing by at the hangar. Over a quick breakfast, David and Michael listened quietly to the latest news.

"Looks like you got out of the States just in time," said Irving through a bite of chicken. "Mossad says one of our guys was killed on the trail of an Arab agent last night."

Michael frowned and looked at Angela, who showed no emotion at the news. "Well, Angela got one of their guys. Little Arab fella barged into her room. Tore the place apart and tried to kill her."

Irving studied her with a new interest; then he interpreted for Claudio who looked at her with respect. "I was wondering why you brought a dame along," said Irving.

Angela bristled slightly at the use of the word *dame*, but decided it was not worth the trouble to comment. *Only a few more hours . . .*

The gray, solemn city of Prague stretched out below them. Never was there a more welcome sight to the eyes of David Meyer than the shining, bespectacled face of Avriel. Since shortly after Partition had been voted, this little man had roamed the surplus arms markets of Europe under a false passport and had managed to purchase everything needed for a well-equipped infantry. From canteens to backpacks, the future of a nation's fighting force lay secreted away in warehouses and hidden in crates marked "tractor parts," or "farm machinery." David and Michael had been with him one cold December day when he had purchased fifteen German-made ME-109 fighter planes. But their transportation to the Holy Land would have to wait for another day.

Four loaded trucks stood waiting as the plane taxied up; Avriel sat in the lead truck out of the rain. David laughed as the little man jumped from the truck and waved his arms broadly, then stood swaying with anxiety as the Czech arms merchant stepped out and stood dourly beside him. The arms merchant opened an umbrella and lit a cigarette, but Avriel stood beneath the weeping sky, wringing his hands and looking over his shoulder as though any moment the new Communist authorities would come to impound every last precious item on the cargo manifest: one hundred forty Czech M-34 machine guns, seven-hundred and thirty rifles, thousands of rounds of ammunition, grenades, one dismantled artillery piece with shells, and eighteen bazookas. It was admittedly not enough, when David stopped to consider the fully equipped Arab armies poised to invade in just one month, but it was a beginning. And maybe it would be enough to hold Jerusalem.

David hooted with joy and slapped Avriel on the back as the

crates were loaded one by one onto the C-47.

"How much cargo will this plane carry?" asked the Czech arms merchant, as though he knew something Avriel did not know.

David frowned and blinked at the question, then looked at Michael who shrugged. "You're looking at a couple of fighter pilots," David said. "We got this baby here with an empty cargo bay. A full belly is something else again."

The Czech looked at Avriel in amazement. "You Syrians! Are you in such a hurry then to destroy the Jews that you cannot have your materials properly shipped? This cargo will be at least five thousand pounds overweight." He returned to the cab of the truck to retrieve a clipboard.

David leaned close to Avriel. "We're Syrians?" he whispered in astonishment.

Avriel nodded. "You don't think Jews could buy weapons, do you?" He put a finger to his lips as the merchant returned, flipping through the invoices on his clipboard.

"Why don't you ship the excess with your other order?" The man asked in clear English, untainted by accent.

"The other shipment?" Avriel scanned the invoice the merchant studied.

"Did I not tell you before? The *large* shipment bound for Syria, which will leave here,"—he searched the page—"Yes. Only next week. We have obtained a freighter for shipment. You could easily add this tiny excess to that order." He tore an extra sheet from his notes and handed it to Avriel, who scanned the sheet with fascination.

Six thousand Czech rifles and eight million rounds of cartridges had been purchased by Abdul Aziz for shipment to the Arab Legion within days. Avriel noted the name of the freighter, the port of departure and the destination. "Leaving from Fiume," he said, pointing to the manifest. "But its destination is Beirut, Lebanon, not Syria. No, I think it best if we simply transport these weapons as arranged."

"Syria. Beirut. All Arab, anyway. As you wish. But this is a heavy shipment for only one plane." He looked at David with curiosity. "You have not flown cargo before?" he asked.

David did not answer him, but turned to inspect the engines of the C47 as the fuel tanks were filled to capacity. No doubt with this kind of load, it would take every drop for them to reach their destination.

"Maybe we should leave out the field piece," Michael said in hushed tones. "That and the spare fuel tanks are going to be pullin' on us, Tinman."

"If we get her off the runway," David said, touching the hot metal of the engine cowling, "we'll make it. I've heard of guys flying the hump in Burma ten thousand pounds overweight. We can manage."

Michael shrugged and nodded his head in reluctant agreement. "I guess we don't want any artillery going to Beirut with the Arab Shipment," he smiled. "Might end up getting sunk by some nasty Jewish bomb."

Angela walked along the apron of the runway as the cargo was loaded and the plane refueled. Her chestnut hair shone, and Michael looked at her and sighed. "She's somethin' else. I feel like I got her into a mess with all this," he said.

David considered his words, then answered carefully, "I have always had the feeling she wanted to be in the middle of it. Well, now she's got it. The whole ball of wax."

As the arms merchant supervised the last of the loading, Avriel walked to where David and Michael stood near the wing of the plane. He slipped them a folded piece of notepaper. "They know you are coming," he said in a tense voice. "They'll be waiting at Beit Darras airfield. You are code name *Hassida*. Stork." He looked over his shoulder. "The Arabs know all about this too, somehow. Mossad says one of our fellows was murdered last night. You got out just in time."

"We heard about it," said Michael grimly.

"I knew the chap. Worked with the underground—" Avriel stopped short as he saw a glimmer of confusion cross David's face. "What is it?" he asked.

David squinted his eyes and stared at the toes of his scuffed boots. Martin had said that the fellow who had tailed them went by the name of Rosovsky. The Jewish name that sounded Russian. An impossible thought entered David's mind and he looked up toward Angela as she sauntered toward them. She smiled and raised her hand in greeting.

"All ready?" she asked. "A short stroll. I feel one hundred percent better. Almost home." She took Michael's arm and winked at him.

Impossible. David dismissed the thought as they boarded the now-packed airplane and slipped awkwardly between crates to the cockpit. Angela sat behind them on a red wool blanket and stared at a stack of machine guns that had been unpacked from their crates to save weight.

The engines coughed and roared to life and the gooney bird taxied slowly out to the runway. "Hold on!" David said when they were cleared for takeoff.

The plane lumbered along, too slowly, eating up the runway. Michael drew a deep breath and Angela gripped the back of his seat in fear as the loaded bird lifted awkwardly into the air, clearing the runway's end by only a few feet. Flying an empty C-47 was an entirely different experience from managing a reluctant, overweight mammoth. The fuselage groaned and the starboard engine hacked and coughed.

"Give it a little more pressure, Michael," David instructed, and the coughing cleared up as they circled low over the city, low enough that they could see tiny ant-people walking along the sidewalks below them. As David brought the aircraft to an altitude of eight thousand feet, Michael plotted the flight plan that would take them home. "It's going to be after dark, Tinman, and we never did have our instrument check. Personally, I'd rather not bump into anything solid along the way."

Night swept in early with dense cloud cover, and David found the muscles between his shoulder blades were twisting into a string of knots. There would be no relief; no sleeping on this leg of the journey. It would take both Michael and David to reach the shores of Palestine.

Sudden down-drafts caused the plane to shudder and slip, bucking through the sky like an angry, aged bull. In spite of the cold of the altitude and the storm front that they were passing through, David felt hot and sweaty and looked forward to a shower.

Angela sat almost wordlessly behind them through the hours, until her presence was nearly forgotten. At last, as they passed near the tip of Greece and over Crete, she spoke quietly.

"How much longer?" she asked wearily.

Michael glanced over his shoulder. "You been asleep?" he asked.

"No. How much longer?"

"Listen to this," Michael said. "She sounds like a kid on the way to camp."

"Not quite." Angela's voice had an unfamiliar hardness to it and Michael frowned as he looked at her.

David answered, clearing his throat and shaking the exhaustion from his brain. "Not long. Egypt is due south. Palestine is east of that. A couple hours, maybe. Maybe more."

She returned a hard, cold smile to Michael's curious stare. "What is it?" he asked. "Are you okay?"

"How far is it to Damascus from here?" Angela replied, pulling a loaded pistol from beneath the blanket.

Michael laughed nervously. "What is this?"

David still had not seen her weapon, but something in the dark edge of her voice filled him with dread. Thought of the impossible again reared up, and then he turned to look at her face, lined and stone hard with purpose. "I want to go to Damascus," she said in a low, earnest voice. Then David saw the gun.

Michael laughed again. It was a laugh of disbelief, but also of fear. "Come on, Angela. Knock it off."

Her expression remained fixed, her tone level. "Damascus, if you please." She raised the pistol and touched Michael beneath the chin.

"Quit foolin' around, Angela." Michael's words were angry but impotent against the cold barrel of the gun.

"She isn't joking," David said, the calmness of his voice surprising him. "And her name isn't Angela, is it? And the little dead guy in your room wasn't really an Arab. He was Jewish Mossad assigned to look after our skins and find out who Montgomery was and where the leak was—"

"No!" Michael shouted. "Tell him this isn't true, Angela!"

Montgomery smiled. "You are bright, David. A bit slow on the uptake, but bright, nevertheless."

"Angela—" Michael pleaded.

"Shut up!" She shoved the barrel deeper into his throat. "You are a well of information, but it is no wonder you are named so well—Scarecrow."

Michael gazed back at her in the horror of full realization of the truth. He blinked and swallowed hard, and then a wave of rage swept over him and he lunged for her. "You! . . ." he shouted, coming over the back of the seat.

A deafening roar of the gun sounded and resounded in the

plane and Michael Cohen's blood spurted out against the windshield of the cockpit. The C-47 moaned and rocked.

"Michael!" David shouted above the pitch and roar of the plane. "Dear God! God! Michael!"

"He's dead!" shouted Montgomery. "You fool! He is dead!"

Seconds passed as David sagged, then stared out the window of the plane as it rapidly lost altitude. "Michael," he said as Montgomery kicked herself free from the weight of Michael's body and lunged forward to grasp David's face, nicking his cheek with her fingernail.

"The plane! You fool!"

David looked at her. She was covered with blood. There was blood everywhere. Then he took control of the plane as they emerged below the cloud cover to see the black Mediterranean a mere thousand feet below them. The huge gooney bird skimmed above the sea like a pelican, and then began a long difficult ascent once again.

"Damascus," were the whispered words of Angela's warning. "And perhaps you will live, David Meyer."

35 Waiting

Moshe's message never arrived over the dead receiver of the Old City's Haganah radio, but Rabbi Vultch did not tell Rachel the grim news that he had heard about Moshe. One more sleepless night was spent holding Tikvah as Stewart prolonged his arrival in the Old City to escort Rachel and Yehudit out.

As night fell on the Jewish Quarter, Dov and Rabbi Vultch, Hannah, Shoshanna, and Joseph gathered in the apartment to bid Rachel farewell.

Tikvah's condition had remained the same through the long hours, and Rachel herself was sick with worry and unable to eat. She sat in the rocker and held the child close to her as she gazed up at the faces of her friends for the last time.

"Captain Stewart said that the best time to leave would be under cover of darkness," said the kind rabbi. "Yehudit will be here soon, as well."

"Poor child," said Rachel. "She has repaid her unkindness to me a thousandfold by this act. She risks everything."

"She had no choice but to leave," said Vultch. "Her father will certainly discover the call was made from his own home. It could have been no other."

Rachel's eyes were shining with emotion as she looked at each dear face. "I don't know when we will see one another again," she said quietly.

"Soon, soon," said Hannah. "If it is God's will."

"I will pray for you all. And I will tell the world of your courage."

Rabbi Vultch took out his small, leather-bound copy of the Siddur, the prayer book, and thumbed through the pages. "On this earth, perhaps we may not see one another again, yet, as we pray together let us remember, as Rabbi Jochanan says, to recall God's mercy." He lifted his hands in blessing over the little band and chanted in a sing-song voice, "Sing ye unto God, extol him who rideth above the clouds by Jah, his name, and exult in his presence. The father of the fatherless"—he touched Rachel on her head as he continued, "and the judge of widows, is God in his holy habitation. May he not forsake us. But ye who cleave unto the Eternal, your God, are alive, all of you, this day. For the Eternal comforteth Zion, yea, he comforteth all her ruins . . ." He lifted Rachel's chin and said to her. "Be comforted, Daughter of Zion, God has not finished with any of us who yet live." His warm brown eyes were full of compassion and admiration for Rachel. There were words, she sensed, that he had not been able to speak to her, and she searched his eyes for an answer.

A soft knock sounded at the door and Joseph opened it to Yehudit. She stood outside on the step, hesitating to come in.

Rachel stood and extended her hand to her. "Welcome, Yehudit," she offered. "Welcome home."

The girl stepped in, then walked slowly toward Rachel. Her head was covered with a shawl and she carried a bundle which she laid on the floor as she took Rachel's hand.

"Thank you," Yehudit answered in a hushed voice. She looked to each face and saw the spirit of grateful acceptance.

No more needed to be said. Yehudit touched the baby lightly. "She still lives. I am so thankful."

Tikvah's heavy breathing filled the silent spaces and crowded everything else from each mind.

Rachel went to the top drawer of the bureau and took Moshe's tallith from where it rested. She handed it to Dov. "It was Moshe's," she said. "They tore it from him but I mended it, and now it belongs to God . . . to this Holy City of Zion. I may never return here, but always on Passover I heard my father pray, *Next year in Jerusalem*. Please, Dov, take this. Passover is only a few days away, and I will not be here to share it. But I can see the top of the Hurva Synagogue from Hadassah Hospital. I will look here on the first day of Passover as the sun rises, and I will pray with you all, *Next year in Jerusalem* . . . in freedom! In Israel!"

Dov cradled the tallith in his arms and gently stroked the fabric. "Sunrise the first day of Passover," he said. "I will not forget, dear Rachel."

"God be with you all," she said as the heavy knock of Captain Stewart sounded on the door. "God . . ." she faltered, ". . . bring us together once again in a happier day."

Rachel and Yehudit slipped out the door and were instantly surrounded by a dozen British soldiers. Stewart said very little as they marched out through the crooked alleyways of the Old City to the final barricade of the Jewish Quarter and beyond. Rachel held Tikvah close and turned to look up at the moon-drenched cupola of the Great Hurva. *Oh, Lord, remember your promise to comfort Zion. Oh, Lord, do not forget those who loved you without knowing who you are* . . .

––––––––

The three hundred trucks, loaded and waiting, circled the soccer field like a wagon train settling down for the night. Dozens of campfires burned brightly in the center, as disgruntled truck drivers shared meals with homesick recruits, fresh out of the training camps. Boys and girls, most not over eighteen years old, had brought with them suitcases and personal belongings that now had to be weeded down to what could be carried in one knapsack. As Luke strolled through the makeshift campsite, he shook his head in wonder at the youth and inexperience of these young soldiers. Never before had he commanded women among his troops. He winced as one young girl sifted through her belongings and wept as she laid a small volume of poetry aside.

Cooks recruited from the civilian restaurants of Tel Aviv ladeled tin plates of stew at the north end of the field. If David's plane were on time, if the weapons were there, this would be the last meal for many of these young people. There was very little laughter among the small groups who sat on the hard ground to savor their stew. Yesterday afternoon this began as an exciting outing, but it had suddenly turned stale and harsh in the reality of what lay ahead.

Whether the targets were Jewish men or women, Luke knew, would make little difference to the enemy. The Arabs were men seasoned by hatred and fear as the heat of the Mufti's cry for Jihad rose higher and higher. The Arabs were unorganized, to be sure, but they had grown up with weapons in their hands.

By the glow of the fire, a young woman with dark braided hair sat cross-legged writing a letter on yellow lined notepaper. His shadow fell over her as he stood quietly with his hands clasped behind his back and watched. She glanced up at him and smiled at his curiosity, her eyes warm and alive.

"A letter to my boyfriend," she explained. "He is holding Kfar Etzion Kibbutz. The Jihad is very fierce there."

Luke nodded, then looked toward another fire. "Don't let me interrupt you." He did not want to know anything more about this lovely young Haganah warrior. *She is too young for this*, he thought. *But they are always too young.*

Behind Luke, a surly truck driver of about thirty sipped his coffee and complained loudly about his hijacking. "My wife is about to have a baby and here I am driving a truck to Jerusalem! They can't do this to me!"

Luke grinned as an idealistic soldier ten years his junior told the man to shut up. "This cause is more important than one man's life or one man's child! You talk like a coward!"

"And maybe I am!" snapped the truck driver. "Better to be a live dog than a dead lion, I always say!"

"And if all felt like you there would not even be any live dogs left!"

The young fellow is right, Luke thought, *but it is the truck driver who more clearly understands the value of life. It is one thing to have a great cause to die for. It is another to have a wife and child to live for.*

He looked up to see Moshe and Ehud standing beside a transport truck, deep in conversation with Fergus and two other Haganah commanders. Luke stood in the shadows and studied the lines that furrowed Moshe's brow. *And here is one man who fights*

*for a great cause and loves deep enough that he would offer his
life for one woman.* Moshe was a soldier, yes. But he was also a
man who knew the meaning of living. Luke breathed a prayer for
Moshe's safety this night in Bab el Wad; then he drew himself up
and strode toward the small knot of commanders.

Moshe spotted him with relief. "I sent three fellows out to
look for you," he said, taking Luke's arm.

Luke peered at the face of his watch. "Am I late? I thought we
were not to meet again until nine."

Ehud thumped the truck. "A few of us are going out to the
airfield to wait. We thought you would like to come since you
were in ordnance. You can show us how to load the weapons."

"I hope you are joking," Luke grinned uneasily. "Our troops
do know how to load and fire weapons, don't they?"

Moshe patted Luke on the back. "Never mind Ehud; tonight
is not the night to joke." He lowered his voice. "The last communique came from Prague about an hour ago. That will put the
plane in Beit Darras probably between one and two. Bobby
Milkin surveyed the airfield in daylight and says there is a bit of
work to do before a C-47 can land there safely. We're taking a
crew out now."

"Where is Ellie?" asked Luke.

"At the airfield, where else? She is hoping, I think, that some
magic wind will push David home to her six hours ahead of
schedule." Moshe smiled, and in his smile Luke saw his thoughts
of Rachel. "I wish there were such a wind."

Beit Darras was an airfield that had been held by the RAF
until the end of World War Two. It was only one small runway,
scarred with holes; it had no tower or electricity, and only two
small wooden hangars stood abandoned at the edge of the field.
Cans of fuel were stored there.

As the trucks pulled up in total darkness, fifty Haganah troops
jumped from beneath the canvas flaps and silently took positions
on the perimeter of the runway. A crew of forty more began the
backbreaking work of filling in holes while Moshe assisted setting up the radio in the back of a truck. Ellie worked side-by-side
with the repair crew until her hands were blistered from the handle of the shovel. Throughout the long hours of preparation, she
would stop and listen for the hum of an airplane engine, only to
be disappointed at the sound of a distant car, or the testing of
the generator. She had dressed in her prettiest blue wool slacks

and had even found time to curl her hair, but the thought of David landing on an uneven runway had caused her to forget her appearance. David would take one look at her, and she would feel beautiful again once she was in his arms.

Someone had had the foresight to send along a huge drum of coffee; as the runway was finished and lights strung and hooked up to the portable generator, Ellie finished her evening of service by handing out warm cups of coffee to grateful crews and sentries who gazed into the dark olive groves while the others looked up at the clouds.

It was only a little past eleven when the radio shrieked and whined to life and the message was sent far out over the waters of the Mediterranean. *"Hassida,"* the operator called. "Stork." There was no reply.

Those who had helped prepare the runway for its first Jewish traffic sat down and scanned the cloudy sky. Except for the persistent call of the radio operator, "Hassida. Hassida. Come in please. This is Mama. Hassida . . ." There was no reply but the wind.

As the hour came and went when David was supposed to arrive, a sense of desperation settled over everyone there . . . *Suppose we have worked for nothing? Suppose the men and food and equipment and all of this is for nothing?*

"Hassida . . ." Ellie sat quietly between Moshe and Luke on the tailgate of a truck. "Hassida . . . come in, please. This is Mama."

With an exasperated sigh, the radio operator began again. Calling and waiting for a reply that never came. "Hassida . . ."

"What could have happened?" Ellie asked in a barely audible voice. A thousand images flashed through her mind: David in the stormy sea, clutching the wing of a sinking airplane; the ammunition exploding in one great fireball that eliminated every trace of David forever.

Moshe patted her gently on the hand. "Maybe it's just his radio. Perhaps it's gone out." He stood and called to the man who sat near the portable electric generator. "Flash the lights, Samuel. Five seconds on and thirty seconds off."

"Right," came the reply, and in an instant the field was awash with light; faces of the crew and sentries were clearly visible for five seconds, then vanished in darkness again.

"Hassida. Hassida! This is Mama. Come in, Hassida!"

366

Ellie found herself counting quietly to thirty until the lights flashed on again, and then to five, when the darkness returned. "Hassida! Hassida!" . . . *four, five, six, seven* . . . "Mama!" . . . *ten, eleven, twelve* . . . "Hassida! Come in, Hassida!" *Twenty-nine, thirty* . . . *David* . . . *David. This is Ellie. David, if you can hear me, David. I'm waiting here for you. Praying for you* . . . *nineteen, twenty* . . .

36 Flight of the Stork

Michael's blood trickled into a small dark pool near David's boots. With the gun aimed at his right temple, David did not look as they flew thirty miles beyond where the lights of Tel Aviv beckoned off the right wing tip.

"You should be able to hear them call you from here," Montgomery said in an amused voice. She switched on the radio and laughed as the frantic calls rasped over the receiver of the C-47.

"Hassida! This is Mama. Do you read, Hassida?" A long pause filled with static hissed at them. "Hassida! Hassida! This is Mama! Come in, Hassida!"

David wondered if they could hear the cough and drone of the weary engines. Ellie would be there, he knew, waiting at the other end of the radio for his reply. *Mama, I'm up here. Michael's dead. I trusted someone I knew I shouldn't trust, and I'm dead too. Everything is dead. Go home, Mama. Put your dreams to bed; nobody is going through the Red Sea this Passover.*

"Hassida! Hassida! This is . . ."

Montgomery cocked her head coyly to one side and smiled as though she had merely won a hand at bridge. "You are quiet, Tinman."

At the mention of this special name, he turned on her with a look so full of anger that her eyes hardened again.

"Come in, Hassida . . ."

He did not answer her, but looked at the pistol with disdain and turned again to stare out the black windshield.

Her laugh was low and cruel; she touched him lightly on the

ear with the barrel of her weapon. He flinched away and then sat rigidly as her free hand stroked his thigh. "Does the Tinman have a heart, after all?" she asked seductively. "You know I would rather have been with you than Michael."

Revolted by her touch, he set his jaw in silent fury. "Is this how you get your kicks on slack time?" He spat the words and she laughed again.

"Hassida. Hassida. This is Mama . . ."

"Come now, David, you can't say you weren't even a little envious of Michael. I saw the way you looked at me . . ." She massaged his leg, and he slapped her hand away.

"Yeah. I was always wondering what he saw in a broad like you."

She laughed again, confidently, and settled back into her seat, the gun still aimed above his right ear. "I don't believe you," she said matter-of-factly. "However, if it makes you feel better in retrospect . . ."

". . . come in, Hassida! . . ."

"I should have booted you out the first minute—"

"You're not alone in that, David. I could name a few British officers who will be quite astonished when they begin receiving little love notes from a girl they knew in North Africa. A girl they loved and told their plans to during the North African offensive against Rommel. There were a few Americans, as well. I liked Americans—"

"Your next career is blackmail, huh?" David cast her a sideways glance.

"Hassida! This is Mama . . ." The call grew more faint with each passing moment.

"It is all documented," she said smugly. "It is remarkable how talkative an officer can be when his uniform is off. We almost won the war—"

"We?"

"The Reich, of course. And now though you think it is all over, the quest for the Final Solution still lives. As do the majority of the German High Command in South America. Haj Amin Husseini continues the work. Palestine will be the rallying cry that will draw the world together at last against the Jews." She stroked his face with the gun barrel, then drew it slowly downward until it rested in his thigh. "And that will be the end. This little shipment that we are bringing to Haj Amin to celebrate your Jewish

Passover; this will also speed the beginning of the end."

The cry from Beit Darras finally fell away, ". . . Has . . . come . . ."

Sweat trickled down David's back, and now he laughed nervously. "Michael was right about you. You are one smart cookie."

"Yes?"

"You had everybody fooled, Angela. Really clever. I thought you were a hard-nosed reporter out for the Pulitzer."

"I have been a thousand things. Men and women. A maid. A shepherd. A whore . . ."

David resisted the temptation to comment on her last occupation. "You should have been an actress."

"But I am, David. The necessity of war simply gave me a broader stage on which to perform, wouldn't you say?"

"Now what?" he asked flatly as she ran the pistol slowly along his ribs and then raised it to his neck again.

"I collect a rather large reward for this little prize—and you. And then I go on to other things . . . the little love notes we spoke of earlier perhaps. I should have a considerable pension on which to live." She laughed. "I have considered buying an estate next to Winston Churchill. He is one fellow I have never met. I should like him, I think." Her words became suddenly demanding. "Begin your turn to the north-east now."

Obediently, David banked the plane slightly to cross the darkness of the Valley of Jezreel and beyond that the tiny Arab town of Nazereth.

"Very good," she said. "You are a man who loves life. I have seen that in you." Her words were soft again.

"Your friends in Syria know we're coming, I take it," David answered her with a question.

"Of course."

"Good. We're flying over Golan, where every Syrian tank and antiaircraft gun in the Legion's arsenal is sitting. We've lost a couple of observation planes up there, and I don't want to be a sitting duck, if you know what I mean."

Montgomery laughed. "Ah yes, David, the Mufti knows we are coming. Your tricks will do no good."

"Just wanted to let you know, lady. If I didn't care about living, this plane would already be on the ground. I could put an end to this without the help of Syrian antiaircraft guns."

"Yes," she smiled. "It would be a pity for all of us to lose this cargo. But I think, David, that you are playing the old trick on me. Like your American story of Brer Rabbit and the fox, eh? Don't throw me in the briar patch." She chuckled and jammed the barrel hard into his ribs. "I sent a wire to the Mufti," she said in a menacing voice. "They know we are coming. Kadar, Haj Amin. They will be waiting for us at the airfield in Damascus, and there will be trucks to carry this cargo back to Bab el Wad to our own men."

With a sense of desperation, David tried yet another tack with her. "I can guarantee you that the Jewish Agency would outbid your deal with the Mufti. Let me turn the plane around, and you'll get every penny you want and more . . ."

She laughed louder, then said in a cool voice, "And I suppose that the Jewish Agency will give me safe conduct into Syria, so that I may die with a bullet in the head for betraying Haj Amin?" She laughed again at the absurdity of the suggestion. "You are a Jew to the end, David. No thank you."

David sighed and fell silent again as she fiddled with the radio in an attempt to pick up a call signal from Damascus.

"We're still too far out," he told her, then, as they passed over the northern tip of the Sea of Galilee, he thought, *Mama, this is Hassida. I tried . . .*

"When will we pass into Syria?" she demanded.

"A couple of minutes." The engines moaned wearily on and David studied the near-empty fuel gauges. They had just enough to lift them over the Golan Heights into Damascus. Only just enough. *What poetic justice it would be if we ran short,* David thought, *and nobody got the guns!* For an instant he thought again of how near the hard earth was, and how easy it would be to end the contest. Still, he remembered Ellie and racked his brain for a way out of this mess short of a fiery end on the rocky slopes below. *God, this is Hassida . . . Forty-five minutes and it's all over for me one way or another. I know you don't want the Arabs to have these guns, and, Lord, there doesn't look like there's any other way for me to solve this little problem.*

He glanced toward Montgomery, and the decision was made. *Better I take this dame with me than end up with a bullet in my head and her manage to land this baby.* He leaned forward to adjust the pressure on the starboard engine.

"What are you doing?" she shouted as the engine coughed and sputtered.

"Something's not right with the engine," he said, lowering the pressure.

"It was fine until you started adjusting it . . . stop that!" She poked him hard with the Walther. "Put it back like it was right now!"

Still the engine hacked and complained and, as they passed over the border, a streamer of flame and smoke erupted from beneath the cowling and the plane rocked violently. A loud roar penetrated the cockpit and the sky around them lit up.

"I said stop it!" she shouted.

"It's not me!" David fought to hold the overloaded aircraft steady as a hail of explosions erupted around them. "Okay, God," David muttered. Syrian antiaircraft guns blasted away at the unidentified plane coming in low over their border. "Okay, you don't need my help!"

Montgomery picked up the radio and began to scream into it. From angry and frightened Arabic, she lapsed into German and then English. "You fools!" she shouted as a terrible flash bucked the aircraft. "This is Isabel Montgomery! You fools! I am bringing weapons to the Mufti!"

Tracer bullets followed one another into the C-47, puncturing the fuselage, and a stream of gasoline sprayed out.

"I thought you said they knew—" David fought for control of the bucking plane as it sank lower in the sky until the fire from the artillery below was plainly visible.

A brighter burst of flame exploded as the starboard engine received a hit, and pieces of shrapnel flew into the air and left little streamers of fire in their wake.

"They've hit us!" Montgomery shrieked, and the gooney bird moaned and tried to roll in a final contortion of death. David held the controls with all his might, pulling the wounded beast up. *Keep her nose up! Nose up!* The aircraft shuddered violently as he held her, and the ground loomed below. Another grinding thud hit the undercarriage, again sending the plane into convulsions. Fire spread along the wing of the starboard engine. Holding on to the control with all his might, David shouted to Montgomery, "Feather the engine! Hit the switch to the—" His words were drowned out, and in a flash of light, he saw Montgomery slumped in the copilot's seat. She was a mass of blood-soaked flesh and a large hole gaped through the side window.

Again the plane shook violently. Rudder damage and damage

371

to the flaps fought against David as he struggled to hold her aloft. Bursts of gunfire pursued him, and the dark shadow of a rocky mountain loomed ahead. With all his strength, he argued with the dying ship, alone now in his battle. "God!" he cried out over the rattle of the shuddering plane. Frigid wind howled through the open wound in the cockpit. "Dear God!" David cried, unable to pray any other prayer as he faced his own end and fought against it. "Nose up! Bank her 30 degrees!" The blood left his hands as every muscle in his body strained to pull the gooney bird against the gravity of the mountain slope.

Montgomery's body thumped to the right as the miracle of a turn began to happen. David panted with the exertion; the darkness of the mountain slipped by to his left. He cried out in a temporary moment of exultation as death was forestalled. "God! This is Hassida! God! Get me to Mama!"

————

The British armored vehicle of Captain Stewart wove through the Arab-held New City quarter of Sheik Jarra. Yehudit sat very still and quiet next to Rachel as the baby struggled to breathe.

Rachel could see Stewart's half-profile; his face had the look of a man in pain.

Rachel opened her mouth to speak, then closed it again. She frowned and looked at the darkness outside the slit windows.

"I want to thank you," she began. "For the sake of my baby—"

He interrupted her harshly. "Well, now that you're out, don't expect to enter the quarter again. Rules are rules. Once someone leaves, that's it. Rabbi Akiva knows that, and he also knows how dangerous the Old City Quarter is. That's why he sent you out." He addressed himself to Yehudit who simply swallowed hard and looked away. "Of course, nothing is any better here in the New City for you Jews." He sounded angry. "There are rumors Tel Aviv may be planning a big offensive. Well, I'll tell you, we have orders not to lift a finger to help. Not a finger. Let the slime . . . the deserters and the terrorists like your husband just try to get past Kastel! It isn't going to happen."

Rachel stared blankly at him, "Like my husband?" she asked.

"I'm of the opinion that he and that traitor Luke Thomas have made their way to Tel Aviv. After all, they haven't found any bodies. No sign of violence. The drivers of the van carrying him and Ehud Schiff to Acre to be hanged only *heard* gunfire."

Rachel looked to Yehudit, hoping for some explanation. Yehudit frowned and took Rachel's hand. "You don't know! Of course, you couldn't know," she said quietly. "Two nights ago a police van carrying Moshe and Ehud was hijacked. At first everyone thought it was Arabs—"

Rachel gasped and her expression looked stricken. "Oh no," she whispered.

Yehudit added quickly. "Now they are saying that perhaps it was not Arabs but British deserters. A fellow named Luke Thomas who commanded the Old City garrison before Captain Stewart. I don't think you ever met him."

Rachel felt the world spin around her. Moshe was undoubtedly *free*, if Luke had anything to do with it. But she did not let her expression or words betray the fact that she knew Luke Thomas.

Bitterness was thick in Stewart's voice. "That Thomas was never loyal to what we are trying to do here."

"And what are you trying to do here, Captain?" Rachel asked.

"Keep the peace," he spat, turning onto the road that led to Hadassah. "An impossible job when it comes to Jews."

Rachel did not reply, but sat in silence as they wound up the dark stretch of road to the top of Mount Scopus and Hadassah Hospital. He stepped from the vehicle and waited for Yehudit to get out. "Your father seems to have a little sense, anyway. Although I'll never know why he wanted you to leave with this woman."

Yehudit looked him straight in the eye and said boldly, "Why don't you ask him, Captain Stewart? Tomorrow is the eve of Passover. He will be in all day. Why don't you ask him?"

Yehudit took Rachel's arm and helped her in through the doors of the hospital. She took Tikvah from Rachel as Rachel walked quickly to the reception desk.

Moshe is free—maybe coming to Jerusalem! Rachel held tightly to the countertop as worry and excitement and days without food swept over her senses. She seemed to be seeing the world through a yellow tinge. The receptionist looked up at her curiously; then her face became concerned. "Do you need to sit down?" she asked Rachel.

Rachel put a hand to her forehead. Tikvah coughed, and she heard the rush of footsteps behind her as her knees began to buckle. "My baby—" she managed to say; then the world grew dark around her.

37 The Miracle

The hours passed, and still the promised Jewish aircraft did not arrive. Haj Amin raged at the news that Syrian forces had shot down a large aircraft just over the Golan Heights into Syria. Empty army trucks stood on the cold airfield just south of Damascus waiting for a cargo that now would never come.

Kadar stood silently beside the distraught Palestinian leader. His hands were folded before him and he shook his head slowly in the realization that for the first time since he had known her, Montgomery had indeed failed.

"The Syrians have betrayed us!" Haj Amin cried out. "They have destroyed the aircraft simply so that we will be powerless to defeat the Jews unless they come to our aid! Traitors! The Arab League has betrayed the people of Palestine!"

"The plane is destroyed," Kadar said in a quiet, resigned voice. "This is the will of Allah. Still, we will hold the pass of Bab el Wad. Even if the Jews had guns and cannon, Haj Amin, our Jihad Moquades number many more than they. Our warriors will hold the pass, and the Zionists will come to their end. We will see the certain power and will of Allah in this."

Haj Amin paced in front of the bright headlights of a truck. "You must return to the pass, Kadar. Rally our forces. Call our men to battle against the Zionists, if they are still foolish enough to mount an offensive without their precious cargo. Crush them utterly! And in so doing, give us a martyr in Fredrich Gerhardt. He becomes an embarrassment to us politically. He is a madman!" Haj Amin's eyes seemed half-crazed as he spoke, and Kadar simply bowed low to him, backed up a step and turned to enter a waiting automobile that would speed him back to Jerusalem and his command at Kastel.

The distant, unhappy moan of the crippled C-47 was first heard by Bobby Milkin, who had slept for hours in the cab of the truck. He leaped from the seat and stood stock-still in the blackness, and then he shouted, "I hear her!"

"Hassida!" The voice of the radio operator became more urgent. "This is Mama!"

A faint reply crackled over the receiver. "Mama, this is Hassida; I'm bringing this baby in!"

Ellie cried out at the sound of David's faraway voice and the approaching drone of the engines.

"Get the lights on!" Moshe shouted as Bobby rushed toward the end of the runway.

Lights beamed on and glowed upward, hitting the gray clouds. A cheer rose from the crew and the sentries as Bobby raised his hands to the sky like a director of a symphony choir. Then he shouted above the joy, "Quiet!" He listened with one ear cocked upward. "There's somethin' ain't right with her!" he said loudly.

"Mama, this is stork," David said again. "We've lost the engine starboard and the hydraulics on the landing gear are shot out. We'll need plenty of room in the nest."

Ellie's heart gripped with an instant apprehension. David, always so glib and cheerful about flying, had an edge to his voice that she instantly caught.

Bobby Milkin cursed and shouted to the crew. "Get back. This crazy plane is going to take up half of Palestine when she comes in!"

"Mama, do you read me?" David was worried. "Whatever patch you've got for me to land on won't be enough. Clear the field. We've got a belly full of ammo here!"

Ellie jumped into the cab of a truck with Moshe and Ehud, and they pulled ahead beyond a vineyard, another 100 yards. Ehud turned the truck around and aimed his lights back toward the postage-stamp runway where David would begin his slide for home. The other trucks followed suit, illuminating the vineyard as though that, too, were part of the runway. The rickety wooden hangars appeared to be dangerously near to where the gooney bird would land. In the back of the truck, the radio operator still called. "Hassida! This is Mama! We're giving you plenty of room. You're going to wipe out somebody's wine crop for the next year!"

"I've got your lights on visual, Mama!" David replied. "Bringin' her in." The roar of the engine loomed in the black clouds. Ellie searched for the shadow of the plane but saw only the darkness, the vineyard, and the runway beyond. David's voice said through the static. "So you got me a vineyard to land in, huh? Sounds a whole lot softer than an olive grove."

"Watch the hangars, Hassida," the radio operator warned. "They're full of fuel."

"Now you tell me!" said David. "Bringin' her on down, boys!"

Ellie prayed, wanting to close her eyes against the frightening sight of David's C-47 scraping against the runway without landing gear. But she kept her eyes open, jumping from the truck stand at the edge of the vineyard. *God, this is Ellie. Hold him up, Lord. Hold him.*

"One mile south of you, Mama. Listing a little starboard. I'm going to try . . . to keep her nose up." His voice was full of physical strain. "Easy does it, baby. Right in line! Flaps down, boys." The roar of the engine drowned out David's final words as the nose of the enormous cargo plane suddenly appeared in the light at the far end of the runway. Ellie screamed and put her hand over her mouth as the C-47 dipped and listed to the side of the silent engine. Propeller and wing tip scraped the ground and sparks shot up from the belly of the aircraft as it slammed down with a crash as loud as cannons. The groan of tearing metal overcame all other sounds and drowned out the cries of those who looked on. The plane skidded across the lighted runway in a direct line for the fuel-packed hangars; then, as if lifted by some great hand, it smoked and spun around, its wing tip clearing the wooden building by inches. Crashing through a low fence, it slid through the vineyard like a giant bird, skimming the water. Vines hung from the wings and propellers, and the string of electric lights clung to the round nose of the plane. Only the lights of the trucks now illuminated the tortuous slide of the dinosaur-like aircraft. As others ran for cover, Ellie stood in the path of the beast, as if to will it to stop. Fifty yards, forty, thirty . . . she could not see the face of David through the dark cockpit window. Twenty-five yards, now twenty and finally, the grinding sweep of destruction ended a mere fifteen yards in front of the truck.

The silence that engulfed them was total and profound. Ellie stood like a silhouette, unmoving, in front of the nose that towered above her. Her hand was still over her mouth as she stared up at the black windows. The air reeked of metallic smoke, and a trail of tiny fires sparkled through the vineyard along the path of the plane's skid.

"David!" she cried out at last. "David!" She shouted his name again, not even aware of how close she had come to being crushed. The propellers were twisted arms of metal, and the tip of one wing had been torn away. "David!" she cried again as the sound of running footsteps echoed behind the wreck.

The headlights shone upward, reflecting off the back of the cockpit; slowly, awkwardly, a hand rose to the window. "He's alive!" she shouted, now running to the plane.

Disheveled from their dive into the dirt, Moshe and Ehud and Luke joined her beneath the cockpit window. A cheer rose up from the rest of the men who shouted and jostled around the aircraft. "Get the fire extinguishers!" Moshe yelled to the soldiers. "Get these fires out before the whole cargo blows!"

David raised his head and, shaken a bit, waved down at Ellie. A small trickle of blood flowed down his cheek like a teardrop, and she wept with joy that he was only hurt a little bit. "David!" she cried, but her voice was drowned out by the shouts of the Haganah men as they rushed by with fire extinguishers and pried open the crushed cargo bay door and swarmed aboard to carry David out and lower him to the shoulders of the men who stood below. Singing and dancing, they held him aloft in a hero's welcome as Ellie struggled to break through to him.

"Ellie!" he shouted, searching the sea of faces for her. He spotted her and stretched out his arms to embrace her over the celebration.

"David! Darling!" she called back as Moshe came to her side. "Moshe, make them put him down!"

Moshe laughed and climbed to the wing of the aircraft, raising his arms to silence the men. A hush settled over them as they looked up expectantly, waiting for a speech extolling David's brave deed. "Comrades!" Moshe said, his eye catching David's smiling face. "Our brother has a wife to greet. And we have much work to do!" Still another cheer erupted and David was carried to Ellie and set safely on the ground again. They stood a few feet apart and simply looked into each other's eyes.

Then David took her hand and slowly walked her to the darkness behind the truck. There he pulled her close to him and kissed her forehead, her cheek, and then her trembling lips.

377

"God only knows how much I missed you," he whispered.

She could not speak, but buried her face against his chest and wept quietly with joy at his presence. A full five minutes they stood alone—as though they were the only ones in all the world—while the clatter and bustle of unloading took place.

Bobby Milkin's voice called into the darkness then, interrupting their sweet reunion. "Hey, Meyer!"

"Oh, not Milkin," muttered Ellie, clinging tighter to David.

"Hey, Meyer!" Bobby shouted again. "Hey, there's a dead broad in there! And Michael Cohen!"

David moaned. "Angela. I mean, Montgomery."

While weapons and equipment were loaded onto the waiting trucks, the bodies of Isabel Montgomery and Michael Cohen were laid out on the ground and covered with a canvas tarp. Ellie did not look at the broken body of this vile servant of evil, but Luke Thomas raised the canvas to study the woman who had worn so many faces and discovered so many secrets. "Someone will have information about her, whether it is American OSS or British Intelligence. She is undoubtedly on someone's wanted list."

"She almost won," David said quietly. "But when she killed Michael—" He didn't finish, and Ellie held his hand tightly in her own.

"You need to rest, darling," she said quietly. "How long has it been since you've slept?"

"Maybe years," David rubbed his forehead. "Forever."

"Moshe?" Ellie looked into the sympathetic face of Moshe. "Can someone take us back to Tel Aviv now?"

Moshe nodded and motioned to the radio operator. "Drop them at the red house," he said. "Then get back here. We need the truck. David, I never dreamed you could manage to bring so much."

"Yeah." David's face was a mask of exhaustion. "Sorry about the plane."

David slept on Ellie's shoulder the twenty-minute ride back to Tel Aviv. And when they pulled up to the red house, it took both Ellie and the young radio operator to steer him into the house and lay him gently on the bed.

———

As the weapons were distributed among the forces, Moshe

looked at Luke and frowned. "This isn't going to be easy, is it? Even with all of this." He motioned toward the stacks of rifles. "Even with all of this we will lose many of these young people, won't we, Luke?"

Luke drew himself up and inhaled the night air as the line of soldiers filed past, each taking a weapon and a bandolier of bullets. "It is never easy." His voice was low. "It never has been. Four thousand years ago the man you are named after was telling Pharaoh to let his people go. Tonight, I suppose, we are doing the same thing."

"Parting the Red Sea," Moshe smiled. "We have been trying to reach the Promised Land for so long, Luke. All my life my people have dreamed of returning to Zion."

"It is never easy to part the Red Sea, my friend. I look at these children and I think that a nation will stand or fall . . . Zion will live or die based on what they will do in the next few days. And then I remember that the children of Israel left Egypt and walked through the water as frightened slaves. They entered this land forty years later as warriors."

"You're right," Moshe said. "Funny. I almost forgot it was Passover, too." He glanced up as a large truck rumbled past, and Ehud poked his head out the window and shouted.

"Hey! Hey, Moshe! Luke! Look at the bumper, will you?"

Moshe laughed out loud as he read the Hebrew letters drawn carefully on the bumper of the truck that carried three tons of matzo bread for Passover.

"What does it say?" Luke asked as Moshe gave Ehud the thumbs-up sign.

Moshe wrapped an arm around the shoulders of Captain Luke Thomas. "If you are going to be a citizen of Israel, my friend, I shall have to teach you to read Hebrew, eh?" He laughed again and pointed to the bumper. "It says, *THIS YEAR IN JERUSALEM— IN FREEDOM!*"

———————

Rachel sat quietly beside Tikvah's tiny crib. A bottle of IV fluid hung above her head and she was covered by a clear oxygen tent. Through a long night the baby had fought for life, and every breath was an effort of will for survival.

Tears came to Rachel's eyes as she studied the now-sleeping child. Wisps of black hair clung to her face, and her breathing still wheezed and whistled. The doctor had told Rachel that the battle was not over yet. It was not yet won in spite of some improvement in the infant's grave condition. *Dear Lord,* Rachel prayed for the thousandth time, *you hold this little one in your hands. You know when the sparrow falls, and you care. I can do nothing but trust you and wait.*

Yehudit poked her head in through the door. She carried two steaming cups of coffee and her face was alight with a surprise.

"I have called your grandfather and Howard Moniger," she said. "They are here."

Rachel stood as Grandfather and Yacov and Howard filed in past Yehudit. Grandfather's arms were outstretched and tears streamed freely down his face. "Rachel! Rachel! Dear little girl," he said in a shaking voice as he embraced her. Yacov simply wrapped his arms around her waist and held close to her.

"Grandfather!" Rachel cried. "I wondered if we would ever meet again in this life!"

Grandfather patted her gently on the back and pulled a handkerchief from his vest pocket. "There now, my child," he crooned. "Our dear professor has taken good care of us. You should not have worried. Oh yes," he said as he stroked her hair, "he has made us and that jackal of a dog his own dear family, you see."

Rachel looked up to where Howard Moniger stood quietly beaming by the doorway. "Thank you," she whispered through her emotion. "God bless you, Professor Moniger."

He winked and nodded, then closed the door behind himself. "Rachel," he said quietly. "We heard from Ellie last night."

A look of shock crossed Rachel's face. "Ellie? Ellie *lives*? A fresh burst of tears erupted and she sank back to her chair.

Howard's face looked intensely pained. He was unaware that Rachel did not know about Ellie's safety. "I am so sorry." He spread his hands helplessly. "I . . . I. . . well, she had some good news for us. She has seen Moshe," he whispered.

Rachel wept harder at those words, and Howard's brow furrowed with worry. "Moshe," Rachel wept softly. "And little Ellie, too. Oh, thank God!"

Grandfather pulled yet another handkerchief from his pocket and handed it to Rachel. "You may need another."

"Where are they?" Rachel asked. "Are they together? Is David all right?"

"Ellie and David are together in Tel Aviv," Grandfather answered gently. "Moshe is right now in the battle for Kastel to break through to Jerusalem."

Rachel's tears suddenly ceased. "But he is well."

"Indeed," said Howard with as much assurance as he could muster. "Ellie saw him and he is very well. And full of hope. He told her to tell us that he is full of hope."

"Then I musn't weep," Rachel drew herself up. "I will be strong and pray that God may let me see his face once again in this life also." She blew her nose.

Grandfather's face softened as he looked at the baby. "So this is the child of Leah and Shimon? The child God in his mercy has given you." He lifted his aged hands over the baby. "So, I am a great-grandfather at last," he smiled.

Rachel leaned forward and rested her head on Grandfather's arm, taking his hand in her own. "The doctors say she has a fight to survive, Grandfather. They still worry that she may not live." Tears came again.

"Ah," the old man answered. "So the world has been saying about us Jews for centuries. And now they say as much about Zion, nu? But God has not forgotten His promises, nor will He forget this little one. We shall pray for her."

Rachel did not take her gaze from Tikvah as Grandfather spoke. The child's eyelashes fluttered, then her blue eyes opened in the predawn light. A faint, recognizable protest bleated from the child, and a feeling of calm entered Rachel.

"Oh, my goodness!" Howard exclaimed, "I almost forgot." He rummaged in his pocket and pulled out a white envelope. "Here is a letter for you from Moshe. It was written while he was in prison, and a British officer dropped it by yesterday."

Rachel took it from him and held it gently, gazing at her name, scrawled in Moshe's unmistakable handwriting below Howard's name and address. She held it to her heart. For the first time, Yehudit spoke.

"Go on," the girl whispered. "I will stay with Tikvah. She loves me. Go on and find a quiet place to read the letter."

Rachel looked up into each face. "You will excuse me, please?" She wiped her eyes with the back of her hand and stepped out into the hall. As the door swung closed behind her, she looked at the nurses' station. The doctor who had examined both her and Tikvah glanced up at her just as she was about to steal away down the hall.

"Mrs. Sachar!" he waved his hand. "Could I have a word with you." His face was pleasant, but lined with concern for all that he had seen in the last few months.

Rachel met him midway in the hall and he smiled briefly at her, then flipped through a clipboard full of charts. "We got your tests back, Mrs. Sachar." His voice was serious. "You are, of course, malnourished. Everyone in Jerusalem is malnourished. And of course, when a woman is pregnant, every bit of nourishment her body gets goes to feed the baby she carries. It is no wonder you fainted. To be pregnant again so soon after having just delivered . . . How old is Tikvah?"

Rachel blinked at him, not comprehending what he was telling her. "Tikvah is my child, but not of my womb," she said quietly.

"Then this is your first pregnancy?" he queried.

"I am with child?" Her words were so soft that he could barely hear her.

"Yes," the doctor answered matter-of-factly. "And Jerusalem is not the best place for a woman carrying a baby right now. You need good food and rest. You're worn out; that much is obvious."

"I am carrying Moshe's child within me!" she said in quiet wonder. "Then . . ." her voice trailed off and she turned away from the doctor midsentence. He scratched his head and called after her.

"Plenty of rest and good food . . ."

Epilogue

High atop the Hadassah Hospital, Rachel carefully opened Moshe's letter as the first rays of sun glistened in the east. In the distant west, Rachel thought she could hear a sound like thunder that echoed up the pass of Bab el Wad.

She closed her eyes for an instant and prayed for Moshe and those who fought beside him for the salvation of Zion. Then she unfolded his letter and studied each line.

My Dearest Wife, My Only Rachel,

Tonight I will not write to you of dying, only of living. No moment passes but you are here beside me, smiling and whispering words of comfort and love to me. I have searched my heart for words that would comfort you now in this hour of our separation, and I can only say that I believe that our love was created by God himself. It is this love that makes miracles of strength and courage; it is this love that is stronger than time or even death. Our Lord has said that nothing can separate us from His love, and since we are both in His care, nothing, then, can separate us from one another. I carry you always in my heart, as I know I am also in yours . . .

Rachel smiled and blushed and touched her stomach. Indeed, she carried a part of Moshe.

And so, remember me always in happiness. This is not an easy battle, but somehow, someday, the Red Sea will open for us once again . . . With all my love, Moshe

Thus, the first dawn of Passover came to the Holy City. Far across the valley, she heard the sound of the shofar calling the people to freedom as it had that first morning of Passover so very long ago. Now, as then, there were miracles yet to be performed. Red Seas to part . . .

Rachel shaded her eyes as the shofar sounded again. She stared at the cupola of the Great Hurva Synagogue and waited for Dov to fulfill a promise. Suddenly, a wind came from the west, and the white silk of Moshe's tallith unfurled and glistened in the sunlight. Blue bands bordered the gleaming banner, and very clear in its center, a blue Star of David sparkled with golden thread long ago woven into the fabric.

"This year in Jerusalem," she prayed, "This year in freedom . . ."

---

*If you would like to contact the authors,
you may write to them at the following address:*

Bodie and Brock Thoene
P.O. Box 542
Glenbrook, NV 89413